FLOODTIDE

Helen Claire Gould

Helen Claire Gould Books

First published in the UK in 2015 by Helen Claire Gould Books,

Peterborough, Cambridgeshire.

FLOODTIDE copyright © 2015 Helen Claire Gould

Cover Art © by Alex Storer

ISBN: 978-0-9930812-1-7

Printed and bound in England in 2015 by
Berforts Information Press
www.bookprinting.co.uk

To Mike and Jason for their love and faith,

and to

Tim, Phoebe, Phil, Carolyn, Julie, Carol-Ann, Julia, Ange,
Lene Lovich, Peter Vincent, David Piper, Pete Irving,
and Maureen Speller Kincaid
for their invaluable feedback.

THUNK!

Jordas blinked awake. The luminescent fungi's glow split the lava tube's darkness, and metres away a skylight filtered in grey rays from the surface. Chill air raised the hairs on his arm. He tucked it back under the sleeping bag, then noticed a scatter of rubble beneath the skylight. Surface water dripped on it.

Rockfall, he thought. *That's what woke me. But I was dreaming –*

Fragments replayed. In the dream, he was two people at once. Jordas's hand scraped against lava as he, Yado and Soolkah crept forwards. He rubbed the rawness to ease it, and was surprised to see Yado frown and massage his own hand. And when Yado and Soolkah lay together nearby, it was the most passion Jordas had ever felt.

His turn.

Soolkah allowed him to pull her closer.

He opened his mouth to speak.

But she laid her finger against his lips and said, "Shh, Jordas. It's because you and Yado are mindlinked that we're here together now..."

I had that dream, he realised, *to tell me that.*

CONTENTS

CHAPTER 1

"FIELD TEAM SENT NEW PROBE TO CAVES last night. Big surprise!" Ray Travers' voice exceeded lightspeed in excitement.

Jordas Krata suppressed a smile at Ray's enthusiasm and hurried into the monitor room with a quick greeting for his colleagues. Neither acknowledged him.

"What did it find?" Marcus Carlin was Project Leader and Chief Scientist.

"More Naxadans than we thought."

"*What?* Are you sure?" For once, Jordas noted, Marcus's composure was shaken.

In the holotank along the west wall Jordas glimpsed what the probe saw: a lava tube, wide enough for several people to walk abreast in, colonies of luminescent fungi encrusting the rockwalls, and ahead the gape of a cavern with its ice-cave roof.

"Must be another group. Others don't look like *him*. See?"

The probe cruised into the chamber. There was some scrubby blackish-red vegetation, but the cavern wasn't divided up into plots like the farm cavern. Nor did it look like a sleeping cavern. A streamlet wound between boulders in the centre of the chamber. And looking this way and that, a dark humanoid form crept through the underbrush.

As Jordas saw the creature his awareness *slid*. He clamped his eyes shut against the surge of vertigo, clutching at nothing. His seat was three metres away. He wouldn't make it. He staggered and braced himself against the wall.

"Change of plan, Jordas –" Marcus began.

Jordas breathed in, legs wobbling. He took a step forwards, hand at his head, but swayed and fell before ever reaching his chair.

As if from a distance he heard Ray exclaim, "Jordas! You all right?"

"...Probably heat exhaustion," someone muttered. Hands rolled him onto his side. Jordas fought waves of giddiness and confusion, and couldn't quell the sense of intrusion into his mind.

Someone slapped his face. "Come on, Jordas!"

He forced his eyes open to gaze up at Marcus. "Whaa –?"

"Ray – get some water! And put the hololink onto record."

The whirl of impressions in his head slowed. Jordas felt an arm under him, helping him up to drink. Liquid splashed onto his overshirt as he tasted its sharpness and chill.

"What happened?" Marcus looked concerned.

"I don't know, I –" A change in the background hum told Jordas the live hololink was off, and he realised they were waiting for him to speak. "I fainted...I think," he said, "though I've never done that in my life before." He clambered to his feet, leaning on a chair for support.

"I could do without you going sick right now," Marcus said. "I was going to ask *you* to pick up Senator Hartmann from the airport at nine – I'll need to look into our calculations and costings again now..." He frowned. "But perhaps you should go get yourself checked out instead."

"I'm fine now," Jordas protested, straightening. "It'll be a waste of time going over to Block B. I'll go for the Senator right away."

"If you're sure...Take the pool car. I'll notify airport security."

Jordas nodded and left the room, willing each step firmer than the last. He hadn't taken a day's sick leave since joining the project four years before and didn't intend to now.

As he settled back into the seat and instructed the car to take him to the airport he couldn't help regretting that Senator Hartmann had been assigned to their case. *If he'd acted sooner the famine on Mourang wouldn't have claimed so many lives,* Jordas mused, then chided himself for making judgements without having met the man.

By the time the car had parked itself it was several minutes past nine. At Security the officer was scanning the crowd as if seeking someone. Jordas hurried over. The security man peered at Jordas's collar ID, took a notebook from his breast pocket and consulted it, then nodded and escorted him over to an angular man standing nearby.

The senator's holo in his own notebook must have been retouched, Jordas realised. Hardened creases ran from nose to chin. The senator's long upper lip sloped, etching a permanent sneer onto his face. The eyebrows zigzagged at obtuse angles above ice-chip eyes. The cranium, softened only by a few strands of greying hair, reflected the artificial light into Jordas's eyes. But the strangest and most noticeable thing to Jordas was the senator's total lack of emotional leakage. It felt as if a steel wall had slammed down around the man.

Unwilling to surrender to first impressions, he inhaled, reminding himself that the project needed the Committee's help. He stepped forward, hand extended. "Senator Hartmann? I'm Jordas Krata."

The politician looked Jordas up and down. "I won't speak to the Press."

"I'm not the Press," Jordas said. "I'm Marcus Carlin's senior assistant."

Senator Hartmann moved a slender document wallet from one hand to the other. "I was expecting Dr Carlin," he said as they shook hands.

"He sends his apologies – an urgent matter needed his attention, so he

12

asked me to collect you."

"I see. What was your name again?"

Jordas told him.

"You *sound* like an Anglo," Hartmann said, "but your name doesn't."

Jordas squashed down his resentment at the comment. "My father's from the Scandinavian states, but my mother was English, and I grew up there."

"Ah-huh?" Hartmann turned to the security officer. "Get my luggage!" he said, heading for the doors.

Jordas raised his eyebrows, but sent the security officer an address from his own notebook, then hurried after the senator. He caught up with him at the doors, keeping his tone mild as he said, "They'll send your luggage round."

Hartmann didn't even acknowledge that.

Heat struck through Jordas's lightweight loose clothing as the doors swung open.

"God, I hate this planet!" Hartmann muttered behind him.

Jordas turned to see him extract a silk handkerchief from a suit pocket.

"I especially hate whir-flies." He swiped at an insect which buzzed too close. It fell, iridescent wings silenced forever. Hartmann put his foot on it and ground it into pulp.

Jordas stared. Whir-flies were one of the few flying life-forms to have evolved on Goranon, and quite as beautiful as dragonflies.

"Is it far to the hotel?" Hartmann asked, mopping his forehead.

After what he'd just seen the conversational tone grated on Jordas, but he swallowed his anger. *So much for reserving judgement!* he thought, and forced himself to answer. "Actually, it's not a hotel. The hotels are in Rorvik, and I'm sure you discovered on the way here that it's an uncomfortable trip in and out. We had accommodation available, and thought you'd prefer to be on-site." Jordas wondered if he'd imagined the brief frown that corrugated Hartmann's forehead. "The apartments on the other side of the complex are very comfortable. You won't get any noise from the landing area, so you can relax before getting down to business." He gestured towards the vehicle park. "I have transport."

Jordas waited while Senator Hartmann blotted perspiration from his forehead and stowed the handkerchief away, then made for the vehicle park. Indicating the pool car, he opened the door for the politician.

Once seated, Jordas swung the wheel and the car sped away from the airport. He could have left the vehicle on auto, but driving gave him an excuse not to speak. Blue-white sunlight barred his hands on the wheel, skipping between the trees and defying the UV protection the windshield offered. This

13

section of the settlement abutted the edge of the compound. Above the perimeter fence the forest loomed, black and uncompromising; eerie purplish shadows diffused light in the rainforest, half-veiling the distant mountains which scarred the jungle. Goranon was a planet of contrasts: walls of foliage, split only by limestone ridges above which updraughts rioted, stretched in every direction around Axos Research Station; the deserts sandwiching this equatorial belt would fry a man's blood at midday.

"I came here once before, many years ago," Senator Hartmann remarked. "The climate hasn't improved."

"Official business?" Jordas asked.

"No." Jordas was less surprised than relieved to sense Hartmann's barriers go up again. *I don't trust him,* he thought. Several kilometres clocked up before they entered the residential area, where blue-black multi-stemmed pseudocedars competed with roofs for light. Jordas pulled up before a two-storey block.

"The apartment's this way," Jordas told him. "I'll call for you at eleven. You can rest until then, acclimatise yourself."

Hartmann grunted, but followed Jordas to the door and allowed his handprint to be recorded so he could use the apartment.

*

"Senator Hartmann? Marcus Carlin." The voice of the Chief Scientist was as cool as his smile.

Gerrold Hartmann shook hands with Carlin, noting the beard which the man kept trimmed to a point. *What vanity!*

"I'm sorry I wasn't available to meet you this morning. An intriguing discovery here required my attention so I had to delegate that honour," Carlin explained. "However, my Senior Geologist and Assistant Astronomer, Dr Krata, is trustworthy and efficient."

An unconvincing excuse. Hartmann wondered if he was being deliberately affronted. The explanation about his accommodation was reasonable enough; he knew from previous visits that turbulence made air travel on Goranon unpleasant. It irked him that this boffin gave his work precedence over meeting him. *Surely Carlin was the one who called in the Committee?* But there was need for circumspection in his dealings with these people, so he ignored the thought and looked around.

The air boiled despite the telltales streaming at air conditioning vents. He sniffed; rooms crammed with machines all had the same sort of atmosphere, not quite at the level of a definite smell.

One wall was taken up by the vacant cuboid of a holotank. A series of

14

instruments and terminal monitor cubes were ranked on workstations, while a semi-circular table bore four connected tanks; from previous Committee assignments he recognised the equipment as a telescope downlink station for processing data. In a corner stretched a highly-polished desk, probably made of wood from renewable sources. Hartmann thought of the oak desk in his own office. *There are ways around the eco-laws if you know the right people...*

Beside Carlin's terminal rose a tray tower stacked with notepads, styli, printouts, and boxes of holochips the size of a man's thumbnail. Krata was seated at a workstation, pointing to the tank and conferring with the third member of the team. *Travers, that's his name.* He remembered it from Asthorn's briefing at Committee headquarters. Travers was the Assistant Geologist: in his late twenties, with a kinked quiff that looked as if it were about to overbalance, the tinted corneal lenses fashionable in blue-star systems, and an earnest expression. His speech was a quickfire mix of words and handjerks.

Hartmann ran a finger between his neck and shirt collar, hoping the meeting would end before the hottest part of the day; besides, the first whore would arrive from Rorvik that afternoon.

"Have a seat." Carlin pulled one forwards. "Ray, organise some drinks, will you?" He seated himself beside the politician.

Travers crossed to the drinks dispenser and dialled. The machine took just seconds to deliver.

Hartmann accepted a beaker and sipped. *Iced orange juice; no whisky.* He grimaced. "The report I received glitched, so I couldn't read much of it on the way here," he said. "I know you've found some aliens but that's about all."

"I'm sorry about the report – we'll give you a complete update. These people face two threats to their existence." Carlin spoke over his shoulder as he crossed to the holotank console. "Here's the map of this sector of space."

Of course, Hartmann remembered, *Carlin's Senior Astronomer as well as Chief Scientist.* He watched him insert a holochip and set the controls. A three-dimensional starmap appeared in the tank. Hartmann spotted the Terran system in the northern quadrant. Towards the centre of the map the Charidas Interchange, staging-post for the several systems in the quadrant, hung like a jewel on a necklace, orbiting the gas giant Theona once a day. He'd often amused himself on-station whilst awaiting connections. Charidas itself was a small orange binary star. Toward the western quadrant lay the Kiai and Declaini systems, and eventually Vanjeyno and Mourang. *I had a lucky escape after that business on Mourang. I suppose this'll be another desperate race against time with no room to manoeuvre.* That thoughtstream led to danger;

15

Hartmann steered his thoughts back to the tank.

The holotank view zoomed in on the eastern quadrant. "Here's the Lyrica star system," Carlin said, leaning forwards to finger-trace Goranon's greenish-blue and yellow disk as it rotated around Lyrica. "We're here – Goranon, second planet out. Our system lies above and east of Malory's Star."

He pointed to a nearby system. The holo focused in on the fourth planet in the Malorian system, glittering blue and white. "Naxada." Beyond it a belt of asteroids whirled about the star. "The farthestmost Malorian planet out is Chryo – a supercool gas giant. And this is asteroid Hamorrah. It's presently on the opposite side of Malory's Star from us – but our space telescope can see it."

He gestured towards the dotted yellow tracer line linking asteroid to planet. "Its trajectory is decaying towards Naxada." Carlin drew in a deep breath. "Five years ago Hamorrah fragmented into a string of rocks held to their orbit by gravity. We thought it would hit Chryo, but when it was realised it was going to collide with Naxada instead, our project was started. Our field team's keeping tabs on Hamorrah and observing the effects of regular minor yearly impacts on Naxada. Although it's lost some mass, it's not small. The larger final impact will occur in a few weeks' time – this is the first threat."

"What do you expect to happen?" Hartmann asked.

"I'll show you. Graphic of impact with Naxada."

The tank cleared, and Hartmann saw a close-up holographic view of Naxada. The asteroid's fragments were ranged above the ice planet, lined up ready to impact. As the planet rotated below the in-falling space rocks, a storm of micrometeorites with embedded larger fragments bombarded the planet. The first major collision site vaporised, along with the asteroid fragment. Strings of secondary impact craters formed behind it as debris was ejected. Some meteors detonated in the atmosphere, but others fell into the oceans, creating tall columns of water.

"Oscillating tsunamis – as high as the depth to the ocean floor," Carlin murmured. "The blasts will be so powerful that the tsunamis will come in pulses." He pointed to the trail of impacts as a line-drawing graphic in red traced the progress of seismic waves as they raced around the planet. "We don't yet know where the biggest fragments will hit, but a major shock on the opposite side of Naxada could cause volcanic activity near our aliens, because the crust is already thinned there." The graphic swooped in with a close-up of rocks tumbling from a fault. The faultline heaved rocks aside as it propagated outwards in several directions. Carlin waved a hand at it. "The hallmark of an impact – jumbled terrain."

"So...where does the Committee come into all this? All you have to do is get your people out before that happens – isn't it?"

"Not quite, Senator. There are unforeseen complications. Of course, you're right, we *will* have to evacuate the field team soon, but that cost was built into the original project funding." Carlin paced up and down between the rows of monitors, tapping steepled forefingers against his lips. "The evacuation of the Naxadans is what concerns us now. *That's* where the Committee for Resettlement and Colonisation comes in."

"What's the other danger?"

Carlin indicated the man who'd met him at the airport. Krata sat watching his monitor cube, forearms resting on his thighs, but Hartmann already knew he was of only average height for a human male, with regular features. He regarded him with more interest than before. His hair curled to well below his collar, dark as the night sky. The firm mouth spoke of determination, but it was his eyes that arrested the attention: an intense blue even at this distance, the iris muscles were highlighted by flecks and streaks of white.

"Dr Krata will explain the geological background to the discovery of the Naxadans."

*

"I'll get some maps up," Jordas said, resetting the controls by voice command. The holotank filled with a 3-d satellite mosaic. "Naxada has four continents, paired around the poles and heavily glaciated. The oceans are ice-free only around the equator. Like Earth, Naxada is geologically active, with plate tectonic, volcanic and seismic activity. The small axial tilt produces minor seasonal temperature variations." He sipped his caffeine freeze, then cleared his throat. "Our base lies near a volcano whose flanks are honeycombed with lava tubes."

"Lava tubes?"

Jordas ran an animation. Lava poured downslope, with golden seams and sparks licking its red and black crust. "Like caves, but they form during runny basaltic eruptions, when the tops and sides of lava streams running down the mountain cool in air." The tank resumed its satellite mosaic. "When the lava inside drains away, it leaves a tunnel. The Naxadans live in their upper levels."

"That sounds highly dangerous."

"This volcano has long been dormant." Jordas pointed on the map. "Here's our base, near this mountain chain where the continent's splitting apart. Climate change, driven by tectonic activity, rifting and intense basaltic volcanism, has led to glacial melting. Soot on the slopes has decreased the ice's reflectivity and increased this effect. Our field team have been there for four

17

years. Two months ago Matt Johnson fell into a lava tube while sampling ice cores."

"Lava tube roofs sometimes collapse," Ray volunteered. "Leaves holes called skylights."

"Or there can be a thin layer of glassy rock, sometimes weathered away to nothing, with thin ice still on top. On the surface, the glacier usually covers the tunnel roof, but in some places that's exposed, or lightly covered with snow," Marcus added. "That's how Dr Johnson fell in."

"Many planets' volcanoes, including Earth, have lava tubes, though not on this scale. On Naxada, some tubes interconnect, but erosion has destroyed some at the surface," Jordas added. "This lava is quite fluid."

"How come there are so many tunnels there?" Hartmann asked.

"Successive eruptions have built up many layers of ash and lava tubes." Another voice command and the holovid swept in on a view of mountains, covered by snow pierced in places by dark rock outcrops. Jordas pointed to the bulge on the side of the Naxadans' mountain. "See this new volcano – this swelling here – forming on the flank? It's growing quickly, metres every day. They share a magma chamber. The original volcano may also erupt again, but the problem is that the mountain is glaciated. These blue contours indicate the extent and thickness of the ice sheet.

"Where volcanoes erupt under glaciers, floods follow. Meltwater gets dammed up under the ice until later eruptions release it. When it reaches the lower levels of the lava tubes it'll enter through the skylights and flood our Naxadans out. – if the lava doesn't get them first." He turned to face Hartmann directly. "That's the second threat to them. We expect the meteor impacts at about the same time."

Ray smirked. "Caught between a rock and a wet place."

Jordas cast a rueful glance at him.

"How does the glacier above the volcano stay frozen, with that heat from below?" Hartmann asked.

Jordas made a throwaway gesture. "The ice is thick, and rock acts as an effective insulator. Above the skylights, where some heat *can* escape, it's formed ice caves. But if the ice starts to pile down into the caverns, it melts."

"The original reports on discovery of the planet indicated Naxada was uninhabited," Hartmann said.

"On the surface," Jordas agreed. "But these people live underground, and heat trace monitoring is impossible through rock, especially hot rock. So like the first space explorers we use remote sensing methods, and our probes are small and pre-programmed to seek concealment –"

18

"I know all about the probes," Hartmann interrupted.

"Indeed. Then you'll know how beneficial they've proved in past first-contact missions. But nobody had used them in such confined spaces before, so working underground presented special problems. Ours rove at times, and use a network of concealed terminals to relay holovid or transmit live. Programming can be changed only when they're hooked up."

"Ah-huh."

"The thing is, microwave radio is subject to rain fade and other precipitation-related problems, and can't pass through rock, so an expedition would have to use cablephones to communicate with us. But they could use the probes' system." Jordas turned. "Ray?"

"Matt broke his pelvis. All excited when they rescued him. Bones in the caves. Sent hoverprobes in. Mapped caves, laid system for probe transmissions. Found more bones. Standard practice – observation before contact. Brought back interesting holovid. Naxada field team very excited." Ray's hands signalled at starship speed.

"Ah-huh."

"Acquired samples." Ray's semaphore intensified. "Unexpected: plants, animals, insects. Life in the caves!" He paused for breath, hands finally at rest.

"The field team's exobiologist confirmed that Naxada's oceans contain plant-like organisms which help maintain the atmosphere. In addition it's an evolved atmosphere, so we expected to find other life forms, and we know surface conditions were different in the past." Marcus sipped his drink. "But without evidence of current surface habitation, we thought any animals other than plankton and fish had simply gone extinct."

"When it turned out they were underground, everything fell into place," Jordas added.

"How can life survive down there?"

"There are streams and hot and cold pools. A surprising range of creatures lives underground, one of which has grown in size, adopted an upright, bipedal stance, and developed into humanoids, like apes on Earth, or Kiai saurians. But we're not sure whether life developed underground in the first place or moved into the caves when the climate became colder."

"I suppose it was predictable," Marcus said, "with humanoid life-forms scattered throughout the galaxy. It's a widespread form because it's versatile and adaptable."

"And have you seen these – er – natives?"

Marcus locked gaze briefly with Jordas, then stared at the senator, and for an instant Jordas saw his dislike of the politician in his eyes. Then they

19

flickered and cleared. "Yes," Marcus said, "we have holovid. Better still, we can go live." He gestured towards the tray tower on his desk. "At present one probe's surveying an inhabited cave."

"Very well," the politician answered. "Show me."

"We knew from the fresh bones that humanoids probably lived in the caves," Marcus said, "and our probes found what we were looking for." He concentrated on his own tank for several moments, then said, "Ah, here."

The holotank filled with the image of a cavern. In one corner of the tank, a lava tube led away into darkness. Through the ice-cave ceiling far above daylight filtered in, revealing streaks of colour marking outgrowths of minerals, crystal formations, and occasional clusters of fungi whose eerie glow enhanced the light from the ceiling. The variety and beauty of this world never ceased to amaze Jordas.

"Are these caves formed like the tunnels?"

"Magmas and lavas contain a lot of gas," Jordas said. "These caves form when gas blisters burst during cooling. They're on a huge scale here, but even on Earth they've been used as living space. The gas escapes upwards and forms these holes – also called skylights – in the cavern roofs."

Hartmann peered into the tank. "I can't see any natives."

"It's dawn there now. They're sleeping in crevices in the rock. Look, far left of the tank –"

The probe focused in on the mouth of a crevice. Several humanoids wrapped in cloth slumbered inside, the smallest obviously children of various ages. Of the adults, two were smaller than the others: females, Jordas guessed. The males looked to be a little shorter than the average human. All had white hair.

Jordas leaned forwards, fascinated. The probe had never observed these people so closely before.

"Their use of both spoken and signed language and their high degree of social interaction support their intelligence," Marcus said.

"How long have you been observing them?" Hartmann asked.

"About three weeks."

"You must have a lot of holovid of them."

"Loads. We have a program which deselects anything very private, though, in accordance with our guidelines." The whole team had undergone intensive training and counselling before using the probes.

"Of course," Hartmann echoed.

One of the females moved, kneeling beside the other and calling her till she awoke. Jordas was struck by the humanity of the action. The female stretched, yawned, pulled cloth slippers on, and climbed upright. The lens zoomed out. She left the crevice, speaking in an undertone all the while, the other female following. Both were clad in short woven kilts, their skins almost as pale as their hair. White peach-fuzz covered most of their bodies, though not their faces.

One female resembled the other enough to be her daughter, and looked younger, even allowing for their alien appearance. They spoke quietly together, mixing speech with hand signals, as Ray did.

The smaller female turned to face the probe's hiding place. She *was* young, and her narrow face had a singular beauty despite her furred torso and limbs. Crimped hair came to just below her ears. Jordas noted the flatness of her chest with surprise; the mother's upper body bore six small breasts, which nevertheless looked engorged.

Her features darkened like thunderclouds as she looked into the probe lens concealed in shadows, and Jordas could have sworn her river-green eyes held an appeal to him. A shock tore through him. He couldn't look away from the holotank. *But she can't know we're watching.*

The mother spoke again, and the daughter replied, tossing her hair. Jordas could hardly hear their voices, but from their gestures, they seemed to be arguing.

*

"You should be *pleased* that they want you, Soolkah!" Gujas watched her daughter stir the dirt with one foot.

"I'm *not* going to marry them!" Soolkah glared. "Chixi's fat and old, and his brothers are ugly."

That wasn't true of all of them; the youngest, Lorr, was at least pleasant-looking, but Gujas saw Soolkah's muscles bunch around her mouth in anger. She felt a moment's apprehension; experience had taught her that this expression always preceded some act of disobedience from Soolkah.

Chixi wasn't all that old; he had a little over forty highwaters, though few Shiranu lived much past sixty. Gujas's own mother had died in her fifties, worn out by hard physical labour and childbearing for several men. *A body can only stand so much punishment.* "I'm sure I don't know where you get this haughty streak from. Chixi's amaaj has high status – their plots are always better-positioned and larger than ours, and he's been negotiating with your fathers for many lighttimes. You should be flattered that he wants you."

"But Mother, when he takes me he'll squash me!" protested Soolkah.

"Don't be crude! Nobody will want to *take* a ganzu at all!" retorted Gujas. Soolkah's temper rivalled a ganzu's, which had led to much teasing within her family group. "In fact, your fathers and I have been wondering who would take you on – we're really pleased that you're to be married, and so quickly after reaching adulthood." When Chixi and his brothers had offered for Soolkah, it had seemed the perfect solution. But Gujas and her husbands had all known there'd be opposition to the match. She sighed. *It just goes to show how right the tradition of the surprise wedding day is!*

Gujas had been married for many highwaters, and felt strong affection for all three husbands. She'd given them five live offspring, including Soolkah. That was good, compared to some women, and because she'd borne two healthy daughters, Gujas had acquired status within the tribe. "You'll soon learn to love them all," she continued, "when you go with them. It happens that way."

"So you keep saying," Soolkah said, shoulders tense.

She's not convinced. "Well, it happened in my case," Gujas said in a tone which she hoped would quell further argument. She could understand that Chixi might not appeal. *He's considerably older than Soolkah, but that isn't unusual for Elder brothers – and, of course, he's very overweight; but the others aren't bad-looking.* Besides, every woman must be married on reaching child-bearing age. She'd never thought to question her marriage, so why should her daughter? *The tribe treasures its women for their rarity, though our lives are tempered by work and hardship for all that.* Gujas thought Soolkah's husbands would cherish her all the more for her beauty of both form and face. *I love my daughter,* she realised, *despite her strange ideas.* She picked up a basket woven from streamside rush stalks. "Look sharp, now! Get me some vegetables so I can prepare the wedding feast."

Soolkah took the basket, mumbling under her breath.

"What's that?" asked Gujas.

"If the family's so low-status, why do we have to hold a feast just because I'm being forced to become amaajni with four men I loathe?" Soolkah muttered. But she walked towards the farm cavern tunnel anyway.

Gujas gave her a piercing look, hoping she wouldn't voice her defiance too loudly. She turned away. The rest of her family lay sleeping. *Thank the volcano none of the others are so rebellious!* she told herself, and stared after Soolkah as she vanished into the dimness of the tunnel mouth.

*

"Our hyperspace hololink with the research base can also receive transmissions from the hoverprobes," Jordas explained. "Of course, the Naxadans don't know they're being watched."

"Good. Good. We like to minimise cross-contamination of developing

22

cultures where possible," Hartmann said. "I guess I should speak to Naxada field base."

Jordas made the connection, and shortly afterwards there appeared in the tank the holo of a middle-aged man; unusually, he wore spectacles.

Marcus moved nearer and introduced Hartmann, ushering the senator to stand beside him.

"Matt Johnson here...Chief Scientist, Naxada Base field research team. Ah, Senator Hartmann, it's good to speak to you at last, eh?" Matt's words were tinged with a Canadian accent, unlike Hartmann's almost uninflected speech.

"Good day, Dr Johnson. Tell me more about your native problem."

Matt blinked, and when he spoke again his manner had lost its veneer of politeness. "The Naxadans aren't a problem, Senator. We just need to make contact with them and get them safely off-planet and resettled."

"Dr Krata said they weren't aware of your presence on the planet," Hartmann said, "so how do you propose to accomplish this?"

"Surely that's where the Committee's expertise comes in, Senator?" Matt parried. Light glinted off his spectacles to match the steel in his voice.

"But how do we know that these – people – are any better than animals?"

"Should that be a criterion for rescue, Senator?" Matt said. "We expect to find that, like the Kiai and Zarduthi, their mindset and some behaviours will be different from ours. We also expect some behavioural similarities."

Jordas finished his caffeine freeze and laid the beaker on his workstation. "The thing is, Senator," he said, "they have a fully-fledged society based around vegetable farming. And there's a mystery here: we believe, from the skulls' dentition, that these people developed as omnivores. Meat is available, yet they're apparently exclusively vegetarian, from choice."

"I'll show you a sign of civilisation our holoprobes found," Matt said. "One even *you* can't dispute!"

"What?"

"Watch, Senator!"

The holotank image changed. Ice-filtered light revealed a cavern in which structures stretched into the distance: unmistakeably buildings, despite the toll of centuries and seismic activity. None bore a roof, though whether by intent or destruction was unclear.

"Ah-huh?"

"It's a city, Senator..." Matt's voice rang with passion. "Built by the ancestors of those who still inhabit the caves!"

CHAPTER 2

JORDAS WATCHED FOR A REACTION, but Senator Hartmann camouflaged his emotions with impassivity.

"From the probe," Matt added, "we observed that this city was built over several centuries." He paused. "These city-dwellers were skilled engineers – a hypocaust used geothermal water to heat the whole city."

The senator's eyes remained fixed on the holotank. "How old is it?" he asked.

"The earliest buildings are about two thousand years old. Some are younger, and we're not yet sure when it was abandoned, or why. But the most interesting discovery *here* is that although these people never developed writing, they recorded events."

The probe's view floated between windowless buildings whose doorways were simple rectangular absences of wall.

"Don't think much of the architecture," Ray muttered.

Then the probe reached the encircling wall and focused in on it, and Jordas saw again the frieze carved in the stone. The holovid moved round the buildings, but he never could distinguish the scenes; dust and age had blurred outlines and dimmed colours, and blocks had tumbled in places. The city couldn't have been inhabited for centuries. Finally the holovid view dissolved to Matt Johnson's image.

*

"Conditions aren't favourable above ground, even with a fur coat. There's nothing to eat up here," Matt said.

"It's a wonder they've even survived," Hartmann commented.

"That's why we need the Committee's help. See for yourself." At his voice command the scene switched; the holoprobe panned round, seeing only icy plains stretching in three directions. The whiteness of the light jangled the senses; the shadow of the landing area shocked the eye, emerging as it did from the snowfields. Against the southern horizon clouds of smoke and ash hazed mountains, lingering like a bad smell in the thin still air. Matt saw this view from the research base every day, but the landscape never bored him. Its aridity and grandeur reminded him of winter at home, though Naxadan forests only grew waist-high; hardly as impressive as the swathes of conifer he remembered.

The holoprobe roved on, showing mountains as sharp as dog's teeth rearing up behind the foothills surrounding three sides of the research station. Among the black rocks piercing the snow flowed rivers of blue-white ice, and to the north and north-east, two of fire. Between and before the volcanoes, a meltwater lake stretched for kilometres. Rocks nearby were scoured by wind and ice, distorted into sculptures of the strangest forms, streaked with the subtle colours of mineral formations. But the land itself spawned only mosses and lichens, and occasional groves of stunted trees.

"Everything the Naxadans need is below ground. The mapping expedition brought back plant samples which our exobotanist, Abdel Tairik, compared with surface samples. He found their DNA was similar, yet differentiated enough that they probably evolved millenia ago. In other words, they developed to their present forms in that underground environment."

Matt watched Hartmann carefully but could detect no reaction.

"Thank you, Dr Johnson." Hartmann turned back to Marcus Carlin.

Matt nodded and cut the connection, glad to let Marcus deal with the senator.

*

Marcus noticed Ray Travers hovering beside his desk, shifting his weight from one foot to the other. He crossed to him. "What is it?" he asked in an undertone.

"More holovid coming in – from the other cavern. Think we should view it. Might help sway senator."

Marcus nodded. "Put it on now, Ray."

Ray gave the voice command, while Marcus explained to the senator what he would see next.

Moments later the holocam lens swooped in on the humanoid hiding in the bushes. Despite the light level in the cavern, Marcus saw again that this Naxadan's skin was darker than that of any of the tribespeople he'd seen so far. The image grew in the holotank, features resolving by the second: a young male, compact and tightly-muscled. Now Marcus could see that his fine fur differed in texture from that of the other Naxadans; it splayed out in whorls about five centimetres across, with a tiny bare patch at the centre. On one arm was a band of beaten copper; the light-skinned Naxadans wore no jewellery.

"We think he's from another social group." Marcus felt his back muscles tense. He'd recalculated the costings while Jordas had been fetching the senator, but without any idea of how many extra people were involved he could only guess at numbers and costs. *That doubles the projected budget, and could still be wrong.*

As they watched, the Naxadan put a hand to his head.

"Uuuhh..."

Marcus had all his attention on the holotank but turned when he heard the groan from behind him.

Jordas knelt on the floor, hands pressed to his head. "What...?"

"This happened last time we had live transmission from this cavern," Marcus snapped. "Ray – take him to the Medical Centre – *now!*" He brushed past the senator and pulled Jordas to his feet, supporting him under one arm. Ray took the other and they got him onto a chair.

"I'm a bit dizzy, that's all. There's no need –"

"Jordas, listen! Go see Dr Blumenwald."

"I'll be fine soon. I don't want –" Jordas seemed disoriented.

"Jordas," Marcus said, "you may be my senior assistant, but *my* word is law. I'll call and tell her you're on your way."

"I don't want to let you down," Jordas argued, "especially now."

"You'll be letting me down more by not getting yourself checked out," Marcus retorted. "Go with him, Ray – he can't stand by himself."

Hartmann stepped back to let them pass.

At the door, Marcus added, "Don't come back till you're fit. Understand?" Jordas nodded.

It must be serious, Marcus thought. "Make sure he gets there, Ray."

"Will do. Here, Jordas." Ray supported Jordas down the corridor.

Excusing himself to Hartmann, Marcus made an internal holophone call. When he'd finished explaining to Dr Blumenwald's assistant and extracted a promise that the doctor would let him know what she found, he turned back to the senator. "Let's find out what's happening on Naxada," he suggested.

*

The youth staggered back against a boulder, scraping his arm and side. The dizziness and confusion ebbed, but his legs felt as unsteady as the last time.

Twice in one lighttime now he'd felt, in that whirl of emotion and sensation, something which had been a stranger to him for two highwaters and more: the embrace of sajamu – the sharing of the physical senses. The texture of rough cloth against his limbs, moving as he moved. Touching and holding things that ought not to exist, things he could neither name nor understand. Unfamiliar words filtering through his mind. He tried to dispel the confusion with a headshake. *This cannot be,* he thought, lowering his hand, outstretched as if to ward away the sensations. In a heartbeat they were gone, though their ghosts lingered against his flesh.

He squatted against the boulder, hands pressed to his head, waiting for his strength to return in full measure. He needed it all in Shiranu territory, though it was many highwaters since Shiranu had fought Sargussi. There were so few of either tribe, now, that neither dared risk actual warfare. The numbers of his tribe had leached away over the generations since leaving the city.

His fur prickled and lifted from his skin like a ganzu's rage-spines as his proximity sense activated. He bent a branch aside to look around again, but the cavern seemed empty. Yet as the dizziness faded he couldn't rid himself of the sensation of being watched. It made him feel as vulnerable as a hunted bachu.

Despite the danger of discovery, game here was plentiful, and this being Shiranu territory, the bachu were unafraid. *I might eat well, can I but stay away from the Shiranu.* It wasn't that he feared them; but it made no sense for a lone man to take on a whole enemy tribe.

By the cavern entrance he paused, surveying the rocks and cocking his head to listen. There was no sound from the tunnel behind, nor in the cavern. *The safety code hurts no-one.* He stepped forwards on feet leather-clad against ground that tinkled and crunched as shards of glass cracked underfoot. He moved so as to make the least noise possible as he explored, senses extended against danger. He used the shadows of rock and bush in a way that no Shiranu could, his skin and fur providing its own camouflage.

Ahead, a movement. Eyes tracking on it, he recognised the shape of its back leg: long for bounding, slender yet strong. Good meat. His stomach gurgled its emptiness. He reached for the handspear with its tip of bronze slung at his back. His only living father, Maru, was named for the hunt. *I'm nothing if not his son,* he thought, and his lips parted in a grin.

*

Soolkah marched along the tunnel, hating the feel of the mud clinging to and weighting her slippers. The last few seasons had been unusually damp, water often leaking in from Outside to flood the lower-lying passages ankle-deep.

She wandered along, lost in thought, pace slowing. *Seven lighttimes till blow-out.* Before that they'd pack up and leave the area for another seven seasons. The food had to be harvested before the journey. That was why her parents wanted her married quickly. *But I must find a way to avoid becoming amaajni with them!*

Ever since her coming-of-age earlier that season, she'd been dreading the lighttime when one of the unmarried men of the tribe would offer for her. It was inevitable, with few females of marriageable age and nearly twice as many unmarried older brothers. And each had at least one or two brothers, mostly three or four, and in one amaaj, six. No Shiranu woman ever had it easy.

27

They'd arrived at the cavern just before her coming-of-age. She remembered Mnanga's claws probing the private place between her legs, the stretching sensation before the tough membrane inside snapped, the drip of blood down her leg; the approval of the other women. She sighed, remembering her terror; she hadn't understood *why* Mnanga, the Eldest woman, was performing the ceremony – until the women's mysteries were explained to her afterwards. Then she'd been able to let go of her fear. But when the blood of her first course had come only lighttimes later, she'd been scared again. Not, this time, because something was being done to her body without her consent or understanding, but because her body was doing something of its own accord that she hadn't experienced before.

"Why are you crying?" Gujas had asked. "You're grown up, a woman."

"I'm *sure* to get pregnant now!" Soolkah had snuffled.

"No, no, child! Not until you become amaajne. And perhaps not straight away even then."

Over several lighttimes the shock and fear had faded. Now desperation filled her instead. As a child, she'd been content. As an adult thrust into an unwelcome situation she couldn't stop asking questions. Why had Chixi offered for *her*, and not some other girl? Why him, and not another Elder brother? Why did she have to marry at all? Why, why, *why?* She stamped her foot. The thought of Chixi's flabby body heaving against hers made her feel sick. Her mother had told her that sex felt good, but she couldn't imagine it being even bearable with Chixi's bulk on top of her, hanging down either side of her body. And though some of the tribespeople had Chixi's condition, none were as tall and fat as he. *I must get out of it,* she told herself. *But how?* She mentally reviewed the tribal stories. No other woman had ever refused marriage, as far as she could remember. And who would have her if she rejected Chixi? Her duty towards the tribe was clear, and to refuse would diminish her origin-amaaj's status.

If the Sargussi hadn't been our enemies perhaps I could have married into their tribe. Her face tightened into a grimace as she remembered how Sargussi ways differed from her own tribe's. She sighed. *I'm trapped.*

She looked around, realising that she'd neglected her safety, something girl-children in particular were taught as toddlers. Not enough daughters were born, and not all grew up. *My parents would be furious if they knew I'd ignored the safety code.*

Soolkah shivered. The mud had penetrated her slippers. She looked around. *The tunnel's empty.* But she couldn't help feeling uneasy.

Smoothing a hand down her kilt, she hitched the basket more firmly under

28

her arm. Almost there now. She'd see how much more produce remained to harvest, then all four of her parents could plan how to gather it in. *But I won't be there to help them. I'll be helping Chixi and his brothers instead.* The shock of realisation churned her stomach and dried her mouth. *Tonight is my wedding night.*

Her parents hadn't told her until it was almost too late, though she'd seen Chixi and his brothers speaking with her fathers just lighttimes before. It was common practise for marriages to be contracted quickly, especially at harvesttime. But Lorr, the youngest brother, hardly took his eyes off her every time they met, and his coming-of-age had been only lighttimes ago. *Chixi had to wait until then. And it's said that he beats Lorr because of it. He might beat me too.*

She walked on, thoughts racing, until she rounded a bend. The tunnel opened out and the farm cavern was spread out in front of her. Light – accompanied by spatters of water – diffused through the ice ceiling, showing plots terraced on a slope heated from below by the volcanic. Glow-cakes lined the walls, the shadows between them forming a pattern on the rockwall as they shed their cold light on the rows of crops. Digging out the irrigation channels again had been hard work, but now their land was fruitful. This season the stream level had risen again, drenching paths and turning dust to mud. There had been a glut of edible fungi this season; but who wanted to eat chillcaps all the time? *I'll get a few,* Soolkah thought, *but I'll get mostly vegetables.*

She surveyed the cavern before entering. Later, others would harvest food for the coming season, but for now she was alone.

She hoisted the basket onto her hip, wondering where to start. Being alone thrilled and frightened her. Although she had privacy for thought, an accident to a lone Shiranu could be fatal. There was always the risk of a rockfall; and she feared attack from Sargussi hunters, though they didn't usually come this far south of the city. It was rumoured some even lived in Keramanthu itself, though *that* couldn't be true; she was sure no Shiranu had dared visit the city after the plague.

She'd picked a great pile of spicepods before the idea came to her: *Why not run away?*

But how could you survive? she argued with herself.

Simple. By staying near enough to scavenge food from your family's plot each season, came the answer. *After all, it's not as if you haven't worked hard yourself – and you still could, at darktime. There's always light from the glowcakes to see by –*

Impossible, she told herself. *That's what it is. An impossible dream.*

All the same, she moved on to the next crop and started picking. She had enough spicepods now, and some chillcaps from the streamside; she needed fruit and root vegetables too. Some black-grey luthu roots would do, and mathnafruit were delicious. She could dry some along with purplish spicepods. She could grind aldu cereal into gritty powder and mix it with water and a little pressed vaazi oil for baking into breadcakes, and... It wasn't long before she realised she was only picking her favourite foods, and only enough of anything to last a few lighttimes.

I'll find somewhere to hide, she thought, as the basket filled. *I daren't come back here for food for a couple of lighttimes, but if I leave it too long, the place will be stripped.* That made her pause, then add more food, though if she took too much it would spoil before she could eat it. But the heat from below could be used to dry some of her harvest. Her mother would do that to keep food edible over the approaching season. *When I need more I'll have to come back at lightbreak or darktime.*

Basket full, she set off as if returning to the sleeping cavern. Her haul was heavy, but she had no intention of starving. After about a pythet the passage diverged west, the only possible escape route since she needed to stay close to her tribe. She couldn't work a plot on her own, without tools; and she'd have to move on when the tribe did to avoid the blow-out. She'd trail them when they moved on; she knew the route by heart.

Then why not leave first? They needn't know she'd arrived first. They'd think she was dead, attacked by Sargussi hunters. She could conceal herself, become their shadow, taking part of their harvest to live on.

As she thought of the consequences of her audacity she shivered and felt all six nipples harden on her chest and stomach. All she'd ever learned about personal safety tumbled through her mind; she moved forward slowly and almost silently. The tunnel's gloom was split only by occasional glowcakes. *All to my advantage.* She crept forwards in search of a hiding place.

*

What the hell's happening to me? Jordas asked himself.

This time his head spun so that the corridors passed in a blur. Ray led him with a limp, sweaty touch on his wrist, their arms twisted together, the posture further disorienting Jordas. When they went out into the heat the stormclouds had amassed for the lunchtime downpour. Jordas squinted across the compound at the Medical Centre. Its noviglass windows, darkened to exclude the sun's rays, cleared as they approached.

The last time he'd been there was when he'd first come to work at the research station. A medical check was compulsory on arrival, and yearly

30

thereafter. That was where he'd met Nina. She didn't matter to him now; but he remembered why they'd broken up, and had avoided Block B ever since.

He sighed, and the first raindrop fell, a splash of water that burst on the sealcrete with a *splat!* Ray hurried him across the compound and inside the steel doors.

"Hello, Dr Krata, Dr Travers," the receptionist greeted them. "Dr Blumenwald's expecting you. Go through."

Jordas followed Ray, his heart thudding against his ribs. *I wonder if Nina still works here?* He swallowed and stepped through the door.

"Hello, Jordas," Nina said. "We've been expecting you."

Oddly, seeing her wasn't as confrontational as he'd expected. *Well, it was years ago,* he told himself. Yet she looked exactly the same: smooth bronze skin, laughing eyes and shiny chestnut-coloured hair.

"How are you feeling now?" Nina asked.

"I'm fine." Jordas wasn't, but nor was he going to let this woman guess that, or that coming here unnerved him.

"Sure you are. Well, go in there and strip off to your underwear." Nina waved a hand towards the changing cubicles. "I'll just get the medicheck calibrated for you. Have a seat, Ray, if you're waiting."

She'd already moved to the control console of the diagnostic machine which dominated the room. Jordas guessed she was loading his file. He shrugged, a gesture more for Ray's benefit than his own, tottered over to a cubicle, and, once inside, pulled off his long cotton overshirt and loose vest and trousers. As he folded them on the bench he realised this was the same cubicle he'd used when he'd first met Nina. His hands were shaking. He pushed his sandals into a corner and tried to empty himself of all emotion.

When he stepped outside, Dr Blumenwald was waiting. A chunkily-built woman who contrasted with Nina's daintier figure, she pumped his hand, just as she had four years before, and boomed a greeting. Jordas concentrated on ignoring Nina and smiled at her instead.

"So. Dr Carlin says you fainted. Twice. We better check this out." Her accent matched her form. "Lie down here. Nina!"

Jordas climbed onto the reclining seat at the side of the medicheck machine and lay still while Nina wired him up for the scan. Her touch made him feel acutely uncomfortable. At last she finished and stepped away, and the machine began its work. He could hear the two women conferring in the background. "...Negative scans...Vital signs okay apart from unusually high blood pressure for this subject...Indications of high stress levels...No signs of any viral or other infections. Other than the stress factor, it compares well to

31

his previous profile...Hmmm. But look at these alpha waves." Dr Blumenwald came over to Jordas. "How do you feel? Any pain anywhere?"

"None. I just went dizzy and fainted, like this morning." Jordas lay back, too drained now even to feel embarrassment at Nina's occasional glances at him, or wonder about his alpha waves.

"No obvious problems apart from some signs of stress. But you didn't come to see me each year," Dr Blumenwald boomed.

"I felt fine." Jordas glanced at Ray, who was examining his fingernails. *He couldn't have failed to hear.*

"Sure. So this is what happens when you don't have your yearly medical. It's stressful when you have to catch up all at once!" Dr Blumenwald smiled good-naturedly at him. "I am getting a strange result from one test so I'd like to run all the scans again."

Jordas nodded, aware of Ray's gaze on him. "You ought to get back," he said to him, trying to firm up his voice.

Ray searched Jordas's expression. "Sure?"

"Go on, Ray. Marcus needs you there – go help him."

Ray nodded and raised his hand in a half-wave, then scurried out of the door on tiptoe.

"Another complete sweep, Nina."

The machine ran through its repertoire of tests once more. It seemed to take longer this time. Dr Blumenwald conversed with her nurse at her usual volume. Just when Jordas had become desperate for the scan to end Nina came over to him and released the sensors.

"You can get dressed now."

Jordas sought refuge in the cubicle, relieved to don his clothes again, though he was sweating despite the air conditioning, and not just because of the noon heat. He wriggled his feet into his sandals and left the cubicle.

Dr Blumenwald was examining two charts in the scanner's holotank. "I'm comparing your brain activity with your previous profile. We should be able to decide if anything unusual's going on, but don't expect miracles." She checked the time. "Have you had anything to eat yet?"

Jordas shook his head. "I'm not hungry right now."

Dr Blumenwald shrugged. "Nina! Get me some lunch, will you?" She watched Nina leave on her errand, then said, "Nina thinks you avoided your medicals because of her."

Jordas hesitated, then shrugged. "Okay," he agreed. "What of it?"

"You could have called me and explained your difficulties."

"Maybe."

"I don't want to pry, but why didn't it work out for you two?"

"It's not really your business," Jordas said. "Why don't you ask her? You've obviously been discussing me."

She shrugged again. "I was interested to hear your side of the story, since it seems to have affected your ability to follow instructions!"

Jordas acknowledged that with a throwaway gesture and thought back. He'd known he wouldn't forget what Nina had done to him; but it was hard to explain to anyone else. "She wasn't ready for the kind of relationship I wanted, and I wasn't prepared to share her."

"Hmm." Dr Blumenwald pointed to a chair. "Wait here, Dr Krata. I'm just going to analyse your results."

Jordas seated himself, reached for his notebook, and drew his earpieces from the storage facility on the side of the device. Then he looked up Senator Hartmann on its Infosearch facility.

Nina returned and entered Dr Blumenwald's office. Jordas could hear them talking, but ignored Nina's glance at him and concentrated on his research. The notepad's miniature projection tank filled with the head and shoulders of a holovid newscaster.

"Senator Gerrold Hartmann has tonight been cleared of any culpability in the delay in release of funding to the Mourang famine zone two years ago. Five thousand colonists starved to death, and for more than a year their offworld relatives have lobbied for an inquiry into why supplies took so long to arrive. Senator Hartmann, also a member of the World Government on Earth, is one of several politicians who liaise directly between their governments and the Committee for Resettlement and Colonisation on resources and funding. He was accused of vacillating over the release of supplies, but evidence against him was circumstantial, and the Inquiry collapsed. One of his colleagues has been implicated by Senator Hartmann's evidence..."

"Okay, Dr Krata, you better come in here."

Jordas stowed his notebook away and crossed the room. On Dr Blumenwald's desk lay half an egg and cress sandwich in its wrapper. He sat down in the chair she indicated, feeling more relaxed now. His hands weren't shaking any more and the dizziness had finally leaked away while she'd been checking his results.

"We-ell, I can't find anything actually *wrong* with you –"

Jordas stared at her. "Are you sure? I felt pretty rough back there."

"Well – there is one thing which is...unusual. Both profiles show enhanced psi sensitivity." Dr Blumenwald didn't so much shrug as lift her square shoulders in a gesture which travelled throughout her body. "I don't know if it's significant, but there are much higher residual activity levels in the new profile. It may be that which caused the dizziness and fainting, if you were in contact with an equally sensitive person."

"I was tested once before, for the Meiller study," Jordas said. "They said I was a highly sensitive subject."

"Really?" Dr Blumenwald didn't seem very interested. "Well, I did find definite signs of stress, so I'm putting you on a week's sick leave –"

That was probably because I had to come here. "I'm working on a very important project," Jordas interrupted. "I can't take time off for *stress!*"

"Ach, that's the trouble with you obsessive compulsives!" Dr Blumenwald permitted herself a grin. "They can manage without you for a week," she boomed. "I'll fix it. I know Marcus Carlin. He's totally dedicated, but knows the benefit of fit and healthy staff." She smiled this time. "Forget about your project for a few days. I think you need a break from your work."

But will the Naxadans survive? Jordas opened his mouth to protest again, but Dr Blumenwald forestalled him.

"There's nothing more to be said. I've already entered it on your records and I'm just going to call Marcus and tell him. Go home, Dr Krata. Rest."

As he rose, it occurred to him that he'd got over Nina a long time ago after all. Even his anger had seeped away over the years. *Maybe I won't have to avoid the medical next year.* He opened the office door. Nina was watching him. He summoned a smile and said, "Goodbye," in a careless tone, and left.

Outside, water was still pounding the ground, though it was almost time for the rains to cease. Jordas stepped out, into the rain. The water cooled his flesh. He walked slowly across the deserted compound, fully upright. He usually kept out of the rains but this time he didn't mind getting soaked. His clothes clung to every inch of his body. It didn't matter.

Nothing can touch me now, he told himself. *I'm free.*

And I'll never let any woman hurt me again.

*

Marcus Carlin flicked off the holophone, hoping he could conceal his dismay. In a corner of the monitor room, Hartmann was talking to Ray and Bill Borthwick, the anthropologist who worked part-time on the project. Marcus could just hear the conversation.

"So what happens to the holovid screened out by your privacy filter?" Hartmann asked. "You must lose some useful information."

"That's true, because once edited to archive chips the originals are deleted," Bill agreed. "The only time the filter doesn't operate is on live transmissions."

"I see."

Marcus beckoned Ray over. "Can you come in a couple of hours earlier tomorrow?" he asked in an undertone. "Jordas is on sick leave. Bill will cover the live hololink monitoring, but he'll need an update, and with the senator here we'll be hard-pressed."

"Sure," answered Ray. "Dr Blumenwald say what's wrong with Jordas?"

"Stress. He comes back on the last day of the senator's visit." Marcus sighed, pressed his lips together and turned towards Hartmann, intending to continue their lunchtime discussion.

"So about these troglodytes," Hartmann said.

Marcus frowned. "You mean the Naxadans?"

"Yes. I'd welcome more holovid to study at my leisure. Send your young assistant over tonight to discuss my requirements – I'll need copies to take back with me."

"Ray will call round with a selection when he goes offshift."

"Even better. I need to find out what they could offer the Federal League."

"Senator, does that matter when sentient creatures will die if they stay where they are? I think that's a good enough reason for resettling them. So do my colleagues."

"You see," Hartmann continued, just as if Marcus hadn't spoken, "I have to justify the rescue to my superiors, and I don't see any great advantage to the Federal League in them becoming members."

You're not getting away with that one! thought Marcus. There had been no mention of such necessity in the procedures he'd checked before applying for the CRC's help. The politician puzzled him. What advantage could delaying or not authorising the rescue project bring? He remembered Mourang and changed tack. "Senator, what do you *think* we want from you?"

"Money," Hartmann said. "That's the only reason the Committee would be asked to get involved. You contacted us so we could raise and allocate funding to a resettlement project for these indigenes, then oversee that process."

"Precisely." Marcus paused. "But I want funding for two purposes. First, I want to get those people out of there before they drown, and resettled on another compatible world, where they can continue their way of life with minimum disruption. Second, since the city will be destroyed, and it's probably of historic or even religious importance to these people, I want to put an archaeological team in there with adequate holorecording resources to reconstruct it and, if possible, preserve its artefacts."

"I see. Do you have estimates for the amount of funding you need?"

35

Marcus extracted the notebook containing his latest estimates from his desk and handed it to Hartmann.

The senator skimmed through the report.

Marcus watched him and waited as he studied the financial summary intently. When Hartmann looked up, he said, "You asked about benefits to the League, Senator, but it occurs to me that there's a benefit to yourself in authorising the rescue, particularly after Mourang."

Hartmann paled. "In what way?"

That's got him, Marcus thought with satisfaction. "It wouldn't exactly do your reputation any harm," he countered. "In fact it would make you very popular within the scientific community, and might even increase your political reputation."

Hartmann's brows met in a zigzag for an instant before his usual lack of expression reasserted itself. "You'll have my decision shortly after I get back to Earth."

"Oh no, Senator, the situation's too urgent!" Marcus retorted. "I need a decision from you while you're here. Otherwise the city will drown and these natives will die along with it."

CHAPTER 3

A BURST OF STATIC ANNOUNCED that the robot arm of the probe had disconnected itself from the terminal again. Ray Travers had ordered the probe to follow her when he'd seen the young female on her own.

No time now to get what Senator Hartmann had requested. He'd watched the female fill her basket with food from the terraces of black and dark red vegetation – colours Abdel had suggested the plants had evolved to absorb as much light as possible. The surface might be too cold for many plants to survive, but in the caverns roofed by ice caves, they could cling to life; the mixture of volcanic heat, sulphur-tinged springs, and light from both the surface and the luminous fungi had provided potent nurture.

At last the holovid reconnected itself. Concealed from the female's view, it panned around the mouth of the passage, which had widened out into a cavern again. The female shivered. Ray could see the peach-fuzz of white fur on her body better now; the holoprobe was close behind her.

Hitching the basket on her hip, looking around her, she darted from one piece of cover to another, working her way further inside the cavern. But here no Naxadan hands had irrigated, planted, fertilized and nurtured the terraced plots. Here fewer fungi augmented the light; although mosses and lichens, similar to surface species, had patterned the cavern floor with red and brown-black. Scrub and bushes clustered around a stream which ran through the centre of the cavern, despatching tendrils to chase light. Though no farmer, Ray was sure they weren't cultivated – they didn't resemble any of the crops in the farm cavern.

He shrugged. The female had worked her way round almost a quarter of one side of the cavern while his attention had wandered. He saw her reach a crack in the cavern wall and squeeze inside it. Minutes later she reappeared without the basket, glancing around as if she suspected the presence of a watcher. She slipped from one pile of boulders to another until she reached the stream. A few metres along, the rocks formed a screen around part of the brook. She worked her way along the streamside until she could take cover there and was lost to view.

The probe remained connected to its terminal. Ray wondered again why she was there. It was unusual for a Naxadan woman to leave the cavern alone, and so early; the people usually moved about in groups, probably for protection. He tried to return his attention to the tank before him but thanks to the extra shift he was too tired to concentrate. Marcus and the Senator would arrive later. His thoughts wandered. *Jordas suffering from stress, eh?* He yawned. *Bet he's madder'n Marcus at being off for a week!*

*

Jordas reached for the next handhold. He hadn't tackled this climb before, but he was glad of the challenge. He needed a distraction.

His gloved hand connected with the rock. It seemed solid enough, though roots had sliced through the cliff-face, making climbing hazardous. He tested the boulder before daring to transfer his weight. *It'll hold.*

He'd gone straight home from the medical centre and picked up his climbing gear. *It's true that I haven't had any leave at all this year,* he reflected. *But I can't believe that faint was caused by stress, and it's a damned nuisance that it should happen now.*

The next handhold was to his right. Jordas looked for a toehold that would enable him to move across the cliff-face, spotted one and hammered the piton into the crevice. A brushplant was growing out of it. As he transferred his weight again, its stiff spines quivered against his foot. Part of the rock around the crevice crumbled and fell into the forest below. *Shit!* He recovered himself and shivered, though the day was as hot and clammy as ever. *I'll stop on the next ledge,* he promised himself. His hand reached out sideways and found the hold he sought. A quick glance upwards as he felt for the next handhold told him he was nearly there.

Seconds later he hauled himself over its lip onto a limestone pavement. Trees had sprouted through the rock in places, arching overhead, some several metres high, though many were only seedlings. A pseudocedar and its broadleaved cousin almost completely obscured the hazy disk of Lyrica. Jordas lay on the rock, panting and as glad of the shade as he was of sunscreen shots.

He could hear water nearby. *This would be a good place to make camp.* When he'd recovered, he set to unpacking his belongings, but found his mind still following its previous tack. *Dr Blumenwald didn't take much notice of the results of that brain activity scan. Strange.* He thought about the faints and tried to remember the sensations they'd brought, but it was no use: the memories teased him, then slithered away. He shrugged. It probably wasn't important. *And yet – I wonder what really happened. I went dizzy, and I don't know why – but twice it happened when that dark-skinned Naxadan was on the live hololink...*

Although alone, Jordas shook his head. He laid his sleeping bag on the ground to sit on, then prepared to boil water. He knew it would do him good to be away from work for a while, but he couldn't entirely banish thoughts of the Naxadans.

38

*

"Araz?" Gujas couldn't help it; she'd held back from asking him for too long.

Her eldest husband turned. He was knapping a new harvesting knife from glossy obsidian. Several sharp slivers lay beside him, ready for spear tips. "What?"

"Have you seen Soolkah? She knows I need those vegetables for tonight's feast."

Araz looked troubled. "How – how did she take it?"

"Not – well." Gujas wouldn't touch him, even with Lagi and Ulon out of their sleeping niche, though she longed for him to hold and reassure her. Her other husbands were in an unused sleeping niche, boiling dyes for the cloth Benna's amaaj wove. The hot dry reek filled the air. But Gujas had justifiable pride in the quality of the dyestuffs her two younger husbands produced; their goods were sought after throughout the tribe, and Araz' knapping skills had also brought their amaaj status amongst their people. "Araz, I'm worried about her. It's almost mid-lighttime. She should have been back long ago."

Araz wrapped the rest of the blades in a piece of cloth and laid them high on a ledge for safety before answering. "I'll see if I can find her. She might need help carrying everything."

Gujas nodded, though his reasoning hadn't convinced her. *There's surely something wrong.* She hadn't forgotten Soolkah's expression when she'd told her she was to become amaajni. For a moment Araz stood at the mouth of the niche, face turned in the direction of the dye-cave. As her Eldest husband walked away, guilt pierced Gujas. *Should we have told her before? But every daughter must be claimed by one amaaj or another, and only Chixi and his brothers offered for her.*

Gujas rubbed one swollen breast. It was time to feed Teffen again. He was shifting coloured stones around on the floor into patterns; they were large enough that he wouldn't swallow them, and not easy for a child of a little over one highwater to lift. Gujas settled herself down cross-legged against the rockwall, a sleeping cloth protecting her from its rough surface. "Teffen! Come here! Feed-time!"

Teffen understood much more than he said; with two brothers ahead of him, how could it not be so? His smile showed he had nearly all his even white teeth now.

"Come on!" She held out her arms to him. He left his stones and ran across, laughing. She laid him down in her lap and pushed one of the lowest pair of nipples into his mouth. He was sucking contentedly when Araz' form blotted out most of the light from the main cave. From his breathing, he must have run back.

"I've checked the farm cavern," he said. "She's not there."

*

Ray gasped as the holotank darkened, obscuring the cavern. The holovid's view cleared as a shape slipped forwards from below it: the young male he'd seen earlier. He recognised the copper band on his arm. No taller than the pale Naxadans and a little shorter than a human, but proportionally more powerfully built, muscles flexed under dark skin. The leather kilt hem was ragged, following the shape of some animal's hide. A belt of thicker leather bore a thirty-centimetre scabbard, from which the hilt of a knife jutted.

Abruptly the Naxadan turned, as if sensing observation. His face was distinctly masculine, but as hairless as the female's. As if perplexed, he tapped at his chin with one talon. His hands bore four fingers and an opposable thumb; though the claws curved, flashing like scimitars as he flattened himself back against an outcrop for concealment.

"What's *he* up to?"

Ray hadn't realised how involved he'd become with the holotank scene until he heard his own words. *Call Matt – see if he knows what's happening? Don't want to miss anything.*

The cavern's ice ceiling muted the light, camouflaging the Naxadan's form against the rocks. He stood unmoving for a minute before dropping into a squat, to edge past the rocks in one fluid movement.

The holovid swung up so the dark shadow below it was still partly visible, but now it included most of the cavern in its field of view. There was no sign of the female but the male lifted his head and sniffed.

Must rely on scent for info. Uh-oh, thought Ray. He watched, wondering whether or not the Naxadan had seen – or scented – the female.

Still crouching, the male moved further into the cave. The holovid's lens followed him, seeing what he saw.

Ray gave the command for direct contact with Matt.

*

"Chixi?"

He opened his eyes, blinking to clear his vision. His condition tired and irritated him at times, though resting towards mid-lighttime helped.

The focus came back all at once. Araz stood in the mouth of his sleeping niche: Soolkah's eldest father, a man two or three highwaters older than him. He looked worried.

Chixi drew himself up to his full height so that he towered over Araz.

40

"What is it?"

"I asked Lorr and he said you were here. I –" Araz' mouth worked as he sought words.

Just say what you have to say and let me rest! Chixi thought, trying not to show his impatience. *I'll need my strength for tonight.*

"It's Soolkah," said a woman. Beyond Araz, Chixi saw Gujas, her youngest son in her arms, his mouth attached to one of her middle pair of breasts. "She's disappeared."

"Disappeared?" After a moment Chixi realised he was gaping at them, so he closed his mouth and spread his hands, palms down, in the gesture of misunderstanding. "Impossible!"

"I sent her to the plot for vegetables early this lighttime and she hasn't come back."

Rage invaded Chixi's mind. His visions of being amaajne at last died like a ganzu in a rockslide. Squashing the urge to grasp Araz by the neck and shake him, he croaked, "Then we must search for her. Now."

"What about the harvest?"

"The harvest can wait," Chixi growled. "My wedding can't!"

"I'll get Hanook," Lagi muttered from beyond the niche.

Chixi hadn't known he was there, though he supposed in the circumstances all Soolkah's fathers would be. "Good." It took an effort of will to say the word. He turned to Gujas. "When did you last see her?"

"At lightbreak, when I told her about the wedding and sent her to get food from our plot for the feast."

"Then that's where we must look first." Chixi struggled to keep his temper in check. He concentrated on his brothers to divert his anger. Sajamu from them told him they were still in the farm cavern. "I'll meet you at your plot with my brothers." Chixi turned aside and picked up his spear and knife, made by Araz himself and traded for plants two seasons before, when the mathna bushes on Araz' plot had withered from soil-plague.

"What are you doing?" asked Araz.

"She may have been taken by Sargussi."

The smaller tribesman's pupils dilated in shock. "There haven't been any near our lands for many highwaters, Chixi."

"Doesn't mean to say there can't be now!" he retorted, and pushed past all of them, stomping towards the tunnel which led to the farm cavern.

*

Soolkah sat on the rock outcrop, dipping her feet in the shallows. The streamflow was fast, the water cold, but she disliked the sensation of mud and dirt squelching between her toes even more. As she lifted her feet out, she shook water from them, then rinsed her slippers and pulled them back on. She yawned. *That tunnel must be ten pythetu long.* She knew they'd search for her today; but with the harvest they might not search up to darktime. *They've enough to do without worrying about one missing bride! Have they discovered I've gone yet? I'd better hide now.*

She hoped she hadn't left a trail in the cavern's earth floor, and wouldn't leave water drips on the way back to the niche. She rose, intending to collect branches and twigs to make a switch and brush the earth to conceal her tracks.

But as she tried to get to her feet a hand clamped over her mouth and nose and an arm locked across her stomach. She couldn't breathe. All she could see before her were coppery-skinned fingers. The cave blurred around her. The fur on her captor's forearms tickled her throat and stomach, making her own fur stand on end as she strove to speak.

"Be silent!" came a growled command from behind.

His speech sounded strange – old-fashioned and oddly accented. Soolkah felt the warmth of her assailant's chest at her back as she struggled in his grasp. *He must be Sargussi, not that I've ever seen one before.* Anger boiled up in her that he should break the touch taboo and not care. *But if he's Sargussi, that would explain it –*

A noise in the distance alerted her. Chixi and his brothers – and her fathers – would be out searching for her now. She *must* get under cover.

Her teeth closed on the finger pressed against her mouth.

"Mmmmf! Shiranu ganzu-bitch!" The Sargussi moved his hand slightly.

It was enough – she could breathe. "I've got to hide!" she gasped. "My amaaj are searching for me!" It was a direct appeal, but she couldn't think of anything else.

"Why would you run from your own amaaj?" the Sargussi demanded. "And why would you think I should help you?"

Soolkah thought hard. "If they find you, they'll kill you," she hissed.

The Sargussi stood still for a moment, nostrils flaring, head cocked, fur lifting from his skin. For an instant curiosity overcame fear as she realised that the rumours were true: their enemies still possessed the proximity sense her tribe had lost after abandoning hunting.

"Where were you thinking to hide?" he demanded, shaking her.

"You shame me by touching me!"

"*Really?*" His voice was mocking. He never relaxed his grip. "Answer me!"

The fear came back in a rush. Soolkah could feel his knife hilt digging into her hip. Sargussi didn't take prisoners. Hunters and carnivores, they were rumoured not just to kill Shiranu but to eat them as well. Fear gave her more strength than she'd known she had. She twisted round in his grip and stared up into the face above hers. "Th-the crevice in the rockwall over there —" Trying to keep her hand from trembling, she pointed.

"Quickly, now!" he muttered. "If you speak truth, we may have little enough time." Pinioning her arms behind her back, he pushed her along before him. "Show me!"

Soolkah stumbled round the outcrop again. Her ears strained for the slightest sounds of pursuit, though as a child she too had learnt to move like a silent shadow on the glassy rockfloor. The cavern and tunnel beyond were silent. But she couldn't flee further. The tunnel ended in this cavern.

At the niche entrance a hard shove from the Sargussi almost tore her arm from its socket, but pride kept her from complaining. She glanced at the ground. "What about our tracks?"

"Let *me* deal with that!" he answered. "Now in there with you!" He thrust her forwards, sending her sprawling on the floor. She twisted, trying to rise, and saw he'd followed her inside. He took a length of vinerope from his belt pouch.

She shrank back against the rockwall behind her. "Wh-what are you going to do with that?"

"Tie you, of course! I've yet to decide what to do with you!" He reached for her hands, breaking the twine with his teeth when he was done, and started on her ankles. He moved with efficiency and wasted no breath on speech.

That didn't surprise Soolkah; her tribe also kept silence unless necessity demanded, for fear of discovery by Sargussi hunters and to avoid causing rockslides.

Rolling her on her side when he'd checked the tightness of her bonds, the Sargussi ducked out of the entrance to the cave.

"Where are you going?" she whispered, though her voice sounded loud even to her own ears.

It was enough to detain him.

At last the light fell full on his face. He was young, her own age.

"Tracks," he said. "Be silent!" Then he was gone.

*

Lorr was cutting mathna fruit from black stems when Chixi found him. He kept the privacy shield raised, forcing his brother to use spoken language.

"Daydreaming again?" Chixi asked.

"That's not fair," Lorr muttered. "I work as hard as any of you." *And I don't have to rest in the middle of the day.* But he knew from past experience that with Chixi it was a case of least said, soonest mended, so he crouched down to cut the next couplet of reddish globes. The stalks were tough, the fruit slippery and hard to grasp. There was little room between the branches. It took a practised flick of the wrist to extract the fruit whole. "Come to think of it," he grunted, "why aren't you resting?"

"Soolkah's missing. You'd have known if you ever lowered your mindshield."

Lorr stared up at his brother. "Missing?" he repeated. "But – she was here this morning. I saw her leave the sleeping cavern." He swallowed on a dry throat. "We – we'll become amaajnu with her this evening."

"No need to remind me of that," Chixi rasped. His brown-green eyes were hard as stones, and there was a chill in his voice. "There could have been an – accident. We have to find her now. Leave what you're doing. Fetch your weapons. I'll wait for you here."

Lorr nodded. He put the fruit he'd gathered into the basket and hurried down the tunnel without glancing back at his elder brother. He didn't need to; he could have shared thoughts easily. The effort came in not sharing. Lorr chose to use the privacy shield more often than any of his three brothers, knowing Chixi would bait him if he learned of his feelings for Soolkah. *I won't lay myself open to his sarcasm,* he resolved, and tried to swallow his fear for their bride-to-be.

In their sleeping-niche Lorr grabbed spear and knife. His head ached with the effort of keeping the privacy shield going but he ignored the pain. *We must find her. Please be safe!* He ran back to the farm cavern. Lorr joined the cluster of men had gathered about Chixi; his brothers Jeene and Vru stood beside him.

Hanook, the Eldest man in the tribe, led them towards the tunnel mouth again. "We've already searched the farm-cavern twice," he said. "She's not here. I suggest we search the nearby tunnels and any caves we come across." He led the way back into the tunnel. Lorr followed his brothers, aware of the urgent pounding of his heart.

*

The Sargussi had been gone so long that Soolkah began to think he wasn't coming back, and wriggled about in an attempt to free herself. The floor ground into both fur and skin as she moved; she only succeeded in gathering scrapes and tightening her bonds. Her wrists and ankles smarted from the pressure of the vinerope on them.

All at once he was back, almost filling the entrance to the niche, all broad shoulders and solid muscle. On a submerged mental level she realized he was

44

quite good-looking. In his hands were some dried pricket twigs; his fur bore bloodstains from the thorns. She noted with pride she'd drawn blood on his finger, too.

He laid down the twigs, then propped something else up against the rockwall. In the gloom it took her a moment or two to identify it as a metal-tipped spear. "We were safe from discovery now," he said, "provided you keep silent." She heard satisfaction in his voice. He didn't even bother to glance in her direction as he spoke, concentrating instead on levering rocks out of their resting places and building up a mound near the entrance to the little cave.

"What are you doing?" she asked.

"You ask many questions, Shiranu!" He positioned one boulder on top of another. "I'm concealing the entrance."

"Will we be able to breathe?"

The Sargussi stopped for a moment and turned to face her. He bared his teeth, but he wasn't smiling. Meeting her eyes, he raised one brow and asked, "Now what would make you think that's going to matter to *you*, Shiranu?"

CHAPTER 4

THE SARGUSSI YOUTH KEPT HIS FACE EXPRESSIONLESS as he looked over his shoulder at the Shiranu girl on the ground behind him. She looked about sixteen or seventeen highwaters – his age – and was very beautiful despite her exotic appearance.

"A-are you going to kill me?"

"If no other game offers," he replied in as non-committal a tone as possible.

"Huh! I'd rather die than get married anyway!" she retorted, struggling against the vinerope. "Ouch!"

"What *now*? I must concentrate on building this wall!"

"I hurt myself moving. Look, untie me and I can help you with that."

"There isn't the time," he answered. *Why would she help me with her own capture? It makes no sense.* "Any time saved by you helping me would be lost in untying you, and anyway, Shiranu haven't *this* skill of wall-building. Now be silent!" He fitted another boulder into place, and the light in the crevice decreased further.

The wall stretched upwards under his hands. Once he stopped to listen; the cavern and passage beyond were quiet as a dried-up river. *But she said her people will be looking for her.* His hand strayed to his belt knife. If they found him.

"If you don't hurry up with the wall it *will* come to a fight," she hissed.

He shot a puzzled glance at her before continuing his work. *Why would my enemy choose captivity over returning to her tribe?* He realised he'd only find out with leisure for discussion, but couldn't quell his curiosity.

At last darkness almost totally filled the niche; only a concealed airhole remained near the top of the stones. He crossed to the girl's side and knelt near her, hesitating. He considered putting his hand over her mouth again – until his finger throbbed. *Is it truth that she's left her tribe, or must I be on my guard now?* He laid his knife against her throat instead.

"Keep quiet when your folk come," he breathed, "until I tell you it's safe to speak." In the remnants of light leaking in he saw her nod. He spread his furs on the rocks, leaned back against a boulder, and stretched his legs out before him, resting his hunting knife across his thighs.

*

Lorr followed his brothers: Chixi, Jeene and Vru. He sniffed. *She's been here. I can almost taste her.* Blood thundered in his veins.

46

They walked on. The tunnel twisted, dipping before rising again. In the distance Lorr saw the brighter half-circle of another cavern ahead. His heart jolted, filled with hope. Now they must move as quietly as possible, so he dropped his mental barriers in case Chixi needed to mindspeak with him.

The group halted at the cavern mouth. Hanook stared around it, then signed to Chixi to follow him. Lorr noticed then that Hanook's brothers weren't in the group. They must be searching the sleeping and farm caverns again.

Despite his size Chixi could move as silently as any other Shiranu. Lorr watched him circle the cave, Hanook and Nulma flanking him. When they returned, signing to the rest of the group that the cavern contained no threat, he realised he'd forgotten to breathe and had to gulp air in.

"You can search now," Hanook told the rest of the group in the signing-speech.

They spread out in pairs. Lorr stood beside Jeene, sniffing the air. Was his conviction that Soolkah was still alive just hope or a shadow of the proximity sense?

<What is it?> asked Jeene in the mindspeech.

<I'm sure I can sense Soolkah nearby,> Lorr answered. Chixi might dismiss such a statement, but Jeene wouldn't.

<Where?>

Lorr shut his eyes. He circled on the spot, ignoring the other men. He didn't care if they thought he was as mad as Chixi – he *knew* he wasn't. He let the thoughts float out of his mind and tried to relax. Awareness pounded at him. He twisted about. <There,> he told Jeene, pointing.

He opened his eyes. Hope was at once damped: before him lay a mass of boulders.

<Can't be...though I think there used to be a niche there.> Jeene moved forwards and prodded at the pile of rocks with his spear.

*

The Sargussi tensed as the wall he'd built shifted slightly, and held his breath until his head spun and his heart thumped. When the man outside moved away he guzzled in air in relief. He'd known the Shiranu were nearby, but hadn't expected to get this close to them. But survival in the face of such danger would surely earn a newly-adult male much-needed status.

He cocked his head in the darkness. The searchers made little noise; they must have been using sign language and the mindspeech, as his own folk would have. As his eyes adjusted to the dark he was able to make out the Shiranu girl's face, and he stared, amazed at her impassivity. It really did seem she didn't want to be found by her tribe. He wondered what was happening in the cavern, but he'd made the airhole twist so nothing would be visible from outside the rock barrier, and he dared not even move lest the searchers heard him.

It was hard to keep still for so long.

*

Disgust twisted Jeene's face. <There must have been a rockslide since last highwater.>

Lorr nodded, unable to even mindsend for the disappointment blocking his throat and prickling behind his eyes. *I suppose he's right – there's no chance I could have got the proximity sense back...*

Chixi walked back to them. <She isn't here,> he sent. <I still think Sargussi hunters must have taken her.>

Hanook was beside him. As they reached Jeene and Lorr, he made the hands-spread gesture for "What?"

Chixi repeated his message in the signing-speech.

Hanook nodded. "There's no other exit from this cavern. We should leave when the others finish searching. There's nothing more to be gained by this, and we have a harvest to gather in." His eyes held kindness as they rested on Lorr. "Perhaps she didn't come this way at all," he suggested.

You're wrong, all of you. I'm certain *she was here.* But Lorr's hands stilled of their own accord; he couldn't find the signs to argue. And who would listen to a younger brother?

*

The lighttime passed slowly without activity to fill it. At last the Sargussi's proximity sense told him that the searchers had indeed left. Still he made himself wait many moments before dismantling part of the barrier. Light seeped in, blinding him. As his sight adapted again the blur resolved itself into the cavescape, and his eyes confirmed what his instincts had already told him.

"Are you going to untie me?" the Shiranu girl asked.

He glanced back at her. Her face was paler than ever. *Mayhap her bonds are too tight.* He nodded and leaned over her, cutting through the rope with his knife. "Hurts, Shiranu?" he asked, grimacing as he stretched his own limbs.

She made no answer but rubbed her wrists and ankles to bring back circulation.

His eyes wandered over her: flat chest with pink nipples, slim build, straight back, blue woven kilt with paler patterns, slippers soled with woven reed stalks. "We are so alike, yet so unalike," he mused, allowing his gaze to meet her cool green one.

"Do Sargussi have names?" she asked.

"Of course," he answered, surprised. "Hungry, Shiranu? I am."

"I brought food with me," she answered, trying to gesture towards something he hadn't noticed before. At the back of the niche lay a basket.

"Vegetables!" he snorted. "We Sargussi eat only meat."

"I know that. I wasn't offering *you* any!" She reached for a pod from the basket and crunched on it with enjoyment. He watched, and his own stomach rumbled.

"So what *is* your name?"

That took him by surprise again, but he quickly recovered. "Oh, no. You don't fool me that way!" he muttered. *Does she think she were safer if I thought of her as a person, rather than just my enemy?* He looked up at her again. "Do you never stop asking questions? Are all Shiranu as inquisitive as you?"

It was her turn to stare at him. "Inquisitive?" she echoed. "Just because I asked what your name was?"

"Tell me yours first," he said, and got up, giving her no time to reply. "I have need of meat," he said, and reached for the package containing his kill.

She grimaced in distaste. "I *thought* I could smell blood. Here." She tossed him something. It landed on the floor before him. He bent and picked it up. It was a root of some sort. He sniffed it.

"Well, go on, eat it!" she urged him.

"It looks...old, wrinkled –"

The green depths of her gaze gleamed with laughter.

Could it be poisonous? he wondered.

"Mmm, luthu taste *so* good! If *you* don't want it, I'll have it."

He watched her again. She had a way of tossing her head that made the fur shake and bounce, and each time he saw her do it he realised he was waiting to see her do it again. It was...different, interesting. He hadn't taken much notice of the females of his tribe until recently, but like the men's, their whorled headfur never grew long. He touched his own fur, remembering the feel of her fuzz-covered limbs as he'd bound them. *So similar, so different...* There was something about her –

"Well, eat it then!" she commanded him, shifting position.

He looked down at the root in his hand. Traces of earth still clung to it. Pride fought caution. He didn't want to appear afraid in front of her. He brushed at the thing, then bit into it and chewed. "Pah!" he coughed. "It tastes sweet." He spat the lump of root out. "How can you eat such a thing, Shiranu?"

*

Soolkah pulled out a handful of mathna globes out of the basket. Their

49

juice would help quench her thirst.

The Sargussi slid his knife from its sheath. Soolkah thought of her own knife, her father Araz' handiwork, lying at the bottom of the basket. *I won't use it yet.* When she saw him set the point of the knife against the bachu's flesh she screwed up her face and turned away.

"This led me far on the chase," he remarked, concentrating on his task. When she didn't answer, he added, "It's true, then? Shiranu eat no meat?"

Soolkah wondered if his taunts were intentional. "It's true." Her voice was a whisper. "That smell – the blood – makes me feel bad –"

"You won't *be* sick, will you?" he asked. "*That* smell's one to make *me* feel bad!" He edged away from her and turned his back as he continued to skin the creature.

Soolkah's nausea ebbed; she could still smell the blood, but at least she couldn't see the meat now. But when the Sargussi turned back to her, his knife dripped a liquid dark as mathna juice. *How can he do it?*

He watched her with narrowed eyes for several moments. "Are you still afeared I'll kill you? One man couldn't eat so much!" He grinned again.

Soolkah saw that some of his lower teeth were crossed. But she felt her face lighten with relief.

"Are you alone here, then?" she asked. "I thought Sargussi always hunted in groups."

"I'm on my initiation quest. I've just had my coming-of-age."

"I had mine almost a season ago," Soolkah said, "when the tribe came here."

"Season?"

"Oh, I suppose you wouldn't keep the seasons like we do – it's the length of time it takes for a harvest to grow," she explained, watching his reaction. She thought he probably didn't like to show ignorance before his enemy. "About fifty lighttimes, not counting travelling time between farm-caverns. It's based on the length of time between blow-outs. Don't you have anything like that?"

He nodded thoughtfully. "We measure time by the rise and fall of the rivers, and the length of the lighttimes we can see through the ice above," he told her. "And we know our age by the highwaters which come from meltwater from Outside."

"So do we."

He surveyed the cavescape before replying. "I have need of a cooking stone –"

"You're not going to cook meat in here?"

50

"It's safe inside here. If I cook outside I risk the smell drawing your folk should they come this way again."

"It'll smell in here," Soolkah objected.

"Can't be helped." He tapped the ground. "It's hot enough down there! But I'll need a good stone, one that's already hot...so I must tie you."

"I'll come with you and help you find one," she offered, rising. "Don't tie me again."

He stood up to bar her way. "How am I to know you won't run and fetch your folk to kill me?" he demanded.

"I *won't* go back to them."

"Yes, why?"

"Now who's inquisitive?" Triumph blazed in her amazing green eyes for a moment. "I can't go back – they're trying to make me marry into an awful amaaj –"

Surprise spread over his face. "And you ran away, just for that?"

"It's all very well to say 'just for that'," she grumbled. "I suppose you're an Elder brother, and will have the choice of your woman. Just remember, when you do, that no tribeswoman ever has a choice!"

"No," he answered after a pause. "I'm no Elder brother. Mine died in a rockfall, two highwaters ago." He squeezed his eyes shut. "We were just two, Uvvuz and me. I shall remember him all my life. I...I'm glad I had no other brothers I couldn't bear that loss again. I felt him die, and a part of me died with him."

So Sargussi do have feelings, Soolkah thought.

The Sargussi straightened his back as he opened his eyes again. "You – *help* – me?" he murmured, shaking his head. "I must be mad to deal with you. After all, you are Shiranu!" Then he made the pushing gesture, as if he'd made a snap decision. "Let's be quick, I'm hungry."

They entered the main cavern, looking about. Soolkah couldn't rid herself of the feeling of being watched every time she came out of the niche, though the Sargussi had said he was alone. She shook her head and concentrated on finding a cooking stone. It didn't take long. They both knew what to look for despite the difference in diet: a large flat stone, heated by the slumbering volcano below. There were several to choose from.

The Sargussi handed her a bachu-skin.

Soolkah looked at it in distaste.

"Wrap it like this." He wound another around his end of the stone to protect his hands from the heat.

She copied his example. Together they dragged the stone inside the crevice. Soolkah watched the firm back muscles moving under his skin as the Sargussi pressed it into the dust just where the floor felt warmest. "What do you have to do for this – initiation?" she asked when strips of meat had been spread out to cook.

He stared at her. "Do your boys not leave the tribe to be reborn as men?"

"I've never heard of such a thing. Tell me."

"I must stay away from the tribe for twenty lighttimes and return with meat."

"Ah. Don't you have the cutting, then?"

"The circumcision?" Surprise was back in his eyes. "Of course. No Sargussi man could be reborn without it – or wed, though there's no bride for a man without brothers. But surely it's the same for Shiranu?"

She nodded. "But not the initiation – because everyone's needed for working the land, I suppose." She thought of her knife again. "What if you don't return?"

"I shall." His voice was firm, and he breathed in until he seemed to grow a little taller. "I shall at least be known as a great hunter, like my father Maru before me."

*

The doorbell rang. Gerrold Hartmann turned down the volume on the holotank by voice command, checked the time, pasted a smile onto his face and got up from the sofa to answer it.

At the door, his smile subsided somewhat. Ray Travers stood there, hair flopping over his eyes, shifting his weight from one foot to the other and fidgeting with something in his pocket. "Uh – holovid delivery, Senator," he mumbled, standing up on tiptoe as if trying to see past Hartmann into the apartment.

"Thank you, Dr Travers." Hartmann held out his hand for them.

"Had a lot of trouble recovering this stuff. Not supposed to watch it. Hope it's more to your taste than mine!"

Hartmann couldn't help noticing the gel inkstain on Travers' fingers as he took the package and put it in his own pocket. "I'm sure it will be."

Travers continued to stand there, still hopping from one foot to the other. "Just on my way home."

"Then don't let me keep you," Hartmann said curtly. "I'll see you in the morning."

Travers nodded, stepped back into the purple dusk and mumbled "Goodnight."

Hartmann shut the door. He examined the package, counting. All ten chips were labelled with the time and date, though the writing resembled a spider and some labels bore inky fingerprints. A quick calculation of the time difference told him which ones would be of most use when the next whore arrived, and he extracted them and laid them beside the holotank console.

Another ring of the doorbell. Hartmann opened the door. A woman stood there. "You're late."

"It's a rough ride," she said. She was pale and sweaty and her mascara had run. There was a lighter stain on the bodice of her black dress and she smelled of too much perfume.

"You'd better come in and clean up."

*

The Sargussi watched the girl go to the basket in the corner of the niche, every sense alert to discover whether he could trust her. Should he believe her reason for leaving her people?

My suspicion might have been less were she ugly, he realised. *But were I Shiranu, I'd be proud to be amaajne with her.* As she'd helped him drag the stone back to the niche, he'd caught himself watching the play of shadow and light about her legs under her kilt, and had hastily averted his eyes, wondering if she'd seen up his own kilt then. A man had more to conceal than any female. The situation between them was awkward enough as it was.

"Should we cover the place where the stone was?" she asked. "Someone might come for another look here, and a hole in the ground would look suspicious."

He nodded. "I'll attend to it." He allowed a smile to show his approval. "You have the makings of a good hunter," he said, and was surprised by the look of revulsion on her face. *I meant it as a compliment.* To cover his mistake, he asked, "Where are you thinking to go when you leave this cave, if not to your tribe?"

"I'll follow them round the farm cavern circuit," she said. "They won't know I'm there. They'll think I'm dead, and won't be looking for me."

"I thought you were running away," he said.

"I still need food. Vegetables. Fruit." Her eyes went to the meat. She made a face and pinched her nostrils with finger and thumb.

"Good smell!" he declared, and crossed to the bachu skin. "I must prepare this for use. I keep the skins for clothes and sleeping furs." He stared hard at her kilt till heat came to her face. "They say you Shiranu weave and dye cloth."

"Yes. From luthu fibres, with sheddings of our own fur mixed in for warmth, or from machee pelts. We make a fine string out of their fur and weave that. They're so slow and stupid, it's easy to get them and cut their fur off – it soon grows again...And sometimes from anzu bolls –" She broke off as if some thought had struck her.

"What is it?" he asked.

"I'll need bolls to soak up the blood when my next course comes." She averted her face. He wondered if there was the same division of knowledge in her tribe as in his own. He knew nothing about women and how their bodies worked – except what they'd told him after the circumcision at his coming-of-age. "What do your women do, without them?"

He spread his hands palms down. "I don't know – use strips of leather?" As a child he'd seen his mother hang up stained strips of wet leather to dry in their sleeping caves and had always wondered what they were for. This was an insight into women's ways. "You can have some leather if I can get the right sort on my next kill."

The girl shuddered, but said nothing. He worked at the skin, scraping with a knife he'd made himself.

He wondered how long it would take him to rejoin his tribe. They'd move on when the game dried up, and often did so every few lighttimes. They used any suitable caverns, but had no set circuit in their wanderings, unlike their enemies, and usually only returned after a couple of highwaters' absence. He remembered some of the caverns he'd lived in over the last few years. Some had been rather wet these last few highwaters. One had been unusable. "Have your folk noticed much flooding lately?" he asked.

"The water's been very high in the streams these last few seasons," she answered. "More water helps things grow better but too much is dangerous. It kills plants and washes soil away. It *is* strange –"

"My tribe thought so too. We followed the game towards this side of Keramanthu, then I left the others and came on here. The ground's higher at the city – better for avoiding floods. If there were game there it were a good place to live again. The plague can surely do nothing more to us." He scraped at the skin again. He wiped the fat off the blade into his spare lampcup, setting in it a wick of the twine he'd used to tie the Shiranu with. "That should solidify soon." Then he checked the meat. It was cooked. The girl sat watching him while he ate, disgust twisting her face.

"I don't know how you can eat something that's been alive, Sargussi," she said.

He laughed. "Nor do I understand how *you* can eat something from the ground!" He looked across at her. "I must hunt more bachu for darktime's meal," he said. "Must I also tie you again?"

"I'm here from choice, remember –" She met his gaze, diverted from her protest. "Do you only eat bachu?"

"Bachu means any small animal to us, as well as these jumping ones," he explained, gesturing with the meat as he spoke. "Shiranu, don't think yourself free. And don't fetch your folk to kill me –"

He tore at the meat with sharp teeth to underline his meaning.

*

Hartmann sipped his champagne cocktail, eyes fixed on the holotank. It was a quarter of the size of the one Carlin and his two assistants used, but it would do.

The chip bore 'EDITED HIGHLIGHTS' in joined capitals on the label. Travers had chosen well indeed. A group of the troglodytes were slipping away up the dim tunnel from the main chamber: three males and a female. That looked interesting. Their white fur gleamed in the dusk. Hartmann sat forward on the sofa in anticipation.

The troglodytes passed a bend in the tunnel. One of the males spread out a length of cloth on the ground. The female and he laid down on it. She pulled her own kilt up, then reached under his as he mounted her. The other two males squatted or lay nearby, reaching under their own kilts.

Hartmann beckoned the whore over. "Undo my trousers," he said. She obeyed and knelt between his legs, put a hand inside his trousers and began to rub him. Hartmann ignored her efforts as the scene unfolded in the holotank, but when she'd succeeded he suddenly stood up and shoved his cock into her mouth.

None of the troglodytes spoke, even at the climax, though they all seemed to enjoy it. It didn't take long. Soon the group left, and another took their place. It wasn't long before Hartmann's own semen spurted. He sipped his drink.

Below him, the whore swallowed hard and relinquished him. She turned to watch the holotank again, eyes wide. "I've seen plenty of alien porn, but I've never seen aliens with six tits before," she said. "I was told you were an important client, but just who *are* you?"

I'm a little more sophisticated than that, he thought, *but nevertheless there's something very odd about these troglodytes.* "Ask me no questions and I'll tell you no lies," he replied, swallowing the last of his cocktail. "Get me another drink, then I'll remind you of how a human does it. And by the way, the walls *are* soundproofed."

*

The darktime was descending Outside, but the glowcakes never slept.

Soolkah watched the Sargussi. He was sewing the latest skins to the larger sleeping fur he already had with a bone needle, much like the slippermakers in

55

her own tribe. *We're so alike,* she realised. *Yet our tribes were always enemies except when we lived in the city, and even then Shiranu, Sargussi and Chabira always kept apart from each other.*

He wasn't watching her; he was concentrating on his work. Her hand stole into the basket where her knife lay. He was squinting now, turning the skins this way and that to make best use of the light as he sewed in small, neat stitches with fine leather thongs. "I'll get you a glowcake," she suggested. "You'll see better then." He turned his head to look at her, but she got up on her errand before he could stop her.

She soon found one and detached it from the rockwall, holding it so that the liquid at its centre wouldn't touch her skin. When she got back to the niche, the Sargussi stood at the threshold.

"You'd dare touch this for me to see better?" he asked.

"And me." She tried to push past him. "It will die if I don't refasten it and feed it quickly."

"And had it occurred to you that we could be found if your folk return, just because we have a glowcake here for light?"

"Had it occurred to you that we could be found because the threshold of the cave is open now?"

"I have the means of light," he argued.

"Ugh, burning animal fat smells horrible. Pursuers would smell that, and still see the light."

"Glowcakes are also disgusting." But he stood aside then, and watched as she found a shallow depression in the rocks to lay the thing on. She pushed it against the rockwall, then walked back past him into the main cavern, crossed to the stream and lifted a large pebble. There in the exposed soil wriggled zulchi worms no longer than a fingerjoint. She scooped some up and replaced the rock, then hurried back to the niche. The worms didn't bite, but she'd never liked the feel of them in her hand. She tipped them into the glowcake's exposed digestive juices and hurried back to the stream to wash her hands. The Sargussi still stood watching her when she returned.

"So that's true about your folk, Shiranu – what the legends say, that you learned to use the different animals and plants and fungi here in the caves to suit your own ends." He walked back to the corner of the niche and picked up the skins.

Soolkah spread her hands, palms down. "We survive in our way. As you do in yours." She'd never felt so aware of the differences between them.

"Also, Shiranu, while you were gone just now, I found *this*." He held her obsidian knife in his hand.

56

Soolkah's heart thumped so loudly she was sure he must hear it. "Yes, it's my harvesting knife."

"Hah! Stone." But it was her turn to stare as he flung it against a boulder. It broke into the usual curved slivers. "Did you think to kill me as I slept?" he asked. "Well, now you shall not."

"Without it I'll starve," she replied. "And...that was the only thing from my origin-amaaj." She swallowed hard on tears, but the anger wouldn't go away.

"Then you're truly on your own, are you not?"

There was nothing for Soolkah to do but lie down on the floor and pretend to sleep; but the tears wouldn't be stopped this time, and she wished she'd hadn't given in to the impulse to light the niche.

*

Yado opened his eyes. He'd been dreaming. He thought the light from the main cavern had awoken him until he heard the girl move nearby. The glowcake on the wall still shone. He shivered despite the warm ground. He missed his own sleeping fur, which had been large enough to cover all of him. But after this he'd be reborn in the eyes of his tribe: an adult male, capable of survival under even the most difficult conditions; and he'd never use that sleeping fur again. Maru would have burnt it before the rest of the tribe by now; it represented his childhood. Blinking, he looked over at the Shiranu girl. She was asleep, but restless.

He felt his uchaan through the leather kilt. It didn't seem so sore today. It had hurt constantly after the circumcision, and walking so far hadn't helped, though it was normal for a young Sargussi male to travel quite some distance on his initiation quest. *Mayhap I should try it out since I've no brothers to disturb!* He eyed the girl, wondering what her reaction would be if she woke to find him touching himself, and what it would feel like to have sex with a woman, whether it was different from the self-touching. He remembered waking far into the darktime once, several highwaters ago, when all his amaaj had been alive; his parents had all seemed to enjoy it. And Sargussi men had to relieve themselves until a woman became available to marry. From what the girl had said, he assumed it must be the same for Shiranu men. At the thought of her his uchaan throbbed and hardened without any encouragement from him – and he realised it still had healing to do.

"Shiranu? Are you awake?"

"Mmmm..." came the answer.

I could have killed her while she slept, he thought. But that had never been his intention. *And what is?*

The dream came back to him. It was as if his thoughts and ideas had crystallised while he slept. The darktime had spoken to him, just as Aa'kam, Eldest man of his tribe, had said it would.

"Shiranu?" he asked again.

"What?" She leaned up on her elbow and regarded him.

"I'm sorry about the knife. I should have trusted you more." *But I didn't have the dream to guide me.* "I'll make you a new one – of metal."

"You trust me with a knife?"

He nodded. "I'm going to Keramanthu. I dreamed of it last darktime. Mayhap I'll bring back a piece of the Prophecy!" He grinned to himself. "I want you to come with me."

"You'd take me with you, even though you thought I was going to kill you? Why?" she asked.

"For company?" he answered, and watched emotions whirl across her face.

"I can go part of the way with you," she agreed, then added, "But not as your captive."

"Fair speech, fair terms," he agreed. "Shall we make truce, then?" When she nodded, he wasn't surprised: truce with a Shiranu was unheard of, but so was running from a wedding. She was a strange creature, but he had confidence in the true-dreaming which came as part of the initiation; and instincts he'd always relied on were also telling him to trust her. "My name is Yado. What's yours?"

"Soolkah."

"That's an odd name to have."

"It's a good Shiranu name!"

Yado liked her spirit as much as her company. *But I wish I weren't so attracted to her.* Still, it needn't make things awkward. He could just find somewhere private if it became necessary to relieve himself. "I shall cook another bachu for breakfast," he said. "Shall you take meat with me?"

He watched her shake her head, pale fur bouncing in several different directions. *It's almost worth asking her something just to see her do that,* he thought.

As he set the meat on the stone, he heard the sound of teeth crunching on vegetables.

*

"Why didn't you want to be amaajni, Soolkah?" Yado asked.

"Chixi's horrible," she answered. "I'd rather not be amaajni at all than marry him. I'd rather die."

58

Her voice brimmed with distaste. *I hope she never loathes me like that,* he thought. "Is he cruel, or just ugly?" he asked. "I thought it strange that you feared me less than him!"

"I'm not sure that's true," she answered, walking on and speaking over her shoulder, "but I won't go back to find out!"

He smiled to himself in the gloom, and followed her down the tunnel.

"He's fat and ugly and lazy, but he's also a nasty man." She hesitated, then added, "Some say he's mad, but I think his heart is full of bitterness. There's a big age gap between him and his youngest brother, so he often beats him —"

Yado lingered on the sense of her words. "You mean — because he had to wait to marry?"

She nodded.

They were going to the farm cavern get food for the journey. She'd told him that the place would be crawling with Shiranu during lighttime until the harvest was over, so they must do their own harvesting at darktime. A few glowcakes lit their way, at the same time warning off unwary fingers. Yado heard the buzz of a ruzli fly being digested alive as he passed one of the things. He shivered.

"Have you ever been in a Shiranu farm cavern?" Soolkah asked at last, a hint of pride colouring her voice.

"Once or twice I passed abandoned ones on the way here," he answered. "And sometimes we use sleeping caverns your folk have also used in times long past. But I've never been in a working farm cavern, nor seen one in full blow-out."

"There used to be more when our tribe was larger," she said. "My fathers have pointed them out on our journeyings."

"Sargussi are also fewer now," Yado agreed. "There were no females born these last three highwaters, and a lack of females means fewer marriages and babies." He sighed. "I have no maaj'gar, no thought brother now." That pain was back, as sharp in his mind as ever, an intangible amputation nothing could erase. "It's forbidden in my tribe to become amaajni with only one man."

"And mine," she answered, "and I don't expect to marry now, either. As far as I know, no woman's ever refused to be amaajni before. It would mean loss of status for my amaaj if I went back. It's better that they think I'm dead."

Yado glanced sidewise at her.

The farm cavern was lit by many glowcakes, though it was the darktime Outside. Yado saw masses of vegetation; he scraped up a handful of the soft black soil. Once he felt the chill of a droplet of water on his back and looked up through the skylight to the ice cave's ceiling. "Keep watch," Soolkah said, "and growl twice, like a jumper-bachu, if anyone comes. I'll get the food." The scene looked alien to him; but Soolkah plunged among the leaves, basket ready at her hip.

Nothing stirred. She soon returned, basket barely half-full. "We should have come before – it's six lighttimes now since I left the tribe. They've taken almost everything. This stuff is hardly ripe, too small to harvest. It won't last me." Bitterness tinged her voice. "They must have left already. So should we." She handed him back the scraper he'd lent her in place of her knife.

Yado grinned at her. "You must learn to eat meat, Shiranu!" They started back down the passage. "D'you know how to reach the next farm cavern?"

"Of course –"

A rumble split the air.

"Quick – it's a tremor!" She grabbed his hand and pulled him down the tunnel as the ground shook. He made the sign for *can't hear*, and she nodded and switched to sign language. "It's not a bad one, but the vent will blow soon. Hurry!"

The breath rasped in his chest as they ran. Once or twice stones struck them. A couple of glowcakes had been dislodged and lay on the tunnel floor, still emitting light. He skirted round them, glad of the protection of his moccasins. They slipped and slithered along the passage. It was further than either had realised. As the din subsided and the ground steadied, their pace slowed to a walk, but their breathing took longer to catch up.

If this isn't a bad quake, I'd hate to be in one that was! Yado's tribe avoided caverns in blow-out. But the Shiranu depended on the volcano. Soolkah had explained the relationships in the food chain, and he'd realised that, as meat-eaters, the Sargussi were another part of that chain.

Finally Yado pushed Soolkah inside their refuge, almost falling on top of her as he stumbled over a rock at the entrance. The basket slipped from her grasp.

"Idiot!" she exclaimed. "I was going to test the floor ahead. The tremor could have opened it up!"

"Sorry," he muttered, resenting the rebuke. "Our hunting grounds aren't much affected by quakes." He rubbed bruised shins and looked around. A small crack had opened up at the back of the cave.

"It's not safe to stay here now. There could be aftershocks. We must follow my tribe at lightbreak. Let's get our things outside."

They had little to move out into the larger cave, mainly Yado's few possessions.

60

"It's colder out here. I don't know how we'll keep warm." Soolkah shivered, eyeing his sleeping skins with a mixture of longing and revulsion.

"Come here," Yado whispered. "Lie next to me. We can keep each other warm."

She'd been his enemy. Now they were friends. He laid the skins under them both, and his arms closed around her as if of their own accord. In the distance, the ground had stilled.

CHAPTER 5

JORDAS PASSED ONE HAND OVER HIS EYES, remembering Marcus's reaction, on his return to work earlier that day, to his worry about live transmission work.

"Nonsense!"

"But you must have read Dr Blumenwald's report?"

"Of course. She described you as 'quite stressed', and that's exactly what we've been without you here!"

"Didn't she mention my high psi sensitivity? I thought she might have."

Marcus had looked surprised, then sceptical, and suppressed both expressions.

Jordas had raised his own eyebrows. "I just don't want to faint on you again."

"Jordas, if there's a problem we'll deal with it as it happens." And he'd had to be content with that.

Marcus had updated him on events concerning the two young Naxadans on his return, but he hadn't dared check on them. It was night on Naxada; families had slept through Jordas's daytime in their niches. The Naxadan day, at twenty-eight and a quarter standard Terran hours, never quite matched up with the Goranoni day of twenty-five and a half hours. Jordas yawned. A nine-hour shift was a long stretch.

It was Senator Hartmann's last day at Axos; he and Marcus hadn't returned to the monitor room after lunch. Ray was off-shift. Jordas checked the seismometers again. *Tremors from the parasitic volcano. The magma's on the move. I wonder what's happened to the others now?* In the holotank the main group were resting in a small chamber, part-way along the lava tube, where the probe was currently connected to its transmission terminal. Silence smothered dimness in the chamber; only a few luminous fungi shone, their glow not yet augmented by light from above.

Jordas hesitated, then made up his mind and switched over to the two young Naxadans. Ray had originally said the female was a prisoner, but that morning during hand-over Bill had told Jordas he'd seen them speaking together and smiling and laughing like friends during his last several night shifts. *Perhaps they reached agreement during my sick leave.*

Neither had been injured in the quake, but Jordas noticed their belongings, scattered on the ground beside them in the main cavern. Dawn had brought enough light for him to see them asleep in each other's arms, their fur mingling where their bodies touched. *Funny how alike and yet different they look,* he thought. The scene was curiously erotic. Jordas knew a moment's affinity with the tribesman and for a moment almost envied him, remembering that shock as the female had stared into the camera's gaze. *But this is an alien female,* he reminded himself, and retreated behind a scientist's professional detachment.

He crossed to the 'scope console and checked the predicted co-ordinates of Naxada and Hamorrah. *Seventeen days until Hamorrah becomes visible from Naxada again. Less than six weeks before it hits – so little time to evacuate the Naxadans. I hope Marcus can persuade Senator Hartmann to help them.*

Jordas turned back to the calculations for Marcus. He hoped his weight estimates were accurate. A mistake could mean people were left behind – *if* they could make intelligible contact with them in the first place. They knew roughly how many of the white-furred people there were, but in Jordas's absence Matt had directed a third probe to locate the dark-skinned people. As it hadn't found them yet they had no idea how many of them there were. And there could be more than just these two racial groups. He sighed and seated himself beside the holotank console.

"Mmmm..."

A rush of sensations left Jordas swaying in his chair. He raised a hand to his head and glanced back at the holotank. The Naxadans were waking up. Through a curtain of dizziness, he heard speech between them. He leaned forwards, as if pulled by the tugging which had returned to his mind, along with a powerful eroticism. Jordas couldn't distinguish what they were saying, but he could see the male touching the sleepy female's face and chest. It looked like a very private encounter indeed. And because it was a live transmission it wouldn't be filtered out.

He distracted himself by checking the seismographic display again. But it made no difference. His head whirled so as he moved that it was less disorienting to stop fighting the dizziness. That receded when he allowed himself to be sucked into the deluge of passion. He felt so drawn into it he might have been there with them. *It's not much different from what I used to do with Nina,* Jordas thought, aware of his discomfort as his own desire for sex grew. *I should have more self-control.*

The female was reaching down and lifting the male's leather kilt, looking at his genitals as if she'd never seen any before. Finally, she touched them, giggling as they became erect. The male's genitals resembled a human male's, but hairless, and he'd been circumcised. He grinned when the female touched

63

him and reached for her own kilt. Her chest, flat only moments before, now carried six small swellings, the nipples and aureoles enlarged. Jordas's head swam with the vertiginous thrust of affinity and his own arousal.

They didn't kiss. *Perhaps they don't.* The female's whisper as she touched the male's face was unintelligible. She was still giggling. *They're a lot like us,* he reflected, fascinated. He felt guilty at watching them, especially without their knowledge, but couldn't avert his eyes. If he had he was sure he'd still have known what was happening. *The counselling and training we had when we first started using these probes didn't prepare me for* this! He tried to tell himself scientific interest had him rooted to the spot, but it was a half-truth. Seeing the female straddling the male, he swallowed hard on the thought that the field team might be watching. The young couple deserved their privacy, and he hated himself for not switching off. But he couldn't tear his eyes away from the tank. Of their own accord his hands sought the holotank console settings, his mind scarcely registering their actions.

The male thrust against the female. As his passion and urgency spent itself inside her at last, impressions exploded in Jordas's mind, and the hot wet surge in his own loins answered the Naxadan male's, an assault of shared ecstasy. Fur-covered limbs moved against his own flesh. He sucked in gasps of air. Urgent movements slowed as tensed muscles relaxed. Daylight licked his flesh through an icy roof. Jordas smelled leather; through the skins under him he felt the rockfloor and heard the crunch of ground glass.

"It's as if I'm him as well – what's happening to me?" he whispered; but he had no answers. His mouth was dry. He pulled his overshirt around himself, hoping no-one would come in.

He still felt the ghost sensations in his limbs and body. It was as if one set of sense impressions was constantly overlaid by another. He hadn't been aware of them before. Questions tumbled through his mind. *What's happening to me? And why? I hope it's not permanent. If it is, how will I cope?*

He tried to concentrate and be the professional he'd always taken pride in being. *Calm down. You're in shock. You've just had a strange experience. Right now you have to get to the gents'.* He rose and pulled his shorts from his locker, then hitched his overshirt about him, intending to walk to the toilet a few paces down the corridor; but his attention was caught before he could move away.

"We'd better leave it another day before we move on. We don't want to get too close to my tribe," the girl said.

How come they speak English?

"I hope there are no more tremors," the male murmured, shuddering.

64

"That wasn't a bad one last darktime," the girl replied. Her tone was mild, but her eyes flashed with the intention to tease. "The Sargussi must indeed be a faint-hearted tribe!"

He shot a look at her from under his lashes, lips pursed in amusement. "I'm hungry," he announced. "My fathers often said sex causes hunger. Now I see it's true."

"You're *always* hungry, Yado!" she giggled.

No, Jordas thought, concentrating on hearing the sounds again. *They don't speak English. It's me. I understand* them.

*

Matt Johnson cupped his hands around the beaker of black tea, smiling. In the last six months Yue Xiao had weaned him off coffee. He emptied the beaker and pushed his spectacles up his nose until they rested more comfortably in the groove they'd made. *Now what's the second tribe up to?* He supposed he ought to let Marcus's team know that they'd located the other aliens, but as he watched he decided to call shortly.

A female cut meat on a cooking stone to give to her two elder children, suckling the three youngest as she did so, each attached to a different nipple. Matt could almost smell the meat and felt his mouth water as he watched.

At least his shift would soon be over. He hated the early morning finish. *You miss the best part of the day.* Yue Xiao would be turning on her side, thinking about getting up, while he'd be able to sleep soon. He didn't like being on a different shift from her, but everyone else here had to put up with it at least sometimes, and he believed in leading by example.

I'll just check the other probes. Matt flicked open the channel to the young couple's cavern and without warning, the holotank image folded in on itself.

Strange, he thought. *There must be a problem with the probe...I hope the hyperspace link is still intact.*

*

Jordas fastened his shorts and hurried back to his post, only to find the tank view had split to accommodate Matt's image.

"Where the devil were *you*?"

"Sorry," Jordas mumbled. "Nature called. What's up?"

"We've got a problem with our holotank. I tuned in to the probe following that young male and female and the image just went offline," grumbled Matt.

"I've got perfect reception here." *Perhaps it would have been better if I hadn't!* he thought. He felt heat rise in his face and hoped Matt hadn't noticed. "It must be your equipment."

"I've run the usual checks, and it's in perfect working order. I just can't understand this –"

Then Jordas remembered touching the controls as the Naxadans were about to make love. "Let me try something." His hands flew over the controls again, restoring the links. "Check that out."

"Nothing yet." Matt's voice followed a delay longer than could be accounted for by hololink transmission. "Oh, I almost forgot to tell you. We've established visual contact with that young fellow's relatives."

"Oh, good." Jordas was relieved to change the subject. He wasn't ready to discuss his strange experience with anyone. "How many are there? We've assumed similar numbers in both tribes but our calculations for funding and evacuation facilities will be out if that's wrong."

"We'll count and get back to you."

"You found them just in time. Hartmann's due back any minute and Marcus is trying to get him to make up his mind before he leaves. Make it quick with that head count, will you?" Jordas paused, relaxing slightly. "How's your reception now?"

"Just coming back online."

"Probably channel drift, then. Look, Matt, I'll call you back later." Jordas cut the contact, needing to think through and understand what had happened to him, and turned to face the holotank again. The man was laying a skinned carcass on a boulder they'd dragged out into the main cavern while the girl munched vegetables.

As he watched them, he puzzled over the experience. The double sensations were as strong as ever. *It's like being in two bodies at once.* Jordas's thoughts whirled like a maelstrom. *And how can I understand the language? What is it that links me to this alien – this man?*

As that thought entered his mind, the tribesman scanned the cavern, then swung to face the holocam lens. His gaze, the colour of citrines flecked with topaz and tiger's eye, locked with Jordas's own, and it was as if the alien could see inside his soul.

Jordas pushed his chair back, scraping it against the floor. He grimaced, then remembered himself the tribesman couldn't see or hear him since the holocam only transmitted one way.

"Yado, what's the matter?"

"I'm not sure," he answered. "My proximity sense tells me someone's watching us, and since we made love –" He broke off mid-sentence. "Do you think – would this be how it feels to be haunted?"

"I don't understand."

Fear convulsed his face. "Maru couldn't give Uvvuz a proper burial when

66

he died."

"You mean – you're afraid he's haunting you?"

The man gave a dip of his head, almost a nod. "It feels – as if I'm sharing again. As if Uvvuz still lived."

Jordas stared, his thoughts whirling. *Who is Uvvuz? What is this "sharing"?*

"Ah." The girl gave her version of the nod. "The sharing. What's it like?"

Yado's answer came after much thought. "It would doubtless feel strange to a woman – none in our tribe have the sharing."

"Nor in mine."

"Although I'm alone now, I well remember sharing thought and feeling – when my brother or I wished it. Knowledge too, though that must be an act of will." He turned away from the lens and back to her, and added, "And then there are the physical sensations. A man with brothers is *never* truly alone."

Jordas's eyes followed Yado as he stared once more around the cavern.

"I don't understand, Yado."

"Nor I!" He stared at her for a second, then opened his eyes wide. "The sharing *is* returned. But not with Uvvuz."

"Then – who with?"

"It feels like no man I know, or have ever known."

Yes, thought Jordas. *That's it!* His confusion was clearing. The fever of sex had left his mind and body. The press of sense impressions had faded to a more manageable level and was crystallising into a pattern. He was sometimes aware of the uneven cavern floor, occasional pebbles beneath the alien man's moccasins, the heat in the tunnels. He knew with sudden, incredulous clarity that what had overwhelmed him at first was the sheer rush of information.

It's telepathy. And something else. Telepathy plus. Jordas remembered what Yado had said. *These people are telepathic, and it's a familial characteristic. A male phenomenon.*

But how could this happen? We're not even of the same species, let alone related!

*

Yado hauled himself upright, gripping the rockwall, wincing as the ghost sensations caught at him again: heat in the humid air; a feeling of perching on something off the ground rather than squatting as the tribespeople did, the touch of loose clothing around skin which felt indefinably different from his own, and an awareness of many nearby objects whose purpose was unclear. Yet the mind which touched his must often check them. And quite apart from the fact that the sensations were strange, there was no sense of comfort or familiarity from that mind, only an awareness that the sharing wasn't its usual state. Yado sensed a puzzlement his own mind could only echo.

He wouldn't have Soolkah see him so affected by the new mental link. That was prideful; but it was so much accepted among the Sargussi that the brothers of one amaaj shared sense impressions, an awareness of emotions, mindsendings, and knowledge, if required, that he found it hard to accept the touch of a mind unused to those things.

He sought Soolkah. She was reweaving her basket of food into a backpack so as to leave her arms free as she walked. The reeds creaked in protest. Yado watched her for a moment or two, a smile curving his lips. That often happened when he looked at her. Then he felt the stir of the stranger's mind against his, and the urgency of his need to find out who it belonged to.

It's the overspill of this man's mind that makes me dizzy, he realised. *There is much to take in at once. And it feels so different – yet right.*

*

Jordas checked his wrist chronometer. Sixteen fifty-seven. Two hours to the end of the shift. He wondered if Marcus had persuaded Senator Hartmann to allocate funding for the project. He'd sensed their mutual dislike every time he'd seen them together.

He rose from his seat and wandered over to the drinks dispenser. His favourite mixture of ice and cool liquid sploshed into the beaker. When he returned, the girl was scooping dried vegetables into her pack. The man Yado had left the cavern. But at the thought of him, a torrent of information poured into his mind and for a moment vertigo threatened again, until Jordas closed his eyes and allowed the sensation to flow in. Yado was...creeping...through tunnels? The floor was uneven beneath his feet, the rockwall to one side brushed the fur on his arm. He felt something in that intangible hand which paralleled his own right; something hard and straight which reflected light from the clusters of fungi. There was a movement ahead and the hand drew back, the hunting instinct fuelling his arm for the kill –

Jordas came to with a shudder. *How can I be getting someone else's sense impressions, when they're light-years distant?* But even as he repudiated the idea, he thought he could see the answer. His own psi sensitivity had always allowed him to tune in to other people on an intuitive level. *And I only fainted when Yado was live on the hololink.* He sipped his freeze, remembering the fainting spells, his medical results, that sense of affinity with the tribesman. It was as if the link worked on several levels; the sense impressions were just one. *But does he get them too?*

<Who *are* you? I felt Uvvuz die.> Fear underlay the communication.

68

<I'm not Uvvuz. Who is he?> Jordas's mind demanded of the voice in his head.

<Uvvuz is – was – my brother. He died two highwaters ago, when I was fifteen,> the answer came back instantly.

An answer. Jordas hadn't expected to get one. <Don't be afraid. I'm no ghost. I'm alive,> he told the voice. <If Uvvuz was your brother, am I right in thinking you're the tribesman, Yado?>

<My name *is* Yado. How can you know that?>

<I...heard you two speaking. You mentioned the name Uvvuz earlier, to the woman. Girl.> Neither were long past adolescence, by the look of them.

<We *are* both adults!> came the reply.

<Sure.> Though still unfamiliar, the contact was beginning to feel more comfortable. <My name is Jordas Krata.>

<Where are you, Jordas Krata? I feel you in my mind – why can I not see you?>

<I'm in a far distant place,> Jordas answered. <You won't be able to see me unless I come to your land.>

<What is it you want? And how can you mindspeak with me?>

Jordas sensed the fear behind the voice in his mind. There was no time to reply. The door swung open. Marcus stood there with Senator Hartmann.

"How soon can we get the mission under way?" Marcus asked.

Hartmann's voice was brisk. "As soon as you've got those figures for me – I can set the financial wheels in motion from the ship. Though I'm not yet sure how I'm going to sell it to Asthorn."

"Would telepathic communication be a skill the Federal League could use?" Jordas enquired.

"Why?"

"Because they use it," he answered. "And I'm in contact with one of them. You might find that a useful selling point with your Committee." *If you really need one.*

*

Telepathy indeed! Marcus Carlin leaned back in his seat. "I still don't understand. You're not even remotely related to the Naxadans."

Jordas sighed. "I know." He raked a hand through his hair. "I don't understand how it happened, either, but it's a fact."

"If it really is a fact," Hartmann said, "then I'm sure that people other than just the Committee would be *very* interested in this ability."

"Quite so," Marcus murmured, and turned back to Jordas. "Prove it, then." He sighed. "I've always found you such a *truthful* person."

"I'm telling the truth *now*. Listen. The young man's name is Yado and he's from the Sargussi tribe. I don't know the girl's name or tribe. They're both just turned adults – in their terms. Yado told me so." Jordas paused for breath, meeting Marcus's speculative stare. "I know it sounds crazy, but I'm not lying. I'm sure it's connected with my fainting last week. You remember we noticed it was whenever Yado was on the live hololink? It's clear as daylight now."

It was anything but, to Marcus.

"Don't you see? Thinking back, that dizziness was caused by too much information rushing in at once. Yado's own brother died some while ago and I've – taken his place."

"Prove it," Marcus repeated, folding his arms across his chest. "I'm sure the senator here –" he indicated Hartmann, "– would be interested to see you back up this claim."

"Fine!" Jordas said. "Matt's probe has made contact with the second tribe. He's calling me back as soon as he's done a head count. I'll ask Yado how many people there are in his tribe. If they tally –"

Marcus caught his drift. "Very well."

Jordas nodded. "It won't take long. He's been waiting for me to continue our discussion ever since you came back into the room." He crossed to the holotank, where Yado and the girl were still squatting on the cavern floor, speaking quietly together.

Marcus observed Jordas. He stood before the projection tank, muscles rigid with concentration. The female kept glancing about her, and clung to the male as if for reassurance. Once, she pointed straight up at the holocam.

"She's seen the probe," Marcus muttered.

Just seconds later Jordas said, "He says there are just under five hundred and fifty people in his tribe, about fifty less in the other tribe."

"We already know how many of *them* there are," Marcus objected. He had to admit it was an accurate estimate as far as the female's tribe was concerned. But he knew he wouldn't be satisfied until he had Matt's head count. The habit of exactitude was too ingrained.

The tank split to show Matt's image on the left. "I've got those figures for you," he said. "There are five hundred and forty-seven. That gives a total of one thousand and fifty-six people to transport, which Yue Xiao confirms as a large enough genetic pool for successful breeding once in a less dangerous environment."

"Thanks," Marcus acknowledged. "Over." *There's no way Jordas could have cheated on that answer.* He had to accept it. He reached for his notebook. "Fortunately, that's very close to the calculations we made when the second group were discovered." He turned to the Senator. "I'll just recalculate the costs —"

"Don't forget to include me in the contact team, Marcus," Jordas interrupted.

"Include you?"

"If I can meet up with these two, they can help us to contact everyone else."

"Sorry, Jordas. I need you here. Anyway, do you have any idea how much it would cost to replace you?"

"The total amount's already pretty large," Jordas pointed out, "so what difference will I make?" He put both hands on Marcus's desk and leaned towards him. "Besides, it could make all the difference to the success of the mission. As I'm the easiest means of communication with these people, surely I should be in the contact team?"

"Jordas, you're our link to these people," Marcus said, "and our back-up if we should lose the cable lines."

"He's right, you know, Dr Krata," said Hartmann. "Your abilities are needed here." He held out his hand to Marcus. "Contact me at the spaceport with your amended figures. There isn't much time if I'm to make my flight."

Marcus nodded as he stood up and laid the notebook on his desk. "I'll ask them to hold the shuttle for you," he offered.

"Thanks." Hartmann shook hands with him, then left, almost colliding with Ray at the doorway.

"Okay, Jordas – shift's over," Ray said to Jordas.

Jordas Krata snatched Ray's arm and shook it. "We've got it!" he said.

"Funding?"

"Yes!"

"Excel*lent!*"

"Before you get too excited, I want you to know I'm not pleased." Marcus waggled a finger at Jordas. "I don't appreciate you trying to manipulate me in front of someone like Hartmann. This isn't a day trip to the Moon, you know."

"I know that, and I had no intention of manipulating you. I just thought it would be easier if you only had to recalculate the funding once."

"Recalculate funding?"

Marcus ignored Ray. "That won't work, Jordas. I need you here. Not only would it be expensive to replace you, there'd be a delay before your replacement arrived. And Ray's already had to cover for you while you were off sick."

"Replace Jordas?"

Neither Marcus nor Jordas were listening to Ray.

"You can replace an astronomer or a geologist," Jordas retorted. "You can't replace a telepath."

"Telepath? Someone tell me what's happening?" Travers asked. "Know I'm the junior. Still part of the team. What's going on?"

"Tell Ray," Marcus said. "And by the way, I see you couldn't resist the urge to wear your shorts this afternoon, even though you knew Hartmann would be around."

"I need to wash my trousers – I had an accident with my caffeine freeze." Jordas summarised the afternoon's events for Ray.

When he'd finished, Marcus couldn't help feeling Jordas was holding something back. However, he contented himself with murmuring, "Well, Jordas, you're off-shift now. We'll see you tomorrow."

CHAPTER 6

JORDAS OPENED THE DOOR AND ENTERED HIS HAVEN, bought soon after his arrival on Goranon, around the time development at Axos began. The house was compact but comfortable.

The first thing I'm going to do, he promised himself, *is have a shower.* He entered his bedroom and stripped, savouring the coolness of air conditioning on his perspiring body. Then he stepped into the shower. On Earth steam showers were the norm, but there was no water shortage here; and Goranon's heat made a cool shower of real water as welcome as air conditioning. He turned the dial and let the water squirt over him, soaped himself, and felt his tension dissolve away and follow the suds down the wastewater disposal.

Hair dripping moisture as it sprang back into its curls, Jordas towelled himself, wrapped his bathrobe around himself, and wandered into the lounge. He felt too disturbed to eat, but as he looked around the room, the familiarity of his possessions comforted him. The brass Vanjeynish dancing girl; his lamo-harp, also from Vanjeyno, beside it on his grandmother's half-moon table by the wall; the tall pitcher of bluish Kiai glassware; a pair of Zarduthi swords hanging crossed on the wall. On another occasional table lay the carved box containing the antique Colt .45; the only thing, apart from his education, that his father had ever given him. It had been in his father's family since the twenty-first century. Old then, though still in working order, Jordas had learned to shoot with it. And there were three bookcases of first editions, both textbooks and classical literature. He picked up Malory's *Le Mort d'Arthur* and leafed through it, wiping dust from its cover with fingers which were already perspiring again. His gaze fell on familiar passages and well-loved lines, but his thoughts were elsewhere. He replaced the book.

He took a beer, slippery with condensation, from the fridge. Thumbing open the catch, he sucked liquid into his mouth. Its chill was wonderful. But he still felt shell-shocked by the afternoon's events, and was unsure how to deal with them. He settled back against the leather of the couch and composed himself for the mindspeech, knowing he couldn't put it off. For the moment, the sense impressions were distant, and Jordas felt more comfortable with them now.

<Yado?>

No answer. *Perhaps he's asleep,* Jordas thought, aware of the sensation of fur against fur. *Or perhaps they're making love again. At least this time –*

<Why were this time different from the last?>

Jordas sensed Yado's surprise as the memory of his reaction to the rush of ejaculation returned unbidden. In retrospect the sensations seemed even more intense.

<Why shame for something so natural?> Yado asked.

<Natural, maybe. Socially acceptable, no. Not among us, in a public place,> Jordas protested, wondering how to explain about the time difference between Goranon and Naxada. <I was working. Anyone could have walked in on me, and there would have been nothing I could do about it. It would have been very embarrassing, and it wasn't as if I wanted that to happen.>

Yado hesitated before sending, <I know, and I'd have known if you were touching yourself.>

<We don't – at least, not in public, when we're at work.>

<Nor we, but in my tribe, the Sargussi – and the Shiranu – it *is* acceptable between brothers.>

Jordas was getting used to the voice in his head now. It was even beginning to feel as though it belonged. But he squashed his curiosity about Naxadan sexual customs, afraid to offend Yado and lose the chance to help his people. <Are the Shiranu the other tribe?>

A shift in mood signalled the affirmative, followed by an ironic pause. <The enemy. Soolkah's tribe.>

<And Soolkah's your – wife?>

The affirmative mood-shift again. <My *amaajni*.>

<Right.> Jordas thought it best to change the subject. <I promised to explain to you.>

Even before he'd finished, Jordas sensed the dread washing over Yado, felt him square his shoulders in an effort to set it aside, then perceived a barrier to him within Yado's mind, and recognised his reluctance to share his unease with him. <When shall this happen?>

<We think the new volcano under the glacier will erupt and trigger flooding in about fifty or sixty of your lighttimes. We'll need to evacuate our own people on the surface pretty soon, too, but your caves will flood first as the water passes down inside the mountain through rock pores. There's no time to waste. We need your co-operation to save both tribes. I know it's awkward, but you must trust me.>

<The problem is,> Yado sent, <how should I know to trust you? We share the mindspeech, but unless you let your barriers down I can't –>

Jordas sensed Yado's surge of disquiet. <What is it?>

74

<You haven't the privacy safeguards?>

<What?>

<I would have asked to share more deeply with you so I'd know if you could be trusted, but there aren't the barriers I expected anyway. How can you mindspeak without privacy safeguards?>

<I'm not sure what you mean, but do what you need to. If you can't trust me I won't be able to help, and I really want to.>

Jordas felt the barrier Yado had raised between them dissipate and the contact between them deepened.

<I do trust you, my *maaj'gar*.>

*

Yado stared into the darkness above Soolkah's shoulder, arm curved about her. His mind shied away from the human – *human?* – man's revelations. He couldn't take them in.

He brought to mind what Jordas Krata had shown him and forced himself to examine it once more. He understood about *temperatures* – everyone knew ice melted into water when heated. He pulled the sleeping-skin around him as he remembered what Jordas Krata had told him: that heat from inside the ground, where a new volcano – child to Kerui itself – was growing nearby, would melt the ice above the lava caves, and landslides would cause flooding, within sixty lighttimes – a Shiranu season...And that a chunk of rock would hit their world at about the same time and could even destroy Kerui.

How can Kerui die? For many highwaters our people have travelled these caves seeking game; a thousand highwaters ago our ancestors lived in Keramanthu. He'd told Jordas Krata that, and had been shocked when the human had replied, <Nothing is forever.>

But the information excited him too. Yado hadn't realised heat and cold could be measured, just as the Shiranu had their seasons for measuring shorter intervals of time than a whole highwater. *With such knowledge my folk could become even better metalworkers.* Every Sargussi man forged his own belt knife of iron, the grip wrapped with twine. Both men and women wore bronze, copper and gold jewellery. Soolkah's people had never learned to work metal, though Yado had heard it said that they worked stone as if lived. He'd promised Soolkah jewellery if he could return to his tribe. The relationship growing between them made it important that he should do so, but he feared the tribe's reaction if he returned with a Shiranu amaajni. His fear was not for himself; but as a son of the tribe, loyalty denied him recourse if she were attacked. His amaajni commanded loyalty too, but that would put him in the same position with his tribe as Soolkah was now in with hers. *And one man*

75

without maaj'garu has no right to a bride in tribal law. How could they return to either tribe?

But now new problems teased him. *Were our own safety relevant against that of the whole tribe? Will I compromise my tribal loyalty by helping this man Jordas Krata for the good of both Shiranu and Sargussi? And how shall the Humanu protect each of us from the other's tribe?*

There was also kazmo'ra. If Soolkah returned to her own tribe, as Jordas was asking them to do, she would owe status-debt to her parents for the shame brought to their amaaj for running from her wedding, and he would owe status-debt to the man Chixi and his brothers for taking their bride. He didn't even want to imagine how Shiranu Elders would allocate repayment of that to a Sargussi.

In the darkness he heard the stirring and spitting of a ganzu. It sounded far distant. Yado ignored it, sighed, and turned on his back.

*

Jordas became aware first of the couch under his shoulder, then of the darkness in the room. *It must be late,* he thought. *But at least Yado knows what he needs to now.*

The sun had been low on the crags in the distance when their discussion finished. Jordas had realised it was later than his usual mealtime, and had gone to the food dispenser. He'd brought his plate into the lounge, but before he'd emptied it his appetite was satisfied.

Breaking contact with Yado, he'd been aware of the sadness and fear of the tribesman, and had wondered if Yado would sleep again that night. He'd promised to do his best to get them off-planet, but they both now knew what they faced. He'd told Yado what he needed to know, but had gained few answers for himself. And from what he'd learned, more questions had sprung. Revolving them in his mind, he'd dozed off.

Rolling over onto his back, he stared up at the ceiling. He needed some coffee. He rose. "Lights on."

He tucked the lamo-harp under one arm, wandered into the garden, beaker in hand, and perched on the stone boundary wall, under the eaves of the jungle, swinging his legs. He held the instrument on his lap, reaching into the circular splay of strings to pluck notes and draw from its belly a melody which floated away into the night and mingled with the scent from a flowering shrub nearby. He sipped his coffee without registering its taste. He had no reservations about being mindlinked with Yado, if it would help the Naxadans, but the young female was something of a complicating factor.

He remembered that shock the first time Soolkah had stared directly at him. Her youthful beauty was exotic yet strange. *But how can I be attracted to an alien female I've never even met? And she's married.* His stomach churned. *To Yado...my 'thought brother'!*

Jordas reviewed the situation between the tribes as he caressed the instrument's strings, hoping the music would soothe his jangled senses. Thanks to the enmity between the tribes, Yado and Soolkah's relationship placed them in an awkward situation. Yado's mood changes during their "conversation" had flagged the difficulty of untangling it. And adopting tribal ground rules, as the Committee preferred, might take too long.

Yado had mindsent, "But they'll listen to a stranger," and the phrase kept coming back to him. It made sense. If he could speak to the tribes' leaders, they might just listen.

It wasn't just a question of rescuing the Naxadans now. It was personal, and the more urgent for that. He *must* go to Naxada with the rescue team. *I might even get the answers* I *need.*

Jordas shivered. The hour's lateness had chilled the air. He jumped down and headed inside the house, the lamo-harp tucked under his arm.

It was the first time ever that it hadn't brought him solace.

*

The Shiranu Eldest man couldn't sleep. At the edge of his mind there was an awareness of events out of kilter. *Am I the only one in the whole tribe to feel it?* he wondered.

He listened. The waystop was silent. He sat up and looked around, avoiding disturbing his brothers slumbering beside him. *It won't hurt to check,* he told himself, *and it will set my mind at rest.* He rose and crept from his place.

He stepped over the members of one amaaj after another, brothers huddled together, children stirring as he passed, mothers cuddling babies, husbands snoring nearby. In a waystop there were no private niches. He spotted his elder daughter, Nahru, and a sense of unease pervaded his mind and body.

Things haven't felt right ever since we noticed the higher floodtides, and especially since Soolkah disappeared. At the mouth of the tunnel that had brought them here, he stopped to listen. Nothing reached his ears other than the sounds of regular breathing. The glowcakes gave enough light to see by in the waystop, but the passages to and from it were holes receding into darkness. Hanook stared into the tunnel, then went to check their way onwards in the morning. The sense of strangeness wasn't enough to send his hand to the knife at his belt. It felt more like change than danger. But it existed.

77

And that, in itself, frightened him. Since leaving Keramanthu nearly a thousand highwaters before the Shiranu had remained in a state of opposition to their traditional enemies. Looking back over his life, and thinking about what his parents had told him as a child, Hanook realised that there'd been no change in the tribe's way of life during that time. It must be the same for the Sargussi. Even the *idea* of change filled him with apprehension. *What other way could there be?*

Only half-reassured, Hanook crept back to his place, laid down and pulled his sleeping-cloth around him. As he stared up at the ice roof, unwelcome images filled his thoughts, and, later, shaped his dreams.

*

The morning dawned bright and hot as usual. By the time Jordas had reached the compound, wisps of steam were drifting up from the jungle. The avenue which formed the backbone of the research station was lined with pseudocedars which shed hot acrid shade. Shafted by ultra-violet emissions from Goranon's blue sun, the humidity was building up under the plate-like foliage, where insects swarmed. Jordas stared up at the branches. The first colonists had tried to grow Terran plants, but the soil was too alkaline for most, though fertile for native plant life. Lyrica's second planet was a strange world, Jordas reflected; but not more so than Naxada.

Jordas had dreamed of the ice world. He'd seen tunnels, caverns filled with burning gas, ice-cold streams rushing and hot mud springs bubbling. He wondered if Yado had tried to contact him as he slept. Then he reached the monitor room, and his musings stopped.

Ray was waving his hands and talking at top speed to Bill Borthwick. He'd been drafted in part-time from another project for anthropological support on discovery of the Naxadans, and spent several nights each week analysing holovid accumulated during the day. He smiled a greeting at Jordas, then nodded to Ray and strode down the corridor. Jordas entered the monitor room.

"Well?" Marcus was standing beside his desk. Despite his cool demeanour there was an air of impatience about him this morning, tempered with pleasure at having got what he wanted from Hartmann. "Have you explained the situation to your – friend – on Naxada?"

"He knows." Jordas changed into his shorts, hung up his trousers in his locker, and turned to find Marcus holding out a beakerful of caffeine freeze for him. "What about the arrangements for the rescue?"

"Hartmann promised me there'd be a team standing by in a couple of days," Marcus said. "Did you tell Yado?"

78

"I explained that we haven't much time to get them out of there. I just hope the team can get there in time to help them." Jordas settled himself near the holotank.

"What did he say?"

"Yado can't understand how it is that brothers here don't 'share'." He made inverted commas in the air as he spoke. "By that he means mindspeech. He calls me his *maaj'gar*, his 'thought brother'." Jordas cast a glance across at Ray's back, hunched over his notebook, and sipped his drink, knowing he was stalling and unsure how to continue. He felt a frown gathering on his forehead to match the headache underneath it. At last he faced Marcus and said, "The biggest problem's going to be getting the two tribes together."

Marcus raised his eyebrows. "I thought the team might have some hard negotiating to do when they go in. But there must be a way. If *both* tribes have this telepathic ability there must be some common ground between them. Let's hope the Committee can help on that one."

Jordas shook his head, wondering how to explain the difficulty.

"What? Come on, man, spit it out!"

Jordas took a deep breath. "According to Yado the only contact between the two tribes for centuries have been food raids and territorial disputes. He says if the Shiranu find him they'll kill him. If he takes Soolkah back to *his* people they'll kill her. Prejudices like that will be almost impossible to overcome. And she can't return to her own tribe or she and her family will be in very serious trouble for running away from a marriage she didn't want."

Marcus's response was to smooth his beard. Jordas had sometimes wondered if he used it to filter out emotion. Then he said, "Are you telling me we're talking to the wrong people?"

"Hardly – they're all we've got. But Yado says it would be better if I went there to make contact with the tribes – he thinks the tribes are more likely to listen to a stranger – especially someone older than either of them. After all, they are just teenagers, even in their terms. And they venerate age."

"That's true," Marcus said. "Bill says the tribal leaders are old people. He thinks you should go with the rescue team, although you're not exactly the vintage model! He agreed that they wouldn't listen to two youngsters in their current situation, but they might just listen to an outsider. The trouble is, I need you here too." Marcus paced the room. "The fact that Yado and Soolkah have overcome their differences must count for *something*. Let's hope we can bridge the gap between the tribes with their help."

"Perhaps," Jordas echoed. "But can we take anything about them for granted? They aren't human. Nor are their customs."

"Well, you'll find out about their customs from Yado, won't you?" Marcus stretched, and yawned. "We'll just have to hope the rescue team can come up with something and rely on the mindspeech in the meantime."

"You believe me?"

"I do now, and I spent half the night tracking down the final report on that Meiller experiment." Marcus reached across the desk and handed Jordas a holochip.

"That's –"

"I know. You were tested at university, along with several thousand other undergrads. I checked back with Dr Blumenwald after you left last night, and then compared her report with the Meiller paper."

"I tested very high on the psi scale. I never tried to develop it, though I've always been very intuitive about other people." He shrugged. "We never heard the results of those experiments. In the end I forgot all about it." Jordas tossed the chip up in the air and caught it again. "I'd be interested to read this."

"I thought you might. Take it home with you. The paper was eventually published five years ago. The original survey generated further research and it was a while before they reached firm conclusions. They decided that there *are* various types of psi talent, and that some subjects do have a latent telepathic ability – usually twins, or people who find it easy to empathise with others, especially if stimulated by contact with a subject with a similar or greater level of ability."

"That makes a *lot* of sense to me," Jordas said, eyes wide. "You stayed up all night just to check this out?"

"Not *all* night. I passed on the recalculated costs to Hartmann at Rorvik spaceport as well. Including your travel and replacement."

Jordas gaped. "You changed your mind?"

Marcus smiled. "There's a ship leaving for the Charidas Interchange in three days' time. I plan for you to be on it." Then he leaned forwards. It was the closest he'd ever come to intensity in all the time Jordas had known him. "Look, Jordas. The Committee will want results from their involvement. If Yado and Soolkah can't persuade the tribespeople to leave...well, we can't afford failure. Tell Yado that."

"I will," Jordas said. "It's important to me on a personal level now."

Will we get there in time? Will I even survive? It hadn't occurred to him before that he might die on a strange planet. *I might never see my home again, or any of my colleagues.*

But it didn't matter. He wanted to leap in the air from sheer excitement.

"Yado's sleeping now. I wish their day matched up better with ours."

"Will in about a week's time," Travers interjected. "For a day."

"Only you'll be there then," Marcus said. "*If* I can sort out your connections this morning."

Out of the corner of his eye, Jordas caught sight of Ray's envious expression.

CHAPTER 7

IN THE GREY LIGHTBREAK Gujas rose before anyone else. Of its own accord her hand sought her daughter's shoulder, as it always had; then she remembered Soolkah was no longer there. *Nor would she have been if she'd married Chixi and his brothers,* she reminded herself as tears welled up. She scrubbed them away. The priority was to feed her surviving family.

"What's the matter?" Araz was her eldest husband, and though by custom all three husbands claimed the credit, Soolkah's determined jawline, and her occasional mutinous expressions and mutterings, had been exactly like his. "You miss her?"

She felt the concern accompanying the words. "Don't you?" she croaked. *Was it our fault?* she asked herself, as she often had during the lighttimes since her daughter had disappeared. *Did we drive her away by contracting her to marry Chixi? And even if that's the case and she hasn't had an accident, how long can she last without food?*

But she knew, even as she thought of it again, that there had been no alternative. At the last Women's Council, where Soolkah had sat with pride as a new adult, Mnanga had explained, "Our tribe now has fewer members, so it's every woman's duty to marry as large a group of brothers, and bear as many live children, as possible. This must be a concern of the women of the tribe, especially as more adults die than babies are born. Accidents kill people of any age, and not all infants survive." Gujas's own fathers had been lost in an unexpected blow-out, well before old age.

Araz's arm came round her shoulders. "Of course I miss her," he said, hugging her. "But getting upset won't bring her back."

Gujas felt tears coming again.

He nuzzled her face with his chin. "I didn't sleep so well last night, either." He stroked her face.

Gujas felt her heart would burst with sorrow. "I'll prepare food." She disentangled herself with a gentle shove, having seen Lagi and Ulon stirring behind Araz. *Being married to three men at once isn't easy. I can't show favouritism, though when it comes to accepting comfort from them, Araz will always be my first love.*

Grinding up aldu meal for bread and porridge gave her something to concentrate on. She looked over to where the children lay asleep, and wiped more tears from her cheeks. *Half of it's guilt,* she realised. *If only –*

She shook herself. *There's nothing to help it now.* Clamping her teeth onto her lower lip to stop it from trembling, she added water and oil and began to shape the dough, pounding it with her clenched fists to relieve her feelings.

At last Araz came to her saying, "The firestone's free for baking." Gujas seated herself cross-legged and began to express milk. "Mix it in well," she warned her eldest son, Go'ti. He nodded, stirring the warm sticky mass with his fingers. Sprinkling a mixture of luthu chips and yellow beans into the dough, she took the cakes and porridge to the communal firestone. Soon they would eat. Now she turned her attention to the children. The two eldest boys and Alsa would sup hot porridge, mixed with her milk. The baby, Teffen, and Alsa, a child of three highwaters, she would feed herself. She woke them and wiped their faces with a strip of wet cloth. "Get porridge from the pot," she told her sons. "Enough for Alsa too." The two boys ran to the firestone, returning with filled bowls.

She lifted Teffen into her lap and placed a lower nipple in his mouth. Alsa she gave one of her upper nipples. The child knelt to suck while her mother stirred her bowl. When she had finished, Gujas gave her the bowl and swopped Teffen to the other side while she munched on a bread cake Ulon brought her. Despite her grief, the previous day's march had used much energy, and she must eat to keep milk coming.

When the tribe had eaten, the firestone was covered up to conceal the traces of their occupation. They moved off, Teffen slung at Gujas's back. To her surprise Hanook was looking around him, concern on his face. The Eldest man usually concealed his emotions well.

What's he worrying about? she wondered.

*

Hanook looked back at the tribespeople. His two brothers flanked him. Their sons, Nadna and Geem, and their daughter, Zuas, who would have her coming-of-age later this highwater, followed them. In addition to Hanook's status as Eldest man, his amaajni Lulla had brought status to their amaaj by bearing equal amounts of live daughters and sons. But the previous highwater she'd died of the coughing sickness. Hanook himself had just had a bout of it.

His eldest daughter, Nahru, had been married for five years. She trudged some way behind them, hidden from Hanook by a bend in the tunnel. Following his unease the previous darktime, Hanook felt the need to speak with her, so he told his brothers, Kayas and Brach, that he would wait for her. The tribespeople filed past him in amaaju of three or more – and often five, six or seven – adults, children walking behind them, carried, or clinging to their parents' hands.

He watched most of the tribe pass; his daughter's amaaj was towards the

83

back of the march this lighttime. When he saw Chixi and his three brothers walk past, packs loading their backs like everyone else, but no woman among their group, he was reminded again of his sleeplessness the night before. He couldn't bring himself to feel very sorry for Chixi; few liked him. But Lorr's downcast eyes spoke of grief which resonated in Hanook at the place where he carried his memories of Lulla.

As Nahru came into view, he dismissed thoughts of Chixi and his brothers and fell into step beside her, greeting her and her five husbands.

"What brings you to our side, Eldest?" Nahru asked, smiling to see him there.

"Are you all well?" Hanook asked. His glance included all the adults in the group; he scratched at the baby's shock of head-fur which bounced as Nahru walked. He couldn't rid himself of the idea that he should make the most of this meeting.

"Thank you, we are." Nahru smiled at Hanook again.

"Shall I carry him for a while?" Hanook took Gili into his arms. He was almost two. He stared at Hanook; even the Eldest hardly understood the true nature of the blood relationship between them. *The only old-word for blood relationships – from the time before the fall of Keramanthu – which makes much sense to me is gare. Our modern word, maaj'gar, reflects the mindlink between brothers. Now there are only words for husband, wife, mother, father, daughter, son, brother, sister, and amaamu – ancestors – for the dead.* Hanook shook his head. *I can't work it out either. It's enough to know he's the son of she who was my daughter.*

He stayed with them for some time, chatting as befitted the tribal leader, then made his way to the front of the march. His brothers turned at his approach, though he'd made no sound.

<My thanks for deputising for me!> he told them.

Brach grinned; Kayas smiled slowly.

<Anything?>

<There doesn't seem to be any da–> Brach was interrupted by a booming growl from ahead. With one accord the tribe halted. The ground began to shudder. Brach's face was paler than breastmilk.

"Flames of the volcano!" Hanook swore. He waved the rest of the tribe back the way they'd come. Nobody panicked, but his anxiety overrode everything else. *If the tremor sets off a rockfall –*

<I'll scout out the passage ahead when it stops,> Kayas volunteered.

<As long as you get out at the first sign of danger!> Hanook agreed. As Eldest he must remain with the rest of the tribe. <Brach, go to the back of the

84

group so I can contact them through you. When I mindsay, return and scout with Kayas.>

When the noise and vibration stopped, Hanook sent to Brach: <Tell them to rest now.> Nadna, Geem and Zuas he pulled into the circle of his arm. The tribespeople needed rest after their flight. Zuas was gasping; her breathing was often harsh and wheezy at night. Hanook often wondered how she'd survived childhood, and if she'd survive marriage as well. He'd decided to find her an amaaj with perhaps just two or three brothers, who wouldn't make too much work for her. *I must ask Mnanga for more of those herbs for both of us,* he added to himself.

Soon Brach appeared at his side, also puffing and blowing. <Rest now,> Hanook told him, <Then go ahead with Kayas.>

There were only minor aftershocks. When Brach and Kayas looked at Hanook for guidance he nodded his assent. They set off together. They knew the routine. Whatever happened, one of them must report back before the tribe would move on.

*

Soolkah reached for Yado's hand and played with his fingers. He sat cross-legged beside her on the sleeping-fur, staring at the glowcakes. His face had hardly lost its look of anxiety since the contact with Jordas Krata had begun. "Yado? What is it?"

He looked at her and smiled then. "I wouldn't wish to cause you to worry." But shadows darkened his eyes, golden in the glowcake's light.

"I'm scared, and all the more so when I see *you* fretting," she admitted. "What d'you think Jordas Krata meant about contacting our tribes? You know I can't go back to my people."

Yado sighed. He took her hand into his and examined it, stroking the fuzz on the back of her wrist with a talontip. "I did tell him so."

"The Shiranu certainly won't believe a Sargussi, and they've no reason to believe an ancestor either." Soolkah tried to smile at her own joke, but her lips were trembling. "Did you tell him my origin-amaaj think I'm dead?"

"I told him the whole tribe thinks so, and that they must," he said.

"What did he say?"

"I think – he didn't understand. He kept saying everyone must leave Kerui so both tribes can survive."

"Leave Kerui?" Soolkah echoed. A shock passed through her, so that she almost missed Yado's nod. A moment stretched into silence. At last she added, "But where would we go? There's nothing Outside."

"Jordas Krata says his tribe are seeking a new place to for us to live – he doesn't yet know where."

"I'm confused," Soolkah said.

Yado nodded. "I too."

"Do you trust him?"

Yado looked more troubled than ever. "I would have trusted Uvvuz with my life," he said. "He was my maaj'gar, always there, and brothers can only hide thought or feeling from each other with the privacy shield. But Jordas Krata doesn't have that. My instincts tell me to trust him, but he – *feels* – so different from Uvvuz. He's a voice in my head and some sajamu." He sighed. "What should I think?"

"It's harder still for me to know whether or not to trust him. I don't even have a voice in my head!" Soolkah paused and pointed upwards. "And that – thing – up there..."

"He calls it a *camera*," Yado said. "He says it shall follow us and tell his people where we are for them to find us. Small wonder we thought someone was watching us! At least it's proof I'm still sane..."

Soolkah caught the irony in his voice as she eased her legs out in front of her and leant back against the rockwall.

"Jordas Krata didn't know of the hostility between our tribes." Yado hesitated before adding, "When he said I must return to my people I told him it's not yet the time for that, and why, but he said there were times when traditions and customs must be sacrificed for safety. I explained that the safety code was something else, but I think he misunderstood." He breathed in and out before continuing, as if weighing up answers. "He said he'd asked to come to Kerui, with the men of his tribe, to meet with us, but was refused permission at first. I think his tribe's ways are much different from ours."

"Sounds that way," Soolkah agreed. "When will these people come to Kerui?"

"Soon."

"What kind of people are Jordas Krata's tribe?"

"That's what I'm thinking."

*

Chixi couldn't take his eyes off Gujas's amaaj.

He wondered if his brothers had noticed his scrutiny. He imagined Soolkah grabbing at the streamside, her hand missing rocks and vegetation, slithering through the mud, then the chillcaps, the stalks breaking as the hot currents carried her down into the heart of Kerui.

But the search had revealed no sign of any such struggle; Soolkah had just vanished. He recalled his anger and frustration in the tunnels and caverns they'd searched – though not as diligently as he'd have liked – despite the tribesmen sacrificing most of a harvest-lighttime. If not for the approaching blow-out, he'd have gone back and searched again himself, and insisted that at least his brothers help him. *Surely it wasn't an accident,* he thought. *And if that's the case...*

The other tribesmen had been more concerned about gathering in the harvest before moving on. Even in the cavern where there had been a rockfall, they hadn't looked as carefully as he'd wanted. The smell of newly-turned earth had stung more pairs of nostrils than just his own, but that was more likely the result of the rockslide than makeshift toilet arrangements.

He glanced at Lorr again. The boy had kept silence since their return to the sleeping cavern without Soolkah. Although Shiranu skin was light-coloured there was an unhealthy pallor about him now. He'd eaten nothing for lighttimes.

Chixi squeezed between Jeene and Vru and came to his youngest brother's side, noticing his dull eyes and slack mouth. "What's this, self-pity?" he growled.

Lorr made no answer.

"You aren't the only one who was looking forward to being married," he said. "But perhaps one of the other girls...?"

At this, moisture spilled from Lorr's eyes. "I don't want –"

"As you wish," Chixi interrupted. *He'll come round when there's a woman lying beside him in his sleeping cloth,* he thought.

"She *can't* be dead!" Lorr exploded.

Chixi's arm flailed Lorr's shoulders, skimming his backpack.

Fear stalked the faces of the tribespeople and stilled their march. Their eyes watched them.

Chixi stared back, daring anyone to challenge him. For once he didn't care if others saw him break the touch taboo. Neither Sargussi hunters, nor a rockfall, nor shame for his amaaj and possible kazmo'ra, could touch him while his emotions seethed so.

<You'll make our ancestors walk again if you carry on like that!> he grumbled at Lorr. <If you must speak, use the mindspeech rather than draw attention to us.> Lorr nodded, but kept his mind as silent as his mouth and his eyes downcast. They walked on, rock shards on the tunnel floor occasionally snagging the soles of the slippers they themselves had woven.

<I still want to be married,> Chixi sent to him after a while. <I take it you've no preferences?>

Lorr shook his head.

<I'll talk to the others.> He lumbered forwards.

Vru and Jeene were more receptive to his ideas.

<Who did you have in mind?> Vru asked. At just over thirty, he was the brother nearest in age to Chixi. Their sister Ledew had already been amaajni for two highwaters when Lorr was born. <I don't mind Kassi or Beya.>

Jeene was adamant that while Kassi and Beya were acceptable, he preferred Mzana, daughter of Tarchon, Finnus and Urdin.

<But she's not had her coming-of age yet,> protested Chixi. <I'd have to wait till later in the season before I could offer for her. And I've waited longer than anyone else in the tribe.> *That's because of the way our parents spaced out their pregnancies.* It was more than three highwaters since Jaak, Reevun, Eelel and Feyzu had been killed in a rockfall during a quake. Being old and suffering from the sickness Chixi had inherited from her, Feyzu had been unable to get to safety in time. Her husbands had tried to rescue her and died with her instead. Although Chixi had grieved for them, he hadn't been able to squash down the feelings of resentment at having to wait that he'd carried inside him for so long. He'd always felt it was their fault, though in his heart he knew no woman could control when she became pregnant.

<What does Lorr think?> asked Jeene. <He won't let me in. >

<He doesn't care,> answered Chixi, remembering that they'd had similar discussions before he'd offered for Soolkah. Lorr had been keen enough then.

<He's still in a bad mood.> Jeene cast a glance at Lorr.

Chixi grunted.

<That won't bring Soolkah back!> Vru commented.

*

Lorr welcomed the stinging in his shoulder where Chixi had cuffed him, the fatigue in his legs, the cramp knotting his calf muscles. At least focusing on the misery in his body distracted him from being too aware of his emotional anguish. He tried to ignore it during waking time. But in the darktime he grieved as his brothers slept.

If some of my enthusiasm for Soolkah had spilled over into my brothers' minds, they might have continued searching for her, and found her, Lorr reflected. When Chixi had suggested offering for Soolkah, he'd been jubilant. He'd always liked her, but since her coming-of-age he'd realised just how much and had been apprehensive as to whom Chixi might choose once he was old enough to marry. He'd guessed his Elder brother wouldn't delay, for he probably had only twenty or so highwaters more to live at most. *And with his size...Such big people can be less fit than other folk,* he remembered thinking, *and lethargic, and prickly as ganzu spines besides, when they feel poorly!* Yet

88

his mother had been as loving as Chixi was spiteful.

They trudged on. They'd been walking for two lighttimes and were still many pythetu from the next farm cavern. He hefted his backpack into a different position on his aching shoulders. *Chixi always knows where to hit to hurt.* Lorr had realised long ago that Chixi didn't have his own capacity for emotion and affection. He knew other tribespeople whispered about him; only fear and loyalty to his amaaj kept him from confirming the rumours and bringing shame to the others, and certain kazmo'ra to Chixi. *Because that would make things worse.*

He felt the water gathering in his eyes again, and was relieved that nobody was looking at him. He knew no shame would attach to his grief; after all, he'd been going to marry the girl; but he preferred to keep his feelings private. He was grateful for the privacy shield. He could join in at any time if he wanted, but hadn't the heart. This was too much all at once. *How can Chixi be so cold? Doesn't he care at all about what happened to Soolkah?* If she wasn't alive to wed he didn't care who else the older three chose.

Stop it! he told himself, *you're just torturing yourself by thinking about her. Accept it. She's dead. You'll never see her again.* He swayed on his feet at the finality of what his body and mind were trying to learn, and put out a hand to the tunnel wall. He remembered Soolkah's face. He pictured her cool green eyes just as if they were watching him from the rock.

As he saw the vision, the doubt in his heart and mind crystallised. Tears streamed down his features. *Surely she must still be alive! I don't know how, but I sense she's not dead!*

But I don't know where she is.

*

The lighttime was well advanced before Hanook received a sending from his brothers.

<Aagh! The light here's too bright!> Kayas told him.

But Hanook already knew that. Sajamu had told him about the cold, too, and the water on the tunnel floor.

That was impossible. Unless...

<We're going forward,> Brach reported. <But the air's like ice, and we're shielding our eyes with strips of cloth from our packs. The water's getting deeper.>

That was all Hanook received for a long while, during which he could only comfort himself with the thought that he'd have known if any harm had come to either brother.

<It's the next waystop.> Kayas sent at last. <The ceiling's collapsed and

flooded the tunnel. Feel how cold it is!>

Hanook shivered, and his eyes burned and stung at the brightness of the light assaulting his brothers' eyes. A sajamu-tide of freezing water swirled about his ankles. "Ghasru!" he exclaimed. Difficult situations demanded hard words, even to the point of swearing – he'd forgotten the presence of the two children at that moment. The volcano ruled their lives. <What about beyond?>

<We're checking,> came the reply. <It's slippery with the water from Outside! Hanook, how can this happen?>

The Eldest had no answers for him.

*

"What *is* that?"

Aa'kam turned at Raaza's half-touch. She was pointing to the centre of their sleeping-cavern, one the Shiranu had abandoned. The tribe would pass the darktime here and continue on their way at lightbreak.

A hunter's eyes were quick to spot movement, from habit and instinct. But this wasn't just the movement of one animal. Aa'kam leaned forwards, peering down at the ground. It seethed like boiling liquid –

"It's a mass of zulchi!" he exclaimed. He stepped closer and squatted to better observe them.

Raaza followed him.

The worms wriggled and jostled against one another as they left the cavern. Yellow-tinged from the sulphur which nourished them, they formed a stream two handspans wide, undulating towards the tunnel mouth. Aa'kam felt his scalp tingle; he disliked zulchi, and to see such a mass of them made his head-fur prickle upright.

"Which way are they going?" Aa'kam's middle brother, Jeeban, had approached in silence, followed by Ghura, his youngest brother.

"North-east, like the game." Aa'kam straightened. "Towards Keramanthu."

"It's as well we're headed in that direction too," said Raaza. She was always the practical one in the amaaj. "What did you catch for our meal, Jeeban?"

He spread his hands wide, palms up, in the gesture for empty. "We must move on for game, I think."

Ghura moved nearer, grinning. "Surely you were too noisy, Jeeban!" He held his own hands out. Two animals dangled from them, back legs knotted together with vinerope. "Even were you without catch, Jeeban, we shan't starve. I've a ganzu to bake in mud this darktime and a gahle for the next two lighttimes." The tinge of pride in his voice mingled with laughter at Jeeban's chagrin. "Ready your cookpot, Raaza!"

Raaza smiled. "Bring them, Ghura, and I shall do just that." They walked back to their niche, the game swinging from Ghura's shoulder. Aa'kam and Jeeban watched them disappear into the crack in the rockwall.

"This migration worries me," Aa'kam said. He watched the zulchi again. "First the game, now even the insects."

Jeeban nodded, frowning. "I was after a jumper-bachu when several umi-beetles flew past me. They swarmed on the bachu and stung it, or we should have had more meat. But umi-beetles don't usually fly together."

"Where was this?" Aa'kam's voice sharpened.

"In the disused farm cavern, back along the tunnel. Would you see it?"

"Show me."

Jeeban led Aa'kam out of the sleeping-cavern. The cavern was a half-pythet along it; they were both panting by the time they reached it, though Jeeban was younger by seven highwaters.

Despite its ice ceiling, the cavern was lit by a few self-spored glowcakes. Towards the centre of the chamber a clump of blackish vegetation clustered around a pool of stagnant water. Jeeban stepped across the streambed which led to it.

Flow-patterns marked the fine black soil of the cavern floor; water filled Aa'kam's footprints. <Where were the umi?>

Jeeban pointed towards the plants round the pool. <The bachu was eating leaves,> he answered. <It should still be there.>

They approached with care. Jeeban parted the leaves of a wild spicepod-plant. Beyond it lay the bachu. Its hind leg had ballooned under the coat of dark brown fur. Death must have been quick, though painful. The carcass had already begun to smell.

<I was lucky the beetles didn't sting me,> Jeeban observed. <I was near enough.>

<But why were they were flying together?> Aa'kam prodded the animal with the blunt end of his spear. <Something strange is happening this highwater. Even the insects know it. Since they and the game think Keramanthu is the safest place, then we should follow with all speed.>

CHAPTER 8

HANOOK TURNED HIS CHOICES OVER IN HIS MIND. He must act decisively. They couldn't go back; going forward they risked cold and flooding; but they'd starve if they stayed here. Further tremors might occur wherever they were, as they often did at blow-out time. Though the waystop ahead was useless, they could reach the next by walking all darktime, then catch up on sleep there. *That's surely the sensible decision?* Travelling time lost meant planting time lost too, and plant growth couldn't be hurried.

Hanook sighed. He pitied the children; babies and toddlers could be carried, but from four and five highwaters children walked with the adults. The three pregnant women and their amaaju would have to follow at their own pace, resting as necessary.

Hanook gathered the tribespeople together. When he'd finished explaining the situation, the Eldest Woman spoke up.

"The tribe has never been split before," she said.

She's right. If something should happen – if I've made the wrong decision... Aloud, Hanook said, "We've never seen such swollen rivers before, either, but we can only cross one if we meet it."

"True, but is this right for the tribe? What about the amaaju who follow us? Remember these women carry future tribespeople in their wombs."

"I haven't forgotten, Mnanga." He wanted to add that in caring for the interests of women in the tribe, the Eldest Woman was undermining his authority and confidence. But he contented himself with replying, "We must do as circumstances dictate," so as not to lose status.

<It's the best choice,> Kayas reassured him. <We'll wait here for you.>

They approached the waystop cavern. Wind blasted through the tunnel, whipping kilts around shivering legs and flailing head-fur into eyes. The body fur of the tribespeople was little protection against the ice particles in the air, scouring skin unused to such assault. Kerui's warmth was all they'd ever known. Hanook wrapped his sleeping-cloth around him, and many of the tribespeople copied him.

He was glad to see his brothers, and gladder still of the darktime falling beyond the cave's ceiling. But he couldn't resist staring up at Outside as they passed through the waystop. He thought he could see a faint sprinkling of lights above. He shuddered with fear at the strangeness of them as he remembered the old-word for them: bazu. The word had dropped from the language since the tribes had come to live in Kerui. *Stars! They're beautiful, but terrifying.*

92

<How far can we get this darktime?> Kayas asked him. <We *must* make up the lost time. >

<I know,> he replied. <We'll stop for food and rest in the tunnel beyond, then move on. The smaller group can follow and you can travel with them so I'll know what's happening.>

<Good idea,> Kayas agreed. <But for now, I must get out of this wind and wet.> He shivered. <I'm bone-chilled.>

They stumbled forwards, slippers snagging rocks unseen in the flood. Hanook felt forwards with his feet one step at a time. Once, he looked up to see a huge chunk of ice bearing down on him. He flattened himself back, shut his eyes and caught Zuas close. He felt the block's chill invade their bodies as it floated past. When he dared look again he realised everyone had stopped behind him. The whole tribe was following in his exact footsteps as best they could.

The waters were still rising. As he neared the hole in the ceiling Hanook tipped his head back to look Outside again. Water and chunks of ice still cascaded over the lip of the rock above. Droplets splashed in all directions. The ice cave above the waystop itself must have shivered, crumbled and melted; *that* was what was entering where the ceiling had been. More water and ice were swilling down towards them. Fear and vertigo seized Hanook; he averted his eyes. The wind screeched and flung particles of ice against his face. The hairless areas of his body shrivelled. His fur stood on end. His eyes smarted. His hands shook. The pack on his back weighed heavier with each step. They crept forwards...He coughed. *I must get those herbs –*

<Hanook!> Brach's exclamation clutched at his awareness. It was accompanied by a shake to his arm, acceptable only because of circumstance.

"Wha –?" he muttered, but his words were drowned by the roar of wind and water. He looked round. Zuas was behind him, shivering but upright, the boys clinging to her hands.

<Hurry! Not far now.> Brach pointed to the tunnel mouth ahead, where glowcakes offered more welcome than Outside. <Everyone's waiting for you.>

Hanook coughed again, nodded, and moved on.

*

Exhausted by the crossing, the Shiranu dozed where they sat. Chixi drowsed at one with them. Lorr's stew had lacked much; a tunnel was no substitute for a sleeping-cavern with well-used firestones. But his belly was full.

"Give us a story, Kayas!" somebody said nearby.

"Yes, yes, a story!"

Chixi raised an eyelid.

"Which one?" Kayas asked.

"You choose."

"Very well...I choose the story of how the tribes came to live here in Kerui, since we've just seen the Outside for ourselves." Kayas paused. Chixi opened both eyes to see why he'd stopped speaking; the older Shiranu was settling himself into a more comfortable position. Kayas was a particularly accomplished story-teller; the traditional role of next eldest brother of the Eldest man suited him well.

"In the past," he began, "when men lived Outside, they had no knowledge of Kerui. Men shared Outside with bachu which jumped and ran, with creatures which flew through the air, with fish in the rivers and seas, with creatures which glided along the ground without legs, with their scaled brothers who had legs, and with all manner of creatures. Men spoke the language of the three tribes as well as their own tongues, and there were enough women for each to have only one husband." He looked round at each of them in turn. "But this was long ago, and the tribes were small, scattered groups of Shiranu, and Sargussi, and Chabira. They moved through the land, foraging as they went, or hunting animals, drinking rainwater. Sometimes there were wars, but everyone was happy, and every woman had several daughters and sons.

"Then winters grew longer and summers became shorter, and gradually plants and animals became rarer. With less food for everyone there was conflict, but at last the Elders of the three tribes met to decide what they should do about it. Then Mekar of the Chabira told of how he'd taken shelter in an ice cave during a storm, and had been surprised to find rock caverns and tunnels below, with occasional holes in the ceiling which allowed in light. One of those caverns now houses Keramanthu, the Place of the Tribes. And because there were plants and animals in the caves, much like those Outside, he thought the tribes might live in safety and warmth there, as the volcano was dormant."

Chixi had heard this story often before, so he tried to hear where the changes would come.

"So the tribes came together to explore and live in the caves. They named them Kerui, our own place – the only place left to us. For during the building of the city of Keramanthu, the forests Outside died, leaving only mosses and dwarf forests, and nothing above ground to eat. The animals perished or also moved underground as it got colder. And Shiranu lived beside Sargussi and Chabira, and all walked together in peace, trading skills, crafts and goods. As the prophecy says –"

"The prophecy is wrong!" Chixi interrupted. "Sargussi shall never walk with Shiranu – why, they would eat us while our backs were turned to gather in the harvest!"

<Elder brother, you shouldn't question the prophecy!> Vru reminded him. <Nor interrupt the storyteller.>

"I *will* interrupt if I want!" Chixi retorted, too angry to remember to use the mindspeech. "If Sargussi hunters could steal my amaajni they can do anything, even flood a waystop!" Rage thundered in his veins. "If I ever see a live Sargussi I'll tear him to pieces with my bare hands!"

<Elder brother, please stop,> Jeene begged, <before our amaaj loses status!>

"I will *not* stop!" Chixi ranted. The loss of his amaajni goaded him like a pricket thorn. He had to blame someone. "I'll have my say, and you'll all listen to me or die in their next attack. It's Sargussi mischief that's broken open the waystop!"

"How could they have done that?" asked Lorr. "You're mistaken, Elder brother. The quake broke open the waystop and flooded it."

"They're miners and metalworkers – they'd find a way, and have the tools to do it." Chixi started to rise.

Hanook glared at him. "Sit down! I'll hear no more of this nonsense. Chixi! Be quiet or you'll cause a rockfall!"

*

"Gather, Sargussi!" Aa'kam called. "I would speak with you."

Long ago, Shiranu had made this sleeping cavern comfortable with regular use. But without light they couldn't farm their plots in the cavern nearby. Now this abandoned cavern was fast becoming unable to support the Sargussi either. From the corner of his eye Aa'kam saw another glowcake flicker out of existence.

He regarded in turn every amaaj, every brother, every wife, every child – over five hundred people in all. They waited for him to speak.

"You all know," Aa'kam said, "that strange things are happening now in Kerui." Though fatigued, his voice held authority. "We've seen migrations of zulchi, umi-beetles and ruzli, whose husks feed the glowcakes which by Shiranu trickery make plants grow. We've seen game migrating north-east, and the water has gradually risen in Kerui for several highwaters, and still more quickly recently. To survive we must head for the higher ground around Keramanthu, as the insects and game have. Only there shall we find enough food to survive." He looked around the tribe. Even the smallest children were listening. He nodded, satisfied.

"We daren't delay. Already some glowcakes have died without food; soon

95

darkness will come to these tunnels, blind us for travelling or hunting, and so starve us. So we must change our ways. To adapt or die, we shall march every day, so hunting must be cut to the minimum for survival. But marching people need food, so each day three of the unwed amaaju shall hunt for the whole tribe. But for this to work, each adult must eat less than usual." Those without children would move faster anyway, and could catch up or make their own way towards the city if separated from the rest of the tribe.

<Aa'kam? This weren't our custom,> Jeeban objected. <Each amaaj always hunts its own food supply. >

Thank the volcano for the mindspeech, Aa'kam thought. But he could see Ghura preparing to side with Jeeban. <I know,> he sent, <but new conditions demand decisions. Pay attention, now!> He was reluctant to split the tribe – and who knew *what* they should find at the city? But there was no choice.

The tribespeople made no protest; loyalty and obedience were the law. They would accept his orders if it meant survival as a tribe, though individuals might suffer or die. Aa'kam took a deep breath.

"Next lighttime," he continued, "Jeman, Gwa and Rowak's amaaju shall hunt for us. The following lighttime the responsibility shall be Morra's, Lakar's and Adi's amaaju. That pattern shall continue until we reach Keramanthu, the rest of us to walk."

Aa'kam regarded the Elder brothers of the six unmarried amaaju in turn. Then he spotted Yado's father Maru shifting position. *Yado was always independent, especially since his brother died.* When he returned from his initiation quest there would be another two excellent hunters to help. "Questions?" Aa'kam asked.

This time there were none.

*

Hanook rubbed his hands over his stomach, warmed by his sleeping-cloth, fed with hot vegetable stew and freshly-baked aldu bread brought him by his former daughter Nahru. He longed for sleep now his agitation with Chixi had abated. He hadn't enjoyed making him look small before the tribe, but ill-feeling against the Sargussi would be inappropriate in this crisis. His cough tore through the tunnel again; shame to his amaaj, though illness couldn't be helped, and none would dare shush the Eldest. Hanook hoped the water in the breached waystop wouldn't rise to trap the slower party, and allowed himself to doze with the others.

They pushed on before lightbreak, their way lit by glowcakes. He'd sent Brach ahead with two others. As they walked, Hanook mused on Outside, surely an impressive sight. *If it were possible to see it without being blinded.*

\<Hanook!\> Brach's mindsending.
\<What is it?\>
\<Rockfall. Our way's blocked.\>

CHAPTER 9

HANOOK HAD SEEN MANY ROCKFALLS. <Check for a gap, Brach,> he ordered. <I'll be there soon.> He beckoned to a nearby man.

"Keep everyone moving, Nulma. I'm going on ahead."

Nulma bobbed his head in acknowledgement.

Hanook quickened his pace until he passed the bend in the tunnel. Few glowcakes lit this part of the tunnel, but as he rounded the curve he saw Brach surveying the pile of rocks that blocked their way, talons scratching at his headfur. The tang of disturbed earth hung in the air.

<Well?> Hanook asked, reaching Brach's side.

<It's not good, Eldest. Not the slightest breath is coming through to tell us how far ahead the tunnel's blocked.>

Brach's fear, frustration and anger mirrored Hanook's own. He raised the privacy shield, not wanting Brach to realise how afraid he was of making the wrong decision. *He'll be looking to me for guidance, and I've none for him,* he thought. "What choices?" he asked in the signing-speech.

Brach's hands flashed a message back. "Shift the rocks or go around it. I don't know of any other route to the next farm cavern."

"Me neither," agreed Hanook, noticing Brach's trembling fingers. While he was Eldest man, his brothers shared his responsibilities.

It may be our function to lead the tribe, he thought, as they trudged back, *but everyone has the right to say what they think. Including Mnanga. Perhaps someone else has a better suggestion.* He sensed Brach's mind clamouring to know what he was thinking and feeling. <I'm not ready to share my thoughts with you yet, brother,> he told him.

"Well enough," Brach said.

The Eldest sensed his withdrawal.

*

Lorr walked on, trying not to think about anything, ignoring his brothers. Chixi lumbered in front of him, his shadow now huge and black, now pale and smaller as they approached, then passed, each colony of glowcakes. The tribe had made good progress that lightbreak.

Ahead the passage curved. Once past the bend, the light from behind dimmed. Lorr was surprised to see Hanook walking back towards them, hands held up palm outwards, telling the tribe to stop. Around him footfalls ceased as everyone obeyed.

Hanook still held up his hand. "No further. I must speak to everyone. Pass the message back – we'll go back past the curve so everyone can hear."

The tribe retreated until their forms, distorted by their backpacks, were once more silhouetted against light seeping into the tunnel along with water from Outside. They knelt or sat cross-legged on sleeping cloths spread on the tunnel floor. Soon the passage was full. The Eldest moved to a place where he could see everyone. When they were everyone was seated and focused on him, he began to speak.

In the distance, Lorr heard the roar of water entering the waystop. Hanook's voice carried against even that. "We've another problem ahead – there's been a rockslide."

The tribe's shock flooded the passage. Wife looked to husband in horror, husband looked to brother for reassurance. Lorr watched as Hanook held up his hand again for everyone's attention.

"We have two choices, though one may be no choice at all." Hanook paused and looked around him.

Lorr glanced about him too; despair and fear warred with hope and trust on most faces. *They expect Hanook to solve this problem,* he realised, and recognised that the weight of responsibility, bound to him as tightly as a baby to its mother's back, had bent Hanook's shoulders. *Luckily I have little chance of becoming Eldest man.*

"We can either move the rocks or find another way to reach the farm cavern." Hanook paused. "I don't know of any other route. But if anyone else does, he or she should speak now."

The tunnels confused even those who used them regularly, so the tribe stuck to certain routes. They knew roughly when blow-outs would occur in the farm caverns, and kept to the tunnels to avoid them. The blow-out would have come as usual and their destination would be ready for planting up. There was always the danger that a blow-out would fail, as sometimes happened, or occur later. But Lorr was certain, from the quakes they'd faced, that wasn't the case now.

He surveyed the faces before him. Nobody spoke.

Then Chixi said, "Supposing a group went back and tried for another way round?"

"What did you have in mind?" Hanook asked.

"Perhaps my amaaj could find a different route to the next farm cavern."

Lorr felt the chill of apprehension curl through his stomach. But it was no use saying anything to Chixi. He exchanged a glance with Jeene that held the thought, <He'll kill us all to be a hero in the eyes of the rest of the tribe.>

Jeene shook his head, warning Lorr to keep quiet. <Just do what he says,> Jeene told him, <and you won't get hurt. He'll have his way anyway, because he's bigger and heavier than any of us.>

Lorr acknowledged the truth of this with a nod. They'd all felt Chixi's fists at times, though Lorr was the usual target. Chixi always got his own way. He wouldn't listen to a man without status; Lorr was well aware that to Chixi he had no value.

He turned his attention back to Hanook just as Mnanga spoke.

"We should move the rocks," she said. "The tribe shouldn't be split again." And she turned an accusing stare on Hanook.

*

Hanook followed Chixi's amaaj back down the tunnel. The sound of water became a roar, and the light brightened as they approached the broken waystop. The chunks of ice had disappeared; melted, probably. The water level in the tunnel had risen again. The air from Outside flowed like water around his body. He shivered. Lightbreak had given way to full lighttime; far above the sun spat light into his eyes. He shielded them with his hands; ahead he glimpsed Chixi and his brothers doing the same. He edged forwards.

A group of Shiranu were at rest inside the tunnel mouth as they approached: a pregnant woman, her four husbands and two children. They looked exhausted. Hanook smiled encouragement at them and sat with them. He looked up as Chixi and his brothers settled behind them. Loja's amaaj were just crossing: three men, one supporting a woman with hugely distended stomach. Azhee shuffled forwards; she'd surely give birth at the next farm cavern. A boy of about three highwaters rode on the shoulders of the second man, and a five-year-old held his hand. An older boy followed.

"Why did they wait so long?" Hanook asked. "Surely it would have been better to cross before the light got too strong?"

"It was also colder," said the woman beside him.

Hanook's misgivings returned with the force of a highwater. Then he realised that if they'd been on time they'd all have died in the rockfall, and his confidence seeped back.

He studied Chixi, seated below the flicker of a dying glowcake. *He's brave to the point of recklessness,* he thought. The sickness was known to change a man's personality. Chixi either saw no danger, or felt he had little to lose –

A shout of surprise and fear grabbed his attention. As he focused on the amaaj crossing the flood Hanook forgot to protect his eyes. Light assaulted them. His "Aaagh!" was drowned by the *crack* of ice. He shut his eyes, but afterburn images remained – water gushing into the waystop, a huge chunk of ice falling from the ceiling. He blinked tears away, screwed up his face to see what was happening, and watched, paralysed.

The flow became a highwater. Fear froze Loja where he stood as the ice bore down on him and his eldest son. The boy clutched at Loja's kilt. The rest of the amaaj stood as if crystallised in place. Harsh white sunlight petrified them into shapes rising out of the torrent. For an endless fraction of a moment nothing moved except the tide.

The ice struck Loja. He keeled over backwards, arms thrashing. A swirl of water sucked the child under.

The ice moved on, leaving no trace of Loja or his son.

*

"You on that hololink again, Matt?" Abdel asked from the doorway.

"We brought you your lunch," Yue Xiao said. "We thought you'd rather not stop."

Matt swung his chair round to face them.

Just then Yue Xiao caught sight of the holotank scene. "What's going on?"

Matt explained about the accident. "I don't like the look of this. The quake's breached the glacier just where a sub-surface river drains it. Look." He pointed. "Water's percolating down through the skylight."

*

"Ancestors!" Hanook breathed.

The amaaj jolted back to life. The two younger boys clawed at their throats, drawing blood. The woman took the youngest in her arms to quiet his choking sobs. The two remaining husbands clung to each other. Hanook saw their faces, contorted as if by the effort to breathe.

Azhee moved forwards, hauling at each husband in turn. They might as well have been frozen in place, stiff with grief, horror, shock and pain.

Hanook was on his feet. Water lapped over them, soaking his slippers. "Help them!"

Lorr jumped up, followed by Jeene and Vru. Chixi fumbled in his backpack, then splashed after them. Other men followed. A glance upwards told Hanook they were safe for now, but the remnants of the ice ceiling had another large crack across it.

Vru and Jeene reached the two men and guided them through the water. Lorr dragged the elder son to safety. Azhee followed with her youngest son.

Hanook stood ready to help the survivors onto land. *Where did Chixi go?*

The first family group to have crossed moved further down-tunnel. Lorr

101

reached the shallows first, still gripping the boy. Azhee stumbled after them, helped by the men of the first amaaj. Finally, Jeene and Vru brought the surviving brothers and child ashore, eyes vacant but with water overflowing down their faces.

Hanook stepped out into the flood. Its roar filled the enclosed space. He strained to see Chixi across the waystop. *Where* is *he?*

Something bumped against his leg. He looked down, still shielding his eyes. The shape of a man floated nearby. Behind the body was a smaller one.

Tears blurred Hanook's vision. *It's my fault. I should* never *have split the tribe into two groups.* He turned to Lorr. "Help me get them out," he signed.

Lorr handed over the child he'd been leading and set to with him. It took their combined efforts to retrieve the dead. They weighed as much as firestones. At last, gasping with effort, they hauled the child out and laid him on Loja. Hanook sank down into a squat, coughing. Mnanga would make much play on this disaster, he was sure.

He remembered Chixi as he got his breath back. A scan of the shadows at the tunnel mouth opposite showed him, tall and steady even against the flood. He'd almost reached the far side. "By my dead amaamu, where does he think he's *going?*"

Then he realised that Chixi had seen what he'd forgotten. The third amaaj still hadn't crossed.

*

Matt had little appetite after the accident, but he took the rice salad, still focusing on the holotank. One giant Naxadan male caught his attention, striding through the rising water, a mass of rope coiled round him from shoulder to hip. The lens zoomed in at Matt's command. "He *has* got a rope." He felt like cheering, though he knew that was idiotic. *I hope they make it across.* It proved the Naxadans were intelligent, whatever Hartmann might think. *'Troglodytes' sounds so pejorative!*

The giant had crossed the cavern to where another family stood waiting. There he threaded the rope through a vesicle which had formed a tube. Matt couldn't see any detail but knew the crystals growing inside it could split the rope. When the giant had made it fast, he signed to the group, then walked back into the flood without speaking.

As the giant reached the other side, the old male gesticulated at him again. The giant ignored him and tied the rope round a boulder at the side of the passage. It was stretched taut, half a metre above the water. He beckoned the waiting group across.

They waded forwards, clinging to the rope, all still shielding their eyes.

The holocam panned round after them. As the last Naxadan child was helped into the shallows, the group turned and splashed down the passage, carrying their dead with them.

*

Abdel drew up a chair and seated himself beside Matt. Yue Xiao leaned against the side of the hololink console.

The holovid hovered at a distance, tied to its terminal. Matt noted that the pregnant female from the family which had lost the man and child was with two other males; all were weeping in silence. Although not a sentimental person, he couldn't help but feel sympathetic shock, particularly at the loss of a child. A glance at Yue Xiao told him she felt the same: her lower lip was gripped between her teeth.

At the far side of the cavern an ancient male, blanket-wrapped against the cold, gesticulated and pointed at the younger members of the group.

"Sign language must be useful in a situation like that," Abdel observed. "Ray would get on well there!"

"A handheld translator unit would be useful," Yue Xiao said.

"Or Jordas," Matt mumbled around his salad. "It looks like an argument, eh?"

*

"You took a stupid risk!"

Chixi's eyes were stone-hard with defiance as he regarded Hanook. "I *chose* to," he said. "It got everyone back over here, didn't it?"

Hanook considered Chixi. He recognised the truth of his words. *But because he acted without my authority he compromised my status.* Further up the passage he could hear the sounds of rock scraping on rock, of grunts of effort, the occasional thud and accompanying curse or groan of pain. He made the sign of incomprehension. "Go and help them, Chixi. Your strength is needed."

The giant shook his head. "My amaaj will try for another way to the farm cavern. We agreed, remember?"

Hanook's blood sang in his ears and his face grew hot as meat on a cooking stone. "You expect me to approve that now?"

Chixi's face wore an expression of sullen determination. "I'm going –"

"You may *find* a way," Hanook interrupted, "but don't expect us to use it. I won't risk more men, or women, or more precious children. You see?" He spread his hands wide, palms down again. "It would be pointless risking yourself and your maaj'garu if the tribe doesn't use whatever you find. And I *forbid* such a waste of time, effort and useful lives."

103

Chixi opened his mouth to speak.

"May I remind you," Hanook added, "that there is such a thing as loyalty to the tribe, and that it's demanded above all else, even above loyalty to the rest of your amaaj?"

Chixi closed his mouth and nodded.

"I'm not ungrateful to you," Hanook continued. "If it hadn't been for your quick thought and bravery, we could have lost another whole amaaj. Only *you* could have done that." He sighed. "There are bodies to be buried. Come with me."

Another nod.

They tramped back towards the rockslide and the passage grew darker and darker; the rockfall had extinguished many glowcakes. Beside the corpses, Mnanga sat with the grieving Azhee, stroking her head-fur and giving her an herbal decoction. She didn't even look at Hanook. The omission spoke her disapproval. Her assistants sat with the remaining husbands and sons.

The faces of two sets of maaj'garu reflected only the blankness of the maaj'nag'ur.

*

"Probe, feed a fix on your current location through to the map databanks. Then follow on record." Matt turned to Abdel and Yue Xiao. "That should help us gauge the flood risk in this sector."

The probe detached itself from the terminal.

"Jordas has been analysing that map of the volcano," Matt added. "He says the tribespeople call it *Kerui*. Here – he sent me this." The holotank filled up with a three-d projection of the area showing the last twenty tremors. The epicentres of each seismic disturbance appeared in sequence, linked to their foci above by colour-coded lines. They formed a squashed ring of winking markers on the flank of the volcano. "It looks like this parasitic cone will erupt soon, judging by the pattern of quakes – and our tilt meters have detected the movement of magma through the rock below."

"When will it erupt?" asked Abdel.

"When the magma's emplaced – the quakes will become very frequent beforehand. But I don't fancy the Naxadans' chances when it does."

"Nor me," Abdel agreed.

*

"We must bury Loja and Geffu now," Hanook said to the woman. "Will you lay the first stones, Azhee?"

"Loja was the Elder brother," the woman choked. "And Geffu, my eldest son. How can I live without them?"

104

"Because you have two more husbands and two other sons who need your strength," Hanook said, "just as the rest of the tribe needs you. And your baby." His voice quivered as he spoke. *I should never have split our people.* "Here. You must say goodbye to them now. They shall lie together forever, father and son, so their spirits won't wander and haunt you." He passed her a stone. She took it and laid it on the dead man's chest.

Hanook passed stones into the hands of the rest of the amaaj, and Mnanga and her assistants helped them to place them on the bodies. *The maaj'nag'ur protects brothers while they grieve and adapt, but it will make travel difficult.*

At last he signed to Chixi, "It's good that there are many stones here from the rockslide. It makes our work easier. Help me." They set to in silence. Before long two mounds of stones covered the dead.

The task completed, Hanook turned to Chixi. "We'd best help the others now."

"I can rest later this lighttime." Chixi rubbed his forehead as if to erase fatigue.

Hanook nodded. He was tired too, but must set a good example. Only the grieving amaaj, the pregnant women and Mnanga and her helpers were excused from clearing the rockslide. He led Chixi towards the pile of rocks. "Come on!"

Someone yelped in pain. Hanook glimpsed a woman leading her youngest child in Mnanga's direction, hand pressed against his kilt. He guessed the boy had touched a dislodged glowcake.

There came a sudden *whoosh*: air being sucked into the tunnel.

"We're through!" Hanook said.

Even Chixi grinned.

*

"I'm exhausted!" Soolkah complained as they entered the waystop. "Must we rush along like this? There's no hurry for us to catch them up – we won't be doing any planting!" She sought Yado's gaze as they walked. "At least, I assume you're not planning to help with it?"

Yado grinned. "I'm no farmer."

"Then can't we stay here for the night?"

He looked around, considering. "We could," he agreed. "But isn't the farm cavern due to blow over the next day or so?"

"Yes, but we're in no danger here." She reached behind her to unhook the makeshift backpack.

"Hmmm!" was Yado's only reply. "Being near a vent makes me nervous."

"Well, I need a drink and a rest." Soolkah pointed to the pool at one side of the waystop. "That's odd, it was only fed by one waterstream last time we were here." She moved closer to the pool, sniffing. "The water smells all right, though," she added, examining the trails of water trickling down the rock face. Above them, colonies of glowcakes lined the walls.

"Jordas Krata was right," Yado said. "Changes come now to Kerui." He stood beside her, staring down into the pool. "Flooding is among the things he warned me about."

Soolkah watched him and saw fear flicker in his eyes.

He tried to smile. "Put aside your fright," he said. "Jordas Krata will come to help us, and both our tribes."

He's making an effort not to think about it. Soolkah smiled back in relief, feeling a surge of love and companionship as he laid his arm about her shoulders. "I've never known of anyone with such a long name before."

"It has two parts." Yado leaned back against the rock. "Humanu all have names in several parts."

"Humanu?"

"Jordas Krata's tribe."

"When will he arrive?"

"A few lighttimes."

Soolkah didn't want to think about it just then. "I'll dry these beanpods while you prepare your food," she said, scraping the soil off the firestone with her talons. When it was exposed she spread the pods out on it to dry. Yado cast glances at her between skinning his kill. She'd seen him do this enough times now not to be upset by it, though she still loathed the smell of blood. Soon two jumper-bachu and a smaller dakr, whose long whiskers compensated for its blindness, lay on the firestone beside her beanpods.

"Try some meat?"

"I'm not sure I could eat it," she replied. "It's just not our way."

"Oh, so you prefer to starve rather than eat what I could give you?" he asked, his voice roughening. "Shiranu, you must soon learn to like it! I know *your* food is nearly gone."

Soolkah bit her lip. "True," she agreed with a deep exhalation. "All right, if you'll try some of the bread I made yesterday."

"Fair trade," he answered.

She pulled a cake of aldu bread from the basket. Yado set the meat on the stone and held out his hand. "Not all of it," he said. He broke the piece she gave him in half again and handed one part back. He put the other quarter in his mouth. Soolkah watched him chew, grimace and swallow.

"You'll get used to it," she said. "It's our staple food."

106

"Make love?" Yado asked, catching her hand.

"With that – *thing* that sees us – watching?"

"Jordas Krata said he'd tell his friends to stop it at darktime."

"You trust him?"

He turned her face up to his and looked deeply into her eyes. "I must," he said. "I know his heart and he knows mine." His voice trailed off.

"Is something the matter?" Soolkah asked.

"Well..." Yado's voice trailed off into silence. He started again. "I don't know how I should say this."

"What?"

"He's my maaj'gar." He paused. "I just thought – we should share you."

"What do you mean?" Soolkah felt the blood drain from her face. "You said your maaj'gar was dead, and that Jordas Krata could only see us through that thing that follows us?"

"That's no lie. But now we share thoughts, sensations, feelings. We should also share you, amaajni."

She'd wondered when he would broach this subject. "I suppose we should, if he's truly your maaj'gar," she said.

"Trust me?" Yado asked. He stared back at her, eyes tawny as citrine crystals.

"I trust *you*," she said slowly. "But I'm not sure I trust Jordas Krata. I don't know him, and I don't want to go with a man I've never even seen before."

"He – saw you, and likes you," Yado said.

He seemed distant and distracted. Soolkah wondered if he was in contact with the stranger at that moment. "Chixi saw me and liked me. That doesn't mean to say I wanted him to take me!" she retorted. "What does he look like? I'd like to know who it is if I must go with him." She paused. "You said he's from a tribe called Humanu –"

"Yes. And I don't know how he *looks*, only how he *feels*," Yado admitted. "I think mayhap we're not *much* different from folk of his tribe." He sighed. "I want to treat him with fairness –"

"Yado, remember, he won't know our ways," Soolkah interrupted. "How would he know whether you're doing things properly or not? And it might not matter to him as much as it does to you."

"Mayhap not, but *we* will know, and he will if I do." He reached for his pack.

Soolkah hadn't finished. "Humanu ways may be different from ours."

Yado spread his sleeping skins on the ground, then lay down and pulled

107

her against him. "True. But if he asks concerning our customs, I must tell him." His hands moved over her breasts, feeling them swell and the nipples harden at his touch. "He seems a good man. Shall you really mind if he takes you?"

"Perhaps not if he's kind and gentle. But it won't be the same as with you." Soolkah sat up suddenly. "You aren't playing a trick on me, are you?"

Yado sat up too, bewilderment spreading across his face. "Why would I do that?"

Soolkah shrugged, finding no words to explain her suspicions. "Because – because you're Sargussi and I'm Shiranu," she answered at last. "I thought you'd perhaps find it amusing – to bait me."

"Why?" Hurt sharpened his voice. "I'm telling you the truth as I see it."

Soolkah digested this in silence. "I see." Her words dripped into the cavern. "I'll check the pods."

They weren't ready. Then she felt Yado's hands in her head-fur. He liked to touch it when they lay down together. She twisted round to face him.

"I wouldn't wish to upset you...but I thought you might be angry, or afraid. I never expected to have to share you, either," he murmured, "though I don't mind as it's Jordas Krata. But you –" He searched her face. "You know even less of him than I do." He thought for a moment or two. "Indeed, I never thought to have a – foreigner – as my maaj'gar."

"Do you know what it's like where he lives?" Soolkah asked.

"Only that it's hot, and people live Outside. And he comes from a different place again. He tried to explain, but I didn't know the words. It's so different from Kerui that I can't describe it...Even though I can *see* it, sometimes – he showed me mind-pictures, something Uvvuz never did, but I couldn't understand them. Everything's so different there. But I understand *you* – except for just now." He drew a breath. "How could you think I would play such a trick on you? Shiranu or not, you're my amaajni. I respect you too much for unkindness, and I was thinking you respected me. But mayhap it matters too much to you that we're of different tribes?"

"Oh, Yado!" Soolkah could see she'd really hurt him with her suspicion. "It doesn't matter to me at all. But I thought perhaps it mattered to you."

"How can it, if my beautiful amaajni is Shiranu, but my maaj'gar's tribe is from a different world entirely." Yado asked. "Come, amaajni. Let me *show* you how much I love you!"

Soolkah allowed him to show her, at that.

CHAPTER 10

JORDAS PREPARED TO ENJOY his starship flight. He stowed his luggage in the wardrobe in the pleasant cabin, extracted clean underwear and a shirt, and by reflex checked the safety catch on the Colt.

He'd left Axos in a private aircar and caught the shuttle to this ship which was bound for the Charidas Interchange. There he would catch his connection to Naxada. It was the fastest route Marcus could arrange for him.

He'd just stepped into the steam shower when it was announced that the space yacht was leaving orbit. The shower relaxed his muscles; he felt as if he'd been pummelled all over. *I don't mind space travel, he thought, it's flying on Goranon that my body objects to.*

As the steam jets opened the pores in his skin, his thoughts returned to the Naxadans. *I can't fail, particularly after that discussion with Yado during lift-off.* He'd promised to bring food for them both. Yue Xiao's team were working on that using food synthesisers. He estimated he could catch up with them in just a few days, and once Yado no longer had to hunt they should make good progress.

He scrubbed perspiration from his body with a brush, wondering what Naxada was really like. Extremes of temperature wouldn't bother him; but he was apprehensive about how he'd deal with Yado and Soolkah.

<When shall you arrive?> the tribesman had asked, as the pressure on his body and eardrums had increased.

<I should be there in five of your lighttimes, though I'll have to find you, and I suppose that depends on where I enter the caves. But I want to meet both of you soon.>

<Likewise.>

Jordas hadn't been able to block the flood of desire that had swept through him, so he'd ignored it as best he could. But even remembering it embarrassed him.

The final jet of cold water from the top of the shower splashed down onto him before warm airjets dried him. He shrugged himself into his vest and shirt, and rolled the sleeves up as usual. His loose Goranoni cottons and linens wouldn't look out of place on-board ship.

And no-one would have any inkling of his response to Soolkah, inappropriate as he considered it to be. *Is this – attraction – my own feeling?* he asked himself. *Or is it just because I'm mindlinked to Yado that I feel so drawn to her? Anyway, who'll know, other than me, and perhaps Yado? So why worry?* Yado hadn't mentioned it.

But his reasoning didn't make him feel less adulterous or ashamed.

*

"Wonder what Jordas is doing?"

"He'll be halfway to Charidas by now," Marcus grunted. "I'll just check the account then get the next stage under way. The sooner we can get the archaeology team out there, the sooner they can get on with the job."

"They from Earth?"

"Yes, an archaeologist and two holotechs. They'll enter the city and start work before the Naxadans even get there."

"Don't know much about archaeology. What will they do?"

"They'll build a perfect hologrammatic reproduction of the city for the Naxadans. We can't transport it off-planet bit by bit – there isn't time, and we don't know where they're going yet – but we can give them the holoimage, and preserve at least some of whatever religious or historical significance it has for them."

"Great idea."

"The space telescope's moving into position now. Put it onto record, will you?"

"Sure." Ray crossed to the telescope console. "When does Jordas's replacement arrive?"

"I've selected her –"

"Her?"

"Why not?" Marcus gave Ray a speculative stare. "She's a Kiai geologist with an interest in astronomy – the nearest I could get to Jordas's specialisms. But she has other commitments until next week." He inserted a chip. "Is something the matter?"

"No – no. Nice to get a day off." Ray turned back to the console monitor.

Marcus called up the codes he'd received from Senator Hartmann four days before, humming tunelessly. Information filled his monitor cube. He scanned it for a moment. "Unbelievable!"

"What?" Ray came to stand beside him.

Marcus felt cold despite the heat. He stroked his beard and repeated, "I don't believe it! The account – the money –" He shut down the screen, then called up the codes again.

The screen reappeared, identical information laid out in the same way. He traced the first date with his finger and checked it against his wrist chronometer. There were two entries, one of them the payment for Jordas's

110

passage to Naxada. He'd made that transaction himself.

That's correct, he thought, *and so's the amount.* He checked the next date. He'd only made the one transaction. *So what's this one here?* He became aware of Ray hovering beside him. "Someone's withdrawn some of the money," he said. "I'll have to call Hartmann."

Marcus moved to the holotank console. His stomach felt as if it was being unravelled piece by piece. "I didn't expect problems once we'd got our funding."

He requested a call to the Charidas Interchange and waited. A robot operator took his call, no doubt an export from the free colony on Mars. "I must speak urgently to Senator Gerrold Hartmann," Marcus said. "He should be on-station now."

"I'll check for you," the operator grated. "Accessing now." There was a short pause. "Senator Hartmann has checked out of his hotel. He is booked on the *Zeus*, leaving for Earth in two hours. I could page him at the Departures Lounge if you require?"

"Please."

Within seconds Hartmann's holo confronted him.

"Ah, Doctor Carlin. How can I help?" The senator looked as if he'd been expecting this call.

"There appears to have been an unscheduled withdrawal of funds from the bank account," Marcus replied. "I wondered if you had any idea why and by whom?"

"I'm sure there's no problem," Hartmann said. "Sometimes money's temporarily re-allocated."

"This has happened before with these projects?"

Hartmann nodded. "And often it's paid in instalments."

"You mentioned that," said Marcus, "but you said that wouldn't happen as our project is so urgent. Most of the money has been withdrawn! And it's needed *now*, for *this* project."

"Of course, of course! I'm certain all the money will be back in the account in a few days, but I'll see what I can do in the meantime. You must remember that your project isn't the only one the Committee's currently funding. These things are ongoing for years after resettlement begins – that's how the instalment system came about – and sometimes more financial support is needed than first thought." Hartmann's mouth snapped shut as he stopped speaking and settled back into its usual hard line.

If we could forecast how much money was needed, surely other projects can! Marcus thought. *But some of the other projects the Committee's funded*

111

involved relocating several million lives. *I suppose we are dealing with only about a thousand people.* "Perhaps your superiors haven't realised how urgently this funding is needed," he said. "I could speak to them and see what can be done to speed things up –"

"That *won't* be necessary," Hartmann assured him. "I'll deal with it myself, and the money will be back there in a few days. Now, if you'll excuse me, I've a ship to catch. Good day, Doctor Carlin." The transmission ended.

Marcus felt he'd been dismissed. He sat back, resting his hands on his knees. He inhaled and exhaled, trying to expel his sense of impotence.

"Call bank?" Ray suggested.

"I guess that's the next step." Marcus leaned forwards and busied his hands on the hololink console.

*

Jordas's connection for Naxada wouldn't arrive for some hours. He shoved his luggage into a locker and sought some food. The Charidas Interchange boasted a good mix of ethnic restaurants; he decided to revisit Vanjeynish food, having enjoyed it during his student days. As he sipped chilled yellow wine and munched on a salad of nubbets, edible flowers and protax leaves, with strips of meat in a piquant sauce, it occurred to him that Naxadan delicacies would never grace restaurant tables. Even if other species could eat them, there wasn't enough time to catch animals or collect plants, and the unique ecosystem was irreproducible.

One thing worried him. Marcus had told him that if he hadn't located the tribes by the time the field team's evacuation ship arrived, the whole team was to return to the research base and leave with Matt's skeleton crew. He was determined the mission wouldn't be in vain.

Returning to the observation lounge, Jordas felt he was drowning in impatience. The stars hung motionless, one moment seeming near enough to touch, the next receding into the distance – an illusion caused by the meteor shield. He'd done a tour of duty on the Galatea IV station at university. The star maps were engraved in his memory. Even here he could pick out stars he recognised; constellations were distorted, but the stars stayed the same, just viewed from new angles.

Ships arrived and left. He watched them, drumming his heels on the safety rail, eager to be on his way. Eventually he drowsed where he sat from boredom.

When the summons came, he jerked awake with a start.

"Calling Dr Jordas Krata. Hololink call for Dr Jordas Krata," a tinny voice announced. "Please go to the nearest holotank and indicate your readiness to receive this communication."

Only Marcus and Matt knew he was here, and they'd only call in an emergency. *What the hell's happened?* Jordas was on his feet and moving towards the cluster of private holocubes in one corner of the lounge before the message could be repeated.

He acknowledged the call. In seconds it was patched through to his terminal. Marcus's head and shoulders filled the projection cube. He was pale, and his voice betrayed more agitation than Jordas had ever heard in it before. "We've got a problem. I want you to wait at Charidas for further instructions."

"Why?"

"Some money's been moved from the account. I've –"

"What?"

"I've contacted Senator Hartmann and he assures me it'll go back in, but it means we can't send the other teams yet."

"There isn't time for delays like this! My connection's due to dock soon. If I miss it there'll be a hotel bill which we wouldn't otherwise have had."

Marcus looked even more troubled. "I know, Jordas. I thought of all that before I called you. It'll cost us to rebook the other arrangements, too."

"Every day the danger for the Naxadans increases. They shouldn't have to wait just because some bureaucrat's cocked things up at the Committee," Jordas said. "Why don't you let me go on to Naxada as planned, and I'll go into the caves and see what I can do?"

"What can one man do alone?"

"Perhaps a lot, with the mindlink. Besides, there are other experienced climbers and cavers on-station. The rescue team can catch up when they arrive."

Marcus fingered his beard as if contemplating alternatives. "We-ell...If you're willing to try it, then perhaps that's what we must do."

"Can you call the bank?"

"I've done that. The Manager confirmed that money sometimes gets temporarily re-allocated."

Jordas's anxiety grew as he listened.

"Hartmann said funds sometimes get switched from one project account to another because the Committee puts funding wherever it's needed most urgently. But that didn't sound right. I've been trying to contact Howerd Asthorn, the Committee Chairman, to explain that we need the money now and can he please ensure that none is switched away from our account in future, but he's away and won't be back before the end of the month. It seems that beside myself and Howerd Asthorn, two administrators have access to the account, Corah Whitley and Nevil Floyd, both appointed by the Committee.

113

So far I can't contact either of them."

"They're Committee employees?"

"Yes." Marcus seemed calmer now. "Call me when you reach Naxada, Jordas. I'm glad you were willing to go ahead as your transport's already paid for. Do what you can, and I'll try to sort out the problem from this end." He paused. "Good luck!"

"Thanks. You too. And thanks for letting me know." Jordas walked back to his seat deep in thought, and only remembered to glance up at the lounge's station-time chronometer after he'd sat down. The *Leda* was due to arrive within minutes.

He headed for the locker containing his luggage.

*

Sleeping, Jordas dreamed.

The rough rockwall was at his back, and Soolkah rested in the crook of his arm. A piece of meat had stuck between two of his slightly crooked lower teeth. His tongue worked without success to release it. He reached for a strip of freshmouth, and began to press it between each tooth in turn, relishing the wood's taste and scent.

When he'd finished, his hand touched his whorled fur, then moved over the peach-fuzz of Soolkah's chest and abdomen, seeking her nipples. He wanted to watch her flat breasts swell, evidence that he could make her desire him. It fascinated him as much as her head-fur. Later, when she'd given him children, the change wouldn't be as noticeable, and would disappear during suckling...He watched her wake and turn towards him with a pert smile, urging him on, guiding his hands lower, under the fabric of her kilt...

Jordas awoke. The impressions of Yado's surroundings still felt real, especially the urgency of desire. *I was there, in his mind,* he reassured himself. *And if I know what he's doing now, surely he must know I was dreaming about him. And her.* The smell of scorched meat lingered in his nostrils.

"Light on." His eyes were gritty, his throat dry. Clambering out of his bunk's protective webbing, he caught sight of his wrist chronometer: oh-three-thirty, Goranoni time. He hadn't changed it to ship's time, intending to reset it to Naxadan time on arrival.

He ordered a drink from the cabin's food dispenser. As he sucked the juice into his mouth, he was aware again of the feel of a body pressed provocatively against his own, of his *uchaan* plunging and retreating, plunging and retreating. Jealousy knifed him. He shook his head but couldn't clear the sensations. He felt guilty that he hadn't contacted Yado at Charidas as he'd promised. *Perhaps this is his way of reminding me of that.*

Perhaps not. *Surely I'm just over-tired?* He couldn't believe Yado would deliberately send him impressions he must know were – Jordas stopped himself, fist clenched on the pre-pak, swallowed more juice and climbed back into bed. His voice command darkened the room.

But thoughts circled constantly in his head. It wasn't just because of his growing feelings for Soolkah that he'd avoided mindspeech with Yado. Ever since Marcus's call two days before he'd worried about losing the tribesman's trust if Yado learned of the project's financial problems. How could he even explain them to him? His tribe had no concept of money.

It was hours before he drifted into sleep, to the unceasing motion of steps taken on a journey through a strange land.

*

Yado was worried. He'd shared no mindspeech with Jordas for four lighttimes now, and needed reassurance that all was well. He knew Jordas was safe, was aware of his occasional flashes of guilt, and felt puzzled and hurt that Jordas had broken his promise to communicate with him. But he wouldn't lower his self-imposed privacy barrier as Jordas had no privacy safeguards of his own.

Jordas was ignoring him deliberately. He was speaking, and Yado knew he wouldn't mindspeak with him while people other than his friends were present. Jordas was eating. Yado waited, but the meal seemed to last forever. When he could stand it no more he spoke in Jordas's mind. <There is need for mindspeech between us.>

The contact stopped Jordas's hand midway to his mouth. A dollop of orange paste fell off whatever he was eating. Yado got a glimpse of Jordas's fellow passengers as he scanned round the table. <It's not convenient right now.>

Yado tried to keep his hurt from showing. <Would you be avoiding me?>

<There...hasn't been anything to tell you.> A pause. <I need you to shut off these sense impressions, Yado. They're driving me crazy!>

He still has no understanding of the sharing. <Jordas Krata, I can cut off the mindspeech, but the sense impressions are always there between maaj'garu. Why, Uvvuz told me he felt what I did in the womb...>

<Did your mother know that?> Jordas asked.

Yado sensed his curiosity. <This is men's knowledge.>

<What?>

<Things only men can know. There is also women's knowledge, but *I* know little of that!>

<What about feelings? I know yours sometimes. Do you know mine?>

115

Jordas asked.

<It's part of the sharing.>

There was a silence before Jordas sent, <Yado, someone's speaking and I can't carry on two conversations at once.> There was another pause. <Don't worry. I'll contact you from the field team's base.>

And Yado had to be content with that.

*

Senator Hartmann forked roast venison into his mouth. Why should he stint himself on expenses when on Committee business? It helped to make starship travel bearable, particularly as the line concerned had human serving-staff as a main selling-point. The food in the Huntsman Restaurant excelled even the eating houses at Charidas. *It's real food – none of your food dispenser muck!* He caught the stewardess's eye and raised his empty glass.

As she approached with another bottle of wine the bulkhead newsboard flashed up the headlines: "KIAI SHIP LOST". Hartmann loaded his fork up again. "The cargo ship was carrying, amongst other things, a shipment of exotic glasswares for sale at auction on Earth."

It surely can't be the same cargo ship –

"More wine, Senator?"

He nodded, eyes fixed on the flashboard. The liquid splashed into his bluish frosted wineglass, itself a Kiai export. A droplet escaped onto the tablecloth.

"Oh, I'm so sorry, Sir!" The girl produced a cloth and dabbed at the stain. "If you'll just move back a little I'll clean up."

Hartmann eyed her as she bent over her task, her bodymoulding trousers highlighting the delicious crease between buttock and leg. Without thinking, he ran a finger along it.

At his touch, she jerked upright.

"Do you have any more information about this explosion?" he asked, gesturing at the flashboard.

"I'll try and find out, *Senator*," she gritted out, and hurried away.

Oops! One of the chillier ones, Hartmann thought. He picked up the glass and sipped the wine.

Seconds later the full report flashed up. Hartmann scanned it. "...The ship was four days out from the Kiai homeworld, and about to enter hyperdrive when contact with it was lost. It's believed to have exploded without survivors. Having already negotiated the largest asteroid belt in the system, the incident is being treated as suspicious. The freighter was operator-owned, but the company which produced the glasswares say litigation may take some years,

116

and will depend on what accident investigators find..."

Hartmann refilled his glass, relaxing. *Who'd have reason to blow up a cargo ship, after all?* Then he read the name of the ship and tension clenched him through and through.

CRACK! Shattered glass and red liquid ran down his wrist and into his cuff.

Hartmann looked up. The other diners were staring at him.

CHAPTER 11

JORDAS STARED OUT OVER THE LANDSCAPE, shading his eyes against the dazzle of sunlight on snow. Patches of standing water were scattered across the snowfields. They glittered up at him like eyes full of tears. As the shuttle skimmed ever lower, diamond-sparkles of frost on snow winked at him. Shadows of bare rock broke the surface of the snow here and there.

The flight had been smooth; there had only been a soft double *whump* as the starship had entered hyperspace, then left it again almost at once. After that they'd simply coasted through the Malory system until they approached Naxada. The research station nestled in the lee of a mountain range. The shuttle pilot had located it by radar map, projected in his holocube beside the controls, and by directions from Jordas, his only passenger.

Seconds later the shuttle hovered over the sealcrete landing pad, then eased down and came to rest. When the whine from the jets had died, Jordas unstrapped himself, and clambered down with his hand luggage. The raised landing pad was bare of snow, but Jordas noticed the difference in temperature and pulled on the gloves attached by umbilicals to his thermosuit. The atmosphere was thinner, but not enough to make the helmet necessary. He tucked it under his arm.

Stepping away from the shuttle, he felt dwarfed by the scenery. Snow undulated away in three directions. The sky was purple-black even at mid-morning, and perforated by mountains; Genavora spat smoke in the distance, flames licking the lava spilling out of its cloven crater. This tectonic setting made a volcano chain inevitable. The research station looked nearer than it actually was, and only the figure of Matt Johnson lounging against the wall put it into perspective against the harsh landscape.

Matt hauled himself upright and walked over to meet him. His thermosuit was also minus its helmet. As he approached, light glinted off his gold-rimmed spectacles. Jordas remembered once asking him why he hadn't had corrective surgery, and Matt had shrugged and said that, due to the nature of his sight problem, he wasn't suitable.

They greeted one another and Matt pointed towards a doorway to his left. "I'll call and tell Marcus you've arrived, eh?"

"Leave it a while," Jordas advised, as they trudged through the snow towards the entrance. "He'll be sleeping the sleep of the just right now."

"Okay. You can meet Abdel. He's an experienced mountaineer and caver as well."

"It'll be good to have company in the caves."

"What? Ah – sure." Matt pushed his spectacles further up his nose and cleared his throat. "Abdel's family was one of the first group of colonists on Sarlsworld – another CRC operation."

"When was that?" Jordas asked.

"About a hundred years ago," Matt replied. "Abdel learned his mountaineering skills during military service, before he became a scientist."

"I thought the Arabs were very reluctant to leave Earth because of the sacred places."

"Me too. But Abdel says they're not obliged to go on *Haj* if they can't afford it." The doors peeled open and they stepped inside. "This way. Marcus told me about the funding problems a couple of days ago."

"Yes, he told me he'd keep an eye on it," Jordas said. "Any other news?"

Matt shook his head. "The canteen's through here."

"Have you mentioned to anyone why I'm going into the caves?"

"Only Abdel and Yue Xiao know about your – mindlink. The others know you're coming here to go in with the rescue team. That's all."

"Let's keep it that way, shall we?"

"Okay." Matt led him over to a table and introduced him to Abdel, then went for coffees.

"What's the mindlink like, Jordas?" Matt asked, putting a mug in front of him. "And why you, and not, say, me or Abdel?"

Jordas considered this. For days now he'd spent every spare waking moment trying to understand how he'd become telepathically bonded with Yado. "Who knows? And it's not very private, but I am getting used to it." As he spoke, he realised this was true. Yado's presence in his thoughts *was* growing more comfortable, despite its strangeness and the fact that Yado saw and felt what he did. "Now it's starting to feel like he really is the brother I never had," he said. "And it's reminded me of how lonely I've been since Gran died while I was at university."

"What about your parents?" Abdel asked.

Jordas couldn't resent their curiosity. "My mother died when I was born, and my father moved to New York. Gran said losing my mother broke his heart."

"So you've lost touch?"

"You could say that. He paid for my education, but I've only met him three times. I haven't even heard from him since moving to Goranon, though I let him know my address. We have nothing in common except our name."

119

"Your first name's unusual – what does it mean?"

"'Earth stream'," Jordas grinned. "Good name for a geologist, huh?"

Matt and Abdel laughed too. Then Matt added, "So you're not unhappy, in a way, about this – mindlink – with Yado?"

Jordas thought of Nina. "It scares me that now that I have someone I'm close to I could end up losing them. But I don't regret it." He hesitated again, then added, "Yado knows what it's like to be alone, too."

Later, as he laid out his gear in his quarters while contacting Yado, Jordas asked the station computer for a local timecheck aloud and adjusted his wrist chronometer. As he peered more closely at the display he remembered that he was thirty-five that day.

<Thirty-five highwaters? You're older than me?>

<I am.> Jordas sensed Yado's nervousness during the silence that followed and wondered whether he'd broken contact. <Yado? Are you there?> he asked.

<I am – Elder brother.>

<Couldn't you just call me Jordas, like before?>

<If that were your wish, Elder brother. Jordas.>

Yado seems awed and submissive, but why? He's not acted like this before – oh, of course! They revere age. Jordas shrugged and focused on the electronic map in his notebook. He explained that he wanted to use it to arrange where to meet Yado and Soolkah, but although Yado could see it he didn't understand that it was a plan view of the caves. *Of course, he's never seen anything like this before,* Jordas realised. *And he doesn't know Soolkah's territory.* After another attempt to explain the idea behind maps, he reasoned that it would be easier if he simply shared his own knowledge with Yado, and opened his mind to him, as Yado had shown him before. He brought to mind everything he knew about maps, aware of a deepening of the contact between them, and *felt* the tribesman's mind soaking up information like a sponge.

<*Now* I understand. Show me again where we shall meet!> And this time Jordas was more successful in arranging a rendezvous.

*

"I've tried juggling the money but there's not nearly enough for both the archaeological and rescue teams to travel, despite a payment made into the account the other day. That's without expenses such as salaries and equipment." Marcus sighed. The hololink showed him Matt, Jordas and Abdel in Matt's monitor room. All were dressed casually; the station's heating was efficient. "It's either the rescue team, or their evacuation ship or the archaeologists – unless the rest of the money we asked for goes in by tomorrow latest."

"Bloody hell!" Matt said under his breath.

"I beg your pardon?"

"I said that's a hell of a decision to have to make."

Marcus shrugged. "One of the less attractive aspects of project management. I'd prefer getting those people out of the caves alive and off-planet with a small team to having lots of rescuers and losing everyone for lack of transport. Don't forget," he reminded them, "I'm responsible for *everyone's* safety, including the Naxadans'. If I bring in outside workers and then can't get them out of danger, it's my head that's on the chopping block."

"Of course."

Marcus considered their new decisions. When Jordas had asked about the archaeological mission, he'd admitted that it would probably have to be abandoned altogether. The main problem was the frieze, important, as Jordas had confirmed with Yado, because it recorded the tribes' history whilst living in the city, and contained prophecies about the future. A permanent holo required good quality holovid, and its information would help them to settle the Naxadans when they reached their new home. But the frieze was too dusty to read.

So Matt had sent a hoverduster ahead, programmed to get the worst off the frieze before recording it, and Jordas had an operator-controlled high-resolution holocam with him. But Marcus could have predicted Jordas's reaction from the glint in his eyes. Tomorrow he and Abdel would set off together and try to contact both tribes through Yado and Soolkah. Marcus thought he'd be able to send the Committee rescue team in a couple of weeks' time, leaving a week for them to get there. By the time they arrived the majority of Matt's staff would have been evacuated. "It only leaves a week's margin of safety," Marcus added.

"I know. Damn the idiots at the Committee!"

"Can't you contact these administrators?"

"I've tried, but it appears that Floyd isn't actually based there, and the woman, Miss Whitley, is on leave. And Howerd Asthorn's still away on business. In the end I had to settle for asking them to call me."

"I see. But there's enough money in the account to cover the rescue?" Matt sounded anxious.

"With this pared-down plan, yes. I contacted the bank manager again," Marcus said, "and asked him to notify me as soon as either Corah Whitley or Nevil Floyd make another transaction. It appears that Nevil Floyd deposited some money the day after I called Hartmann at the Interchange, but not the full amount debited." *I'm not usually vindictive,* he thought. *But this is inexcusable.* "Someone at Committee HQ is going to be in a lot of trouble once I contact Asthorn."

*

"There it is!" Abdel pointed through the port at the opening in the rocks, partly veiled by intermittent sleet which turned to slush on contact with the surface.

Jordas leaned forward, shivering.

"Cold?" Abdel grinned.

"Somebody walked over my grave. You're right. It's *not* like Goranon!"

The flyer was circling, seeking a place to drop them. Its jets shrieked as they sank groundwards. "Nowhere to land," the pilot yelled. "Get out now – I'll hover."

Abdel made the thumbs-up sign and ushered Jordas towards the hatch. They shrugged on their backpacks and fastened them securely, and Abdel released the safety catch and heaved at the door.

The pilot was holding them half a metre above the level of the slush. Abdel clambered down the extensible metal ladder first. Jordas stumbled clear of the flyer and Abdel waved "Go!" to the pilot as they roped themselves together. The flyer lifted again, banked steeply, and headed for the research station.

Abdel moved towards the entrance to the caves, clanking as his equipment knocked together. *Moving on ice would have been easier with less gear.* He shrugged the pack into a more comfortable position and moved forwards, glad of his spiked boots. He pointed. "Let's make the rope fast to that rock there."

Jordas nodded and went to test the rock. "It's firm enough," he said, and unwound a length of rope which he knotted around the boulder, then neared the lip of the opening. Abdel followed him.

He peered into the cavern below. It was dark inside. "Yado wasn't kidding about the fungi dying," Jordas muttered, pulling his flashlight from his belt to survey the cavern.

Abdel saw the rush of rocks below the opening where Matt had fallen in.

Jordas turned on his headlamp, clasped the rope, then reversed, ready to lower himself down into the cave.

"I'll go first, Jordas," Abdel offered. "I've been in before, remember? I never did get to the city, though. Too busy getting botanical samples." He took the rope and fed it out as he lowered himself into the cavern. Darkness closed about him, penetrated only by the beam of his headlamp and the sounds of his breathing. He concentrated on lowering himself towards the cave floor. He couldn't see the boulder choke, but when he thought he was near it he extended a foot to feel for it.

Nothing. He lowered himself another arm's length. His foot struck rock, then flailed against empty air. *The boulder choke* must *be close –*

Abdel froze, sure he'd heard something. He looked around, but the lamp only flashed on blackness. "Jordas?"

Something brushed past his foot. Abdel let go in surprise. The rope dashed through his hand.

There was no time to think. He pitched forwards downslope. His knee glanced off a boulder.

Pain forced a cry from his lips. He landed on his side and his headlamp went out.

The only sound was that of his breathing.

CHAPTER 12

"ABDEL? ABDEL! Are you okay?"

Abdel lay still for several moments, winded and only capable of dealing with one sense impression at a time. Darkness enfolded him.

His backpack had absorbed some of the impact of his fall, but the pain in his knee was intense. When he could breathe again, he put out a hand to explore. To his side, his glove rasped on rock. He put a hand up to his head.

The fall had jarred his body and smashed the lamp, but worse, his knee hurt with well-remembered ferocity. He guessed the impact had cracked his kneecap just where a fall had invalided him out of the army seven years before. He clamped his teeth on the pain.

A grating sound, like animal claws scraping rock, reached him from somewhere in the cave. *Whatever startled me is still here.*

"Abdel?" Jordas was calling again. "Abdel!"

His name echoed into the darkness around him. Perhaps the noise would frighten the beast off, whatever it was. "Jordas! I think my knee's broken."

For a moment there was no reply, and Abdel wondered what had happened to Jordas. He grappled with the release catch on his backpack. *It probably saved me from worse injury,* he realised. He felt for the phone, then remembered it was in Jordas's pack. In any case they'd have to find the cable terminal before they could use it.

Jordas's voice reached him. "I'm coming down. I'll call the station and get help."

From where he lay Abdel could just see the edge of the light marking the entrance to the cavern. The silence was punctuated only by the sound of breathing, which got nearer as Jordas lowered himself down the rope. Abdel gritted his teeth against the pain in his leg, the creature forgotten.

Water dripped onto his face. He shivered, remembering the sleet melting as it touched the ground outside, and turned the suit thermostat up with fingertips made clumsy by gloves.

He heard Jordas's feet touch the boulder choke, felt it shift, heard a clatter as one or two cobbles were dislodged. He tried to make himself as small as possible. His knee was sickening agony. The pebbles bypassed him. Now that his eyes were accustomed to the darkness he could see the faint outlines of rock-shapes on the slope. But the water penetrated further than the light. *I must get out of the wet.* He concentrated on trying to turn on his bed of rocks.

The heat began to rise just as the smashed glass from his helmet scraped the suit. The outer layer of insulating fabric ripped open with a hiss and a burst of sparks.

Allah help me! he prayed. The inner layer of the suit would prevent a fire, but he must be careful. He dared not move for several minutes. But he wouldn't be able to maintain this posture. With an effort which sent sweat streaming off his forehead and had him grinding his teeth against the pain, he managed to flop back into an easier position.

The suit cooled around him.

*

Yado stopped, hand half-raised to his head. Soolkah was several steps ahead of him, eyeing the nearest colony of glowcakes. They flickered like flames under a man's breath, forming strange shadows in the tunnel, then became insubstantial and vanished. "Soolkah!"

She halted and swung to face him. "What?" Her eyes were wide, the pupils dilated.

"The man with Jordas is injured. His people will mayhap not allow him to come alone to meet us."

She came to kneel beside him. Shadows gathered in her eyes.

He wished he didn't have to scare her so. His hands sought hers, knowing she'd understand the extent of his worry through his own need for physical contact. "Or there'll be some delay."

"And the glowcakes are dying," she said. "If he can't come –"

"He said he'll try his best." Yado stroked her hand, seeking to give *her* comfort. *After all,* he thought, *there is none here to see. Only Jordas will know, and the Humanu watchers.*

Soolkah freed a hand to stroke his head-fur, following the shape of the whorls with gentle fingers.

Her touch soothed him. "We should move on." He spread his hands palm down. "How can we travel with no glowcakes?"

"Haven't you got your lampcups?" Soolkah asked.

"The light will last only a short time." Yado sighed. "I've made no kill in two lighttimes. Without game I've neither meat nor fat to light our way." He pulled a face. "Bread and vegetables are so much –" he made a big space between his hands "– less satisfying than meat."

Soolkah sighed. "Plants won't grow in the dark. And some bachu live on plants too –"

She'd spat out the scrap of meat he'd given her, Yado remembered, just as a glowcake winked out above them.

*

The air smelled of sulphur. Blackness was all around them.

Jordas switched on both helmet light and flashlight, revealing a silver-suited figure lying scant metres downslope from him. He sat down, peeled the spiked soles off his boots and stowed them in his pack.

His conversation with Yado hadn't reassured him. Kerui was dying, perhaps faster than predicted. A glance up at the cavern roof showed him sleet pelting into the opening. Depression settled about him. "Abdel? Are you okay?"

"I think my leg's broken. And my suit's short-circuited."

Shit! Jordas thought, but he said, "Hang on. I'm coming." He felt his way along the rope until he could hunker down beside Abdel.

"Try and get to the terminal. Over there." Abdel pointed. "The quicker you contact Matt the quicker we can both be out of here." He was shivering. The torchlight revealed his hair, plastered to his face.

Jordas manoeuvred Abdel's rucksack off, took out the sleeping bag and laid it over him.

"Thanks."

"What happened?" Jordas pocketed the cablephone from his own pack.

Abdel told him. "I fell the last few feet and landed awkwardly." He exhaled with a hiss, then added, "I think it was a cave porcupine. Vicious things! One went for Yue Xiao last time we were down here. It might still be around."

Jordas flashed the torch around the cave, but the darkness swallowed the beam. "I can't see anything – maybe our lights have scared it off? You said the terminal was over there?" He clambered downslope, the flashlight outlining the tumble of boulders. On the rockwall opposite he spotted the terminal, hurried across the flatter ground of the cave floor, plugged in the phone, and thumbed the switch on. "Matt? It's Jordas."

"What's happened?"

Jordas explained. "Can you send someone over here to get him out?"

"Sure. We'll have you both out of there as soon as may be –"

"Matt, just get Abdel seen to and I'll get on with the job. I'm fine." Jordas heard Matt speaking to someone nearby.

"The pilot's just leaving now, Jordas. But you shouldn't go alone, and I can't spare anyone else."

"This isn't like limestone caving! I should be able to meet Yado and Soolkah quickly and then I won't be on my own."

"You still shouldn't –"

126

"I know, I know, the insurance! Don't try to stop me, Matt! I'm going. I know the risks as well as you, but a lot of lives depend on me. I can't let them down."

"If anything happens to you, you won't be much help to the Naxadans," Matt pointed out. "Jordas, Marcus called to say the money had gone up again when he checked it today. He'll authorise the rescue ship departure as soon as he can get in touch with the administrators, so there's no need to risk your life."

"It'll be too long before they get here."

"It's safer."

Jordas shook his head. "Meeting up quickly with Yado and Soolkah is our best chance. Between us we should be able to help the rescue team contact both tribes. You know I'm right."

"I know you're a damn fool, man!" Matt snorted.

But Jordas sensed that his attitude had softened. "Just tell Marcus I went anyway."

"Don't worry, I will." He sighed again. "The important thing is to get Abdel out of there and start his treatment. The flyer should be there in about fifteen minutes."

"Okay. I'm going back to Abdel – he's not too good."

Jordas rearranged his pack to take some of Abdel's equipment, along with the phone. His impatience to leave was simmering before he heard the drone of the flyer. Abdel was slipping in and out of consciousness, and didn't really come to when the medical team slid down the rope.

Tim Perry gave Abdel a shot to keep him under and supervised the winching. "Matt says you're not coming back with us."

Jordas picked up his pack and slung it on his back. "No," he said. "I've got a job to do. Tell Matt to let me know how Abdel is."

"Are you sure you'll be okay down here on your own?" Tim asked.

"I have to be." Jordas fastened the straps of the pack. "I'll call Matt at each terminal. I'd better go."

He looked around him again. A tunnel mouth gaped to one side, beckoning him. *That's my route to Yado and Soolkah.*

He didn't look back as Tim swarmed up the rope and out of the cavern.

*

Jordas unsealed his thermosuit and climbed out of it. It was hot in the conduits but he'd need it outside. Re-lacing his boots he stowed the suit away and shouldered his pack again.

The sulphur smell strengthened. Ahead, two tunnels led in different directions. *Which should I take?* He squatted to consult his electronic map. The coloured tracer Matt had used to mark the route to the original Shiranu sleeping cave fluoresced in the glare of his headlamp. Wondering how quickly he could catch up with Yado and Soolkah, he checked his compass, aware that the mental tie with Yado seemed stronger down here than on the surface; he was certain he was headed east. That checked out on the map: both conduits ran east, one further than the other. He set off down the right-hand one.

Outcrops of glowcakes lit the passage. The subtle colours of the rock changed around him: sometimes banded, sometimes blocks of different colours butted up to others with grainy or crystalline textures. He wanted to stop and examine them but the need for speed drove him on. *It's beautiful, yet terrifying; and I can never forget why I'm here.* Sometimes he walked in total darkness, but he could see well enough by his helmet light. As he tramped through the tunnel, glassy rock crunching under his feet, he tried to concentrate on the pull that drew him on like an invisible umbilical whenever he thought of Yado.

He walked for some time, rested, then walked on. By late afternoon his feet ached, his shoulders were stiff and the straps of the backpack chafed his chest. The tunnels twisted right and left as they rose and fell; his ankles were beginning to ache. *Anybody in one of these when they flood would have* no *chance!* He pushed the thought away as he stopped to rest, drank some water, then set off again.

After a couple of hours he no longer needed the helmet light. *Perhaps I'm near another cavern,* he thought. The fungi grew in clumps here, even in the conduits, and there was a plump healthiness about them. He pressed his head against the tunnel wall to peer at the nearest group of them.

With their concave upper surfaces they resembled half an oyster shell. The few which were flickering appeared drier and browner than the rest, which reminded him of pinkish-yellow tongues, with golden fluid at their centres. In some of them were black blobs. Fascinated yet repelled, he peered closer and realised the blobs were insects, half-consumed by the acidic juices at the things' centres. They were securely rooted to the wall. He put out a hand to lean against it –

<Never touch a glowcake! Only Shiranu can safely feed them.>

Abdel became a casualty when he brought one of them back to examine, Jordas remembered.

<It's all right, I know not to touch it.> Abdel had said that the fungi's light was both an attraction and a warning. <I just wanted to look – I haven't seen one close up before now.>

<Then look and be safe! Where are you?>

< Near a cavern, I think.>

<You must be. The glowcakes in this section are dying.>

Jordas had spotted the cable terminal overhead. As he approached it, the familiarity of the cave mouth struck him. Looking into the cavern beyond, he realised why. *It's the sleeping cavern Soolkah's people were using when we found them. It should be safe here. The tribe left days ago.* He advanced into the chamber. Nothing moved. Back in the conduit was the cable terminal from which he'd first watched the Shiranu. He sat down. Tension had grown unnoticed in him. He released it along with the catch which secured his backpack in place.

<Yado? I'll rest here.> Reaching into his pack, he drew out bottled water, self-heating coffee crystals, and a high-energy biscuit. He poured water into his cup to activate the crystals, then delved in the pack. He crossed the cavern and plugged the cablephone into the terminal. From Matt he learned that Abdel's kneecap had been replaced and that Marcus had been less than enthusiastic about him being alone in the tunnels. Replacing the phone, he felt a sense of isolation, and reached for Yado with his mind.

*

In the morning, Jordas woke early from habit and the resolve to move on. He ate a high-energy biscuit and drank coffee which tasted thick and sticky, then called Matt before setting off again. Hoisting the pack onto his back, he stood listening for a moment before striding off into the tunnel.

He'd been walking for nearly an hour when Yado contacted him, describing a cloud of insects he'd seen the previous night. They'd have choked him and Soolkah had he not flung his sleeping fur over their heads.

<I don't know what it means,> he told Yado. <But animals often behave strangely before an earthquake or a volcanic eruption. I'll check with my friends.> He was glad to mindspeak with the tribesman, and gladder still of the excuse to contact the base at the next opportunity. The gathering ache in his shoulders wasn't caused by the weight of the backpack alone; his solitude was wearing on him and he was hoping to meet Yado and Soolkah soon. He fingered the helmet light – which he hadn't needed to use this morning – then sought the shape of the phone near the top of the pack. They were his links to an entirely different reality.

Later he stopped to rest with the conduit walls looming around him. The previous day he'd found the subtlety of the rock colours beautiful; now it just seemed dreary, reflecting the way he felt. But his depression had nothing to do with the flickering of the glowcakes, which was more noticeable this morning. His legs carried him onwards, yet in spite of the urgency to reach Yado and Soolkah, he anticipated their meeting with a mixture of longing and apprehension. *Stupid! What have I to fear from them?*

After a hot drink at the next terminal he allowed his thoughts to drift, having checked with Matt about the swarm of insects Yado had seen. Yue Xiao had confirmed his fears: instinct must have warned the creatures to seek safety, either from the coming floods, the eruption itself or the precursor earthquakes. But when he relayed the information back to Yado, Soolkah had already interpreted the behaviour of the flies. And she'd explained that without sustenance the glowcakes would starve and everything in this underground world would come to an abrupt halt.

<Kerui dies around us,> Yado had sent. <I understand better now. We *must* leave.>Jordas had picked up the tribesman's sadness and fear then, and after that, he'd resisted the temptation to contact Yado and plodded on in silence. His thoughts turned to the research team. Matt, Wong Yue Xiao – how they'd laughed about the meaning of her name back at the research station, and Matt had suggested she should change her name to Hamorrah.

"You're always teasing me, Matt!" she'd declared with a smile which suggested she didn't mind one bit. Jordas had envied their closeness. He drew in a deep breath. When he'd promised himself no woman would ever hurt him again, he'd reckoned without the appeal of green eyes. He couldn't understand the attraction; Soolkah wasn't human, after all. But it didn't matter to Matt and Yue Xiao that they came from different backgrounds and cultures; and it hadn't mattered to his own parents; so perhaps his attraction to Soolkah was inevitable. *After all, how can you help it when you're mindlinked to the guy who loves her?*

<Yado, are you there?> he asked.

<I feel your presence as you approach, Elder brother. We await you at a waystop.>

This cheered Jordas; he wasn't sure why. He finished his coffee, repacked his belongings, and set off with more energy to boost him onwards.

*

Two days later, with glowcakes flickering in each new tunnel, Jordas was sure he was close to catching up with Yado and Soolkah. Crouching beside a dip in the waystop floor, he saw that the ground looked disturbed and leaned forwards to sift it, remembering the firestone in the Shiranu sleeping cavern. His fingers touched stone. He scraped away rock dust and ash with his hands, soon revealing another firestone, with something stuck to it. He scraped it with his fingernail and examined the pale greenish-pink, shrivelled material; a dried bean of some sort. He sniffed it. It had no scent. He covered up the firestone again.

They were here recently. He could sense Yado not far ahead, but was torn between the sensation of fatigue at his back and the need to move on. He drank some coffee and forced himself to plod on, and was rewarded by Yado's urgent mindsending.

<Jordas! I sense you nearby.>

<How far?>

<Mayhap fifty *pythetu* ->

<What? Never mind. How long will it take me to walk to you?>

<I sense…you've just left our last waystop. There's a day's march ahead. We await you.>

<Good.> Jordas forced himself to move faster, aware of his exhaustion. The tunnel walls passed at a punishing pace. Often the ceiling was just centimetres above his head. Each time the light faltered his eyes closed, jerking open as it came back. He wouldn't allow himself to stop, even to eat. If he did, sleep would claim him. But the tunnel seemed endless. He looked into the dark conduit behind him once, and it made him square his aching shoulders and quicken his pace.

In the distance, something spat. Jordas stopped, wide awake, and looked around. There was no sign of life. He moved on, nerves attenuated.

The sound came again: louder, nearer, and with the scrabbling of claws on rock.

He forced himself to tread forwards on first his right foot…Listen…Then his left…Listen…He moved as silently as possible. He reached for the rockwall for balance, and touched knife-edged rock, then something wet and yielding.

His flesh stung. "Yaagh!"

It was the fly-encrusted surface of a glowcake. Digestive acids had overflowed as it attempted to devour the swarm. Jordas crouched, hand clenched between his knees to contain the pain until it eased enough for him to release his backpack and get the water bottle. He poured some into his cup and dipped his fingers in.

<You touched a glowcake?> asked Yado.

<Yes, like a fool! I'm just bathing it.> Jordas stoppered the water bottle.

<Best treatment ->

The creature materialised out of nowhere. It spat as it darted forwards. Fangs sank into his leg. The water bottle somersaulted into the air and rolled out of sight. He couldn't strangle a shout. It echoed down the corridor.

The thing was knee-high and covered in spines. Its eyes were huge black bulbs, blinking transparent lids at him: what the field team had dubbed "cave porcupine".

<We call them *ganzu*.>

Jordas tried to shake it off. But the *ganzu* clung on like the grip of a dead man. Every movement hurt his leg.

He remembered the gun and reached into his pocket. *I'll scare it –*

He fired at the floor. *BLAM!* It sounded like thunder in the enclosed space. Vicious shards of lava sliced through the air and impacted with the cavern wall.

The *ganzu* released his leg and scuttled away.

Jordas collapsed onto his knees, dropping the gun with a clatter. It landed beside the rock-flattened slug.

<Scared it away –>

<Shame – it were a tasty meal!> He felt Yado's amusement at his recoil. <Leave now – you mayhap disturbed its lair.>

Jordas retrieved his possessions, shoved them into his backpack, shouldered it and scrambled upright, shaking. He walked as fast as he could, until he thought he heard a sound behind him and took to his heels. He had no idea how far he ran. He ignored the stab at his injured shin as he built up speed. The light was good and the floor even. His breath rasped in his throat. Cramps jetted between strained muscles.

Finally he saw another cavern mouth ahead. Two shapes stood silhouetted against the semicircle of light, as if people awaited him. But he hardly registered any of this.

Now I can rest –

The light closed up and he pitched forwards.

*

Soolkah followed Yado as he limped towards the fallen man. *He's affected by the Humanu's wound,* she realised in wonder. *More proof that they really are maaj'garu.* She wasn't sure whether to be pleased or not.

Yado hadn't got there fast enough to catch Jordas as he collapsed. He turned him over. A cut oozed blood above his left eye, and the garment which covered his legs bore signs of damage. Yado drew the cloth up to expose the skin, and they saw the ganzu-wound. One finger was striped raw where the glowcake's digestive juices had touched it.

"See how like us they are!" Yado gasped.

Soolkah nodded, not daring to approach too closely. Her eyes were fixed on his face. Though relaxed by the swoon it was shadowed with fatigue. *He doesn't look so different from a Shiranu,* she thought, *except that his fur's dark as a Sargussi's.* She looked at the rest of him and saw that, apart from his black head-fur, which curled almost to his shoulders, his fur was much sparser than theirs, and extended over the exposed backs of his hands and along his arms

132

but not inside them. On his lower half he wore a garment of tough blue fabric which enveloped each leg separately, and on his torso and the tops of his arms a garment of a different texture. It was soaked, but she couldn't tell where the water had come from.

"Help me remove his pack!" Yado said.

As she approached Jordas, she noticed that his scent was peculiar: a sharp tang. She slipped his pack off and carried it to their camp. When she returned to Yado's side, she saw he had managed to bring the man round.

His eyes flickered open. In the fading light from Outside, they were an intense, dark blue. *I've never seen a man with eyes that colour,* she thought, shivering. *He too is to become my husband.* Her stomach tingled with fear and anticipation.

"Is he all right?" she asked.

Yado nodded. "Just dazed," he answered. "The ganzu wound is minor. We can clean and bind it for him. But he needs food and rest." He leaned closer to the man and spoke to him.

"Can he understand you?" Soolkah asked.

Yado held up his hand to her.

He's mindspeaking as well. She knew that intense look of inward concentration well; she'd seen it on her fathers' and brothers' faces many times. Now it was there on Yado's and Jordas Krata's faces. She wondered what they were mindsending to each other. She always felt excluded when Yado mindspoke, though he was otherwise considerate.

But what kind of a husband will Jordas Krata be?

"Come." Yado slipped his arm under the tall, pale-skinned man's to help him up. "Eat and rest."

To Soolkah's amazement, he answered in words she understood. "I shall. I *am* hungry and tired."

Yado's taught him our language, Soolkah realised, as the two men hobbled towards the fire. That Jordas Krata spoke with the Sargussi inflection was the final proof of the bond between them.

Yado wasn't playing a trick on me. They really are maaj'garu.

*

Several high-energy biscuits later, warmed by coffee, Jordas concealed a yawn behind his hand. Soolkah had cleaned his wounds with sulphur-tinged boiled water, then he'd sprayed pseudoskin onto them. He'd taken some painkillers; the pain in his leg was just a dull ache, and his finger wasn't throbbing much either. He'd cleaned his teeth using bottled water. The two Naxadans had watched in fascination. Yado had shown much curiosity about the gun, asking to handle it. *There'll be no secrets from him!* Jordas had thought. He'd removed the ammunition clip before letting him touch it.

After stowing the gun safely away, Jordas found the waystop's cable terminal and reported to Matt that he'd met the Naxadans. Their conversation was brief. Yado and Soolkah watched with interest.

<Are you tired?> Yado asked as Jordas rejoined them.

Jordas nodded, smiling sleepily.

<We shall sleep now. Soolkah is yours tonight. With there being just the two of us, we can take turns with her every other night.> As he spoke, he gestured first to the girl, then to himself and Jordas.

Jordas could feel his jaw dropping open, abruptly wide awake. Too stunned to say anything, he stared from one to the other of them, until Yado reached out and mimed pushing his mouth shut, grinning his amusement.

Jordas couldn't put his thoughts into any semblance of order to reply.

<What's the matter, Elder Brother? D'you not like your wife?> Yado asked. Although he was smiling shadows darkened his eyes. <I know we did it all the wrong way round, but you weren't here when Soolkah and I decided to become *amaajnu*, neither of us having any other chance of marrying –>

<That isn't – a problem,> Jordas interrupted, unsure how to proceed. <And I *do* like her – you must know that. But she's *your* wife, not mine.>

Yado's face showed sudden understanding. <Ah! You don't know our ways. Forgive me, Elder brother. I thought you knew that here women are few, so the brothers in one *amaaj* share the same woman.> He paused. <But you come from a far place, and mayhap there your customs are different?>

Jordas nodded. <And you keep calling me 'Elder brother', but we're not related. I'm not even the same species as you!>

<You are my *maaj'gar*. We mindspeak. We share each other's sense impressions and can share knowledge when we wish it.> He frowned. <I'm not sure why I have a privacy shield and you don't, but it makes no difference. Only *maaj'garu* can do these things. It's –> he spread his hands. <It's the way we are. And it's your turn to go with Soolkah tonight.>

Jordas's heart jolted as he met Soolkah's gaze, half-expecting her to refuse to even look at him.

But she stood up, smiling. "Come, Jo'das."

He remembered that neither tribe made the "or" sound in their language. A tingly feeling ran down his spine at her use and exquisitely foreign pronunciation of his name. He could understand them, but the tongue still sounded strange to him, not like any language he'd ever heard before, English, Vanjeynish or the hard and soft Zarduthi languages. She beckoned, and he

134

couldn't look away. Her eyes were bright as they met his. *Perhaps I'm reading her all wrong,* he told himself, aware that Naxadan body language didn't always equate to the human equivalent. *But she does seem to want me to go to her...*

"Come on, then," he murmured in English, forgetting for a moment that she couldn't understand him. He selected the place that looked least uncomfortable, just out of sight of the spot where Yado had curled himself up under his sleeping-fur, removed the sleeping bag from his pack and laid it on the ground.

<Shall you do such strange things that you don't wish me to know?> asked Yado.

Jordas recoiled physically from the sense of exclusion coming from him. <We do mostly the same as you,> Jordas replied, registering that Soolkah was staring at him. <But sex is private between two people.>

<Yet you watched me with Soolkah the first time,> Yado reminded him.

<I know, and I still feel guilty about it. I just couldn't look away.> He sought the right word. <I was drawn into it. I'm sorry.>

<There is no need for feeling sorry, or embarrassed. Of course you were part of it. *Maaj'garu* cannot help but share such things.>

Jordas breathed out. He felt very uncomfortable. <All the tribespeople share wives? This isn't some politeness custom?>

<It's not a – *politeness?* – custom.>

Jordas indicated Soolkah. <What does *she* think about it?>

<You are the Elder brother. You lead the *amaaj*. She will be yours tonight.>

<And you?>

<I shall feel and share what you do.>

<I was afraid of that,> Jordas answered, and felt the Naxadan withdraw from his mind. Relieved, he turned to Soolkah. His leg hurt as he moved.

"Are you all right?" she asked him. He nodded and smiled at her. They lay down on the sleeping bag, and his arms closed around her, folding her in against him with the fabric. He felt at peace, though he couldn't fathom why. But his leg stopped hurting as he held her close.

It was some time before Yado fell asleep and Jordas felt ready to give Soolkah his love.

Then he tipped her face up and kissed her.

CHAPTER 13

I'M NOT QUITE SURE ABOUT THIS. Soolkah lay in Jordas's arms. *If only I could mindspeak as well, I'd know all about him.* Gentle as he seemed, this stranger was from a place so far away she couldn't even imagine it. But she could see, from the faint lines bracketing his eyes and mouth, that he was older than Yado.

And Yado trusted him. He cared for him like a real brother, so she must treat them both the same.

He turned her face to his. Would he touch his mouth to hers again? *That felt so strange!* She waited, hardly daring to breathe.

But he touched her face with his hand.

So he knows our way too, she thought, then remembered Yado saying Jordas had watched them together the first time. *And we didn't even know!* Anger swept through her, but his face again expressed mingled tenderness and wonder, as if he couldn't believe he was lying beside her. The anger evaporated.

His fingers trembled a little as he touched her.

Her hands lifted to his face.

"Soolkah? Mmm, that feels nice!" he murmured.

She didn't know what she'd expected: it wasn't just that he looked different from Yado. She'd watched him while they ate, and hadn't understood all his gestures. But though no mindspeaker, she could feel almost tangibly that he liked her. She let his hands stroke her face for a moment, then pressed her cheek against his, rubbing tentatively. It didn't feel so strange this time.

He pulled her closer still.

She stared into his eyes. They were the colour of her kilt. Shiranu eyes were green, or brownish-red, or a blend of the two. She decided she liked blue eyes.

"Your people don't *kiss*, do you?" he said.

She shook her head. "Show me again. I –" She pressed her face against his chest. The fabric covering it was as soft as anzu bolls. Her voice sounded muffled even to her own ears as she murmured, "I can learn new things."

"I'll not force you to do things you don't want to do, Soolkah. If you don't want to go with me, I shall – understand." That outdated Sargussi inflection again. The last few words came out in a rush, and he gulped in air.

He is nice, she thought, and smiled to reassure him. He tried to return the smile, shut his eyes, fighting to swallow. He seemed as nervous as she was.

"Do that thing again," she said, "the thing your people do." She almost added, *the thing you like doing,* because she was sure he did like it.

"I...was thinking you didn't want me to." His breath touched her cheek as he spoke; it smelled different from Yado's, though not unpleasant. She remembered how he'd scrubbed his teeth clean after they'd eaten. The smell of that white paste was strong and unfamiliar. *At least,* she thought, *he's clean, and not fat and ugly like Chixi, though his ways are strange.*

His mouth pressed against hers moments later, and Soolkah realised she was starting to like this new way of touching. She stroked his face as well, but when his lips started to move against hers, she drew away.

"You don't like that?"

"It's – different from last time."

"Nicer, I think," he agreed. "It's different again when we put our tongues together."

Shocked, she retreated as far as she could within his arms. "I don't think I'd like *that*," she said.

"I won't do anything you don't like," Jordas promised, loosening his arms about her; she could have got up and walked over to where Yado lay if she'd wanted. It was as if he didn't want to frighten her in case she refused him. *But surely he must know that however scared I am, it's my duty to be his amaajni too?* Soolkah remembered it had been her idea for him to put his lips against hers again, and smiled mischief at him, slipping her hand down across his chest and stomach.

"Uh," he said, as if he couldn't hold the sound in, and drew her closer to touch her mouth with his. She pressed her lips against his, and when his hand touched her chest, her nipples hardened and her breasts swelled under his fingers. *I really do want him!* She caught her breath in surprise, then decided it was all right.

"You wear – lots of – things –" she said, and stopped. Because no-one ever wore anything else but a kilt in the caves, there was no word to describe what Jordas wore.

"T-shirt," he agreed in the Humanu tongue, taking her fingers and rubbing them against the cloth. *"Trousers."* He reached down and opened them, and she slipped her hand inside, exploring. *"Briefs."* He kissed her again. This time she didn't object when his lips moved against hers.

"I'm starting to like this mouth-touching," Soolkah whispered. She hoped that would please him; he seemed to like her as much as Yado did. But he didn't say anything. Her hand skimmed his stomach again. There was fur on the lower part, not whorled like Yado's but curled and bouncy. Her hand slid lower still to touch the smoother skin of his samaachi. It was ready for her. She felt sudden heat between her own legs and drew the kilt up.

"Wait," he said, and disengaged himself to slide the *trousers* down. He settled into a more comfortable position, one arm around her while the other stroked her face, her throat, her breasts.

"What do your people call that mouth-touching?" she asked.

"*Kissing.*" His voice sounded far away.

She moved so that her moist crotch pressed against the top of his leg. "My daazni is *kissing* you," she told him.

"Daazni?" he asked slowly, as if he'd been considering what she'd said. "There's another word Yado would use."

"Don't tell me," she said, feeling foolish. "It's forbidden. We – we don't tell women's words to the men, only to our girl-children at coming-of-age. I shouldn't –"

"I won't repeat it. Though Yado seems to know everything I know." He stroked her face again. "I like it when you kiss me with your daazni."

"Then let me *kiss* your samaachi with it!"

"More women's words?" he asked. His eyes shone amusement at her. "Let me touch you there first." His hand slipped downwards, testing some of the moisture between his fingers. "You feel different from a human woman – but only on the outside..."

It hadn't occurred to Soolkah that Jordas might already have been with a woman. She could think of no reply. His fingers slid in and out, rubbing against the pad of erectile tissue above her bladder opening. "Mmm..." *Yado probably doesn't know to do this. Perhaps there are advantages to going with a more experienced man, even if he is from a far place...* As sensations exploded white-hot in her daazni, she forgot about the differences between them.

"A human woman would take longer to get excited," Jordas murmured. "She'd make more noise, too. Soolkah, I want you, *now!*"

"I know," she said. "Take me, Jordas!" She squatted over him, guiding him inside her, feeling the engorged flesh swell further, and the hot ache of desire as he entered her. He was large and firm, he filled her sweetly; and as he slid in and out the sensation intensified. She knew enough by now to realise that in this position she controlled the pace, and manoeuvred so he'd slip onto the pleasure-place as he came out each time, like Yado. Within moments she was gasping at the sensations, and soon his low moan of pleasure mingled with hers. Finally, they both lay back gasping, the Humanu man's samaachi still inside her.

A few moments later he stroked her face.

"It was good?" she asked.

"Very good," he assured her, and kissed her again. "And for you?"

"Different, but also good." As she said it she realised it was true. Though of a different tribe, he'd made her enjoy sex as her mother had said she would; not quite as Yado had, but in his own special, different way. *I'm glad I ran away,* she thought. *I'd never have wanted Chixi like this.* She realised then what the difference was. Chixi and his brothers had never attracted her, but from the moment she had set eyes on Yado, and then Jordas – strange though he seemed to Shiranu eyes – she had liked the look of both of them.

"Let me go to sleep inside you."

"I don't do that with Yado, and I can't treat you any differently," she answered, squeezing his hand. "I'm sorry." As she withdrew from him she teased his samaatchi with her fingertips, noticing how wet it still was – then bent to examine it. "You aren't circumcised!"

He smiled his amusement at her then. "I hope you shall not insist!"

"But – how...?"

"It isn't *our* way," he told her, and with that drew her back against him to sleep.

*

Lightbreak found all three of them seated around the firestone. Yado's jaw ached from chewing the breadcake Jordas had given him; and it tasted better wet than dry. He dipped it in his drinking water. He noticed that Soolkah had finished hers, and was swallowing Jordas's *supplements.*

"How far to the next farm cavern?" Jordas asked.

"Three days' journey for the tribe," Soolkah answered. "One day for us, if we travel fast."

"No need to hunt, with the food you've brought. How quickly can you travel?" Yado asked Jordas. He'd felt the echo of pain in his own leg from time to time.

He grimaced. "I can cope."

Yado had watched as he scraped a sharp-bladed object across his lower face. Now, as Jordas faced him, he saw the fuzz on his face was gone, and understood why he'd felt his chin and cheeks itching. <Have all your people fur on their faces?> he asked.

<Only the men!> Jordas grinned. Then his expression became serious. "The ceiling in the next waystop has fallen in, and it's flooded. It'll be cold, wet and dangerous to cross. Beyond it the same tremor caused a rockslide."

"Your tribe told you this?" Soolkah asked.

Jordas nodded. "Last darktime. And I must speak with them before leaving here."

Yado watched him take the object he'd named *phone* out of his pack, attach it to something on the tunnel roof at the waystop entrance and thumb a button on it. "Matt?"

Yado listened to his speech. His vowels were rounded, and whereas the Sargussi separated each consonant with a short indeterminate half-vowel, Jordas's language often put consonants together. It sounded utterly incomprehensible.

Jordas finished speaking to his friends and detached the phone from the *terminal*, frowning. "Matt says the Shiranu are working hard at the next farm cavern, but water's entering the sleeping cavern."

"We must reach them soon," Yado said, and within moments the firestone was covered, packs were on their backs, and they set off.

*

Despite Jordas's leg they made good time to the flooded waystop. There, though, he was appalled to find the floor wet for metres down-tunnel, while the wind funnelled cold air in from Outside.

"It's f-freezing here!"

Jordas quelled his instinct to put his arm around Soolkah, taking garments from his pack instead. "I brought these for you both."

"How do we put them on?" Soolkah asked.

"Here, I'll show you," Jordas shrugged into his own waterproofs. Yado and Soolkah soon got the idea, rolling up the sleeves and hoisting their packs on their backs again afterwards.

"You've got *trousers* as well." Soolkah pointed. She looked at Yado and giggled.

<How does she know that word?> Yado sent.

<I told her.> Jordas replied with a tight smile. "We thought trousers would be awkward with your kilts." He rummaged in his pack for webbing belts and snaplinks, and roped them all together before they started across the flood. "Shall we go?"

It was mid-lighttime when they splashed down the tunnel. Jordas knew the light bothered Yado and Soolkah as they edged towards the flood, but there was nothing he could do about it. He walked between them, taking an arm each. They shielded their eyes with their hands. The rush of water filled the air. He couldn't make himself heard. The others gestured at him.

<You know these signs,> Yado sent. <Use them now.>

Jordas remembered they were an integral and useful part of the language.

At the cavern threshold he realised why the noise was so loud. The inrush

140

had formed a waterfall, with its own merciless beauty. The clinking of snaplinks against belt fastenings was lost under the avalanche of sound.

There was the rope, wet and frayed from friction with the crystals, but still looped through the vesicle as Matt had described. Jordas led them forwards, feigning confidence. Water rose about their ankles and entered his boots. "Watch your step and follow me." *They'll find out soon enough about the two Shiranu lost here when we catch up with the rest of the tribe.* He stepped forwards, testing his footing at each step and clinging to the guide rope. For him it was at shoulder level; for the Naxadans, their heads. Water chilled his knees, roaring louder as they moved forwards. Soolkah followed him, shivering, Yado behind her.

Step by step they crept forward. Once, Jordas turned to smile encouragement at Yado and Soolkah. Their faces were swollen and discoloured by unaccustomed cold, but filled with determination. "Come on!" he signed, and added against the waterfall's white noise, "You *can* make it!" in English. Yado's grin told him that he, at least, had understood.

Jordas concentrated on crossing the flood. It was up to his thighs now. Cold numbed his feet. He couldn't feel his way. His leg ached. Meltwater spangled with lumps of ice threatened to sweep them away. The far side of the cavern was metres away, the end of the rope stretched round a boulder at the side of the passage. He hauled himself forwards. His legs felt even colder. A downward glance told him most of them were exposed to air again. He staggered into the tunnel mouth, glad it sloped up from the waystop.

<We've done it!>

A grin of pleasure and determination spread over Yado's features.

Jordas reached forwards to help Soolkah up beside him. She lay gasping and coughing in a heap of wet limbs and waterproofs as a sound like thunder split the ice roof.

"It cracks!" Jordas shouted. Yado wouldn't hear him but he'd catch his thought. <Come!>

He waded back into the flood, reached for Yado's arm but missed, and grabbed the rope linking them instead. *The karabiner must hold,* his mind screamed.

Yado clung to the guide rope.

Jordas tried to pull him closer as ice shards stabbed the flood, lashing its *whoosh*. Water could penetrate the vesicular basalt only to a limited depth as it filled the tunnels.

The level surged up to Yado's neck.

Jordas felt the guide-rope give as the vesicle end whipped into the water.

141

Yado lost his grip on it. The webbing belt cut into Jordas's waist as he tried to pull him closer. He thought his back would break. But he hauled on the rope, hoping Soolkah would retreat up the passage. He forgot that she was still roped to him as well.

The current swept Yado sidewise, knocking him off his feet. It yanked at Jordas's arm until he thought it would part company with him at the shoulder. But he clung on. "Yado!"

Jordas *felt* the fear on Yado's face, the water that swilled into his mouth, felt him gasp for breath, exhausted with the struggle for life, yet aware that he stood firm against the flood.

The pressure lifted. Soolkah had grabbed the guide rope. Once it slipped through her hands, but she uttered no cry of pain. Jordas tried to pull Yado near enough to catch him, but his right arm wasn't functioning properly. He clutched the rope, ignored sense impressions which told him Yado was drowning, disregarded his panic, and breathed deeply. Summoning his last ounces of strength, he hauled on the rope again. Pain lanced his shoulder. He felt sick, but as if through a mist, saw Yado's face bob nearer.

"You did it!" he whispered to Soolkah. *Now all we have to do is get him up here!* He sat down hard in the shallows, too spent to move.

Soolkah helped Yado stagger out of the flood. He collapsed beside Jordas, coughing up silty water and gasping for breath.

*

"You asked me to call you," the woman in the projection tank said.

Marcus studied her: about thirty, dressed in the Terran fashion of body-hugging stretch fabrics which contrasted with her loose leather blouson jacket. Business-like rather than attractive, though the glossy red curls piled in a precarious confection on top of her head were girlish enough to spoil that impression. "You're Corah Whitley?"

"Yes. The bank gave me your message." Her voice had a little-girl lisp. "Sorry I couldn't contact you before. All administrators oversee several accounts."

"Ms. Whitley, I —"

"Miss," she corrected him. "I prefer Miss."

"Quite so. Miss Whitley, I've never had dealings with the Committee before. Tell me: is it normal practice to have two administrators for each project?"

"Oh yes, always." she said. "For security."

"Do you know the other administrator?"

"Nevil Floyd? I understand he's senior to me, though I must admit I haven't worked with him before." She pursed her lips in thought. "But I've only met a few others. Most work from home via online services. I live nearby, so –"

"Have you spoken to him?"

"Not yet. I was surprised to learn of your concern that some of the funding had been spent already – I assumed it was *you* that had used it."

"I did use some," Marcus said. "I needed to send someone to Naxada to make advance contact with the indigenes. But the bulk of the money was transferred out during his journey by someone else." He repeated Hartmann's explanation, then explained the situation on Naxada. "Miss Whitley, I need your help. The Naxadans will die if these problems aren't resolved soon."

"I wasn't told it was *that* urgent," she said, "though I thought when I read the dossier that it should have a priority label."

"Who's your contact?"

"Senator Hartmann."

I might have known, Marcus thought. *This is revolving in circles, and they all come back to the same man.* "How long have you worked for the Committee, Miss Whitley?"

"Seven years. I worked my way up through the department. Why?"

"Is it usual for funding to be reallocated?" he asked.

Corah chewed her lip. "I've never heard of it before," she said, "though I suppose a large, priority resettlement requiring urgent funding might –"

"Would you be able to find out if that's the case now?" Marcus asked.

She nodded. "I'll check the account details." She inclined her head as if some thought had just struck her. The curls wobbled. "One moment." She examined her console. "Hmm...Your budget was fine. The costings were spot on. But you're right, there's not enough money to cover the cost of the archaeological team now." She met his gaze. "I'm so sorry. I don't know why the money was diverted elsewhere. It seems...irregular. Let me look into it for you."

"Please."

"In the meantime, I'll authorise refitting and despatch of the evacuation ship and the rescue team."

Marcus nodded. "Thank you."

"And I could contact Nevil Floyd and ask him why the funding was diverted like that. I could ask him to priority-label it to prevent anything like that happening again. He's got more clout than I have."

"Good idea," Marcus said. "Call me as soon as you have any further information."

"I certainly will, Dr Carlin. Goodbye." The screen clicked off.

Marcus sat still for a moment, thinking. *It's a pity she's the junior administrator. I wonder if she's strong enough to take on Floyd and whoever's giving the orders to divert funding at the Committee?*

*

"We're across just in time," Jordas muttered when his breathing had calmed. The crossing had shown him how deeply he and Yado were linked. "Anyone following wouldn't get through now."

"What happened to the guide-rope?" Yado asked.

"The crystals in that vesicle must have cut through it. Let's go."

Further along the tunnel they found a boulder warm enough to dry their clothes on. Jordas rubbed his shoulder and shin and shared glucose tablets from his pack, which had at least kept his things dry; Yado's sleeping fur was saturated. He hunched, shivering, under Jordas's sleeping bag, staring at the wall.

<What's the matter?>

Yado met his eyes. <Shall we reach them in time?>

<I don't know,> Jordas sent. <We can only move on and hope to beat the flood.> He leaned back against the rocks piled up behind him. They crunched and moved.

"Jordas!"

"What?"

"Th-there –" Soolkah had her hand at her mouth, eyes huge. She looked sick.

Jordas turned, half-expecting to see a *ganzu* poised for attack.

Part of a small, pale foot, with a white peach-fuzz of fur, protruded from the pile of rocks behind him. He recoiled, hand at mouth, heart thumping and stood up, shaking. "I didn't know it was there –" He backed away. His heart slowed. "I'm sorry," he said, then realised it sounded ridiculous to apologise to a corpse.

"It's a Shiranu child," Soolkah said. "What if it's one of my brothers, or my sister?"

"It isn't," Jordas said, moving his belongings and heaping the stones back so that they covered the child's toes again. He had to work with care; his soaked gloves were useless, and the lava was sharp as knives. Yado helped him with the last few.

As Soolkah replied, "How do you know?" he realised the rocks hadn't even scratched Yado as they had him.

"Matt told me. They saw it happen."

144

"You knew, and you didn't tell us?"

"I didn't want to upset you." Jordas sighed. "A man and his son were lost here two days ago. Matt didn't tell me they'd buried the bodies like this. I thought –"

"What man?"

"Matt doesn't know their names. But he'd have said if it was someone in your *amaaj*."

"If two have died, perhaps more have, further on. You said there'd been a rockslide –"

"Matt didn't say anyone else was hurt." Jordas sighed. "I'd no intention to upset you by not telling you about this –"

"It's all right," Soolkah said.

He could see it wasn't. Depression drowned him.

"Shall we move on? I don't want to share space with someone else's *amaamu*," Yado said, mouth full of *aldu* bread, "though I'm not afraid of my own ancestors' spirits."

They struggled back into their clothes. Jordas found the holoprobe hovering above them in the tunnel in record mode. It was then that Jordas wondered whether anybody had seen him with Soolkah the previous night. Although Matt had promised Yado and Soolkah their privacy, Jordas had no idea how he would fulfil that promise. *Last night was probably a bonus anyway,* he told himself. *Don't take it for granted!*

He'd woken to feel Soolkah's weight against his chest, hear her breathing, feel her hair tickling his chin. Try as he might, he couldn't think of it as fur, though the Naxadan word had that sense. He knew she wasn't human, but it was easier to see the similarities between them than the differences. He'd felt at peace.

Then Soolkah had stirred against him. "Muh...Yado?"

Of course, she was used to sleeping with *him* –

How will I feel when she's with Yado tonight? Jordas wondered, as they shouldered their possessions and began to walk once more.

*

<You're worrying, Elder brother.>

<I'm worried about lots of things.> Jordas didn't look round.

Yado felt his hostility like a slap in the face. <Have I upset you?> he asked.

Jordas shook his head.

<Soolkah, then?>

Another headshake. Yado saw Jordas glance at her, then lower his lashes to conceal his eyes, though not before he'd seen their expression. <Our ways are different from yours,> he remarked.

Jordas nodded.

<It's hard to converse when you only get headshakes and nods!>

Jordas only nodded again.

What's the matter with him? Yado wondered. *Were it best to ignore this mood?* He knew better than to intrude on a brother's thoughts, something all maaj'garu learned as children. He concentrated on their surroundings instead.

They'd clambered over the pile of rocks partly blocking the passage hours ago, and had been travelling in silence and near-darkness – punctuated only by occasional glowcake colonies – ever since. Jordas became more morose as they approached the farm cavern.

"Not far now," Soolkah whispered to Yado. "Hungry?"

He shook his head, and indicated Jordas, striding forward, the light on his headgear switched on, leading the way as if he knew it well. "Something worries him. He won't tell me what."

"Can't you sense his feelings? I thought maaj'garu could do that."

"I could at first, but now I can only do it if he wants me to," Yado answered.

"Our ways must be different from his tribe's," Soolkah said. "I thought it was strange that he'd already been with a woman when you said he wasn't amaajne."

"When did he tell you this?" Yado regarded her.

"When we were making love." Soolkah looked up at him. "You did rather surprise him last night!"

Yado joined her chuckle with his own. "Was it – good?" he asked.

"Don't you *know?*"

"He waited till I couldn't keep awake any longer. He likes his privacy, it seems." He couldn't contain his curiosity any longer. "Well?"

"Good, though different from you." She paused, then drew breath as if coming to a decision. "He's not circumcised."

"What?"

"It's true. They don't have to be. I suppose I thought it would be the same with every husband. It isn't."

A shout sounded ahead. Yado looked to where the light in the passage had grown.

"It's the farm cavern," Soolkah said. They crept forwards.

Jordas stood inside the cavern, near the tunnel mouth, encircled by Shiranu.

146

Fear and hostility mingled on the faces of his captors. Every man carried a spear or knife, poised ready to plunge.

CHAPTER 14

AN AGEING SHIRANU MALE pushed his way into the circle around Jordas, signalling to the tribesmen nearest him. The spear-points lowered by centimetres.

"I am the Eldest," the old male said. "Who and what are you?" His eyes raked Jordas up and down.

"My name is Jordas Krata," he said in Naxadan, hoping that what he knew of the Sargussi from Yado held good with the Shiranu. "I'm from – another place. I bring you a warning: the land you call Kerui is about to die."

"You're lying!" The man frowned. "Yet you're neither Shiranu nor Sargussi. Your head-fur –" He raised a gnarled hand towards Jordas's hair, but didn't touch it. Jordas saw doubt in his eyes. "You couldn't be Chabira –"

A movement from the tunnel mouth distracted him: a dark shape followed a pale one into the cavern.

"A dead spirit!"

"*Amaama!*"

"It's the shades of our ancestors!"

The Shiranu cowered and scattered as Soolkah approached.

"I'm not dead!" she answered. "Do the shades of your ancestors wear such things?" she asked, indicating the waterproofs. "Do they also wear the skins of Sargussi?" She waved a hand first at Yado, then at Jordas himself. "He's telling the truth. I'm alive, and these are my husbands."

With a roar of rage, a huge tribesman charged Jordas. Masses of flesh overhung his kilt, reminiscent of a Sumo wrestler. Jordas heard him grind his teeth in rage.

"Hey, what did I ever do to you?" he gasped in English, trying to dodge the fist aimed at his face. The blow glanced off his forehead. Out of the corner of his eye he noticed three Shiranu holding Yado at spearpoint. *Oh shit!*

At that moment the ground shivered under them, rocking the giant on his feet. The brief tremor stopped his next punch, and several Shiranu seized the chance to drag him back. He stood heaving and panting, just metres away, expression sullen.

The cut on Jordas's forehead throbbed. Before he could lift a hand to it his arms were yanked away from his body. He tried to show the tribesmen they were empty, but they held them. He remembered the gun, but said nothing. *Ignorant hands make an accident more likely.*

He looked for Soolkah. When he located her, she was standing amongst a group of people: a woman, three men, several smaller children. Jordas looked closer and recognised the faces; it seemed her family had claimed her.

The adults were speaking; Soolkah looked upset. Jordas wanted to go to her, but daren't move.

<I know you're all right,> Yado said, <though I felt it when that Shiranu hit you.>

Jordas wasn't sure if the Shiranu realised they could mindspeak. <I'm fine, but I'm worrying about Soolkah. They were hostile towards all of us,> Jordas replied. His legs trembled; he wanted to sit down. <Who's that big man, and why did he attack me?> he asked.

<I think that's Chixi,> Yado told him.

<Who?>

Yado explained. < She said he was a giant...and you know why they're hostile to me!>

Jordas felt Yado's amusement, looked up and caught his rueful smile. He grinned back, but curbed the expression on seeing the Eldest approaching. There was no time for further mindspeech. The Eldest stood before him, flanked by two younger men whose features were so like his that they could only be brothers. One cocked his head as if listening to a private conversation and Jordas guessed they were in mental contact. *Do Yado and I look like that when we're mindspeaking?*

His thoughts were interrupted by the words of the Eldest, who had been studying first his face, then Yado's. "Are you the Elder brother?"

"I am," Jordas agreed, "but I don't know your customs. If you're thinking to interrogate me, I request the presence of my *maaj'gar* Yado."

"I can't allow you to conspire with the Sargussi. He'll be questioned separately and killed later." The Eldest gestured, and the men holding Jordas released him, but kept their weapons pointed at his chest. *Peaceful the Shiranu may be in some ways,* Jordas thought, *but they obviously know how to kill, and won't hesitate to do so if they feel threatened enough.*

Jordas showed his inquisitors his hands. He hoped they weren't shaking too much; he dared not look. He wanted to check his equipment still functioned, especially the phone, then wondered if Matt and Marcus were watching.

The Eldest seated himself cross-legged on the ground nearby, gesturing for Jordas to copy him. He did so, keeping his hands visible.

"I am Hanook," the Eldest told him. His voice rumbled like an earthquake. "The tribe is my responsibility. Men have brothers and sons, but I am the father of them all. My brothers help me –" with a wave of his hand, he indicated the two men who flanked him, "but what the tribe does, where it goes, is my choice. On me falls the honour of decision. If I make the wrong choice, my people could die."

Jordas listened with as much attention as he could muster. The ache in his forehead was fading but one of Yado's captors had his arm around the Sargussi's throat. He was gasping for breath, and Jordas felt his discomfort. "I have...worries – for my *maaj'gar* and my *amaajni*," he said.

"Your *amaajni* is with her origin-*amaaj*. She has caused them dishonour, and now she is returned from the dead, she owes them *kazmo'ra*, which you and the Sargussi also owe to Chixi's *amaaj*." Hanook drew a breath and pointed to Yado. "Can you guarantee his good behaviour?"

Jordas nodded.

"Let him sit," he said to the tribesmen holding Yado. Jordas saw one of the men spread his hands, palms down. *The Naxadan equivalent of a shrug.* They released Yado. He sank to the ground.

Jordas breathed a sigh of relief as he turned to face Hanook again.

"How can he be your *maaj'gar*?" the Eldest asked. "He is of the Sargussi. You are..." Hanook hesitated. "You must be of a different tribe, though we were not aware of any others now."

Jordas acknowledged that with a quick nod copied from Yado. "I am not from Kerui. I am of the...the Humanu. But we mindspeak," he said. "We have each other's *sajamu*." As he said it, he felt a shock run through him.

These people had a word for the exchange of sense impressions he experienced with Yado.

And I didn't even realise it before.

*

"I thought I'd find you here."

The cheerful voice penetrated Matt's concentration. He looked round. "What's this, Abdel – a social visit? Weren't you off sick till tomorrow?"

Abdel grinned. He was leaning on crutches, but he looked all right otherwise. "I just can't keep away!"

Matt frowned. "It's good that you're feeling better, but I didn't think you'd need sticks to walk. Those Medicares usually fix people pretty thoroughly."

"Yes, unfortunately I've been fixed before, in the self-same spot, and not by a Medicare. It took ages to heal, and ended my army career." Abdel's lips curled into a regretful smile.

"Bit of a change from soldier to scientist, eh?"

"You're not kidding! Er...I'm not supposed to stand for long periods right now."

"Have a seat, then, and take a look at this."

In the tank, dark faces clustered around a flat stone in the middle of the cavern. On it lay several shapes which women were cutting with metal knives. "Notice the male-female ratio? It's the same as in the family groups of the other tribe."

Abdel's eyes roved around the image. His lips moved as he counted under his breath. "It looks like...between two and six men, with three or four on average, to one woman."

"Does that shock you?"

"Why should it? We can't apply human standards to alien civilisations." He shrugged. "It makes sense to share women if there's a shortage." He wrinkled his nose. "Are those things on the stone cave porcupine?"

Matt nodded. "Baked in mud to remove the spines. These people seem as exclusively carnivorous as the other tribe are vegetarian."

"Probably only Jordas can confirm that. Have you spoken to him recently?"

"Not since this morning."

"Do we still have probe contact with the Shiranu?"

"Oh yes –" Matt would have said more, but the internal holophone bleeped. John Wolfe's face filled the projection cube on his workstation. "Sorry to disturb you, Matt," he said. "Hamorrah has reappeared from behind Malory."

"Thanks." Matt turned back to the main holotank. The Sargussi were seated, listening to the single male who stood there, speaking in a voice which carried to the edges of the cavern.

"What are they doing?" asked Abdel.

"I think they're telling stories. Bill Borthwick says both tribes do this every evening when they've eaten."

*

"Tell us a story, Jeeban!"

"Yes, time for a story!"

<Give them a story, Jeeban,> Aa'kam said. <Take their minds off their empty bellies.>

Aa'kam felt a tingle of pride just hearing the clamour. Jeeban's skill with words made him one of the most popular story-tellers in the history of the tribe.

"This is a story of Kerui from the time before the amaaju." Jeeban stood up, smiling as he looked around him. "It's the story of Chel of the Sargussi."

A hush fell on the tribespeople.

<Mayhap not a happy choice,> Aa'kam sent.

<True,> Jeeban returned. <But sad stories are part of our history and must also be told sometimes.>

Aa'kam raised his hands and made the throwaway gesture of permission to go ahead.

Jeeban acknowledged him with a sharp dip of his head. "When men first came to Kerui they had much to learn about the land. Kerui has rocks, plants, animals, and water, like Outside, but many things about this land are different." He surveyed the tribespeople. He didn't tell this story often, because the tribe liked to hear more positive stories, but Aa'kam knew it was a worthwhile reminder of the safety code in their present dangerous situation.

"Chel knew the water rose and fell in the caves, but it was he who noticed that it came and went with a regularity which reminded him of how the rivers Outside swelled at the greening of the year. So after counting many lighttimes, he realised that the streams in Kerui do indeed reflect the passing of time Outside, and men and women and children began to measure their lives in highwaters.

"Now Chel had two brothers - not his maaj'garu, just garu. In those days, brothers weren't joined as now, but were without the sharing, as women are today. But all three were brave and strong, and would explore Kerui in search of places to mine, for they were skilled prospectors. Sometimes they wandered far from Keramanthu, which was being built at that time, in search of metals."

Jeeban paused. Aa'kam caught his eye and opened his mind to let him to feel his approval. <It's good that you're telling it this way this time. I see what you're about, brother.>

Jeeban continued. "One lighttime they were seeking metals for weapons and tools. They found a cavern with iron, tin, copper, zinc and lead in, but there was so much that they needed help. So Chel's brothers returned to the city.

"On their return to the cavern they heard a thundering, as if the whole mountain were falling down, and indeed, it was a quake. They were afraid, as Chel must have been. Was he lonely, waiting for them, struggling to mine the ores? None shall ever know, for when the brothers returned with other miners, scorching heat drove them back.

"In the cavern, one of those the Shiranu call a 'farm cavern', a blow-out had begun. The rocks vomited gases amid much rumbling and roaring. Fire scorched the air, and hot mud bubbled out of the ground. None dared enter. Doubtless Chel was burned alive. Though the blow-outs renew the soil's fertility and bring us metal to work, in Kerui there is always danger for Sargussi

152

or Shiranu alike.

"Chel's brothers mourned him, but as they were not joined, there was no maaj'nag'ur for them, and therefore they never truly knew what became of him. But they returned to the city with this tale, especially relevant to Sargussi miners. And that's why we – and the Shiranu – now think of the volcano as both the giver and destroyer of life."

Now Jeeban looked directly at the unmarried hunters. "The danger isn't just to miners," he said. "It's there for all, but especially our hunters. Strange things are happening, and we must regard our journey to Keramanthu as Chel's brothers must have on returning to the city. We must beware the dangers of Kerui. 'Our own place' the name may mean, but we have no control over the volcano. Walk with care, my people."

*

Ray had just stretched out his hand for the beaker of coffee at his elbow when the monitor cube beside him lit up, showing Matt's head and shoulders. Abdel was seated beside him.

"Ray? Is Marcus there?"

"Off-shift."

"Are you alone?" Matt peered into the holotank at him.

Ray nodded. "Middle of night. Funny shifts." He wiped his sleeve across his forehead. "Dead beat."

"When does Jordas's replacement arrive?"

"Three days' time."

"Ah. Okay. When's Marcus due in?"

"Tomorrow morning –"

"Can you get him? I'm getting some disturbing stuff on the holoprobe following Jordas and his friends. Here, I'll patch it through." The holovid images jerked as Matt switched channels. "It came in about an hour ago."

Ray saw Jordas pacing through the tunnel, well ahead of the young Naxadans. The light grew as they approached a cavern. When Jordas reached the tunnel mouth he hung back, waiting for the others to catch up with him. He'd turned to watch for them when the Shiranu surrounded him and drew him into the cavern.

For a moment Ray couldn't speak. Then his voice started to work again. "Look hostile. Better call Marcus."

Matt sighed. "Thanks. Ask him to call me back, will you?"

Ray smoothed his quiff back into place and requested Marcus's home number. *Hope I'm doing the right thing, disturbing him – even for this!* he thought. *No telling with Marcus. Never know exactly where you are with him.*

After some minutes a woman's face filled his monitor cube. "Marina Carlin speaking."

"Dr Carlin, please? Ray Travers calling. Urgent."

"He's asleep at present." She hesitated. "How urgent? It *is* the middle of the night."

"Urgent urgent!" he replied. "Sorry to disturb – problem on Naxada."

"I'll get him," she sighed. "Just a moment, please."

Ray waited.

"Marcus. What is it?"

"Call from Matt. Jordas and co. prisoners."

"I beg your pardon?" Even Marcus's composure sounded shaken. "Could you repeat that?"

Ray did.

"Since when?"

"Time of transmission two forty-six. Just came through."

"All right." All trace of emotion was gone from Marcus's voice. "I'll be there shortly."

When he'd told Matt, Ray remembered his coffee. *Cold.* He grimaced, checked the seismographic displays, and turned back to the Shiranu cavern transmission.

*

The tank flashed up Corah Whitley's holoimage. She wore her curls loose about her shoulders this time, though her top and tight trousers were as business-like as her previous outfit. Her leather jacket was draped over the chair behind her.

"Good morning, Dr Carlin – I just got here." She sounded cheerful. "How can I help?"

Marcus returned the greeting, but added, "It's the middle of the night here. I'm calling for a status report."

"Let me get into my terminal. Just a moment." She tossed her hair back and smiled. "There. I checked last night, and the refit's proceeding as planned. They're working round the clock to get it done on time." Her expression became more serious. "Still no messages from Nevil Floyd. I've left several for him re the priority labelling. Have you heard from him?"

"No."

"I'll just check the account. I assume he's had no cause to touch the account, as I'm dealing with you direct. One moment, please." She turned aside to give voice commands to the computer, then raised her eyes to the monitor beside her. *"Hell!"*

"Now what?"

"We're overdrawn. A transaction went through after the refit charges were paid yesterday. Have you taken money out for anything?"

"No. Can you patch it through?"

Corah made the connection and her image was replaced with columns of figures. Sure enough, the last transaction had gone through only minutes before.

"Can you trace it?" Marcus asked.

"I'll try." She looked worried. "I'll have to get onto the bank anyway, to try to make sure they don't freeze the account."

Marcus sat forward, elbows on the workstation, hands pressed against aching eyelids. "That's not the only problem I've got," he said. "My assistant and his friends on Naxada are prisoners."

"Are you sure? Alien body language doesn't always match up to ours –"

"I've seen the holovid. There's no doubt of this. That's why I'm here now." He fingered his beard, sighing. "What action would the Committee recommend in such a situation?"

"That depends on how your man – Dr Krata, is it? – handles his situation. If he can't talk his way out he may have to stay put till the rescue team go in." Corah drummed her fingers on the desk. "That would mean a more costly and difficult operation which would take longer and might overrun our margin of safety."

"I was hoping to get everyone out well before the meteorite impacts. Although micrometeorites will burn up in the atmosphere, at least twelve pieces are up to a kilometre in size. Such a fragment would hit the planet with the force of about 250,000 megatons of explosives."

Corah whistled. "I'll call you back as soon as I have any information for you, Dr Carlin. We *must* find out who's doing this and stop it immediately or the whole project is in serious trouble. We may have to cut the size of the rescue team. I'll try Nevil Floyd again as well. A priority label would prevent any withdrawals without the express written consent of all signatories."

"Thanks." Marcus closed the line and flipped channels to reveal Matt's image again. "Any more news on Jordas?"

"Only what you've seen. Did you get through to the administrator?"

"Yes. Financially, we're in deep water. Drowning, in fact."

"What's happened?"

Marcus told him. "The worst part of it is that we still don't know where the money's going. It looks like this Floyd man's involved, and Corah never seems to be able to speak to him."

155

"Can't you contact Senator Hartmann again?"

Marcus nodded. "But what could he do? And more to the point, what *would* he do? The man I really need to speak to is his superior, and he's not due back on Earth for ten days."

"Where is he?"

"Overseeing another project." Marcus sighed. "No, we'll just have to handle this ourselves until I can get hold of him. Incidentally, I've made all the arrangements for the evacuation of your staff. E.T.A. is in ten days' time. It will take everyone off-planet except yourself, Tim Perry, Abdel Tairik, Wong Yue Xiao, John Wolfe and Frank Doherty. Luckily we're *not* dependent on funding from the Committee for that!"

"Just as well. But what will happen if Jordas can't persuade –"

"From what I gather, that will be the rescue crew's problem. I suppose they might have to go in with stun weapons to round everybody up in an extreme scenario. Hopefully it won't come to that."

"Right," Matt echoed. "Just one moment, Marcus." He swung his chair to the side. "What's happening here?"

"What have you got for me, Matt? Tell me some *good* news!" Marcus's stance mirrored his voice.

"We just had a report from our pilot. He's out surveying the mountain for possible entry and shuttle landing sites and has noticed some large crevasses developing in the glacier. We don't yet know whether they're due to melting or seismic activity. Or both." Matt broke off as the holoimage wavered. "I think that's your answer."

Marcus had sagged onto a seat nearby. "Thanks," he said. "I *really* needed to know that. I'll speak to you later." He cut the contact and turned, just in time to see Ray avert his eyes and check his monitors. It wasn't the first time he'd caught him eavesdropping. "Did you want me, Ray?" he asked.

"No – no," Ray said, shrugging.

CHAPTER 15

"YOU WILL BE HELD apart from the tribespeople," Hanook said, "for your protection and theirs."

"And Soolkah?" Jordas asked. His unease about her had grown as they spoke. *If the giant should think to harm her – no, I don't know what I'd do, but I don't want him anywhere near her.* "She is...our *amaajni*," he added.

"If that's true, she should be with you while we decide what to do with you," Hanook said. "She will be returned to you." He made as if to get up, but Jordas caught his arm.

"Hanook – Eldest –" he began.

The Shiranu leader looked down at Jordas's hand and glared at him. "Even an ignorant stranger shouldn't dare touch the Eldest before his tribe," he said, "if he wishes to avoid owing him *kazmo'ra*."

The word translated as "status-debt", and it wasn't the first time he'd heard it. This time Jordas made a mental note to ask Yado about it. He let go, sketched one of Yado's respectful nods and apologised, but held eye contact with Hanook. He wasn't sure if the Eldest believed him, but after ensuring his companions' safety, he had a job to do.

"Kerui dies." He risked a glance at Yado. "Hence I'm here – to help both tribes survive."

"Enough!" Hanook gritted out. "I won't listen to further lies. Your *maaj'gar* and *amaajni* are returned to you." He put a wealth of contempt into the words. "That's all." He rose with grace, and beckoned to his brothers to follow.

Jordas got up less nimbly. Within moments Yado was being frogmarched towards him. A shove sprawled him at Jordas's feet. He made as if to help him up.

Yado waved him away. <It mayhap were permitted in the Humanu tribe, but public physical contact is shame amongst the tribespeople, except in an emergency.>

Hanook's threat made more sense to Jordas then. <They're bringing Soolkah to us, but they don't believe me about Kerui.>

<I didn't think he would. Try to speak with him again later. They've had many shocks this lighttime. For now, it's enough that Soolkah be returned to us.>

And that was a problem in itself. Jordas wondered if Yado knew of his

157

jealousy, then decided it was the last thing he should worry about just now. *At least we're together again, and still alive.*

They watched as Soolkah approached with her guards. She had to pass near where Chixi was still restrained. It had taken several tribesmen to stop him from rushing over and continuing his attack. As she passed, he spat and muttered, "*Mooska!*"

Soolkah flinched. Her escort led her away from the giant.

Jordas searched his memory. "That's an animal. What does he mean?" Concerned for Soolkah, he forgot to use the mindspeech.

<It's known for its promiscuity,> Yado told him, <I'll kill him if he says that again!>

<Calm down! That won't make them more anxious to listen to me.> Jordas was beginning to wonder whether he'd ever resolve his emotional conflict. He had a certain amount of sympathy for Chixi, especially since it seemed he was also suffering emotional conflict, but that didn't give him the right to insult Soolkah.

She reached them and stood examining them. "Your poor face," she said to Jordas.

"I'll live," he murmured. "Are *you* well?"

She nodded. Their captors began to herd them along another tunnel.

"Where are they taking us?" Yado whispered.

"To the sleeping cave," Soolkah answered. "Let's keep quiet," she added, with a meaningful glance at Jordas.

Their guards ushered them towards a crevice in the far corner of the sleeping cavern. "You three can use this niche," one said. "We'll be on guard outside."

"Yes," said another, "Hanook's deciding what to do with you, and how *she'll* repay her *kazmo'ra*." He gave Soolkah a shove with the shaft of his spear. "Traitor!"

Soolkah stumbled, only stopped from falling by Jordas's grab at her arm.

"In!" the Shiranu gestured.

One by one they filed into a crevice barely larger than the one Soolkah had hidden in.

When their guards had left, Jordas asked, "What *is* this *kazmo'ra* I keep hearing about? It translates as status-debt, but what does that mean? I know your language, but not your customs."

"It's how we ensure good behaviour," Soolkah explained. "If you did some wrong to a member of another *amaaj* – even by accident – you'd owe some of whatever status you have within the tribe to that *amaaj*."

158

"A Sargussi would have to hunt for the *amaaj* he owed *kazmo'ra* to," Yado added, "but I don't know how Shiranu settle it."

"We work it off in the farm caverns," Soolkah said.

"I understand better now." Jordas rummaged in the pack for the phone, the holocam, his notebook, and his gun. They seemed all right. He stowed them away again and crept back to the mouth of the niche. The guards stared at him with suspicion but said nothing as he looked around the main cavern. There was no sign of a cable terminal.

But there was a constant background *drip-drip* of water. Jordas looked up at the ceiling. A huge crack crossed the centre of the ice.

"I must speak urgently with the Eldest," Jordas said.

"You'll speak to him when he has time. He's planting up now, like we would be if we weren't watching you!"

Jordas shrugged, moved back to where Yado and Soolkah sat on his sleeping bag, and sat down, frowning.

"What's the matter?" Soolkah asked. Her eyes went to the phone. "Can't you talk to your friends?"

"Not without a terminal."

*

Yado crept to the mouth of the niche and surveyed the main cave. *In here it's dry – but for how long?* Silence dripped around him, mingling with the *plop* of water nearby. He shivered. One of their guards must have stood under the leak recently; his fur was plastered against skin and scalp.

He wasn't sure why Jordas looked so anxious. <Shall one more darktime make any difference?> he sent. <The Eldest may speak to us tomorrow.>

A nod was the only answer. *I don't understand Jordas in this mood.* But Yado's respect for the privacy code kept him from further probing.

Soolkah washed and dressed his injuries using medicaments from his pack. Then Jordas hunched over his *map*, a frown folding his brows together. His face was closed. He set the *notebook* back in his pack and folded his arms around himself, mouth tight and grim.

From beyond the guards came the sounds of movement and quiet speech. The tribe was preparing food, labour in the farm cavern done for that lighttime.

"Sargussi, what are you doing?" One of the guards had noticed him. "Not thinking of escaping, are you?"

"Hardly, since my maaj'gar and I have urgent need of speech with the Eldest. And I'm wondering how much privacy we shall get tonight!"

"We'll keep at a discreet distance!" smirked the guard.

In the cavern the glowcakes' light brightened the streaks of water slicing

159

through the air, and occasional hisses signalled meltwater splattering the firestone. He scrambled back to the others, reaching out with his mind for Jordas. But when his mind touched the Humanu's, he recoiled. "Jordas?" he asked aloud.

He barely lifted his head.

Yado squatted beside him. <Tell me?>

Jordas shook his head.

Yado looked around the cave, seeking any means of distraction. Then he noticed Soolkah was on her knees, eyes narrowed, head cocked to one side as if listening.

The ground growled. Their possessions shook.

Soolkah's eyes widened. Her pupils glinted in the failing light. "Another quake!"

Jordas roused at her voice and staggered to his feet, though the tremor was already settling. Yado put a hand under Jordas's elbow; he seemed to need the support.

From the cave mouth, one of the guards growled, "All right, you three, you needn't get excited. The panic's over. You don't get out of there tonight."

"Not a bad shock," Soolkah muttered. "But there could be more."

Yado dropped the hand he'd put out to comfort her. *With Jordas here –*

"If I could speak to my friends they might know if more shocks are expected." Jordas lapsed into silence again.

A commotion at the entrance brought them all to their feet.

"You can't go in there!" Yado heard one of the guards say.

"But she was my daughter – I've brought them food. Surely you don't expect them to starve?"

"She has brought your amaaj much dishonour. No woman has ever fled her contracted husbands before in *our* tribe."

An insult aimed at me, Yado guessed.

"Once married, she is no longer part of my amaaj," came the reply, "but does that mean I don't love her any more? *Ghasru masaachifar!* I can't forget she came out of my womb. Let me see her!"

Soolkah hurried towards the entrance, her expression lightening at the sound of her mother's voice. Finally the guards decided Gujas could enter. She stepped inside the circle of light from Yado's lampcup. Her eyes went from Soolkah to Yado, and then to Jordas.

<She's curious about us,> Jordas sent.

<More frightening than the tremor!> Yado replied.

*

Gujas stepped back from Soolkah's embrace, permitted only because she was here to celebrate her marriage. Except for childbirth or other emergencies, it was the last time she would ever hold her again.

She handed the basket of food to her. "I'm so glad you're alive, Soolkah!" she said. "But amaajni – and with two men from other tribes...I don't know about this." She shook her head and turned to examine Yado and Jordas.

The Sargussi she could accept. She'd seen them before, though she associated them with terror and flight. But at least his appearance was more familiar than the other man's. Her eyes swept over his compact, muscular form. *He's certainly good-looking, even if he is my enemy,* she told herself with grudging approval.

She knew she was giving herself time before facing the stranger again. The foreign men stood watching her. She caught the expression in their eyes which told her they were mindspeaking as they waited.

She pointed towards the Sargussi's armband. It glittered in the light from the fire. "What's this?" she asked him.

"Igeeja," the Sargussi answered. "You don't have them?"

"We have nothing like it. You must come of a high-status amaaj to own such a thing." Gujas couldn't keep the curiosity from her voice.

Yado shook his head. "There is only my father and myself now. We're metalworkers."

"And him?" Gujas jerked her head towards Jordas. "Is he also a metalworker?"

Yado shook his head. "He is my maaj'gar."

"They say he's from another tribe altogether. Chabira, perhaps."

The Sargussi inclined his head. "He's neither Shiranu nor Sargussi nor Chabira."

Gujas allowed herself to examine Jordas. The first thing she noticed about him was his height beside Sargussi and Shiranu alike. And his face was broader and squarer than that of a man of the tribes. She looked more closely at his eyes. They were a deep blue.

Unfathomable.

Alien.

Yet not. His features, apart from the furless neck and the sparse covering on his arms, weren't so different from Sargussi or Shiranu features. He had the right number of arms and legs, though his clothing was strange. *Someone in his tribe weaves and dyes fabric.* The cloth was a darker blue than her own kilt, or his eyes. His lips were less full than the tribespeople's; his head-fur curled almost to his shoulders, and was as dark as a Sargussi's. But his nose was as

161

straight as any tribesman's.

I'll get used to his looks, I suppose, she told herself after staring at him for a few moments. He didn't seem any more put out by her scrutiny than the Sargussi.

"Tell me the names of Soolkah's amaajnu," she commanded.

*

"Here," said Gujas, placing the basket of food between them. "You can't have had much of a wedding feast."

Yado sent Jordas a look of consternation as Soolkah shook her head. <You said you can't eat our food, and it were grossly impolite to refuse.>

<I must explain to her. But how will you manage? Everything there's fruit or vegetables.>

<I know.> Yado grimaced. <I'll try to put her off.> "Gujas, we've no wish to offend you, but neither Jordas nor I can eat your food."

"But –"

"No, Gujas," Soolkah said. "Jordas will be ill if he eats it, and Yado prefers meat."

Gujas looked aghast. "But how will you feed them? And how will we celebrate your wedding?" She turned back to the men. "You really should feast with the whole tribe, or at least share food with our family group - seeing as your origin-amaaju aren't here. Without the feast, how will we prevent further loss of status for our amaaj?"

Yado felt the mind-shift that told him Jordas had suddenly understood her concern.

"Gujas, let me explain! I've no wish to cause your amaaj loss of status, but Shiranu food, or Sargussi meat for that matter, will make me ill. I can't even drink the water down here without treating it first."

"I don't understand."

"It's because I come from – from a place further away than even Outside. There the balance of soil goodness is different, so our food is too. Don't be offended, Gujas."

Gujas understood about soil goodness, being Shiranu. Yado could see that in the way her expression changed. "What *can* you eat, then?" she asked.

"Meat, in Yado's case, or these in mine." He produced a carton of high-energy biscuits. "But *you* can eat these if you take this extra sulphur as well." Jordas palmed one of the capsules to show her, then continued, "I can't let you waste your vegetables on Yado and me. You'll need all you have and more in the next few lighttimes."

"Could we still have the feast with some of your food and some of

162

Jordas's?" Yado asked. "Would that answer? Jordas and I have no wish to offend."

Gujas brightened. "That would allow me to recognise your amaaj," she agreed. "If *I* do so, as a representative of the bride's origin-amaaj, the rest of the tribe must." She sighed. "Your guards won't release you for a feast with the whole tribe, but perhaps that can be arranged for later."

"Mayhap," Jordas echoed.

Soolkah investigated the basket's contents. There were dried fruits, porridge in a stone bowl, breadcakes, a vegetable stew seasoned with herbs, and a pot of strong-smelling liquid.

"You eat breadcake, Yado," Soolkah said, "and porridge is similar." She helped herself from the bowl using her fingers.

"You have milk here?" Jordas asked.

"Our own," Gujas said. "It's the custom that unless a bride already has children from a previous marriage, her mother donates the milk for the porridge if she is able to, or another relative if not, to create a symbolic bond between the bride and her amaajnu."

Yado's stomach curdled at the thought, but he guessed a refusal could damage Jordas's chances of persuading the tribe to leave Kerui. "Just a little, then," he said. He watched Soolkah dipping her fingers into the stuff, and when the bowl came to him, he copied her. To him the porridge tasted too sweet, but he chewed and swallowed, then reached hesitantly for a wrinkled reddish globe, which appeared to be some sort of dried fruit.

"What would you eat at a Sargussi wedding?" Gujas asked.

"Meat roasted with special herbs for fertility."

Gujas suppressed a shudder and drank from the pot of red juice, then passed it to Soolkah. She drank, and would have passed it to Yado, but Jordas intercepted it to sniff it.

"You know this smell?" Yado asked.

Jordas nodded. "We call it *al-co-hol,* a strong drink." Jordas reached into his pack and brought out a container of brownish liquid. "I have some with me." Yado didn't miss his hesitation, as he took the container Jordas passed to him. <It's intended for medicinal use – but I think this counts as well.>

Yado sniffed the liquid, then nodded. "The same, or nearly so."

"I'll drink some of mine," Jordas said, "while you have this. What do you call it?" he asked Soolkah.

"Zhahzhi," Gujas replied before Soolkah could answer. "Fermented from mathna-juice, with my milk. Mnanga made it."

"It's very rare," Soolkah added, "so it's kept for special occasions, like weddings, coming-of-age ceremonies, and when people join the tribe."

"People *join* the tribe?"

"When a baby is born, it must be adopted into the tribe, and after that the child's loyalty must be first to the tribe, then to its origin-amaaj." Soolkah looked at her fingers – still pebbled with porridge – then at Yado and Jordas. A frown clouded her expression. "You must understand that by accepting our amaaj, Gujas is taking a great risk to her amaaj's status within the tribe. I wasn't loyal to the tribe when I ran from wedding Chixi and his brothers. I was cowardly, and put my own feelings before the tribe. I bring you no status within my tribe." She paused, then added, "But Gujas is proud, and will not see my new amaaj lose status because the tribe don't acknowledge it." She handed the zhahzhi pot to Yado. "Drink."

He looked at it, then lifted it.

"Doesn't your tribe make zhahzhi?" Gujas asked.

"You forget, we cultivate no fruits," Yado said. He sipped at first, then took a great gulp. "Tastes – good!" The stuff both fired and anaesthetised his mouth at once.

<Not too much – you'll get drunk!> Jordas warned.

"What else happens at a Sargussi wedding?"

"Each brother would give the woman gifts." Yado indicated Soolkah. "She has my knife, but they took it when they put us in here."

"Very good," said Gujas. "I'll speak with Hanook about its return, as it was a wedding gift. And what has he given you?" She indicated Jordas.

Soolkah reached across to their waterproofs, lying in a pile to one side of the niche. "*Jacket*," she said, holding it up. "To keep dry when it's wet, and warm when it's cold."

Gujas smiled her approval at Jordas. "It's cloth," she said, "even though it's made by another tribe. Very good, very practical."

Jordas smiled back to acknowledge the compliment.

When they had eaten, Gujas stood up. "I must go now," she said. "Sleep well this darktime and always, amaaj Jordasafar." She turned to Soolkah. "Keep the fruit and breadcakes, and enjoy them." She picked up the bowls and left.

Soolkah moved the basket of fruit off the sleeping bag. "There'll be stories when every amaaj has shared food," she said. She turned to Yado. "I thought the knife was a replacement for the one you smashed."

"It was," he said. "But even then I thought you were beautiful." He leaned against the rockwall, watching her, until he became aware of Jordas's posture: one hand brushing the head-fur back from eyes shut tight as if to exclude him,

164

the other arm wrapped around his knees. <Jordas? What is it?>

There was no reply, so Yado probed further, edging deeper into waves of shame, the fear of disgrace, and a passion which threatened to spill out and engulf them all: undercurrents of confusion, bitterness and worst of all, sexual jealousy, each cutting into him like blades. <Jordas, there is no need for jealousy between maaj'garu.>

<Your whole mindset is different from mine,> Jordas sent. <Mayhap we're just *too* dissimilar!>

<You can learn,> he answered.

<And lose my sanity in the process?>

<I don't understand.>

Jordas opened his eyes. <I can't cope with these feelings any more than you can understand them, and I'm not even sure if what I feel is real or a reflection from *you*.>

His skin may look pale as ice, but passion flows in his veins, like a river of strong currents, Yado reflected. *And this man is my maaj'gar. What kind of a man can he truly be?*

*

They moved closer to the niche mouth to hear the story.

Jordas settled himself on the sleeping bag and gazed around the cavern, as a heavily pregnant Shiranu woman came into the light, followed by two men and two boys, all four led by other tribespeople. "What's wrong with them?"

"The *maaj'nag'ur* has claimed them," Yado whispered back.

"The sleep of brothers," Jordas translated. "What's that?"

Yado looked troubled. "When one brother dies, the others need to adjust, but during that time they can't do anything for themselves." He bit his lip. "I don't remember anything when Uvvuz died, except the rockfall and coming to many lighttimes later –"

"Hush!" Soolkah raised her hand. "Kayas is starting the story now."

Kayas stood up to speak. "Shiranu, we have strangers amongst us. They have formed an *amaaj* with the woman Soolkah. So it falls to me to remind you how the *amaaju* came about." Kayas surveyed his audience. "When the tribes lived in Keramanthu the Chabira succumbed to a plague. No-one knows where it came from, or why it attacked the tribes, but it came after the Shiranu and Chabira learned to cultivate Kerui's herbs and plants for medicine and food, so perhaps it was something in the soil here. First the Chabira women died, then the children, and lastly the men. Their knowledge of healing was of no use against it."

<It were better had they just eaten meat, like we learned to,> Yado sent.

165

Jordas held a finger to his lips, then changed the sign to a palmraise. <I don't know these stories,> he sent, <and they may contain important information.>

"The plague also attacked the Sargussi and the Shiranu, killing many. Of those that survived, most were men. When more children were born, although they survived, there were always more boy-children than girls. Women became scarce, so woman-sharing began amongst brothers. But often one man would feel jealous of his brothers. Some killed to secure their claim to a woman and her children. Eventually, a public display of jealousy led to loss of status within the tribe."

In the silence in the cavern Jordas heard Kayas draw breath.

"Over time, it became obvious that the plague had changed both Shiranu and Sargussi forever. As the plague-born generations grew up, a bond developed between brothers, first of *sajamu*, which is fitting as touch is the first sense a baby knows. Later came the mindspeech, then the transfer of knowledge and the privacy shield. And soon the *maaj'nag'ur* claimed any *amaaj* which lost a brother.

"Where there was rivalry between the first *amaaj*-fathers over sharing their wives, within generations it had died out. To counter fratricide, the Elders ordered such men banished whilst claimed by the *maaj'nag'ur*. Yet some men still failed to adapt to sharing wife and fatherhood equally. They had to learn to accept and overcome their feelings, sometimes with the help of the Elders' wisdom. The practice of reckoning lineage from father to son died out, and each brother in an *amaaj* claimed all the children as his own, as we do today.

"Later, the sense of proximity, shared by all three tribes when we lived Outside, was much blunted in the Shiranu from lack of use." Kayas's eyes rested on Yado's face, showing his curiosity, before he looked around the tribespeople once more, then stared at Jordas. "To survive, every adult had to put loyalty to the tribe above his or her *amaaj*, as we do today." His gaze moved to Soolkah.

"Now it falls to me, as story-teller, to remind the strangers who are apparently *amaajnu* with Soolkah of their obligations towards her. They must feed her and care for her if she's pregnant or ill, and must protect and defend her from all dangers. She in turn must feed and care for them, bear their children, and ensure that all runs smoothly in the *maajaa*, the home-niche.

"When the Shiranu drifted away from Keramanthu to tend the farm-caverns, the Sargussi chose to follow game animals as they migrated through the caverns with the seasons."

<That were the Shiranu view, of course,> Yado sent. <Jeeban would say

166

it happened differently.>

With a warning glance at their niche, Kayas walked with head held high to Hanook's sleeping crevice.

<Come, Jordas. The darktime is the time for the sharing.>

Jordas shook his head and wouldn't permit himself to look round at them.

<Please yourself.>

For a time he stayed at the niche mouth, ignoring the sounds of Yado and Soolkah's loveplay as best he could. *So that's how the* amaaj *system came about, and how the city was abandoned. I can see why they're locked into the* amaaj *system, but I never expected to have to share a woman, especially after Nina. And it doesn't exactly help that I can feel everything Yado does –*

"...I can't. I should have remembered the time," Jordas heard Soolkah say behind him, her mood becoming serious. "You'll have to do without for once, Yado." She came to the entrance. "I want to speak to Gujas, urgently," she said to their guards. "Fetch her here now, and tell her to bring anzu bolls."

Jordas felt a smile curl his lips. When Gujas hurried up and pressed something into Soolkah's hand, his heart lightened, and he knew Yado felt it too.

I shouldn't feel glad, not in their terms, he told himself. But instead of pulsing with dread the blood sang in his veins. *I can't help it. I'm human, not Naxadan.*

CHAPTER 16

SOOLKAH HAD BEEN HALF-DOZING for some time, trying to ignore the cramps in her lower back. Realising she wouldn't sleep again that lighttime, she eased herself out of Yado's embrace and crept to the niche mouth to look into the cavern beyond.

The sound of running water was louder than the previous darktime. Someone coughed. She couldn't be sure if the next cough was an echo or someone's answering splutter, with the humidity in the cavern.

Of their guards there was no sign, but the firestone depression sizzled as droplets fell on it. Although barely lightbreak, the brightness made Soolkah look upwards, shielding her eyes as tears cleared sleep from them. Instead of the crack she'd seen the previous lighttime, two gashes now punctured the ceiling. She remembered the struggle against the maelstrom of the ruined waystop. *Was it only last lighttime that happened?* It seemed longer, so much had happened.

She shook Yado awake, then turned to Jordas, huddled in his sleeping bag apart from them, frowning even as he slept. At her touch he squeezed his eyes even more tightly shut. Soolkah shook him again.

"Jordas!" she called. "It's starting here too. The cavern roof's going. We must leave!"

Jordas scrambled to his knees in one movement. "Put on your *waterproofs*. Pack everything else up to leave. I must speak with Hanook *now!*" He took the object he had named *notebook* out of his pack, then tried to cram his belongings back in.

"Let me do that," Soolkah said. "The guards have gone – why don't you and Yado go to Hanook? I'm certain he'll believe you now."

"He should, if he's wanting to live!" Jordas beckoned to Yado, then charged into the main cavern without waiting for him.

Soolkah watched Yado go. In a moment, he and Jordas had disappeared into the crowd. The tribespeople stood outside their sleeping niches, looking around in bewilderment. Soolkah spotted Hanook, talking with a group of people on the other side of the cavern. She turned back to her packing, glad of the distraction. *It's good that Gujas isn't too angry,* she thought as she worked, *though I'm sure she's not happy about Yado, and she definitely doesn't know what to make of Jordas.*

The air chilled as the gashes in the pack-ice roof opened up. Streams of

168

liquid poured in. The growing light cast stranger shadows than Soolkah had ever seen before, though it wasn't yet strong enough to cause discomfort unless she looked directly at it. As she worked, she chewed on dried aggifruit from her mother's basket. By the time her husbands had returned she'd prepared everything for them to move on and cleaned herself as thoroughly as time and limited supplies of anzu bolls and strips of damp cloth would allow. Jordas looked only slightly less worried as he pushed the *notebook* back into his pack and sealed it. Even Yado was frowning.

"Well?" she asked.

"I've explained everything – he's thinking of what to do next." Jordas ran a hand through his head-fur. "Whether he believes me is another matter. The Eldest woman was there and heard it, too. Hanook may not understand the danger, but she does. She says Keramanthu is built on the highest level of the volcano, and that we were safer there."

"Are we still prisoners?" Soolkah asked.

Jordas shook his head. "But Chixi's demanding compensation from Yado and me for you. And Mnanga would speak with you."

Soolkah's heart thumped against her ribs. "I'd better go and see her, then."

"She spoke up for you while we talked to Hanook and his brothers. She said you have initiative, besides your strangeness!" Jordas murmured. "Apparently it were a compliment."

Soolkah looked up at the irony in his voice, caught the lopsided smile quirking his mouth and crinkling his eyes. *I like him,* she thought, *though I don't always know what to make of him!* "I'll go now," she said, and shouldered her pack. Quick strides took her to the Eldest woman. She stood apart from the group surrounding Hanook, only half-listening to him. As Soolkah approached, she nodded her approval.

"My amaajne Jordas said you wanted to speak with me," Soolkah said.

"I've been watching you since your return," Mnanga said. "I need your help."

"Me? But I only had my coming of age last season!" Soolkah had never understood Mnanga; she often seemed to inhabit some part of Kerui that no-one else could see. But she waited for her to speak again, keeping her bewilderment from her face.

"Look!" said the old woman, pointing at the tribespeople around them. "They don't know what to do, so they do nothing to save themselves!" she snorted. Wives were feeding husbands and children with leftover scraps of bread and fruit since the firestone was out of use. "Hanook's an old fool at times!" she grumbled. "I heard what your husbands said. We should leave this place now, while we can. If we go we might have a chance." She paused, then added, "We *must* get Hanook to listen to us. He may not take notice of a Sargussi and a stranger of no known tribe, but surely he *will* listen to me? Come! You will speak for your husbands." And with Soolkah trailing her and her sleeping cloth wrapped around her to keep out the chill, Mnanga marched through the puddle towards the Eldest man, then shouldered her way through the group surrounding him to stand before him.

"Eldest, we *must* speak!" There was more than a trace of imperiousness in her cracked and ancient voice. Soolkah remembered that Mnanga was Hanook's senior by more than five highwaters.

"Now?" the Eldest asked.

"You'll regret it if you don't!" She had the air of making a promise.

Soolkah sensed between the two Eldest tribespeople a conflict which had little to do with their status as equal leaders. She'd never understood this before.

"We'll speak in private," Mnanga added, waving her hand at the men and women around them. "Though your brothers may be present if you wish."

*

Hanook realised this was calculated, and was uncomfortably aware of his fear of losing face. "I'm sure that won't be necessary," he said, telling his brothers to eat and see that the children did. Then he sealed his mind to them.

"We'll go to my niche," Mnanga said, and led the way.

Hanook couldn't refuse to speak with Mnanga, but when Soolkah hesitantly followed he had to protest. "How is it that *two* females dare to tell me my business?"

Mnanga spread her hands wide, palms down. "When the volcano speaks a woman may touch *any* man nearby to pull him breathing from the ground – be he her amaajne or not."

Hanook snorted. "Whether the volcano speaks or not, *you* speak in riddles, Mnanga! You have less status than previous Eldest women because your husbands are all dead, you are no longer fertile, and you bore no daughters, though your age demands respect, of course. But you bring with you this woman, who has the least status of any in the tribe, a woman who owes kazmo'ra to her origin-amaaj! Why involve *her*?"

"I have my reasons," Mnanga said, and indicated that he should enter. She followed him and beckoned to Soolkah to follow. "You may sit, Eldest," she said.

"I prefer to stand," Hanook retorted. *To sit in her niche will lower my status*, he reminded himself, though his limbs were trembling. He hadn't yet

170

forgiven her for being right about splitting the tribe.

Mnanga faced him near the mouth of the niche. In the half-shadows her bony features and wrinkled skin looked grotesque. "There is a prophecy on the Wall of the Amaamu in Keramanthu," she began.

"Tell me!"

"'There shall come a time when Sargussi and Shiranu will walk together again in peace,'" she quoted, "'when the volcano speaks his wrath again.'" She indicated Soolkah. "If it is as the stranger says, it will be necessary to form an alliance with the Sargussi."

"Perhaps," said Hanook. He tried to keep his face a mask, as befitted the Eldest man, but knew his anxiety must show in his eyes. "But how would we approach the Sargussi without being attacked and eaten? There are few enough of us as it is."

"So you'll let us be killed here by a sleeping cavern that can no longer protect us from the wet and chill of Outside? Fool!" She took a step forwards. "Don't come to me tomorrow asking for more herbs for your cough, Hanook!"

Hanook stared at the two women. "What would you have me do?"

"Leave this place now, as the stranger says. Soolkah *is* their amaajni, and she and I will vouch for them. It is as they say. The time of the prophecy is come." Mnanga leaned forwards, her voice a growl of suppressed passion. "Isn't it worth abandoning pride for the survival of the tribe?"

Hanook sighed, thinking. "I fear a famine," he said at last. "If we leave this place, we go with less to eat than we came here with."

"And the longer we stay the less we leave with. But the stranger Jordas has brought food with him for all of us, and we leave here alive if we go now. If you delay we'll all die – quickly or slowly, but horribly."

Hanook glared back at her. "I hear your words, Mnanga. I'll consider them. We'll speak again soon." *My voice is strong,* he told himself. *I won't admit to doubts.* But he caught Soolkah's eyes on the hand he clenched on his spear to quell its trembling as he left.

There was a *CRACK* from above as he crossed the threshold into the main cavern again. Hanook looked up. A chunk of ice sliced through the air. Light burst against his eyes. Moisture showered him. He stepped back instinctively, staring.

The ice was already melting, and could no longer support its own weight. Smaller chunks fell as the ice rent above them. The noise was deafening. People screamed and ran in all directions. Hanook saw Soolkah grip Mnanga's wrist, then swing round, searching for her amaajnu.

The volume increased. Someone seemed to be shaking Hanook apart. It

171

took him moments to realise that his unsteady feet had nothing to do with nervousness or frailty. *It's another quake. A bad one.*

Hanook focused on his own sleeping niche and unsealed his mind. The niche was empty, but sajamu told him his brothers were both well. He spotted the precious children running for the cavern mouth with Brach and Kayas. Mnanga and Soolkah edged past him towards the tunnel, carrying their belongings.

"Go!" he signed, waving them towards the tunnel.

"Come with us," Mnanga answered.

He nodded his answer to her, then looked around. The cavern floor was awash. He headed for the tunnel mouth. It was already choked with people.

The cavern floor jerked once, twice. The rock parted. Where the firestone had been there was much boiling and bubbling of water, and with a sucking noise which made Hanook jump, it swilled down to form a whirlpool. Water siphoned into its depths.

The ground tilted. Hanook clung to the rockwall. Ahead, a man grabbed his son's arm to pull him back from the brink of the chasm. Hanook recognised him as he and the boy fled: Nulma, his friend since childhood. *I should have listened to the Humanu. I should have led everyone from this place before Mnanga ever spoke.*

Hanook hauled himself along the side of the cavern. He'd almost reached the tunnel mouth when he thought of Nahru. He turned back toward the cavern.

Confusion was everywhere. Rocks rumbled, ground together and split. The fracture spread. His eyes sought his eldest daughter.

There! He breathed out his relief. People streamed past him into the tunnel. He reached towards Nahru. The baby was tucked under one arm, screaming. She reached forwards to him –

The ground funnelled down around her. His last view of her was her agonised face. Her legs were crushed like sticks, and Gili was ground apart by tortured rocks.

Nahru disappeared.

What's that noise? Even above the din, Hanook could hear strange sounds nearby. It was several moments before he realised what the noise was.

"Nahru! Gili!" he keened. Now he realised why he'd wanted to spend time with them just lighttimes ago. *I knew I'd lose you!*

*

The tunnel walls shivered under Soolkah's hands. She hardly felt the rock scour her skin. The torrent of people in the tunnel almost engulfed her in their panic. She fought to cling to the rockwall as the tribespeople fled.

172

Ahead she saw Mnanga feeling her way along the tunnel walls after the rest of the tribe. Soolkah was surprised at the Eldest woman's agility. *She'll be all right,* Soolkah thought, and turned back to Hanook.

He stood nearby, leaning on his spear for support, staring at the cloven cavern floor like one bespelled by the maaj'nag'ur. Soolkah had to act. She grabbed his wrist and towed him behind her, unresisting. His face glistened with grief and guilt.

"It's my fault," he said. "If I'd made the people go, Nahru and Gili would still be alive now —"

She looked beyond him into the cavern. Nowhere could she see either of her amaajnu.

CHAPTER 17

THERE WAS A SOUND LIKE TEARING MEMBRANES as the cavern floor ripped again. Ground lurched and flowed under Yado, sucking him downwards.

The light brightened as he clutched at the rockwall. He missed. Half the cavern floor reared up to his left. Fear raised whorled fur upright on his skin. His instinct was to shut his eyes. Then he glimpsed Soolkah clinging to the tunnel mouth ahead and felt for the nearest solid object. His hands closed on rock, but it moved and he recoiled.

Jordas grabbed his arm. <She awaits us! Come *NOW!*>

Yado thrust the fear away and concentrated on reaching the tunnel. The floor slid away without warning into the belly of Kerui. He crawled towards the tunnel, scraping even his tough hands and knees at every movement. Time stood still around him and simultaneously flowed like molten lava.

Above he saw Jordas clinging to an outcrop, working his way around the cavern's edge. His *clothes* protected his thinner skin, but once Yado felt him bang his knee. Then Jordas heaved himself up and away from the yawning cavern floor, reaching back to pull Yado after him with a force that almost tore his arm from its socket. Yado scraped his knees over the lip of the chasm, but they staggered to the tunnel mouth, clinging to each other, the last to leave the cavern.

Soolkah *had* waited for them. Somehow she was unharmed and had resisted the tide of people. Hanook stood beside her, dull-eyed and quiescent.

Yado stared after the current of people boiling along the tunnel. "You were safer to go with them."

"I couldn't leave you two —"

"Quick! Let's go!" Jordas gasped, grabbing their arms. Yado pulled Hanook after him and they pounded along the tunnel after the tribe.

The quake was subsiding, though the ground shivered from time to time beneath their feet. Soolkah inspected the floor for cracks, then looked up and gestured. "The tunnel seems undamaged."

The tribespeople huddled together ahead. Yado stopped to listen. With no movement beneath their feet it seemed safe to rest. They sank back against the rockwall for support. Hanook leaned on his spear, gasping.

Yado saw the crowd stir as people parted to let Mnanga through.

She glanced at Hanook. "What happened to him?"

"Nahru died in the quake with her baby," Soolkah said. "I saw it happen. There was no proper burial."

"Kayas and Brach are upset as well – I guessed it must be something like this when I saw them." Mnanga went to Hanook. "Eldest, you owe the Humanu – and the rest of our tribe – kazmo'ra for not listening when he warned you."

Hanook bowed his head and slumped into a squat beside Jordas. "You were right, Humanu, and I was wrong. I'm unworthy to lead the tribe." He looked sideways at him. "As Mnanga says, I've incurred kazmo'ra to them –"

"How will you work that off," Jordas asked, "with no farm plots? And isn't your position a little different from most people's?"

"Indeed." Hanook's face was closed. Yado thought he must be eager to avoid further embarrassment. "And there is also the matter of your own status-debt to be settled. I must think on that. But none will question this. I didn't listen to you, and now my former daughter is dead." Hanook stared at the ground for some moments, tears streaking his face, before looking up at Jordas. "Well. You can work off your kazmo'ra to the tribe in this way: lead us safely out of Kerui, as you have suggested. My own, and that of my maaj'garu, will be to follow you, and be shamed by my folly in not listening to you, Humanu. The Sargussi –" He hesitated, then turned to Yado. "Your task, which I'll impose in the absence of the Sargussi Eldest, will be to warn your people of what the Humanu has told us and make sure they travel to Keramanthu. There we shall meet, and hope that the Way of the Amaaju will be enough to prevent bloodshed and further loss of life between our tribes."

"An ideal solution." Mnanga nodded her approval at Hanook. "No-one else in the tribe can take your place, but they *will* listen to the stranger." Her eyes rested on Jordas, who looked as if he were about to refuse.

<That's your purpose here, Jordas,> Yado reminded him, <to lead Shiranu and Sargussi alike to safety.>

<True.> Jordas looked at Mnanga, eyes narrowed. "I've no wish to usurp anyone in the tribe –"

"No-one else could lead us," Mnanga insisted.

"Indeed." Hanook turned to rejoin his amaaj.

"Without proper burial for she who was his daughter and her child," Yado murmured, "Hanook and his maaj'garu must grieve not just for their own loss, but for Nahru and Gili being denied the chance to join the other amaamu and be looked after by them."

Mnanga nodded her approval at his understanding. "That makes it especially bad that Gili couldn't be buried. But at least he's with his mother, and her spirit will have to do what she can for him." She sighed her sympathy, as a woman of Yado's tribe would have done.

"And me?" Soolkah asked. "What is my kazmo'ra to be? My status-debt is greater than theirs because I shamed my origin-amaaj as well as wronging Chixi's amaaj and being disloyal to the tribe."

"You will discharge all your status-debts by helping me," Mnanga told her. "It's permissible for the Eldest woman to impose kazmo'ra on a woman, and I choose this."

Yado caught Soolkah's look of relief; she'd got off lightly. But there was no time to say anything.

Mnanga sighed and squatted beside Jordas. "Shiranu men value us women for our wombs, but we're still followers, not leaders. No other man would accept my guidance for fear of seeming to be manipulated by a woman and lose status."

"And I will?" Jordas met her eyes again, an ironic smile on his mouth. "Don't forget your customs are strange to me. And I speak like a Sargussi."

"You have a Shiranu wife," Mnanga retorted, "and it will be part of her kazmo'ra to help me advise you. I'll support your leadership, and it need only be temporary. They'll follow you, Humanu!"

<Mnanga is an important ally,> Yado sent. <Even if she's to be the real power behind you, you can't ignore her help.>

Jordas regarded the old woman for a moment, then nodded. "I have respect for your common sense, Mnanga; you listened to me before Hanook did. I can do this, with your support. But we must move on immediately." He rubbed his eyes, and Yado felt his weariness as if it were his own. "And I've seen a couple of pregnant women. I want to protect them, but I'm worried they'll give birth while we travel. That were – difficult – for them and the tribe."

"There are three," Mnanga replied. "Two aren't due yet. The other could deliver any day, but I can give her herbs to postpone the birth until we get to the city."

"I want it done," Jordas said, "if it won't harm her or the baby."

"It won't, I assure you. It's my responsibility to assist at any births. Would I bring distrust and dishonour on my own head?"

"Do it, then," he told her.

Mnanga nodded and made her way back along the tunnel.

Jordas turned to Soolkah. "Help Mnanga as best you can."

"She has assistants –" she began.

Yado put a hand out to hover above her arm. "Remember, you're Jordas's link to this tribe. I'm his link to mine."

Soolkah nodded and hurried after Mnanga.

*

Aa'kam walked steadily. His stomach growled with hunger, but he knew the other tribespeople were suffering similarly.

Around them the glowcakes' light dwindled; they walked in half-darkness. Behind them the tunnels were densest black. *Kerui dies.*

Ahead, Maru hung back as if he wished to speak to him.

Aa'kam summoned up a friendly greeting as he approached. "Fair lighttime, Maru." He saw the anxiety on his face. "What troubles you?"

"My son Yado's safety. He should have returned lighttimes ago."

Aa'kam did a quick count in his head. "You're right, he's four lighttimes late. Keramanthu is eight lighttimes' march away, but he'll surely rejoin us before then." *I hope,* he added to himself.

"Mayhap he's found no food."

"You must be worried, Maru," Raaza said. She put her hand in the air above his shoulder as if to comfort him, and smiled her goodwill at him. "But for certain you'll see him soon."

Aa'kam noticed she was deliberately using the positive future tense rather than the conditional, and took his cue from her. "Walk with us," he invited. "As you've none to share with now, share your fears with us."

Maru nodded his thanks and fell into step beside them, but said no more on the subject.

Mayhap he's now so used to solitude that speaking to us gave him all he needed, Aa'kam thought. Aloud he said, "This journey has been long. We must reach Keramanthu with all haste."

Maru nodded. "But how can Yado know where to find us?"

Raaza answered before Aa'kam could. "He's your son, Maru. Allow him some good sense! He learned his hunting skills from you and your maaj'garu. He must have seen the migrations and worked out for himself where the animals and insects are headed. He'll know to follow the game!"

She always knows what to say, Aa'kam thought. It had been one of his reasons for choosing her.

Ahead the tunnel was dim. Aa'kam had to concentrate to avoid injury.

Ghura said. "Have you oil for your lampcup, Maru?"

He nodded.

Footsteps pounded down the passage towards them.

"Eldest!" It was one of the younger hunters: from Gwa's amaaj, gasping for breath. "Sent me back...to tell you...flooded."

Aa'kam halted the tribe with a hand held high. "Rest. Regain your breath."

177

"Ran most of the way," the hunter said. "Were best to find…another way round."

Ghasru masaachifar! Aa'kam thought. *Kerui floods around us, the game flees, and glowcakes die. The volcano may even speak again before long, this time to destroy us forever.*

*

Static ripped through the air as Jordas detached the holoprobe from the cable terminal. He slotted the phone connectors in place instead, aware that the tribespeople were watching with frank curiosity. Even Hanook, his brothers and Mnanga were staring at him, especially when Matt spoke.

"Jordas? Are you all right?"

"Just about." The relief of speaking English to another human, was incredible.

"Thank goodness. We thought you were all caught in the quake."

"We were," Jordas said. "The whole cavern floor went."

"How many did you lose?"

"Five people only. But two were women – and the tribe can't afford to lose females. The Eldest lost his daughter in the quake and has handed over leadership to me until we reach Keramanthu." Jordas explained to Matt how that had come about.

"But being in charge isn't a problem, is it?" Matt asked. "I don't like to say this, but in a way it's made things easier for you."

"I'm not happy about the way it's happened. But right now, Hanook and his brothers probably *are* too upset to function efficiently as leaders." Jordas hesitated. "The men who lost a brother back at the waystop with the collapsed ceiling have to be led, and can't even feed themselves."

"We saw that. Jordas, be prepared that many Naxadans will have adverse psychological reactions to the situation," came Matt's reply. "We'll arrange counselling for them when we leave Naxada."

I might need it myself if I survive that long! Jordas thought.

"Uh, Jordas…I don't quite know how to tell you this. The rescue team's being cut. It will only consist of the ship's crew, though they are experienced emergency workers."

As Matt brought him up to date on the funding problems, Jordas said, "You mean – it's just me?"

"Yes." Matt paused. "You seem to be doing all right so far."

"That's all very well," Jordas sighed, "but it's a huge responsibility for one person –"

"Marcus *is* doing his best to find out what's going on," Matt interrupted.

178

"I'm sure he'll support you however he can. It's not his fault. You all fought valiantly for the funding, but something or someone's cocked it up at the Committee." He took a deep breath. "You're not the only one who's had the rug pulled out from under their feet, and Marcus has overall responsibility for the whole project."

"I suppose so," Jordas agreed. "Well, I can only promise my best."

"You're doing great just to get so far. Now listen." Matt updated Jordas on the glacial melting they'd observed. "Surface water's entering the tunnel system and flooding the lower parts of the conduits. You *must* reach the city quickly. But we've located a zone where the rescue team can more easily cut through to the cavern where the city is – when they get here."

"Couldn't your staff do that before they get here? We could be cutting it fine if the parasitic cone blows –"

"We only have small drills for collecting rock samples, and most of the staff here are being evacuated in a few days' time." Matt hesitated. "The ship arrives in fourteen days. We estimate it'll take them ten hours to cut through to the chamber where the city is, and everyone should be off-planet two days after that."

"And the Sargussi?"

"They're headed for the city, either intentionally or by coincidence." Matt gave both sets of co-ordinates.

Jordas's smile was one of pure relief as he entered them into his map and was rewarded with a marker.

"There are several terminals in that direction – we'll be able to follow their progress."

"Thanks, Matt. They're ahead of us, but I'll make sure they get there," he said, then disconnected the phone and stowed it in his pack. He pointed on the map to show Yado as the map reference Matt had given him flashed. <Your people are at this waystop now,> he sent, <and this is Keramanthu. They *must* go there, because the Humanu will cut through to us using special diamond-tipped drills there.> He locked gaze with Yado. <Matt says the Sargussi travel as one main group, with a smaller group heading off in a different direction each lighttime.>

<Scouting or hunting,> Yado guessed.

Jordas leaned back against the rockwall, fingering his chin in thought. Moments later he realised the mannerism was one of Yado's. He straightened but dropped the map.

Soolkah picked it up. Her face wore a frown as she tried to make sense of the map. "Mnanga, you are wise," she whispered. "What *is* this?"

179

Mnanga spread her hands wide. "You should ask Jordas," she said. "Unless it's men's knowledge from his tribe."

She was peering at it upside-down. For a moment Jordas watched them both in amusement. Then he said, "Don't worry, it's not," and explained the grid system to them, struggling to find words for some concepts. He pocketed the map and slipped back into the mindspeech. <Yado, I want you to guide your tribe to Keramanthu. Return to them now.>

<A good time to rejoin them – it was time to return from my initiation quest lighttimes ago,> Yado sent. "Keep Soolkah safe for both of us!"

"That's my intention."

"One thing – how shall I prove I speak truly?"

"Show them the probe, or your waterproof jacket," Jordas suggested. "They can't ignore what they see." He shrugged. "Take food with you," he suggested, reaching into his pack for a carton of high-energy biscuits.

Yado took them, but added, "I shall also hunt." He checked his pack. "I have all I need."

He sounded decisive, but Jordas saw and felt the muscles tightening his mouth reflexively and guessed Yado felt less confident than he seemed. His emotions were closed to Jordas. *How does he do that?*

"Keep in mindtouch." Yado stood up, raising one hand.

Jordas returned the wave as Yado hurried into the mouth of the tunnel.

*

Yado was surprised to find Soolkah following him. "Are you not staying with your folk? Mnanga and Jordas need your help and it were dangerous to come with me."

"I wanted to say goodbye in private."

She's afraid I'll die unburied and haunt her. "And Jordas?" he asked.

"He'll manage," she answered with a grin. "I'll be with him for the next few days." Her arms slid round him as they stopped walking. He remembered their time alone together. "Here. I want to show you something."

"What?"

"Something Jordas does. It's nice, though strange at first." Soolkah pressed her mouth against his.

He registered shock at the contact until her body pressed closer and he felt the tingle of desire. He cast his mind back, certain Jordas had never done this while he was awake. "I know we are different," he said. "This is what he does with you?"

"One thing. Do you like it?"

"I'm not sure. Do you?"

180

"Not at first. Now, yes." Soolkah looked up at him. "I'd better go back now."

When she would have released herself he pulled her closer. "Wait," he said. "Show me again, and I'll tell you what I think when we meet again."

Just moments later, Yado released her and tramped off into the tunnel. But his smile lingered for many paces.

*

Jordas pressed his lips together and frowned. He'd felt the imprint of Soolkah's lips against Yado's as if she'd kissed *him*, and his own mouth tingled, but with the tribespeople all around he dared not touch her now he knew of the touch taboo.

She must have seen his expression. She reached out a hand, but didn't quite touch him. "It's all right, Jordas," she told him. "I'm staying with *you* until we see Yado again."

"And then, doubtless, you'll stay several nights with *him* to make up for it," Jordas retorted.

She nodded.

He turned away, trying to ignore the surge of jealousy. He felt out of sorts, frustrated at having to use the tribespeople's language; and even the sight of her hair bouncing up and down as if in agreement with her whole body failed to cheer him until he realised she must have enjoyed his kisses to teach them to Yado.

"I must speak with Matt again. Help Mnanga." He pointed. "She's talking to Hanook's *amaaj*."

Soolkah walked towards the Eldest woman.

Jordas returned to the terminal and reconnected the phone. "Matt? Yado's on his way back to the Sargussi," he reported. "Soolkah and I are travelling with the Shiranu."

"Good job Yado trusts you with his wife, eh?" Matt chuckled.

"He can hardly take her with him." Jordas changed the subject, wondering if Matt really had programmed the probes to switch off at night. "We have two probes here – can one follow Yado?"

"Connect it after this call and I'll reprogram it. Incidentally, the Sargussi hit a flooded conduit and had to revise their route."

"Oh, shit! It's starting already, then?"

"Looks like. We figure it's the quakes."

Jordas thought for a moment. "You'd know if there had been a sub-glacial eruption – Oh, excuse me, Matt."

Soolkah was hurrying over to him. "Mnanga says we must leave now."

181

"Right," he nodded. "Time to go, Matt. I'll just hook that probe back up."

*

I'll see my tribe in three more lighttimes, Yado estimated, *four if they're travelling fast.* He quickened his pace. He'd only stopped to rest at night for the last two lighttimes, driven by the twin needs to find his tribe quickly and avoid volcanic activity.

On the first day he'd found a pair of gahlu, almost as tall as him, no doubt abandoning their nest to seek higher ground like his own people. He wrestled one and took it with his knife, then brought the other down with his spear. The things squealed fit to make the ancestors walk again. They were heavy, so, unable to ignore this piece of good fortune, he boned and salted the meat to preserve it, although it cost him some time. His tribe would need any food they could get; and besides, to be counted a man among them he must return with meat. He cooked some and gulped it down, packaged the remainder in its own skin, stowed it in his pack and set off again. He'd seen no other game the whole time.

When he heard the noise, he turned and cocked his head to listen: another small tremor, but surveying behind him, he was appalled to see a crack in the floor. It reached towards him like a black, clutching finger in the ground. Heart thumping fit to burst he hurried along, stopping only to use his proximity sense to check for game or his tribe. *I'll be glad to know my people are near!* When he'd started his initiation quest – how long ago that seemed – he'd expected to kill a few animals, but much had happened since then. *Will they recognise me at all?*

The proximity sense told him he was alone, so at least they were in little danger from that last tremor. *But they could get caught in others!* As if on cue, another rumble from below. He hastened on, fearing the worst, relieved when it came to nothing.

The light increased; there was a cavern ahead. He hoped it wasn't flooded or breached.

As he rounded a bend in the tunnel, the reek of sulphur clogged his nostrils. Breathing became difficult. The cavern floor was awash with mud which bubbled and hissed as droplets fell from above. Flames stretched out claws of fire. Pallid light penetrated the ceiling; only glowcake spores could survive a cavern in full blow-out. Dead purple-brown leaves, choked with sickly smoke, thrust ceilingwards. This must once have been a Shiranu farm cavern.

Amaamu! How should I cross that? As he hesitated near the threshold, a huge bubble swelled nearby. He jumped back as it burst with a *plop*, all but

182

spattering him with boiling mud. Yado shivered despite the heat beating at him. A check with Jordas told him there was no other way to reach his tribe. *I must cross it.*

The tunnel leading out of the cavern lay paces ahead and to his left – but he'd still have to enter the stinking, boiling cavern. He peered into the steam, looking for a safe crossing.

The ground shook and growled again. Whether these were aftershocks from the quake at the Shiranu sleeping-cavern or the result of the blow-out, Yado couldn't tell. The steam cleared and he saw his crossing-place. Pulling on his waterproof *jacket*, he edged forwards. The mud would scald even his tough skin, but the *jacket* would at least protect his upper half. He wished then for Jordas's *trousers* – if a bubble burst nearby as he crossed, he wouldn't be the only one to suffer.

I have the gahlu skins, he remembered, *and string.* He set to work again. Strapped around each leg they offered protection to well above each knee. Then he tore one of the bachu skins from his sleeping-fur and packed it around the exposed sensitive areas underneath his kilt, using that to hold it in place at the waist.

He stepped onto a fallen rock column lying just inside the cavern. A second piece lay beyond, both surfaces well above the mud. From the second it would be a short jump to safety – if he could keep his balance. The airless atmosphere built up pressure behind his eyelids.

He stepped on the first half of the fallen column. It wobbled but held. He took another step. Then another. Heat clawed through the soles of his slippers, but he had to keep moving.

He reached the end of the first column's uneven surface. He lunged forward onto the second section, which lay lower in the mud, and balanced one foot on each half of the column. Above the continual plopping and splattering of the mud below him, he heard his breathing. The fear of falling pressed down on him.

He breathed in as deeply as his aching chest and raw throat would allow. *Not far now.* But a large bubble swelled nearby. He hurried along the column, anxious to avoid a serious burn. The cavern wall was close. He put out a hand to it for support.

"Yaagh!" he cried, snatching his hand away and almost losing his footing. The leather of his moccasin fizzed as his toe skimmed the surface of the mud. He'd forgotten to protect his hands. He steadied himself and edged towards the tunnel mouth. The bubble burst behind him with a vile sucking sound. Sulphur belched, but he was far enough away for it not to matter.

A quick glance told him the burn wasn't too bad. He unrolled the overlong sleeve of the *jacket* to wrap around his smarting fingers and palm, and rested for a moment. *I shall succeed! Two more steps. One... Two. Then a jump –*

He hit the floor of the passage, coughing steam and hot gas that stank of sulphur from his lungs, exhausted. Another rumble sent him scuttling along the passage, still coughing. His knees were battered and scraped even through their coverings. His hand stung ever more painfully as grit ground into it, but he dared not stop as the growl continued. Finally he dragged himself upright as the grumbling became a rush of sound from the tunnel mouth. Half-darkness descended on the passage, though glowcakes still provided some light.

A glance behind horrified him: the mouth of the passage had sealed itself shut. The rockslide rolled cobbles and boulders in his direction. Flattening himself against the rockwall, he waited for the missiles to pass him.

As suddenly as it had started, the tremor ceased. The rocks had settled for now, but he had to move on. He spat dust. He was shaking. *Shit of my ancestors, only a few moments later and I could have been killed!*

Settling the pack more comfortably on his back, he walked forwards on trembling legs.

*

Soolkah lay against Jordas. Her hair tickled his chin.

In the cavern, only the whisper of people breathing could be heard. His finger pads and the heel of his left hand throbbed occasionally, a reminder of Yado's burn. He tried to ignore the *sajamu*-pain by stroking Soolkah's back.

"How many waystops are there?" They'd walked all day, and he'd been glad to rest, though disappointed at the lack of privacy.

"Eight or nine each trip. Jordas, my course is finished. If you want to go out into the tunnel to make love, we can do that. I should think just about everyone else has!"

He stroked her face, too embarrassed to answer. *I made love with you once – was it only four days ago? It seems like an eternity since then.* "If you wish." He couldn't look at her.

She got to her feet and beckoned to him. He picked up the sleeping bag and tiptoed between the sleepers. In the tunnel, she whispered, "It *is* what I want."

Jordas was surprised. He'd half-wondered if she'd slept with him out of duty. "I'm confused," he said. "How can you accept me for your husband too, when I'm –?"

"Different?" she asked. "Here, lie down. Hold me, Jordas." She pulled him on top of her. "Perhaps it's *because* you're different. Yado is, too." She

184

put her mouth to his tentatively. "Why do you question everything so?"

"My work is in questioning things," he said. "I like to know how things work, why they happen. I know about rocks. And stars."

"*Very* arousing!" Soolkah complained. "Try this instead." She kissed him again, pressing her tongue between his lips as he'd taught her, and between the little probing movements said, "For tonight... just remember...that you're a man...and I'm a woman."

He allowed himself to respond. "Where I come from women only marry one man at a time," he said when she drew back. "I'm not used to the idea of sharing."

"But *you're* not –"

"No, I'm not already married," he said. "And I really *want* to be your *amaajne*. But it's difficult for me to share you."

"But Yado's your *maaj'gar*! That's not like sharing me with someone outside our *amaaj*." Soolkah sounded shocked. "Anyway, you don't have to for the next few days. Touch me, like the other night." She drew his hand down beneath her kilt.

She's as hot for me as I am for her! he realised. A surge of the desire he'd been trying to suppress swamped him. He touched her swelling breasts one by one with his mouth, feeling the nipples harden for him, how the glands themselves grew hot and firm and full. *She turns me on like no other woman!* His earlier jealousy was forgotten. He reached for his belt buckle and unzipped his jeans.

And moments later, plunging into her, he was aware that this time Yado was awake, and knew both joy and pleasure at their lovemaking. *Sajamu*-impressions carried both price and reward: his orgasm, when it came, was more intense than ever before, reinforced by Yado's.

Is this what it means, he wondered, *to be a* maaj'gar?

CHAPTER 18

AT DAWN THE SHIRANU ATE HURRIEDLY before moving on at Jordas's urging. For a while the tunnel ran almost straight, and the tribespeople travelled in silence with Jordas and Soolkah leading them. Mnanga followed, not complaining of the pace despite her age. Hanook's *amaaj* was close behind them, but Jordas could see that guilt fell heavily on the Eldest's shoulders; it was as if the *maaj'nag'ur* had claimed him.

Nadna, Zuas and Geem clustered around Mnanga as they walked. Jordas glimpsed Mnanga's features often cracking into smiles and thought she relished being a substitute parent. Soolkah had pointed out her four adult sons to him earlier.

When the tunnel forked Jordas consulted the map. The right-hand turning would lead the tribespeople to their next farm cavern; the left led to the city. He waved the tribespeople into the tunnel.

They'd been walking for a couple of hours when it grew darker despite the occasional glowcake colonies which lit the way. Jordas switched on his helmet lamp.

"Rest here while I go ahead. Soolkah, stay with Mnanga." He squeezed her fingers in the concealing gloom. "I shall soon return."

"Chixi scares me –" She'd confided her fear of being given to Chixi after they'd made love the previous night. A glance showed the tribesman glaring at him. "Be careful, Jordas."

"I shall," he promised, and strode forwards before she could protest. He switched on his helmet light as the tunnel dipped ahead.

Silence dripped around him, mingling with the faint hollow *plop* of water nearby. His eyes sought to penetrate the gloom. Only metres further on, his headlight beam showed him the answer to the mystery. He reached with his mind for Yado. <The tunnel's flooded ahead.>

<What do the tribe say about it?>

<I'm going back to tell them.> Jordas kicked a pebble in disgust and watched it skim the water for a few metres before disappearing. He trudged back the way he'd come, dreading breaking the news.

The tribespeople had set up camp in the passage.

"It's blocked, isn't it?" Soolkah blurted.

He could only nod; he hadn't the heart to speak.

"Could we get through by going back to the fork in the tunnel?" she asked.

Jordas brought the map out and entered the co-ordinates of the blockage on it, then finger-traced routes on it. "This turning off the route to the next farm cavern goes to Keramanthu – but I don't know how much longer it'll take."

"We could send a crew ahead to scout for blockages," Mnanga suggested.

"They don't have time to go to the city," Jordas pointed out.

"They won't need to. Your *map* shows the tunnel linking up with this one again past the blockage."

Her mind is sharp despite her age, Jordas thought. "Who are the best scouts?"

"Kottas, Deryn, Majee and Gelor. Kottas's brother Goram can tell you what they find."

As Jordas made his arrangements, he had to pass near Chixi's *amaaj.*

A hiss split the darkness. "I haven't finished with you, usurper!"

Jordas stared, heart lurching at the expression in Chixi's eyes. Dislike and distrust filled his mind. Yet the other brothers seemed reasonable enough. The youngest stared at the floor in silent, passive misery.

A flash of insight told Jordas that Chixi had become obsessed with Soolkah *because* he couldn't have her. *It must gall him to have to take instructions from me, and it makes my leadership insecure.* He couldn't show weakness; to ignore Chixi's animosity would be foolish. His responsibilities extended not just to Yado and Soolkah, but to all the Shiranu. *I must deal with it.*

He squatted beside the *amaaj* as he'd seen Yado and the others do, instinct preventing him from fingering his bruised forehead. "I shall be pleased to speak with you after our meal this darktime and seek a solution for you," he said, in as authoritative a manner as he could.

Chixi's expression became one of bafflement. But when he spoke, he matched Jordas's formality. "That would be acceptable."

Jordas gave a nod, rose, and moved on. When he'd gathered his scouts together he used the map to explain what he wanted. "Goram, stay here and tell me what they find."

Goram nodded and squatted beside him as the others set off. He was a small man with a withered arm. He beamed his pleasure that Jordas had chosen him as messenger.

Mnanga nodded her approval as Jordas settled beside her and Soolkah. "While they're gone, the tribe should rest, and we should tell stories to keep the people optimistic."

"Good idea, Mnanga," Jordas said. "Shall you tell the stories?"

"As Hanook isn't acting as Eldest man at present, I can perform this duty."

"Then please do."

Mnanga began to speak. Jordas learned first that the Chabira had been healers and diplomats while the Shiranu were stonemasons and artists and the Sargussi miners and metalworkers. Each tribe had contributed their skills to the culture of Keramanthu.

The conduit's silence formed a backdrop for Mnanga's voice, which held strength, power, and authority despite her age. She explained that where Sargussi axes and picks had cut, nothing would grow afterwards, and Jordas began to understand better the enmity between the two tribes. And as a man of an unknown tribe, he realised Chixi saw him as a threat for another reason. *It's a wonder he hasn't questioned my authority. It's probably only the fact that he fears being publicly disciplined by his enemy – or a woman – that stops him.*

"So, Shiranu, we mustn't let our chance of survival slip away!" Mnanga locked gaze with Jordas for a moment before continuing, "Listen to this man Jordas, who is of neither our tribe nor the Sargussi. Follow his instructions. Only he knows how to bring us all out of Kerui alive. Follow him as long as necessary." She cast a look around the tribe; then her eyes returned to Jordas, no doubt seeing the heat in his face at her description of him.

Goram spoke. "Thank you, Mnanga. You told an old story with new meaning."

Jordas added his thanks. "Mnanga, you've added much to my understanding of the tribespeople's problems."

Mnanga inclined her head graciously. "Would you hear more?" she asked. Jordas saw by the enthusiasm on the faces around him that the tribespeople wanted more stories, so he nodded his agreement.

Some time later, Goram gave him the message that the way to the city was clear. "My brother and his friends can return now or go further ahead."

Jordas thanked Goram. "Tell them to wait for us there." To Soolkah he said, "Check the biscuits in my pack," and shrugged it off for her. He leaned back against the rockwall, calculating the distance the new route would take them off-course. "Going this way adds two lighttimes to our journey. Mnanga, how much food have we got?"

"Enough only if we use these breadcakes of yours."

"And we might find some wild chillcaps or spicepods on the way," Soolkah said.

"We've no choice but to go back to the fork, though. I'll tell Yado."

<I approve your decision,> Yado sent.

<None to be made in the circumstances!>

<When you reach Keramanthu, make sure *you* lead the Shiranu into the

188

cavern. My tribe are never anxious to share space with Shiranu.>

*

"Corah?"

Today she wore a lime-green outfit. "Marcus, good morning!" She looked pleased to see him.

That surprised him. "It's late afternoon here."

"Of course. How are things?"

"Easier now that Jordas's replacement has arrived. And I hear he's leading the Shiranu to the city. And the refit?" he countered.

"Fine. The *Lady of the Lake* leaves Galatea Station in two days' time. E.T.A. Naxada, nine days' time."

"Terran days?"

"Naxadan. Uh, Marcus –" Corah's pile of curls quivered as she moved.

"Yes?"

"My investigations indicate something very – very *strange* going on."

"In what way?"

"Currently there are no large projects which would justify siphoning funds from one account to another. I've set the priority labelling of your project in motion – it'll go through in a few days." She paused. "I couldn't find any trace of those missing amounts in any Committee financial transactions."

"Indeed?" Marcus was conscious of a feeling of irritation. "So how do you account for the money disappearing, then?"

"That's what I'm working on now," she said. "But if the transactions are external, that gives us the whole of the Federal League to look in, just for starters! The only person who knows what's going on is Nevil Floyd, and I still haven't heard from him." She thought for a moment. "Perhaps I shouldn't say this about a colleague, but I'm certain he's involved."

Marcus privately agreed with her. "Can't you contact the bank and stop him from using the account?" he asked.

"Not without proof. I'm only the junior administrator."

Damn! thought Marcus. *It's the same old problem. The project must stay on course for success and none of us can keep this man in check.* "I appreciate your problem, Corah," he said, "but something *must* be done. I've a number of people down on that planet, all of whom could be killed when Hamorrah's fragments hit it –"

"You told me that the other day." Her lipsprayed mouth tightened. "I'm doing my best."

Marcus sighed. "Sorry. I'm not trying to stress you out. Can you find out more about this man Floyd?"

189

"I'll try, but my security clearance is limited. I had to get special clearance to run the internal transactions check."

"Just keep doing your best, then, Corah," he said. "You've done well to get this far. Call me as soon as you have anything."

He surveyed his monitor room again as Ray checked the conduit water level with Jordas's replacement. With a burst of energy Marcus requested a hololink connection to Matt.

*

"Matt? It's Marcus. I need an update on Jordas."

"He was fine when we last spoke." A movement to the side of the tank caught Matt's attention. "Uh – who's that?"

"Alleem Zheutal – Jordas's replacement."

Matt Johnson saw a shape dressed in loose drab linens which did nothing for the dark complexion. "She's tall, even for a Kiai!"

"She's efficient. Not as highly qualified as Jordas, but good."

Matt couldn't resist a grin. "Jordas has other qualifications than just astronomy and geology these days, eh?" Then he pointed towards Alleem again. "But I thought the Kiai had poison spurs on their knees and elbows."

"Only the males."

"Eh." Matt reached for the latest holovid chips. "The Shiranu made a detour due to flooding in sector B three. Unfortunately, it takes them into C three. That last quake damaged our cable system there so we won't be able to talk to Jordas until they reach the city."

"I see." Marcus didn't look best pleased.

"The Sargussi, Yado, hasn't yet reached his tribe, but we have some holovid of his journey."

"Can I see it?"

"I'll run it after this. Uh, Marcus – he's hurt."

"Jordas?"

"No, Yado."

"Seriously?"

"No. But Jordas said he already knew because he'd felt the pain of the burn."

"It's that deep, then, this telepathic link?"

"Seems to be." Matt hesitated. "Actually, it scares me. I don't envy Jordas."

*

Four lighttimes since I left the Shiranu. At least two before I catch up with my folk. They move fast. Yado hadn't even found his tribe's tracks yet, and

190

despite Jordas's reassurances that he was nearing them, he couldn't help but worry. He feared for his people, particularly his remaining father – despite the tradition of non-acknowledgement now that he was amaajne with Soolkah. *Family ties don't just disappear when you marry.*

He'd encountered several small tremors; in a dip in the tunnel he'd crossed a stretch of thigh-high water. But it wasn't deep, and there was no current, just a steady drip from overhead. The rockwalls nearby were alive with glowcakes. He'd bathed and used lather-sap to clean himself; the water had soothed his burns. He'd bound his hand with strips of bachu-skin. After that, the pain had settled somewhat, only searing when he touched something.

He trudged on. <Jordas! I've yet to find my people – are they safe?>
<Matt says so.>
Jordas had always been truthful before. Reassured, Yado turned to check for the probe that followed him. It was intact despite the rockslide.
<Then I'll walk all darktime to catch them up, if need be.>

*

Marcus had just checked Hamorrah's status when Corah's call came through.

She looked flustered and apprehensive. Her desk was more cluttered than ever. "Marcus!"

He left Ray and crossed to the holotank. "Good morning, Corah. You look upset. How can I help?"

"I tried to get an address for Nevil Floyd. In the end I had to get the Payroll Supervisor to help me."

"And?"

"No wonder he hasn't been in touch. He doesn't exist."

"How do you know?"

"The address we had for him is false. I called the number and saw the family. They have no idea who he is, and they've lived there for longer than our records indicated that he has." Corah shook her head. "I felt such a fool when they told me that."

"Surely the Committee would have checked all that?"

"Absolutely. And guess who did it."

"Hmm. Senator Hartmann?"

"Got it in one."

Marcus felt vindicated.

"That's not all. Have you checked the account? More funds fed back in yesterday. The amount matches one of the three original amounts transferred out. It suggests someone – I'm not certain who at this stage – has been

191

'borrowing' the money under an assumed name and replacing it when it's served their purpose."

"Indeed," Marcus agreed, stroking his beard. "Some use not related to the Committee, perhaps?"

"You know, Marcus," Corah said, "this is exactly why the Committee insists on two administrators for each project. So it now puts us in a difficult position because there's only me."

"What will happen?"

"I suspect the account will be frozen pending investigation. That's no use to you, though, is it? So I sent through the authorisation for the despatch of the rescue ship yesterday, complete with the Committee crew, as planned, for the evacuation of the Naxadans. It's already left, so nothing can stop it now. But I've had to report this irregularity, and have an interview with the Project Accounts Supervisor as soon as I've finished this call."

"Corah," Marcus smiled, "well done!"

Her fair skin flushed. "Thank you, Marcus. I expect an uncomfortable few minutes with her. She may want to speak to you, actually."

"She can."

"Good. We have concrete proof of irregularities now, so maybe I'll get more help in finding out where the money's going. I can't understand why it comes back, though. If it was embezzlement or fraud...Anyway, I'll keep checking. If I find anything else, I'll let you know."

*

Jordas rolled up his sleeping bag and packed it away for travel. Just then Mnanga and Soolkah returned, and squatted beside him.

"Well?" he asked.

"I've given Azhee more herbs to retard the birth," Mnanga said. "She'll hold on until we reach Keramanthu."

"We must leave, then," Jordas said. He rose and signalled for the tribe to stand. "Have you seen anything your people can use for food?"

"Not even chillcaps," Mnanga said.

Soolkah pulled a face. "At least you have these breadcakes, Jordas. They fill the belly, though they taste strange."

"My friends are still working on improvements," Jordas said, and gave the signal to go.

They'd passed through the tunnel the scouts had checked the previous day and rejoined the route to Keramanthu when light began flood in.

Jordas fished in his pack. "There's a waystop, just here." He pointed on the map.

Soolkah pulled another face. "This light hurts my eyes," she announced. "I think the ceiling is breached."

"Don't worry. I shall help you cross." He put an arm about her to usher her without touching her, as the tribespeople did. "Let's walk on."

As they approached the cavern, light washed ever more brightly into the tunnel, and Jordas became certain Soolkah was right.

"Wait here," he told the tribe. "*I'll* scout ahead this time – my eyes are used to bright light. Soolkah, help Mnanga keep everyone calm." He caught Mnanga's almost imperceptible nod of approval. *I have her respect and support.*

He strode on. It was quiet ahead. The tunnel floor was damp. Mud soon clogged the cleated soles of his boots. He hurried through floating steam patches. The light seemed bright even to *his* eyes after days underground. Metres from the tunnel mouth he heard the noise.

He hurried on and peered into the waystop. With a sucking *whoosh* the geyser spat into the air. The ceiling had long ago melted. Drizzle mingled with steam and water, in the air and on the ground. *And we have to cross! I should have sent the scouts further ahead.*

He waited, timing the interval between gushes on his wrist chronometer. The next *whoosh* came almost eight minutes later. *We should get across.* He looked for a terminal to check with Matt for tremor warnings, but the cable was broken off near the waystop entrance, sparking intermittently.

Beyond the waystop, the welcome dark of the ongoing passage beckoned. *An adult could cross in a couple of minutes, even carrying a child.* The water wasn't deep. He bent to test its temperature. *Not hot enough to scald.* Exposure had cooled it. *We could probably make it in two or three groups.* He returned to the tribe.

"Well?" Mnanga asked.

The other Shiranu looked as anxious as she did. He told them what he'd found.

"I'm willing to try, Jordas, if you think we can do it," Goram volunteered from nearby. His example encouraged others to echo him.

Jordas acknowledged his loyalty with a smile, aware that he'd made the man with the withered arm feel special and useful. *Now if only I can handle Chixi as well as that!* His stomach muscles knotted, but he ignored it, wondering if he could get the giant's co-operation by giving him some special responsibility. He had to appear decisive now. "Goram?"

Goram came to his side, and Jordas explained what he wanted him to do. Then he picked his way among the tribespeople until he came to Chixi's *amaaj*.

The big tribesman lay sprawled on his sleeping cloth, wrist laid across his eyes against the light.

"Chixi, I have need of a strong man to lead a group of the tribespeople across the cavern ahead. I thought of you."

Chixi didn't move. "You'd best look elsewhere, Humanu!" he grunted. "Travelling so hard and fast doesn't suit a sick man."

"Mayhap surviving doesn't either?" The words were out before Jordas had considered them. *If I apologise now, it will look like weakness.* "Very well, then." He turned on his heel and picked his way back through the tribespeople.

When he reached Mnanga, he said, "Who can you suggest that's trustworthy? I need a leader for the third group? Chixi refused."

"What a surprise!" Mnanga said. "Chixi has his own ideas about what the tribe should do. May the volcano forbid he ever become Eldest man – he'd lead the tribe into danger and away from safety. Why don't you ask Nulma?"

Jordas nodded. Mnanga pointed Nulma out to him. Jordas examined his pleasant, open face and knew instinctively that he could trust him. He explained what he intended, and added, "I'll take Hanook across with me –"

"Let me take him," Nulma said. "He's been my friend for many highwaters, and my *amaaj* will be proud to help his."

"Good. But I want you to lead the group as well, and it wouldn't easy to be in charge of many people."

"We'll manage."

"That's settled then." Jordas turned back to Goram, who had followed him. "Your *amaaj* shall lead the third group. I don't think Chixi will follow instructions from me."

"His *amaaj* can come with us," Goram said.

Jordas nodded.

"Better if Soolkah's origin-*amaaj* was in a different group from Chixi," Nulma murmured. "He's a vengeful, violent man."

"I shall take them across," Jordas replied. "Now, I want one pregnant woman in each group, and special care taken of them. Organise your groups and await the signal to cross in the cavern mouth." He did a head count. "Mnanga and Soolkah, come with me, and bring Azhee to tend to as necessary."

Mnanga despatched Soolkah to fetch Azhee. She soon returned with the whole *amaaj* and that of the five older adults who were caring for them. Azhee's surviving husbands' and sons' blank faces chilled Jordas.

"They're still deep in the *maaj'nag'ur*," Soolkah whispered. "But her origin-*amaaj* are looking after them, so they should also come with us."

Jordas waited until the geyser had sent steamclouds boiling into the air and hot water chasing it. As the mist began to dissipate he waved his group on. The *amaaju* stepped into the cavern, children hoisted onto their fathers' backs. When the last of them had passed him Jordas followed, flanked by Mnanga on one side, Azhee and Soolkah on the other.

All went well until they were about halfway across. Then Mnanga's foot slipped in the mud and she fell. Her face crinkled into a grimace.

"Are you hurt?" Jordas asked.

"My hip, my thigh!" she gasped. It was plainly all she could do to speak. Her thigh had folded underneath her at an angle which brought bile to Jordas's mouth as her wound leaked blood into the mud.

He checked his wrist chronometer. *Four minutes before the geyser blows again.* He held up a hand against the next group crossing. "Take Azhee across, Soolkah. I shall bring Mnanga." Soolkah nodded. He tightened the hood of his waterproof jacket and bent over her. "Mnanga, I've no choice but to lift you to get you to safety despite the pain." He scooped up the frail form in his arms. At first she seemed to weigh nothing, but soon the strain of carrying her stiffened his muscles and slowed his steps. He plodded on, not daring to stop. Her blood smeared his clothes.

A sidewise glance showed him Soolkah and Azhee following the stream of people straggling towards the tunnel. Azhee looked to be limping. But behind him the geyser gurgled. It would blow any second. His instinct was to run, but he dared not drop Mnanga.

The first scalding droplets of steam pressed at his back. Jordas felt their heat but struggled forwards, hunching over Mnanga to shield her. *Four more metres...*

The steam obscured everything. Hot water dripped from his forehead and nose onto Mnanga. *I can't protect her legs!* he thought. *One more step. One more step.*

He was ready to collapse as he reached the tunnel mouth. Gentle hands took Mnanga from him.

"Tell the next group to come," she said. "My sons will carry me."

Jordas hauled himself upright and turned to the four men who held Mnanga. "She were mayhap more comfortable on my sleeping bag. Soolkah, pass me my pack!"

He showed them how to carry her stretcherwise and waved his group down the tunnel. Then he turned. The geyser was spouting again. As it subsided he beckoned to Nulma's group. They crossed safely, avoiding the slippery spot.

Soolkah stood beside him as the tribespeople hurried past. Nulma himself brought up the rear, just as he'd done, supporting Hanook.

"Well done," he told Nulma. "But Mnanga's injured."

"The Eldest will advise you as necessary, I'm sure, if Mnanga can't," Nulma said, glancing at Hanook. "And Mnanga's assistants will heal her."

"The third group waits," Jordas said. "Stay, Hanook. Nulma, keep everyone moving." Nulma nodded, and sent the stragglers on down the tunnel to the accompaniment of the *whoosh* of boiling water. Jordas settled himself beside Hanook.

The Eldest stared at him for a moment. "You've safely brought us many *pythetu*. My judgement wasn't always good of late, and I admit I didn't know whether to trust you, Humanu. But you've proved your goodwill towards the tribe. Are we far from Keramanthu?"

Jordas showed him the map. "Several lighttimes' march still, but my tribe shall cut through the rock there to rescue us from there."

"Your tribe must be much like ours to be able to do that."

"Indeed." Jordas gave the signal to Goram's group. They crossed easily, seeking bare rock wherever possible to avoid mud churned by slippered feet.

"Keep moving!" Jordas told them. "Hanook, let's go."

"Humanu, I've watched you. I should have made quicker decisions. It's because of me that Nahru and her son died."

Jordas laid a hand millimetres above Hanook's shoulders. "You've no need apologise to *me*, Eldest," he said. "A time comes when a man must forgive even himself. Let's just get everyone out of here."

Hanook nodded.

*

The mud made it hard to keep their footing on the tunnel floor. They hadn't dared linger, even to deal with Mnanga's wounds, once the bleeding was stopped. Her sons carried her slung between them: uncomfortable, undignified, but *alive*, and Hanook knew pride that Jordas would hear neither moans of pain nor complaints pass the Eldest woman's lips.

The Humanu's words had shown him he still had worth among the tribespeople. As if from far away he heard himself urging his people on when they were exhausted, and encouraging the hopeless. He even supported Jordas as they staggered away from the geyser waystop.

They splashed through ankle-high watery mud at every dip in the tunnel, but when at darktime it inclined upwards again, Hanook and Jordas judged it safe to stop.

Before resting, Jordas, Soolkah and Hanook picked their way between the

196

resting tribespeople to Mnanga. Her two apprentices crouched beside her.

"Nazahl and Shan. They're next in line for the position of Eldest woman," Soolkah whispered to Jordas. "They learn the healing lore from her. She's in safe hands."

Hanook had forgotten how little the Humanu knew of their ways.

"Are there others who could carry her when we move on, so her sons can rest?"

He seemed very concerned about Mnanga. *Of course,* Hanook remembered, *she helped him and supported his leadership.*

"We would be glad of a rest," Mnanga's eldest son murmured. "It's difficult to carry an injured person, though we want to save her pain. I'll ask if another *amaaj* will take turn and turn about with us."

"Good idea," Hanook approved, and suggested Nulma's or Rejaaf's *amaaj*.

Jordas passed a package of his breadcakes and the *pills* which went with them to Mnanga's sons. "These'll give you extra energy – eat them instead of your own food tomorrow morning."

Mnanga's eldest son dipped his head and thanked Jordas.

Jordas and Soolkah moved among the tribespeople, offering the breadcakes to each *amaaj*. They were accepted gratefully until they came to Chixi's *amaaj*.

Chixi struck the pack out of Jordas's hand. "You promised to speak to me, but instead you bring me poison!"

Jordas's mouth tightened. "It's not poison," he said, picking up the packet.

"Thank you," Jeene said, holding out his hand for it. "Our supplies *are* getting low." He stowed it in his own belongings, ignoring a glare from Chixi.

"Don't expect *me* to eat that!" Chixi's mouth set in a line. "We'll speak now. You owe me *kazmo'ra* for the loss of my bride."

Jordas turned to Soolkah. "Get help to finish the food distribution."

"I'll ask Gujas," Soolkah said, and shouldered Jordas's pack.

"My daughter Zuas will help too." *So the Humanu is trying to solve the problem he and the Sargussi created?* It made sense, Hanook thought, for Soolkah to be elsewhere while he and the Humanu negotiated with Chixi.

"Does your custom not allow Yado and me to perform some service for the good of the tribes as settlement of status-debt?" Jordas asked.

"It does." Hanook spread his hands. "Chixi has no real claim since you're taking us to safety. But I understand his anger and humiliation. No Shiranu woman has ever fled marriage before," he said. "Chixi's situation must be resolved. But how?" He thought for a moment before asking Jordas, "What

197

would *your* people do in such a situation?"

The Humanu hesitated. "Our society is different from yours," he said at last. "Even when a marriage agreement is broken, it's hard to establish legal rights against the other person."

"You could be lying," Chixi said. "What do *we* know of your customs?" He paused, considering. "After all, you may look like a Chabira, but you speak like a Sargussi!"

"I'm no liar," Jordas answered. "But I can't prove it, so you must take me on trust. I'm saying only that when I was in your position there was nothing I could do about it."

Chixi looked down at his hands, big and square like the rest of him, with slabs of fat packed around them except at the knuckles. "I've waited a long time for a woman," he said. "My brothers all had to grow up."

"That's the custom?"

Hanook nodded. "You'd have had to wait until the Sargussi was old enough to be married, had he not already had his coming-of-age."

"I never realised –" Jordas began.

Hanook stopped him with a hand laid above his arm, then turned back to Chixi. "Consider this, Chixi: Soolkah's too independent for your *amaaj*."

"I've lost status by her actions. Now no *amaaj* will give me their daughter."

"I can understand your anger at that." *And after all, why should his brothers be punished too?* Hanook couldn't help feeling sympathy for them, perhaps more so than for Chixi. "I would be happy to perform negotiations for your *amaaj* should you wish it. But the marriage between Soolkah and the two foreigners is a fact, and they are discharging their *kazmo'ra* on instructions from myself and Mnanga."

Chixi struggled to his feet. His face twisted with fury. "I should have known it would be useless to speak to you," he muttered, impaling Jordas with his gaze.

CHAPTER 19

"THIS TASTES GOOD!" Aa'kam turned to Raaza, the chunk of meat on his two-pronged metal eating-fork dripping juices down his fingers.

She nodded her acknowledgement of the compliment. The whole amaaj was seated cross-legged inside their sleeping niche.

"How far to the city?" Ghura asked.

"Two lighttimes' march at this pace," Jecban said, between chewing.

A commotion at the main cavern's threshold brought them to their feet.

Aa'kam peered into the gathering darktime. "I hope the hunting party made many kills – supplies are short again." He sat down to continue his meal.

"Eldest!"

Aa'kam knew the voice, yet couldn't place it. He looked up again, teeth poised mid-bite. A man leaned against the rockwall; familiar yet a stranger at once. His face glistened with sweat and his chest heaved as if he'd run hard.

"Yado!" Jeeban exclaimed. "See how his legs are bound with hides!"

"His face is that of a man now," Raaza approved.

"I'm back... but I've need for rest."

Aa'kam bade him sit with them. "Raaza – bring meat and water for this man." He deliberately used the word *man*, for had he not himself circumcised Yado just lighttimes ago, using the ceremonial obsidian knife kept for that purpose only?

Yado sank to the ground.

"Jeeban, fetch Maru," Aa'kam added. "He would want to know Yado's safe."

Jeeban departed, and Raaza brought a watercup and meat.

Yado's breathing still hadn't returned to normal when he said, "I ran to catch you up." With deliberate movements he removed his backpack and leaned against the rockwall. "We must go to the city."

"Because of the flooding? We know," Aa'kam said.

"Not just that." Yado gulped water, pointing to his pack. "In there – meat for the tribe!" He wiped his chin, then added, "Well? Am I counted a man now?"

For a moment Aa'kam was taken aback by this directness. *Yado seems different, but then, he's been reborn as an adult.* "The meat's most welcome." He turned to inspect Yado's kill, feeling his gaze on him, then allowed a smile to spread over his face in assent.

Yado's grin answered him.

"Gahlu?"

Yado nodded. "There are two skins." He pointed to each leg in turn. "But they're somewhat...singed – I needed to protect my legs as I crossed a cavern in full blow-out."

The others' eyes had grown round with wonder.

"You must truly be a great tribesman, Yado," Raaza said, echoing the thoughts of the others. "All the girls shall want to marry you, despite your status as a man without maaj'garu!"

Yado was too busy chewing meat and gulping water to reply, but Aa'kam thought he saw him stiffen. But then Maru appeared with Jeeban, and made as if to gather his son in his arms.

Yado held up his hands to ward him off. "Maru," he said, "would you shame me? I'm a man now!"

"How did you find us?"

"I shall tell you when I've recovered...I've need of bathing." Yado gulped water.

Raaza gave him some flakes of lather-crystal. "This cavern has a hot spring," she said, pointing to it.

"And when you're rested we shall hear a story in your honour," Aa'kam promised.

"Come with me, Maru," Yado said. "We shall speak whilst I bathe."

His father followed him. Shortly they returned, Maru looking thoughtful.

"Come," Aa'kam said. "Let there be a story."

Yado followed him into the main cavern. Aa'kam raised his arms to draw the tribespeople's attention. "Sargussi," he began, when everyone was watching him, "Yado, son of Maru, the living, and Yeng, Pali, Zaku and their wife Ati, now amaamu, has this lighttime returned an adult.

"His tale is a strange one, but first we shall hear the story of Gan, the first Sargussi metalworker, who became our finest warrior, in honour of Yado, now a man of the tribe, not just the son of Maru." Aa'kam stepped back and Jeeban took his place.

The tribespeople settled down on cured skins on the ground. Jeeban beckoned Yado and Maru to sit beside him, Aa'kam, Ghura and Raaza. Yado sat with the straight back befitting a man reborn, listening as Jeeban told how Gan left the tribe a boy on an initiation quest and returned a man, when the tribes lived Outside. Then, women were plentiful enough to have only one husband, so Gan had just one father; and until they came to Kerui, no circumcision was required. Jeeban told how Gan had discovered metal and returned to his tribe with a knife made of it. While away, he'd discovered that with fire the metal could be worked as required. So the Sargussi had brought their metalworking skills with them into Kerui when Outside became too cold for the tribes. Soon the tribespeople's skin toughened against the sharp lava inside the tunnels. Yado had heard this traditional tale many times when reborn youths returned to the tribe as men.

But after the fall of Kerui, the Shiranu need for food had brought conflict over the very caverns which yielded metals to the Sargussi. So the tribes fought again, as they had Outside. Sargussi slaughtered Shiranu until Gan's descendant, Gan the Peacemaker, made pact with the Shiranu. Then the Sargussi sought the tunnels north of Keramanthu, while the Shiranu stayed to the south. "This," Jeeban finished, "was needful for both tribes to survive, as is the rebirth of boys as men to be hunters and warriors for the tribe." He turned to Yado. "Now you shall hear the story of how this reborn son of the Sargussi tribe braved fire to rejoin us."

Yado stood and looked around him. "Sargussi," he began, "unlike Jeeban I am no wordsmith, nor a weaver of tales as the Shiranu are of threads. I can tell you only the truth, and a strange story it is indeed." He inhaled deeply to steady his racing heart, aware that much rested on the delivery of his story. "Let me remind you that when my maaj'gar Uvvuz died two highwaters ago, in a mining accident, he suffered greatly. It took him almost a lighttime to die. I felt it all, and on my return from the maaj'nag'ur, my status was reduced within the tribe. Such a man will never be permitted to wed." He raised his shoulders, then let them fall.

It was a gesture Aa'kam neither recognised nor understood. He leaned back against the rockwall, weariness descending on him. But he found himself sitting up and listening intently as Yado described his meeting, first with Soolkah of the Shiranu, then with a stranger of no known tribe. "Also, I met a man from Outside. Different from us, neither Sargussi nor Shiranu, though his head-fur curls like a Chabira's. He's my – friend, Jordas of the Humanu tribe, who are Outside and waiting to help us now as Kerui dies. He is *our* friend, come to help us all."

"But there *is* no-one Outside," Aa'kam said.

"Not of our people," Yado agreed. "But there *are* men from another place there."

"Impossible. How could they survive the cold?"

"Their coverings keep them warm – here, I shall show you." Yado reached into his pack and pulled out something. As he unfolded it Aa'kam saw it was dark blue. It rustled as he touched it. "This is a *jacket*. Jordas gave it to me to keep warm and dry." He sprinkled water from his cup on it. Incredibly, the silver droplets simply rolled off. "The stream levels are rising because the ice above the volcano is melting and entering through cracks in the rocks. Jordas told me. He says Kerui shall flood, and that we must leave with him to survive."

"Were he lying –" Aa'kam began.

"I *know* he speaks truth."

"How?"

Yado smiled, though his eyes were shadowed. "I gained a maaj'gar on my quest. I share again, with this Jordas. That's how I know to trust him."

Aa'kam looked at each of his brothers in turn, feeling the surprise spreading from them and stiffening on his own face. *I've never had reason to doubt Yado's word, single brother though he now is,* he reflected. *But if this is true his status within the tribe must surely change.* "How can he be your maaj'gar?" he demanded at last.

Yado made the palms-down handspread to show lack of understanding. "His sharing differs from ours," he admitted. "But let me tell you why we must leave here with him. His people shall rescue us."

It all sounded very plausible, but on Aa'kam rested responsibility for the safety and well-being of the whole tribe. He couldn't just take the word of a stranger – could he? "Why should we trust a man we've yet to meet?"

"You have no choice," Yado said, "or all of us will die."

"And these – Humanu – from Outside, you say. Do they make conditions for our rescue?"

"Only that the Shiranu go as well."

Aa'kam saw Jeeban's eyebrows shoot towards the ice ceiling. "How shall we fight the Shiranu, if they have made alliance with the Humanu?" Jeeban asked. Aa'kam found himself adopting a fighter's stance, and Ghura too stood awaiting combat instructions.

"There is no need for battle," Yado said. "D'you not remember the Prophecy of the Seer of Keramanthu?"

"I do." Aa'kam inhaled and forced himself to relax. *Allowing Yado to tell his story to the whole tribe was unwise, despite custom.* "That's enough!" he barked, standing in an easy movement despite bones that ached when the highwater came. "I'll hear no more lies!"

"They're truth," Yado protested. "I *am* amaajne –"

"With a Shiranu woman, one of our enemies?" *There are six unwed Elder brothers in the tribe. The next thing shall be that they all want to become amaajne with Shiranu women.* "And maaj'gar to a man of a tribe we've never even heard of before? Bah!" Aa'kam spat on the rocks by Yado's feet.

Yado jumped back. "If I'm lying, how do you explain the *jacket*?"

"I shall think more on this." Aa'kam regretted humiliating Yado publicly after welcoming his return so graciously, and sought a way to lessen his disgrace. "You wandered in the maaj'nag'ur for many lighttimes after Uvvuz died – all know you were almost driven mad by his death. Going on an initiation quest alone, without maaj'garu to share with, has turned your mind." *Or you sought to regain status by lying, one or the other.* But Aa'kam wouldn't further shame him by saying this aloud; it was bad enough that he must touch him publicly. He seized his arm and marched him away from the tribespeople towards his father's sleeping niche. "Ghura, Jeeban! Maru!"

"I'm sound in mind, and I speak truth. You *must* listen to me!" Yado tried to push his hand off his arm, but Ghura leapt to his other side before he could run, and multiplied the indignity by pinioning his arms behind his back. Yado's head drooped in shame.

Maru had followed, and stared at Yado, gaping.

"Now listen," Aa'kam said. He signed for Ghura to release Yado. "Do as I say and I'll not tie you."

Yado's only reply was a nod.

"Your father Maru will be responsible for you and keep you confined. You'll speak only to him and me." *That should prevent other tribespeople from being infected by this madness! I must protect the tribe.* But Aa'kam couldn't quite rid himself of the thought that he might be doing Yado an injustice; there must be some explanation for the *jacket*, which after all didn't look like Shiranu work. *And if the Shiranu are going to Keramanthu as well, we shall learn the truth when they arrive.* It looked as if Gan's pact was about to be broken. Shiranu greed for land rivalled the Sargussi need for it.

"What about the Prophecy?" Yado demanded. "Is war with the Shiranu more important to you than the survival of our tribes?"

Aa'kam smiled, but even he knew it was just a baring of his teeth. "What *about* the Prophecy?" he said.

*

As the Sargussi marched on, Matt noticed Yado's hands were bound. Just that morning he'd played back the previous day's holovid. Yado's return hadn't looked at all auspicious, though Matt couldn't be certain of the exact events until he spoke to Jordas.

So he mentally reviewed the evacuation that morning. It had been hard to say goodbye to his team, knowing he might never see some of them again. They'd worked together for the last four years.

A knock on the door interrupted his reverie.

203

"Matt?" John Wolfe put his head round the door. He was aptly named; a shaggy mane and beard covered most of his head and face. His deep-set eyes usually twinkled, but today they blazed anxiety.

"What is it?"

"We've some more exact projections...They're – not good."

"Let's hear them, then." Matt knuckled his spectacles into a more comfortable position on his nose, interlaced his fingers and leant back in his seat.

"Alleem Zheutal – that new woman – compared calculations with me," John said. "She's good. We came up with the same figures independently. Is the rescue ship still due to arrive here next Tuesday?"

"Yes."

"That's the day we think the floodwater entering the tunnels will peak."

Matt snapped upright in his seat. "Damn! Are you sure?"

"Positive. The meltwater's flooded the lowest caverns."

"Jordas reported flooding at lower levels two days ago."

"The water has to percolate down before the levels rise in the tunnels, but it will enter the higher cave levels next Wednesday. They must all be out by then. *And –*" John paused. "That's when the first fragments fall."

"Damn! It'll take at least twelve hours to cut through to them." Matt got up to pace round the room. "It doesn't leave us much time."

"We always knew it'd be tight," John reminded him.

"That's not the worst of it. We can't warn Jordas till he reaches the city."

*

"I must speak urgently with Howerd Asthorn, please," Marcus said.

"I'm his personal assistant. How can I help?" The woman on the hololink was American, probably just over forty, and looked efficient; but he wasn't about to confide in her.

"You can't." Marcus's frustration was infinite; he'd been passed around several departments. "My business is with the Committee's Chairman alone, and I doubt he'll be happy if I'm fobbed off again, once he hears what I have to say."

The assistant pursed her lips. "I see," she said. "And you are?"

"Doctor Marcus Carlin, from the Naxadan resettlement project," he said. "And it's *very* urgent. You could end up with another Mourang unless I speak to him immediately."

"Who is it, Marie?"

The owner of the voice couldn't be seen, but surely it must be Howerd Asthorn?

204

The woman's mouth shut with an audible snap. "Dr Carlin," she said. "He wants to speak to you urgently about the Naxada project. Isn't that the one where the bank account has been frozen?"

"So I'm told. Put him on, please."

With an abruptness which glitched the image, she transferred the call. Howerd Asthorn was seated at a large desk, but he emerged from behind it and perched on the edge, crossing one long leg over the other.

At last! Marcus thought. He did his best to summon a smile and managed to greet Asthorn civilly.

"I know why you're calling," Asthorn said. "You can't contact Corah Whitley."

"She hasn't answered or returned my calls."

"She was suspended two days ago when we froze the account pending investigation."

"That's why I'm calling. I need access to the account for project purposes."

Asthorn turned aside for a moment, checking something in his monitor cube. Marcus studied him: tall, black, solid-framed, with grizzled clipped hair. The flare of his nostrils suggested a remoteness which sat well with his business-like manner. "I gather she authorised despatch of a ship after investigations had already been instigated."

"By both Miss Whitley and myself." Marcus outlined the reasons for the hasty despatch of the ship, then added, "There's only one other person with access to that account, apart from the fictitious Nevil Floyd, and that's you, Mr Asthorn."

He inclined his head. "As you say. I understand the urgency of this mission, and very much regret not being here to assist you earlier. We'll unfreeze the account and reinstate Corah. We've completed the investigation into her actions and I'm satisfied she acted in the best interests of the Naxadans." He paused, resting his chin on steepled fingers. "Our next task is to look into the activities of whoever's masquerading as Nevil Floyd. I'll be giving it my personal and immediate attention."

"Thank you." Marcus felt some of the tension leave his shoulders.

"Like you, I want to know why a non-existent project administrator has been appointed."

"I know very little about internal procedures in the Committee," Marcus admitted. "I'm a scientist, with experience of project management. Who appoints the administrators?"

"The investigating Committee representative – Senator Hartmann, in this case." Asthorn exhaled a breath which wasn't quite a sigh. "He's on another assignment at present, but I'll speak to him as soon as possible."

"I see." Marcus thought for a moment. "Then surely, that means –"

Asthorn raised his hands in a warding gesture. "I never jump to conclusions, Dr Carlin. Without definite proof I can't say who's been raiding the account. But I'll find out, and let you know."

*

Aa'kam was preparing a bachu-skin when the Shiranu arrived.

The tribe had occupied the space before Keramanthu for three days now. At the mouths of the five tunnels into the huge cavern stood guards. They were changed regularly, and uncircumcised boys ran messages between them whenever necessary.

Now one such approached him. Aa'kam recognised F'dal, youngest son of the amaaj of Aneera, Eldest woman of the Sargussi. "Eldest, there are Shiranu!" he signed.

Aa'kam passed his tools to Raaza and stood up. "I'll come."

F'dal led him outside the cluster of skins marking the sleeping-places of individual amaaju. Aa'kam saw nothing that would indicate they were under attack. He stopped and felt for the presence of Shiranu with his proximity sense. *They're coming.*

Aa'kam hurried to the tunnel mouth F'dal indicated and peered past the guard. Sure enough, though they moved with their accustomed silence, the passage was choked with people. White-furred, pale-skinned – other than the man leading the column, who was almost a head taller than the rest and had dark, curling head-fur – the Shiranu limped towards the tunnel mouth.

"Fetch more warriors. Bring Yado," Aa'kam signed. The boy left, but Aa'kam's attention was for the advancing tide of people. He signed to the guard to stand aside for the Shiranu to enter the cavern.

As Aa'kam's warriors took up positions behind him, Yado followed F'dal. His face wore the look of inward concentration of a man mindspeaking. *So Yado spoke truth.* "Stop him!" Aa'kam signed.

The man nearest Yado swung the butt of his belt knife. The blow partially stunned Yado. He collapsed onto his knees.

Aa'kam noticed movement at the tunnel-mouth.

The first of the enemy stepped into the cavern; ancient, leaning on his spear for support. Aa'kam saw the Shiranu Eldest clearly. He gave the signal.

The Shiranu never faltered. The Eldest stepped forwards, ignoring the approaching Sargussi.

Behind him, the stranger from Outside staggered into the cavern, hand against his head, half-supported by a young Shiranu woman. A cluster of armed warriors followed.

Aa'kam smiled to himself. His strategy had worked. The Shiranu had walked into a trap. *And because they travel in their amaaju, those who follow can have no idea of that.*

Behind him a curve of warriors with metal spears and knives formed up to surround the Shiranu.

CHAPTER 20

AS THE SHIRANU POURED INTO THE CAVERN, their exhausted faces and drooping shoulders told Aa'kam that fatigue and desperation, not hope or courage, had led them here. *Some can barely stand. No victory, that.*

Around the Shiranu Eldest, pale faces showed shock at the camp already set up on the slope before the city.

"What's this?" cried a Shiranu who was taller even than the Humanu, and much overweight.

He has the swelling sickness, Aa'kam thought, *like a few of our people. But he is a giant as well.*

The man pushed into the circle of men around the Shiranu Eldest. "These are Sargussi!"

"I *know*," the Eldest said. "Take your own place, Chixi!"

The Humanu stranger could stand without support now. He scanned the Sargussi as if seeking someone. When he spotted Yado, on his hands and knees beside Aa'kam, he pushed aside spears to reach him. Aa'kam watched him approach, taken aback by his audacity and apparent disregard for his own safety – and that of his maaj'gar.

"Well met, Elder brother!" Yado murmured, climbing to his feet. As the Humanu approached, he turned to Aa'kam, scowling and rubbing his head. "Why, Eldest?"

"If you spoke truth before, you would have warned him of our trap," Aa'kam said.

"The pain warned me of *something* wrong," the Humanu said. "Let Yado go!" He turned and beckoned to the Shiranu Eldest.

The Eldest drew breath, pulled his obsidian knife from his belt and held it ready to strike. Then he stepped past the spears, ignoring them as the Humanu had.

"This is Aa'kam, Eldest of all the Sargussi maaj'garu," Yado said, as the Shiranu Eldest arrived. He introduced him in like manner.

Aa'kam was relieved to see Hanook push the knife back in his belt. "You know him?"

"I spent a darktime or so with the Shiranu before rejoining you."

"And they let you go?"

"It was their wish that I return to warn you about the coming death of Kerui," Yado said.

"And this stranger, neither Shiranu nor Sargussi?" Aa'kam queried,

208

pointing to the Humanu.

"He is my Elder brother, Eldest Aa'kam. My maaj'gar. His name is Jordas." Aa'kam could see they were mindspeaking.

"The Shiranu have need of food and rest. We walked for many lighttimes and faced many problems." The Humanu looked worn out himself. "The tunnels flooded behind us. We must settle peace between the tribes now. There can be no more fighting if both tribes would survive."

Aa'kam noticed his speech had the same inflections as any Sargussi's.

"You told me of this man," Aa'kam interrupted, "and said he came to save us." He looked first at Yado, then the Humanu. "I can see he is your maaj'gar, but how? Uvvuz is dead, and this man is truly of a different tribe, as you explained."

"It's true he's not my gare," Yado said, locking gaze with Aa'kam. "But he *is* my maaj'gar." He hesitated, then added, "Speak with him, Eldest. Speak with him or Sargussi and Shiranu alike shall perish, even as the Chabira did."

"I shall." Aa'kam faced Hanook. "Let the Way of the Amaaju be the cause of peace between us."

Hanook nodded. He looked from the Humanu back to Yado, frowning.

"I owe you kazmo'ra, and an apology, Yado," Aa'kam said, inclining his head.

Yado acknowledged that with a nod.

"Which is your amaajni?"

For answer, Yado beckoned to the young Shiranu woman who had supported the Humanu into the cavern. Aa'kam's gesture lowered the spears, and she stepped between them as the Eldest of her tribe had done, head held high. Yado ushered her to stand between him and the Humanu. "Jordas and I are amaajne with Soolkah of the Shiranu," he said. Pride empowered his voice. "We shall be the bond and means of peace between our three peoples."

As she approached, Aa'kam studied her narrow face with its high forehead, the deep green eyes and full mouth, the determination in her jaw. *A good choice of woman – for a Shiranu.*

It went from silence in the great cavern to everyone talking at once. Aa'kam held up his hand for quiet. As he did so, a cry of agony rang out from the back of the Shiranu group.

Soolkah turned. "It's time for Azhee's baby to come."

Aa'kam followed her line of sight. Several Shiranu were clustered near the tunnel mouth. One was hugely pregnant, and had sunk to her knees, supported by an old woman. Nearby stood two men and two boys, their faces blank as if mindlost in the maaj'nag'ur. In the foreground an ancient, shrunken

209

woman lay on a thick blue cloth carried by four Shiranu men. Her kilt was blood-stained.

"Mnanga, Eldest woman of the Shiranu," Yado announced.

"A woman of great good sense and much bravery," the Humanu Jordas added.

Mnanga looked up at her attendants. "Sons, carry me to Azhee *now!*" she commanded, voice strong despite her appearance.

"Let them make camp apart from the Sargussi place," Jordas suggested. "I shall see both tribes are treated fairly if they will also treat each other with fairness."

It was up to Aa'kam to make a decision. He struggled for a moment before words flowed into his mouth. "I see you speak truth, Yado. As this woman is to give a child to your tribe, Eldest Hanook, I agree: let the Shiranu set up their camp apart from ours." He gestured, and his warriors lowered their spears and sheathed their knives.

Hanook addressed his people, ignoring the Sargussi watching to see what would happen. "Make camp here." He indicated a part of the flat space which was unoccupied.

"Humanu, I would speak with you," Aa'kam said.

"I too would speak with you, Eldest Aa'kam," Hanook echoed, before turning himself to the task of setting up camp.

Aa'kam stood watching for some moments, impressed in spite of himself. First Hanook selected the site, some way from the established Sargussi camp, yet as near as safely possible to the higher ground of the ruins. He issued a stream of instructions to various tribe members. The first Shiranu to be laid down was Mnanga, the chosen place having been swept clear of stones. Beside her a place was made for the pregnant woman. As she passed, Aa'kam saw Azhee's leg was bound with a strip of cloth.

"She is injured too?" he asked.

"Scalded," Jordas replied, "on the way here."

One of Mnanga's sons hurried up. "Mnanga requests Soolkah act as her messenger," he said.

Jordas consented with a nod. "I would know how Mnanga is, too," he murmured to her.

Soolkah dipped her own head and followed Mnanga's son to her side.

Aa'kam watched her walk away. "We know Kerui is dying, Humanu, and Yado told me of you. He says you can help, but how?"

For answer, Jordas shrugged his backpack off and pulled out a flat greyish object. "I'm here to help both tribes," he said. "Look." He gestured for the two

Eldest men to gather round him.

Above the grey thing a picture was forming, as if in the air: insubstantial as smoke but rounded as if real. The Humanu used it to explain why the tribes must leave Kerui. The images changed as he spoke. It took some time, but Jordas seemed to have much patience, and explained until both Aa'kam and Hanook understood.

"Well enough," Aa'kam said. Now recent events made sense, and he knew the Humanu was sincere. "My people shall eat. After that we shall tell stories as always, so that these new things seem less strange to them."

"Good. Shall we speak again later?" asked Jordas.

"Were there need."

Both Eldest men acknowledged each other with nods.

"I must speak with my friends," the Humanu said as he faced Hanook. "But my helpers, Soolkah and Zuas, will distribute food to help yours go further, so your people may eat and tell their own stories." He inclined his head to Aa'kam and walked away with Hanook.

Aa'kam spotted Yado speaking with Maru and hurried over to them. "I owe you status-debt," he told Yado. "I silenced and imprisoned you because I doubted your story, but you still have the right to tell it to the tribe." A public apology would entail loss of status but there was no help for it. He'd been wrong, and the whole tribe could have suffered because of him. "Come," he said, avoiding touching Yado as he ushered him into the centre of their camp. "Tell your story to us. We *can* only believe you now."

Yado stared at him for a moment, then accepted. He told his tale while the Shiranu storyteller, whom Aa'kam had learned was called Kayas, told another story in the camp opposite. Aa'kam listened with one ear. In the background came the occasional grunt of pain from the woman Azhee. Her husbands and sons sat nearby, deep in the maaj'nag'ur and oblivious to her struggle to give birth.

"Shiranu!" Kayas began. "This cavern reminds me of a story we should hear, that of how our amaamu learned to cultivate the plants of Kerui in this very place." He flung his arms wide, turning to face each corner of the cavern. "I never expected to see this city, though I have heard stories of it many times. So it's fitting that Chella and Dayu and Raaza should speak to us all through me this darktime."

"When we lived Outside, and even when we arrived in Kerui, all men ate meat, fruit and vegetables. And our three tribes were at war, raiding each other for food, or women, or weapons, and sometimes just for killing. But Mekar of the Chabira had a vision that men of all tribes could walk together."

Kayas glanced round, and his gaze included both Shiranu and Sargussi.

"Mekar had the gift of future-sight, and of speaking to show both sides of an argument. He became known as the Seer of Keramanthu, partly for uniting the tribes, partly because of his visions. He inspired the carving and painting of the frieze which shows our history and his prediction of our future – the Prophecy. So for many highwaters Chabira, Sargussi and Shiranu lived peacefully together.

"Now all the tribes changed their ways while in Keramanthu. In Kerui our ancestors found many animals, plants, the glowcakes, and insects. The Shiranu and Chabira soon became allies through a shared interest in growing plants: the Chabira for herbs for healing and cooking, and our folk for growing plants for food. And Chella is the man of our tribe who first learned to feed the glowcakes with insect husks to make them produce more light, and spores for new glowcakes. He learned that insects feed on the yellow rock, and that plants receive light from glowcakes and heat from the volcano. And those insects help the plants to bear fruit, even as Azhee shall bear fruit this darktime."

The whole tribe turned to look at Azhee. She was lying on her side, exhausted. *But had she been Sargussi, my people were proud of her,* Aa'kam thought, *for she makes little noise.*

Kayas's next words surprised and pleased him.

"Now let me tell you of Raaza, the Chabira Eldest woman of that time. Raaza is known to all for her skill in herb-lore; she discovered the healing powers of Kerui's herbs. And I hear from Yado that though Raaza is today the name of the Sargussi Eldest's amaajni, her skill with herbs is no less than her namesake's."

When the storyteller turned in his direction, Aa'kam inclined his head to acknowledge the honour done to both his amaaj and his tribe. Yado had finished his tale and the Sargussi wondered at its strangeness, but Aa'kam knew Yado's exploits would become part of the body of folk tales of the Sargussi in future years.

"Dayu," Kayas continued, "was the Sargussi who led his tribe to eat only meat, partly because each tribe has its own skills, and Sargussi have never grown food. Thereafter, many Sargussi became aggressive, and when the plague attacked the population of Keramanthu, only the resistance of the Shiranu stopped them from attacking Chabira farm caverns for their metals, as they lay fallow. So this place was the scene of a great battle between Sargussi and Shiranu. Many died that lighttime."

Aa'kam could see that some of his younger warriors were restive. Puffed up with pride at Yado's tale, they'd relished slaughtering Shiranu and had been disappointed, and hefted knives and spears at Kayas's words. Aa'kam stood up. "Lay down your weapons," he hissed. "I have made one public apology this darktime – I shall be displeased to make another to Eldest Hanook, a man with status equal to mine."

The young warriors mumbled amongst themselves, then did as he bade them.

"Now always before," Kayas said, "we have seen the volcano as life-giver more than the Sargussi view of it as destroyer –"

"What do *you* know of our views, Shiranu?" called out one of the younger men.

"How should a Shiranu presume to understand a Sargussi?"

Aa'kam frowned at this rudeness; his stare should have quelled them.

But Kayas ignored the interruption. "Yet now we must view the volcano differently. Kerui floods. The glowcakes die. The ice roofs of our caverns crack open. Tremors destroy our sleeping caverns. We are no longer safe here. The volcano shall speak again, and vomit forth fire to burn us even as we drown."

Although his voice wasn't loud, he'd drawn the attention of Shiranu and Sargussi alike. Aa'kam was impressed once again.

"The reason why Mekar was known as the Seer of Keramanthu has this lighttime become plain to both tribes: peace between our two tribes when we leave this place, as he foresaw, will be mutually beneficial. But peace is made by people, and only they can change their hearts and minds – and only then if they *wish* to make peace."

His words slipped into a silence broken only by a groan from Azhee's direction. Aa'kam decided it was time he spoke of his considerations during the story-telling, and rose. He sought the Humanu, who was standing near the mouth of one of the tunnels, speaking though none was near him. "You know that this man Jordas, the maaj'gar of Yado, has come to lead all our people to safety," he said. "When he returns, I shall ask him to explain to you what he told me."

*

"Yes, Matt, we're here," Jordas said. "What about the ship?"

"It arrived about an hour ago. Two shuttles are on their way down. The first will drop off cutting equipment and personnel on the mountainside. The other will establish a fuel cache here." He paused, then said, "Warn everyone there'll be noise when they start drilling."

"Will do."

"We saw you while the probe was connected up – the tribes seem to be getting along quite well."

213

"There were some sticky moments earlier," Jordas said. "It would have been a tragedy if I'd brought the Shiranu here, only to have them wiped out of existence by the Sargussi."

"Yes, I didn't realise how good you must be at poker till I saw you walk past those spears like that!" Matt murmured.

Jordas heard the relief in his voice. "Nor did I – I thought my number was up for sure. And I don't know why Hanook was so certain they wouldn't kill him, but –" Jordas sighed. "What are conditions like outside?"

"Cold and wet."

"Any news from Marcus?"

"Some more money entered the bank account today. It *looks* like whoever's been raiding the account has decided to put it back before they get caught, but –"

"Wait, Matt, Soolkah's here."

Her eyes were huge with anxiety.

"What is it, Soolkah?"

"It's Mnanga," Soolkah said. "Jordas, she's in terrible pain and I don't know what to do. Azhee's labour isn't going well, and Nazahl and Shan want Mnanga to leave the birth area to rest, but she won't –"

"Let me speak to Mnanga," Jordas said. He turned back to the phone. "Matt, I must go. I'll have the tribespeople standing by to leave tomorrow at those co-ordinates."

Signing off, Jordas ushered Soolkah towards Mnanga and Azhee. As he approached he saw Mnanga's assistants were indeed arguing with her. "What is it, Mnanga?"

"These two want me to leave Azhee because I have much pain and the herbs have run out. There are no more for either of us. And Azhee wants me to stay with her – I think it's a breech birth –"

"Oh, *shit*!" Jordas muttered under his breath.

Mnanga's pain hadn't affected her hearing. Though he'd spoken in English, she chuckled.

"What would *you* wish to do, Mnanga?"

"Me?" Mnanga seemed puzzled that Jordas had thought to ask her wishes, but she replied, "I want to stay here and see Azhee's baby born safely."

Out of the corner of his eye, Jordas noticed Aa'kam heading in his direction. "I'll get help for you, Mnanga," he promised. "Stay here, Soolkah."

Aa'kam met him as he hurried towards him. "Jordas," he said, "I should be pleased if you would explain to the tribe the things you told me earlier –"

"With much pleasure," Jordas said, "but first I have an urgent problem.

214

Who's your Eldest woman?"

"Aneera," Aa'kam said. "Why?" Then his eyes went past him to Mnanga, the two women bent over her, and Azhee helped onto all fours by Soolkah in an effort to stem her pain. His eyes opened wide. "She needs help?"

Jordas explained.

"Come and explain to both tribes and I'll send Aneera to help," Aa'kam promised.

*

Soolkah smoothed Mnanga's head-fur off her face.

The Eldest woman's face was drenched in sweat, but she pushed Soolkah's hand away. "It's Azhee who needs your help, not me," she mumbled. "Go to her!"

Soolkah bit her lip as she looked round at Azhee. The thought of pregnancy and childbirth terrified her, the more so since she could see how Azhee was suffering. She moaned continuously as Nazahl and Shan tried to encourage her into a squat, one rubbing her lower back, the other stroking sweaty head-fur back from her face. They'd removed her kilt long ago, and Soolkah tried not to look at her dilated daazni as she rocked back and forth in agony.

But it isn't always like this, she thought, remembering how easily Gujas had birthed Teffen and Alsa. She'd helped both times.

A shadow fell over her.

"A breech birth, is it?" asked a new voice.

Soolkah looked up.

A Sargussi woman stood beside her, face streaked with wrinkles. Her eyes were yellowish pools much like Yado's, and kindness shone from them. "I am Aneera, Eldest woman of the Sargussi. I shall take charge, and this baby will be born alive."

Soolkah gazed at her, envying her confidence. Nazahl and Shan were busy and Mnanga and Azhee were too far gone to answer. *I'm the only one who can speak to her,* Soolkah thought. *But it feels right for me to do so.* After a moment, she gave her name to Aneera, adding, "Mnanga thinks it's a breech birth too."

"Ah! You're the one who is amaajni with Yado and the Humanu." Aneera laid a hand on Azhee's shoulder.

Azhee flinched and screamed. "I want Mnanga!" she moaned when the intensity of the contraction had passed.

"Mnanga and these women and I will stay with you. You are fortunate, Azhee, to have many helpers, and not one but *two* Eldest women with you!"

215

Aneera beckoned to Soolkah. "Now Soolkah, hold her hand while I examine her. Then, Azhee, I shall give you herbs for the pain –"

"I don't want Sargussi poison!" Azhee gasped, as another contraction came.

Aneera ignored the insult. "And then we shall birth this baby together."

It sounds as easy as breathing, the way she puts it, Soolkah thought. "Azhee's under great stress – her husbands and sons are in the maaj'nag'ur." She pointed to them.

Aneera nodded her thanks, then turned to Nazahl. "Make up this decoction for Azhee and Mnanga, please." She handed some herbs and a metal bowl to her.

Nazahl sniffed at them, then put one or two fragments of chopped dried leaves on her tongue. She recognised their tang, nodded, and went to heat water.

Aneera knelt behind Azhee to examine her. Soolkah saw that she avoided touching her. Perhaps she feared the woman would lose control if she did.

"It's as Mnanga said," Aneera murmured, "and the baby's not quite ready to come. If she'd let me touch her I could try to turn it, but if not, things were mayhap difficult. Hold her hand, Soolkah." She gave Shan some salve. "Rub her back with this."

Shan nodded.

"Azhee, try not to push when the contractions come," Aneera advised. "Let the herbs to take effect."

Just then Nazahl hurried up with the herbal brew.

Aneera tasted it. "It's too hot yet," she said. "While it cools, I shall examine your wound."

"Mnanga! Don't let her touch you!" Azhee shrieked, racked as much by doubt and fear as another contraction.

Soolkah held her and stroked her head-fur again. "Aneera is here to help both of you," she said. "She may be Sargussi, but her heart is as clean and sweet as any Shiranu's."

"Were the pain less, she would accept me better." Aneera's voice became as gentle as a caress. "She's afraid of me and of the pain, but I'm here to help. Lie on your side awhile, Azhee."

"I've had three sons, and none of them was so – aaargh! – difficult *or* painful!" Azhee muttered through gritted teeth. But she did as Aneera told her. Moving to accommodate Azhee's change of position, Soolkah felt rock through the damp sleeping cloth she was kneeling on. Azhee's hand clenched on Soolkah's as the next contraction came. Her face spasmed and a scream escaped.

"We shall use the pain, but not yet," Aneera said. Her voice was as firm as ever. She crossed to Mnanga's side. Nazahl and Shan had done their best with her. The wound had begun to heal in a jagged line. "The bone is well splinted and set," she commented. "Drink this when it's cooler, Mnanga."

"I'll drink it now, if it makes Azhee realise you mean her no harm!"

"Here, then, but it's hot." Aneera supported Mnanga as she held the metal cup up.

Mnanga sipped the brew, then sank back onto her sleeping cloth. "I won't take enough to make me sleepy because I know you want me by you, Azhee. I won't leave you."

"Th-thank you," Azhee said, between gasps of pain.

They're both exhausted, Soolkah realised.

Aneera brought the rest of the brew over. "Drink, Azhee, to ease your pain."

"*Please* drink it," Soolkah said. "You want your baby born alive, don't you? It will surely die if the pain's too great for you to use it properly?"

Azhee's stare clashed with Aneera's until the next contraction forced another groan from her. When it had passed, she sought Mnanga's gaze.

"I'm here," Mnanga whispered. "I won't leave you, Azhee."

"All right," she said. "I'll drink."

Soolkah took the cup from Aneera and held it to Azhee's lips.

Aneera nodded. "When that has taken the pain away I shall try to turn this infant for you." She checked Mnanga's wound again, then wrapped strips of the softest leather around the limb. "Lie as still as you can."

"I am."

Aneera washed her hands and came to Azhee again. She had quieted. "How is the pain now?" Aneera asked.

"Not as bad," Azhee murmured. She sounded sleepy. "But I think Mnanga's right about it being a breech birth –"

"It shall be well." Aneera soothed, explaining what she was going to do. "I'm doing this because Mnanga can't come to you. Try to think of me as her."

The fight had left Azhee; she had little energy. Soolkah helped her back onto her knees as Aneera directed, then held her round the shoulders as the Sargussi Eldest woman slipped her hand inside the birth channel. Aneera knelt behind her for many moments, but at last she withdrew.

"It's all right, Azhee," she said, "I couldn't turn the baby, but the anchor-cords have separated from the womb. I felt them floating loose. The child shall draw breath only when it's safe. Push now. Here, I'll help you – breathe with

217

me."

There must have been something to calm her in the herbs, Soolkah thought. *Or perhaps it's just that she's too far gone to care now.* She helped Azhee into a squat, still holding her hand, though Azhee's talons had drawn blood. Aneera was beside them, Shan holding her other hand, Nazahl rubbing her back.

There was a grinding moan, as if the ground itself were also giving birth.

Azhee's face contorted with effort. She sucked in a breath. "What was that?"

Soolkah had felt it too. "Just a little quake," she said. "We're in no danger here." A distant crash signalled masonry tumbling in the city.

"The baby comes!" Aneera said.

"Well done, well done," Mnanga murmured.

"Last push now," Aneera said.

Soolkah felt Azhee gather herself up for one final effort.

The ground wailed again.

Azhee's face clenched with effort. Her talons dug into Soolkah's palm.

Aneera held her hands out, kneeling behind Azhee.

With a rush of fluid, the baby catapulted into her hands. The anchor-cords, which would gradually drop away and form the nipples, trailed blood across her chest.

Aneera's face glowed with a smile of pleasure and relief. "Azhee, you have a beautiful daughter, and better still, she's alive! You shall gain much status."

The baby cried as the grinding of the ground came again. Soolkah felt a slight shaking, then all was still.

"Here." Aneera handed the baby to Azhee.

"Thank you, Aneera," Mnanga mumbled. "Now I can go to sleep."

"Not yet," Aneera said. "We speak for the women, and must make a pact between all women of both tribes, and influence all the silly men to lay down their weapons too."

"That would be good, for both tribes."

Aneera smiled across at Mnanga. "More water, Nazahl, Shan," she said, "to clean the baby. What will her name be, Azhee?"

"Some suitable name," Mnanga said, "since the child should symbolise peace between our two tribes."

Azhee waited, breathing in more deeply, saying nothing as she gazed at the child she'd fought to birth.

Soolkah saw she was thinking hard.

Finally, Azhee said, "Perhaps she should be named Mneera."

Soolkah understood then that Azhee feared to lose status by admitting her distrust of Aneera. But both Eldest women looked pleased. *And this is a way for her to acknowledge the help both of them gave her,* Soolkah thought, *and symbolic of the union of the tribes.*

Nazahl cleaned the baby, much to Mneera's loud dislike, as Shan replaced Azhee's sleeping cloth.

Aneera washed blood from her hands and chest, then went to Azhee's husbands and sons. "Come," she said to the men. "Your daughter is birthed, and the future of your tribe is safeguarded, thanks to your contribution."

A traditional thing to say, Soolkah thought, *but this time with a very special meaning.* She was glad Yado's tribe shared some customs with hers. *Perhaps Jordas's tribe will, too.*

The men got up, and, with their sons, followed Aneera to Azhee.

"This is your daughter, Mneera," Aneera said, ushering the two men closer to Azhee.

"Our daughter?" the elder of the two husbands asked. His brother started and stared around.

Aneera nodded.

The elder husband rubbed a hand over his eyes as if waking.

"Here," Azhee said, and handed Mneera to him.

*

Jordas looked around in satisfaction. In one corner of the cavern the Shiranu filed up, backs laden with baskets of stones. Sargussi builders fitted them into place, layer upon layer. The rock platform had been Hanook's suggestion, approved by Aa'kam. There was plenty of willing labour to hand, so teams would work through the night. The platform was designed to lead upwards in a tapering wedge which would reach the opening the Committee rescue crew were even now cutting at Matt's co-ordinates.

Grrrrrm!

"What's that?" asked Yado.

"It's the noise of cutting through rock," Jordas explained, realising there was no word for drill in Naxadan.

"Shall I call the next group?" asked Yado.

Jordas nodded. "Before it gets any louder!"

Hanook and Aa'kam had called all the *amaaju* together, so that Jordas could show his holographic animation to all the tribespeople. Once each family group had seen why they needed to leave the caves, the women took the children to care for them. Then Hanook and Aa'kam directed some men to help

219

with the building of the platform, and some to sleep, awaiting the next shift.

Another group, of two smaller *amaaju*, one Shiranu and one Sargussi, approached Jordas, looking apprehensive. Jordas ran the graphic back to the beginning, and started to explain again.

Soolkah hurried to his side. She looked tired, but excited, and was smiling. "Jordas, Azhee's had her baby!" she exclaimed. "It's a new daughter for the tribe."

"Oh, good!" he said. "I'm pleased for her. And Mnanga?"

"She's asleep now."

"Good also." Jordas's voice cracked; he'd explained so many times, and there were still several groups to come. "I have need of a drink," he said, pulling his cup and a sachet of coffee from his pack.

"Of course," Soolkah said.

While Jordas and Yado finished explaining to the *amaaju*, she went to the Shiranu cooking stone for water. She returned with Hanook's daughter. "Zuas will help while I tell Hanook."

As Jordas took the cup from her, he noticed the trails of tears on Zuas's face. "Why do you cry?"

"I'm afraid," Zuas told him. "Men cope better, because they share their fears with their brothers. But I am a woman, and have no-one to share with."

"What do you fear, Zuas?" he asked.

"Things will change, won't they?"

Jordas nodded. "But all shall be well. Your life *will* continue elsewhere, mayhap different from here, but my tribe will help you adapt."

He was touched when she wiped away the tears, smiled, and thanked him. *Don't be fooled,* he thought, watching her slim, straight form walk back to the camp. *You may think it's easier for men, but when you share, you also get someone else's fear to chew on...*

"Any more groups, Yado?" he asked after sipping his coffee.

"One only. But Chixi's *amaaj* is among them."

"We can't treat them differently from the others." He watched Yado go to the remaining group and bring them to him, then saw Hanook approaching.

The Sargussi contingent clustered around him, eager to see the strange thing other tribespeople had described; even Jeene, Vru and Lorr hurried up. They didn't seem to share Chixi's animosity towards himself and Yado; they just seemed depressed, especially the youngest. Chixi followed his brothers with reluctance. Although Hanook had taken over their marriage negotiations with Mzana's parents, Jordas knew that they weren't going well.

I can't help that. He did his best to explain things as the wall of people

220

folded around him; but for the first time, he saw the Naxadans as alien, distracted by the men's beardless faces, the light fur on their skins, the six exposed nipples on both male and female chests. All drew together into a composite, completed by the alien concepts of telepathy and woman-sharing between brothers.

I'm exhausted. I must get some sleep, he thought, then wondered if it was really just that. Chixi was watching him, pupils dilated with chilling hatred. After seconds the huge tribesman's glance flickered away.

As he finished his explanations and the group walked away Chixi glowered at Jordas. "You still owe me *kazmo'ra*, usurper."

"Take your own place, Chixi. This man owes you nothing. He's paid his debt to the tribe by bringing us all here and helping bring about peace between the tribes," Hanook told him. "If you've energy to waste pursuing vengeance, use it on the platform instead."

Chixi cast a sullen glance at Jordas and Yado, then shambled over to rejoin the workers.

"Thank you, Hanook." Jordas looked with narrowed eyes at the Shiranu Eldest. "How did you know Aa'kam wouldn't have his warriors finish you off when you went to parley with him? I was afeard they'd kill both of us –"

"You're a *maaj'gar* and you ask that?" Hanook shook his head. "It's the Way of the *Amaaju*. It's kept the balance between the tribes for hundreds of highwaters –"

"Rest now, Jordas," Aa'kam said from behind them. "Hanook and I will ensure the platform is built. If there's trouble, we shall wake you."

Jordas nodded, hoping the coffee wouldn't keep him awake. But he made his way to the sleeping-place Yado had made for them, aware that his *maaj'gar* and Soolkah were following.

He thought then that he'd never sleep that night, knowing Yado held Soolkah in his arms, but when he lay down, sleep descended on him like a curtain, and neither the *clunk-thunk* of tribespeople building the rock platform nor the growl of the drills could prevent him sleeping.

CHAPTER 21

"YADO AND I ARE GOING INTO THE CITY this morning," Jordas told Matt, "to holovid the frieze."

"We-ell...all right, Jordas – if you think there's enough time. The rescue team should be through to the cavern in the next two hours. And the water's still rising."

"We'll be careful and as quick as we can," he promised. "I have a feeling Mnanga and Aneera will keep the tribespeople from each other's throats even if Hanook and Aa'kam can't!"

Matt chuckled. "Call me with any problems – the first shuttle's fuelling up for the evacuation."

That lifted Jordas's spirits. He knew he'd almost accomplished something important. *My personal difficulties don't matter beside that.* Jordas looked for Yado, and found him watching him across the cavern. The touch of his mind was as insubstantial as the *sajamu* it brought, yet very real; an odd sensation.

Soolkah hadn't wanted them to go. "If there's another tremor the buildings could fall on you."

"We'll leave at the first sign of danger," Jordas promised. "We have to try, for the future of both tribes. We shall return soon."

"I can see I can't persuade you not to go," Soolkah said, spreading her hands in the gesture for incomprehension.

It took only minutes to march the few hundred metres into the outskirts of the city, where blocks of stone spilled over buildings that still stood.

<I'm curious to see inside a house,> Jordas told Yado.

<If we find a safe one we can enter. Shall you show me how to use the – holocam?>

Jordas had noticed his curiosity and used the deeper level of mindspeech to explain the working and use of it, handheld or free-floating. <We can make pictures of the city for your people, like in my notebook,> he added. <A permanent display they can walk through.>

Yado stared at him. <Were that even possible?>

<Certainly.>

They picked their way through the ruins.

*

Lorr stretched his shoulder muscles, wrapped his sleeping-cloth about him and lay down. He'd worked hard; so, he had to admit, had the Sargussi. Between them the tribes had almost completed the rock platform when his team had been sent to rest by the Sargussi Eldest, Aa'kam.

Lorr felt little interest in the rescue proposed by the Humanu. Now that he knew Soolkah lived, the quality of his misery had changed. *Before, I grieved for her loss. Now I know she would risk even loss of status to avoid marriage with Chixi and my brothers and myself.* That hurt. At times he felt bitter anger at the opportunism of the Sargussi Yado and the Humanu Jordas; but also flashes of triumph that perhaps his proximity sense hadn't been extinguished by his ancestors' changed feeding habits. He *had* sensed her presence in the cavern where she'd hid. Soolkah's story had been whispered among the amaaju, though not told publicly by Kayas.

Chixi came to their sleeping-place then, followed by Jeene and Vru. They'd all been in the same workgroup. <I don't enjoy doing a Sargussi's bidding,> he sent to all of them, <especially since I found out that the Sargussi and the Humanu stole my bride.> After a moment, he corrected himself: <*Our* bride.>

Lorr said nothing. His thoughts just then were deeply private. *The way Chixi speaks and thinks of Soolkah, perhaps it's just as well she did run away. At least only I get the occasional thump or talonslash. I couldn't have borne seeing him hurt her, perhaps scar her beautiful face.* He closed his eyes, feigning sleep.

<I only worked because Eldest Hanook required me to,> Chixi continued. <*My* loyalty to the tribe isn't in question.>

Lorr opened his eyes and sighed. <Let it go, Chixi,> he sent. <I don't like it any more than you do, but we all need rest.>

The only answer Lorr got was the sound of Chixi's slippers scraping the rock as he paced up and down. He wriggled into a more comfortable position on the ground and tried to relax. Beside him Jeene and Vru were preparing to sleep – if possible with the grind of the Humanu cutting through the rockwall.

<Where are they?> Chixi peered around the cavern.

<Who?>

<The Humanu and the Sargussi. I can't see them.>

Lorr threw off his sleeping cloth and climbed to his feet. <Chixi! For the sake of our amaamu, let the matter rest! Sleep. You deserve to relax after working so hard.> Chixi's face was lined with fatigue, and through sajamu Lorr felt muscles other than his own aching.

<I won't lie down!> Chixi scanned again. At last he exhaled with a hiss.

Lorr could tell Chixi had found what he was seeking from the triumph which flooded into his mind and the mental picture which pursued it. He followed his line of sight. The Humanu and the Sargussi clambered amongst

223

fallen masonry in the city. Lorr caught the overspill of Chixi's anger, intense enough to convulse his stomach muscles in apprehension. The spasm hadn't subsided when Chixi lumbered towards the ruins.

<No! It's not safe to go into the city,> Lorr reminded him. <Remember the plague?>

<*Amaamu-shit on the plague!*>

<What about the tremors?>

No reply.

Lorr was nearer to Chixi than the others. He ran after him and grabbed his arm.

Chixi flung him off. His shove wrenched Lorr's shoulder and overbalanced him. <Don't *ever* touch me in front of our people again!> his thoughts thundered in Lorr's mind, <and most especially not in the sight of the Sargussi!> His thoughts closed to all of them.

Lorr got up, rubbing his shoulder, while Jeene hurried up. Chixi was gone. Even the sound of his slippers on rock was soon swallowed up against the background noise in the cavern.

<Are you all right, Lorr?> Jeene asked.

<Nothing serious,> Lorr sent. <But I'm worried about Chixi.>

<So am I,> Jeene agreed. < He's obsessed with Soolkah.>

<I know.> Lorr wondered if he dared confide in Jeene. His decision came in a flash, and he sent, <I love her. But I'm certain what Chixi feels isn't the same.>

Jeene just nodded. Vru reached them then, and the three brothers meandered back to their sleeping-place.

<Are you sure you're all right?> Vru asked.

<I'm fine.> The soreness was passing off now, and Lorr was wide-awake; the capacity for rest, though not the need, had left him. <Get some sleep. I'll speak to Hanook about this.>

*

Jordas stopped to survey the city. It hadn't survived as unscathed as they'd thought, after all. Some damage looked recent, though he couldn't recall his first hololink views of Keramanthu with any accuracy. The damage towards the city centre was bad enough to slow their pace.

<This house were safe to enter,> Yado suggested, indicating a building ahead. Its windowless walls opened onto an inner courtyard. <The tribespeople fear to enter the city but our *amaamu* lived here for a thousand highwaters. It's an important part of our history.> He watched as Jordas trained the camera on the five rooms as they explored them.

<Was it a Sargussi house?> Jordas asked, pointing to the remains of a stone grate with a raised block beside it: where food had been prepared, judging by its dark staining.

Yado spread his hands wide, palms down. <Who can tell?> He gestured. <Look!>

Jordas peered through the doorway. Perhaps twenty metres away was a section of frieze. Even at this distance, with dying glowcakes and the melting ceiling overhead for light, he could distinguish carven shapes. Beckoning to Yado, Jordas approached. The duster had revealed brilliant colours and reliefs of Sargussi, Shiranu and Chabira alike. It came to Jordas that past, present and future ran together like a stream in this place. *The city breathes history but holds its own definition of fate.*

<I knew of the frieze but never came here.> Yado sighed. <It's our history, and our future – it contains the Prophecy of the Seer of Keramanthu.>

<We realised the city must be important to the tribes,> Jordas said. <Let's find the start to record the frieze in sequence. There's not much time.>

<It were easy to follow round.>

<But which direction does it run in?>

<Is it important?>

<I should say so!> Jordas grinned.

Yado looked puzzled.

Jordas explained that some Humanu tribes used symbols, writing from left to right, right to left, or top to bottom, to record events and ideas.

Yado crossed to the wall and examined it. <It runs this way,> he said after a few moments, gesturing. But as they turned to trace the tribespeople's story to its source, Yado froze and raised his hand for silence.

<What?> demanded Jordas, standing as still as Yado.

<I thought I heard a scraping, as if something were moving.> Yado cocked his head, listening, then relaxed. <I can't hear it now, but we should move carefully.>

Jordas caught his anxiety. It was swiftly suppressed.

They patrolled the walls, tracing the carvings back to the beginning. Tremors had tumbled stone from buildings in some sections. Jordas set the holocam to work in independent mode, programming its route. It floated into the air. He could hardly hear its hum against the background noise in the cavern. They followed its progress, wondering at the work of the tribal ancestors. The colours caught both eye and imagination: brilliant red, mauve-blue, sulphurous yellow, dull pink and acid green, with black and white, combined in places to produce exact shades. Jordas learned that the Chabira

225

had distilled dyes from plants and refined minerals, as well as using herbs for healing. <Their way of using discussion to solve disagreements was legendary,> Yado added.

<Is this a Chabira?> Jordas asked, pointing at an image.

Yado nodded.

The tribesman's tawny headfur swept his shoulders in waves, curled rather than whorled. Apart from the colour, the man's hair resembled his own.

<The tribespeople think you must have Chabira blood.>

Jordas shook his head. <Though I'm incredibly flattered. But if they were the healers, why couldn't they cure themselves?>

Yado pointed. <See? They all fell ill. In lighttimes they were all dead.>

<It looks that way.> *But a third tribe to rescue would have caused more complications,* Jordas thought, and only realised Yado had picked it up when he heard his chuckle.

<Time to move on?> Yado clambered over the fallen masonry in a missing section.

Close behind him, Jordas hovered a hand above his arm. <Did you hear that?>

Yado bobbed his head, frowning. <It sounds like an animal following us. The game came this way – we were unlucky if a *ganzu* were hiding in the city. Let's not take long over this!>

<I still have my gun –>

Yado relaxed and smiled his relief back.

<Let's get back. The holocam will finish filming and return on its own.> Jordas checked the time. <Matt said the airlift would arrive soon – and they'll need us to help organise the evacuation.> He caught a surge of anxiety from Yado, and laid his hand millimetres above his arm again. <Don't worry, Yado. Everything will be fine, if strange at first. You'll become used living elsewhere.> He thought, then added, <I haven't seen a single tool in the city.>

<Our folk never leave anything useful behind, be it bone, stone or metal,> Yado answered.

<So I've noticed,> Jordas replied. He peered at the wall, stunned by the quality of the carvings. The artists had changed over the centuries, but each face was so real he could imagine each ancestor as live Sargussi or Shiranu. He felt drawn into Keramanthu's past with Yado, and though it was impossible, he couldn't rid himself of the idea, such was the power and vitality of the artwork. It drew to mind the passion of his first shared experience with Yado and Soolkah, and memory set the blood tingling through his veins and his heart thudding. He had a sense that what had been set in motion that day

226

had come to fruition here at Keramanthu.

He pointed. <Is that the last section?>

Yado nodded. <Shall we take a look before we leave?>

Nearby buildings had collapsed, so the end of the frieze lay apart from the rest. They trotted across the open space. The final scene chilled the sweat on Jordas's skin, and *sajamu* told him Yado felt as he did.

*

Soolkah inclined her head. The noise from Outside was louder. She couldn't identify it but at least the tribes would be safe soon.

Where are *they?* She leant forwards, hoping to see her husbands emerge from the city. *I hope they're safe.* She thought back to the bad quake, when she'd got separated from them before, how she'd clung to the tunnel wall though she'd expected it to shiver into fragments in her hands.

There was no denying that she'd missed Yado; their reunion the previous night had been glad, though Jordas had slept through it. He didn't understand her quite as Yado did, not being of Kerui, though she enjoyed his lovemaking – it was different from Yado's. Both had brought new knowledge and meaning into her life. *It was easier than I thought to learn to love them both.*

She swept her gaze around. The water rose faster as it swilled in from all the tunnels. The lower end of the rock platform was already inundated. There wasn't room on it for everyone. People still stood on the opposite slope, where the city lay. The lowest glowcake layers were already extinguished, the light dimmed.

The platform was crowded with shivering tribespeople. Her gaze sought Hanook or Aa'kam, but the press of bodies on the platform was too dense. *When will the Humanu get through, so that we can go Outside? Even if we're blinded, and there's nowhere to go –*

Vibration thundered so, it sounded like a quake. Then she realised it was the noise from Outside. She glanced around at her people. Lorr was watching her as if for inspiration from the remains of the Shiranu encampment. She looked away quickly.

She spotted Mnanga near the top of the rock-platform. Jordas had warned the tribespeople back from where his tribe were cutting through the rocks. Soolkah fought her way upslope to the Eldest woman's side. Jordas's sleeping cloth still cushioned her from the rocks. Bruises encircled her eye-sockets. *She looks so fragile,* Soolkah thought as she knelt beside her. "How are you, Mnanga?"

Since the birth of Azhee's daughter Aneera had kept her mostly sedated. The old woman barely had energy to incline her head, but her eyes blazed courage. "Your husbands will find it," Mnanga whispered. "They'll see, and they'll know the tribes must combine as never before."

"See what, Mnanga?"

"The Prophecy." Mnanga's features creased into a smile. "I came here as a girl of five highwaters. My brothers played in the city with me, and so I saw the Prophecy. Hanook doesn't know. He was born just afterwards." She clutched Soolkah's hand. "Your husbands must hold the tribes –"

The noise grew deafening. Soolkah couldn't hear the rest, but realised what the Eldest woman's words meant. For centuries the tribes had avoided the city; yet Mnanga had been in it. No wonder she hadn't disciplined her more strongly for running from marriage with Chixi, and had supported her marriage to two foreign husbands who shouldn't even have been maaj'gare. *The Prophecy says that our two tribes will walk together in peace when the volcano speaks again,* Soolkah remembered. *All this time, Mnanga knew what would happen. When we're out of here I'll ask her what she saw –*

She laid her hand over Mnanga's brow, then got up to seek her husbands again. She still couldn't see them. She struggled back downslope. The foot of the platform now trailed away into a turbulent river. Many tribespeople had just climbed on, jostling for space and relative safety. With a splash someone fell off nearby. Soolkah saw arms flailing. She fought through the crowd towards the place where the child had disappeared and slid under the waves, reaching for him. Her hand closed on a leather kilt. She hauled the boy closer; he'd seen about eight highwaters. As she straightened with him in her arms, a Sargussi woman approached.

"My son!"

Soolkah handed the boy to his mother. "He's swallowed a lot of water. You need to expel it from his lungs –"

The woman grabbed him. "Thank you," she said.

"You know what to do?"

There was no time for a reply. The mother laid her son on the platform and bent over him as he coughed dirty water from his lungs.

Soolkah climbed back upslope. Dust curled into the air at the rockwall. She watched for signs of a breakthrough. The ceiling dripped streams of moisture. Clouds of dust billowed into the cavern, showering the top of the platform.

Abruptly the grinding ceased. Soolkah squinted across the platform at the place where the Humanu had been working, protecting her eyes from light and grit with her hands. On the rock platform, nobody moved.

A shape stepped through the dustclouds towards her.

228

Silver metal had been plastered molten onto the frieze in a man-like shape. The face was vague, blurred, as if the artist had been unsure of his vision. But eyes as blue as his own stared back at him. The thatch of hair curling on his head was darker than a Sargussi's fur. And Yado's face bore smoky topaz eyes, the mouth half-curved in rueful humour. Jordas was certain he'd heard him cry out in amazement when he first saw the scene. They were followed by a woman as much like Soolkah as could be carved in stone.

"How –?" Jordas began.

"It's the Prophecy," Yado whispered back. "You and Soolkah and I."

Jordas shook his head. "Incredible. Look!"

In the background, some sought the driest parts of a shaking cavern – the artist had even rendered the movement as double vision. A pitiful few Naxadans took leave of the drowning planet: Shiranu and Sargussi stood together, waiting to be swallowed up by the silver mass hanging above them. Volcanoes spouted fire around it. A hail of burning rocks scored the air, trailing smoke, as the planet tore itself apart.

*

Yado shivered at the chilling accuracy of the portraits, especially of him and Soolkah, aware of Jordas transfixed beside him.

"This was Mekar's house, then." Yado's voice was a whisper. "He must truly have had the future sight!"

<I can't imagine carving something I've only seen in a vision.> Jordas paused. <We should leave. The holocam has finished the aerial views.>

Yado bobbed his head in agreement. The holocam lifted and swept above them, towards the tribes. He collected the duster and sent that after it. But as they picked their way back across the scattered blocks, Yado heard a rustling sound. He and Jordas stared at each other.

<It sounds like leaves in the wind,> Jordas sent.

To Yado, the air movement in a cavern at blow-out described the sound better. It got louder and more intense. Nearer.

Jordas scrambled up a pile of masonry, scraping fingers and bruising himself, as sajamu bore witness, in search of a better view.

Yado followed more cautiously.

"The buildings block our vision," Jordas said.

<It weren't safe to climb higher,> Yado warned. In times of stress he reverted to the mindspeech, whereas Jordas spoke aloud. <We must leave now.>

<The city centre's built on the highest land in this cavern,> Jordas

229

countered. <We'd be more at risk of drowning if we left the city>

<But we can't stay here!> Yado beckoned him on. <Come. I fear Soolkah's mayhap in more danger than we are.>

<I'm worried about her too. Pity we're not telepathically linked to her!> They headed across the city. <Though there is the platform,> Jordas added.

Yado felt the floor beneath them shift without really moving. He caught sight of Jordas's expression and stared at him in horror.

Jordas nodded at him. <Earth tremor.>

The ground roared. Water fountained out before them.

Yado leapt back, startled.

Jordas froze, muttering in his own language. <It's the hypocaust. The tremor must have disturbed access to it.>

"What?" asked Yado, though he'd caught Jordas's idea.

Water spurted. Icy droplets splattered. Within moments, Jordas's hair was plastered to his scalp. He clamped his lips shut to keep out the water. They struggled forwards against the pressure of the water.

Yado's waterproof was soaked. Moisture dripped inside it. He felt clammily uncomfortable. Was the cavern roof melting? He looked up. But drizzle blinded him.

Ancient dust mingled with water. Already the slope had become a muddy slide. They staggered through the chill geyser clinging to each other, sometimes half-crawling. Other sounds reached them under the din: the groan of tortured rocks one moment, a scrape behind them the next.

<Mayhap there really *were* a ganzu following us,> Yado suggested.

Jordas could only gasp his acknowledgement.

Yado increased his pace. The floor disappeared under a torrent. Water flowed out of the city towards the lowest points in the cavern. Yado pulled Jordas into the shelter of a house wall. They slumped against it for a few moments, panting.

Scrape! It was nearer this time. Yado drew his knife – though it was hard to grip – and whirled to face whatever stalked them.

Nothing! Silence but for the hiss of the waterspout. But against the rumble that came again just then even that faded away. The building opposite shivered. Blocks tumbled. Another behind them collapsed under its own weight.

<Make a run for it?> Jordas asked.

Another block fell.

"Let's go!" Jordas yelled.

They splashed through the flow, Jordas gripping Yado's wrist. There were too many obstacles to move fast.

<If either trips –>

<Don't think of that. Which way?>

The maze of buildings hazed Yado's sense of direction. He paused for a moment, lifting his head to use his proximity sense. <Over there.> He pointed left.

<How far?>

<Paces only,> Yado assured him. <But –>

<What?>

<I sense someone here. But who –?> It felt much like that long morning when he'd felt with his proximity sense for pursuing Shiranu.

Buildings danced nearby. Terror broke his concentration. Yado had done his best to swallow his fear of quakes, and thought he'd mostly succeeded, though it wasn't easy. He calmed when Jordas gripped his wrist again.

"Come on!" Jordas said, dragging him back to the present. A crash behind them turned the street into a tide splashing around their calves as more masonry slid into the water.

Yado half-turned. He had an impression of someone slipping back into hiding just in time to avoid being seen.

<Jordas! Someone *is* there,> he insisted. <No animal, that – ganzu or otherwise. Someone's following us!>

*

Jordas faced Yado. <Who would follow us? And why?>

<I don't know, but we must leave!>

They struggled towards an open space ahead. Jordas shivered, clothes sodden, boots heavy with water, protection from obstacles their only benefit. <Will this lead us out of here?> He'd overtaken Yado.

< I'll check. I –>

A splash behind Jordas almost drowned Yado's gurgling shout.

He felt the sensation of a huge rough arm around his throat. With his clothes weighted with moisture turning was almost impossible, but he glimpsed Yado dragged backwards.

The water only reached Chixi's calves. As the giant shoved Yado down into the flow Jordas felt water cover his face. *That's impossible – it's only sajamu!* he told himself. He forced himself to breathe steadily, at least to give Yado the illusion of having enough breath.

Chixi turned to face him, still holding Yado under. "I'll get you both!" he cried. A cunning smile turned his features into those of a bloated gargoyle.

"Yado!"

Jordas roared with anger and launched himself forwards. His fist knuckled

231

Chixi's eye and larded cheekbone. It was enough. Chixi let go of Yado. Satisfaction flooded Jordas.

But Chixi growled and rushed back at him. His shoulder thudded against Jordas's breastbone. The blow lifted him off his feet. Water broke his fall as he hit street level. Winded, he fought for breath and footing.

"You won't give me what I'm owed – either the woman or *kazmo'ra* – but I'll get her one way or another!" Chixi mumbled, standing over him. He ignored the grumbling from the ground and rising floodwater. "I've seen the Prophecy. But I'll KILL you!" His hands reached out like grabs.

Jordas could feel and hear Yado coughing behind him. Fear pierced him, not just for himself and his *maaj'gar*, but for Soolkah as well. In a flash he understood why she'd run from marriage with Chixi. He was unusually unattractive for these people; but the darkness in his mind overshadowed even physical impressions.

If neither of us survive there'll be nothing to stop him from claiming Soolkah. I can't let that happen! Jordas felt sick at the thought. He fought for a secure footing so he could rise. "Surely you wouldn't want a woman who's already been touched –"

Chixi glared hatred at him. As he roared his rage again the water surged upwards behind him. A dark form burst from it. Light flashed on metal. Blood streaked the water. The man-mountain above Jordas turned, hand pressed to the wound on his arm.

<Yado!>

Knives flashed. Claws scraped and gouged. The water boiled a disturbingly dark hue. The ground thundered beneath them again, this time a long, drawn-out sound: the keening of a dying world.

Jordas's legs were numb with cold. The waves were above his knees. *For all I know the tribespeople are drowning.* He knew Chixi must be furious about the Prophecy and tried to think how to calm him down. No inspiration presented itself.

Yado's knife disappeared beneath the waves. He and Chixi closed, wrestling. Taloned hands squeezed throats towards death. The waterproof hampered Yado's movements.

Jordas waded forwards and grabbed Chixi's arm. <Shove when I do!>

Yado made no reply.

But as Jordas's hands closed on the giant's shoulder Yado heaved. Together they pushed Chixi away. He stumbled back and hit the wall behind him with a thud. Masonry folded around him. He vanished from sight. His blood swirled into patterns stretched by the flow till they faded.

232

Above the grumble of quakes and the suction of the water, Jordas heard it: the roar of shuttle thrusters slashing the air.

*

Apart from the coating of dust, the man looked much like Jordas. Yet not. He wore on his head what Jordas had named *helmet*, light *beam* piercing gloom and gritty air. A face covering kept dust out of his throat. Behind him Soolkah made out more faces clustered around the opening in the rockwall. Harsh white light slanted through from Outside, piercing dust clouds and making the cavern seem darker. It brought a blast of cold air. Outside seemed as hostile as ever, despite Jordas's assertion that it was getting warmer.

The Humanu came to Soolkah, patting dust from his clothes. His skin was darker than Yado's; she hadn't expected that.

He beckoned for her to follow him Outside. Soolkah shook her head and pointed to Mnanga. The man nodded, and spoke in what sounded like Jordas's language. He beckoned, and two others came in, lifted Mnanga onto an object like the sleeping bag, but with poles on either side, and took her through the opening.

"They're through!" she said. "Go!"

She ushered the nearest man, a Sargussi, towards the opening. He looked at her uncertainly, then nodded and followed Mnanga through into the light, beckoning to his amaaj. The Humanu began to help the tribespeople out.

She fought the press of people, encouraging everyone to leave. Some she recognised: Hanook and Aa'kam, Aneera – with an arm shielding Azhee, who clasped her newborn to her – followed by Azhee's menfolk – and many more of her own tribe. But she couldn't see her origin-amaaj or Maru. Yado had brought him over to introduce him the previous darktime.

I must find Yado and Jordas. She they were on the opposite slope near the city. *How will they escape?*

*

<They've cut through,> Jordas sent. <We must return or be left behind.> He gestured towards the pile of fallen masonry. <What about him?>

<What *about* him?> Yado gasped for breath but still looked indignant. <He would have killed both of us!>

<I know, but – I'll probably have to make a statement about this. It was an accident in the end, but this sort of thing isn't supposed to happen in a rescue!>

Yado snorted. <Nor should one man attack another. Anyway, how could we return him?>

Jordas acknowledged the truth of that, but couldn't help feeling guiltily

233

glad that there was no need to worry about Chixi's animosity. He wanted to embrace Yado out of relief, but wasn't sure enough of tribal customs to do it without checking with him first; and the water was rising. <But shouldn't we bury him?> he asked.

<No time. His spirit must wander unsalved, though his brothers have had scant time to bid him farewell. Let's not make too much of it until we speak to Hanook and Aa'kam. It could cause problems between the tribes. Now come!>

He caught Jordas's arm. They stumbled and splashed through the water until at last they cleared the buildings and saw the open space before the city. The tribes' camping-grounds were awash. Water swilled into the cavern. At the edge it was waist-deep. They could hear the cries of tribespeople trapped on the slopes below the city now drilling had ceased. Confusion was everywhere.

"*Ghasru masaachifar!* I never thought it would be like this," Yado exclaimed.

Jordas swore even more savagely. "*Shit!* We could drown while we await rescue."

CHAPTER 22

LORR WAS DROWNING and being crushed to death at the same time. Water filled his mouth and lungs. The shriek of tortured flesh and broken bones ground all other awareness from him.

Ever since the wall had collapsed around his brother he'd had the sajamu, though they'd faded to grey nothingness, replacing everything in his field of vision, body, mind and heart. A part of him remained on a physically conscious level; he knew his brothers Jeene and Vru were suffering the same death-sajamu. But that level of consciousness was far down among the depths of his being. In the upper levels of his mind, a greater pain was born amid the physical suffering: the pain of severing maaj'gar from maaj'gar.

Chixi is dead; his body lies buried forever in Keramanthu, his mind kept repeating. *I will never see him again.* And: *It's hard to learn that someone's dead when you can't say goodbye to them, can't lay the stone on them.*

Chixi had never been kind to him. Lorr had stored in his memory every blow from his Elder maaj'gar, knowing a time would come when it no longer mattered. *This is that lighttime.* He was fuzzily aware of someone speaking nearby, of being hauled upright and slipping in streams that gushed downslope to join the tides from the tunnels.

I didn't know it would hurt so much to lose a brother I never loved, was his last conscious thought. Then the greyness suffused his whole existence.

*

Moments passed before Soolkah spotted her husbands. As Yado and Jordas walked towards her they gestured. *The handspeech.* They limped across the abandoned campsites, ankle-deep in water. A rush of love for them streamed into her heart. *They complement each other, as brothers should.*

A glance behind reassured her that most of the tribespeople would escape the flood. But those trapped below the city might be swept away. She dipped her feet into the water, knowing she must reach the other side. Gujas might be there, and Araz, and Ulon and Lagi, the children with them. Maru might be there. She shivered, willing herself to enter the water. Fear held her back. To turn an ankle on a stone could mean death. Then she glanced at the city again and saw streams cascading downslope to join the swirling highwater. At the top of the bank three well-remembered figures stood beside Hanook, quite unmoving.

Her heart thundered louder than falling masonry. It was hard to breathe.

How can this have happened to Chixi's brothers?

*

Hanook recognised the maaj'nag'ur at once. He remembered Lorr's warning that Chixi had gone into the city. *So he didn't return.* He scanned for Jordas and Yado. The foreigners were nowhere to be seen; perhaps they hadn't returned either. The need to resolve Chixi's difficulties had been bothering Hanook. If the foreigners failed to return that might solve the problem. Soolkah would be given to Chixi's brothers on their return to normality and the matter would eventually be forgotten. There were enough changes ahead without complications.

Hanook felt a sinking sensation inside him as the Eldest of the Sargussi approached.

"How long since their maaj'nag'ur began?" Aa'kam asked, indicating Chixi's brothers.

"A short while. And all because a Sargussi took a Shiranu woman for his amaajni," Hanook said. His voice dripped bitterness. Then he caught sight of the Sargussi and Humanu, supporting each other across the remains of the camps. "But the situation must be dealt with at once, and in such a way as to keep peace between our peoples."

Aa'kam slanted a look at him through narrowed eyes. "And so *you* don't look less of a leader in the eyes of the Shiranu?"

Hanook acknowledged the truth of that with a half-nod. "Especially since she who was my daughter died, and my kazmo'ra for that was to let the Humanu lead the Shiranu here. I'll send my warriors out, but I won't have the peace disrupted. The Humanu is popular; they must be discreet." He beckoned to Kayas and Brach. <Take two men each. Bring the Sargussi and the Humanu to me.>

Kayas nodded and beckoned to the nearest Shiranu men. "Come," he said, jerking his head in the direction of the city. Brach and four Shiranu picked up their spears and followed him.

"And them?" Aa'kam nodded in the direction of Chixi's brothers.

"That depends on the circumstances that sent them into the maaj'nag'ur," Hanook replied.

*

"I don't believe this!" Jordas gasped, as Kayas and Brach approached with four other Shiranu, spears held at heart height. He didn't doubt they'd use them if they thought fit; they looked fierce and forbidding.

Yado agreed. <We'd best not resist. They're armed, and we're out of breath.>

236

Kayas approached, knife drawn, spear balanced in his other hand. "Come with us, Humanu, Sargussi!"

Jordas held up his empty hands. "We've fought for our lives and haven't breath to resist."

Kayas nodded. "It's well." He stood to one side of Jordas and waved two tribesmen to the other side. Brach and the others flanked Yado.

As they approached the tribespeople clustered on the bank, Jordas wiped perspiration and water out of his eyes. He recognised some faces. Soolkah wasn't among them. He hoped she was already outside. Hanook was talking to Aa'kam. Beside him, silent and patient as gravestones, the faces of Chixi's younger brothers were wiped clean of expression. For a moment, as Jordas's gaze fell on them, his perception of them as living creatures altered, and their bodies had the insubstantiality of shadows. Then life flowed back into the moment, and he saw them as Shiranu *maaj'garu* once more, but with the spark of consciousness dimmed in their eyes.

Hanook spoke. "Humanu Jordas," he said. "Chixi's brothers are the innocent victims of a great wrong this lighttime." He regarded them both with outthrust chin and a speculative expression in his eyes. "How could this thing have occurred?"

"Chixi followed and attacked us in the city," Jordas said. He realised he was trembling. "We had no choice but to fight for our lives."

"Is this truth?" Aa'kam demanded of Yado.

He nodded. "My *maaj'gar* only speaks truth. A wall collapsed on Chixi in the tremor."

Aa'kam's eyes narrowed. "I still owe you *kazmo'ra* for not believing you before," he muttered. "But I know you wouldn't kill without good reason."

"We didn't kill him – it was an accident," Jordas said. "Do you think we'd jeopardise peace between the tribes?"

"There have been past wars between our peoples," Hanook said. "Ever since the plague, the Way of the *Amaaju* has stopped us from losing too many people."

"What exactly is this 'Way of the *Amaaju*'?" Jordas asked.

Hanook looked at him in surprise. "You don't know?"

Jordas shook his head.

Hanook cast a look at Aa'kam, and hesitated. "After the plague, the tribespeople found that when Shiranu fought Sargussi, if one brother died, his brothers couldn't fight."

"So the *maaj'nag'ur* made more than one casualty," Jordas murmured. "I should have realised."

237

"So for a thousand highwaters the Shiranu stayed south of the city, and the Sargussi north of it," Hanook added.

"It were better to avoid each other than fight and destroy both tribes," Aa'kam added. "It ensured our survival."

"You haven't helped matters by taking Soolkah for your *amaajni*." Hanook indicated Yado, then jerked his head towards Chixi's brothers. "This situation must be resolved now." He thought for a while, then began, "Lorr came to me and told me that Chixi had followed you and the Sargussi into the city. If Chixi sought to kill you, he would owe you *kazmo'ra*. But he is dead. If you killed him, the status-debt would be cancelled out against him, but there are still his innocent brothers to consider."

Yado leaned forwards. "It were difficult to repay *kazmo'ra* in this situation, as you have said."

"True," Hanook said, holding up his hand for attention. "But a man shares both pleasure and sorrow with his *maaj'garu*, and without doubt, Chixi's brothers have suffered much, as he has." He looked at Jordas and Yado in turn and sighed. "I may be just a foolish old man at times, but the law is the law. I know how it works. You have again incurred status-debt, though Chixi doubtless brought his doom upon himself, and his action in attacking you cancels that need against *him*. But only his brothers could say for certain what the truth is, and they're lost where grieving spirits wander while the bodies which contain them still live."

"What are you suggesting?" asked Jordas. "I accept that the brothers were drawn into this, though that means I must accept they also had a claim in the first place."

Hanook shook his head. "Not now – that's past. You brought the Shiranu to safety. Your debt to the tribe is discharged." He looked over at Jeene, Vru and Lorr. "You must ensure that they are taken care of until they recover their senses."

Jordas frowned his puzzlement. "But they shall be cared for with the rest of you," he said. "What difference would it make whether we, or the rescuers, look after them? Even if they'd accept help from me –"

"Oh, they'll accept it," Hanook murmured. "They have no choice. At the end of their *maaj'nag'ur*, your debt to these three *maaj'garu* is worked off, if you do as I have said."

"That seems fair," Jordas agreed, though he knew he had no choice.

Yado also bobbed his head in consent. <Soolkah is there,> he told Jordas, pointing to the rock platform.

<She'll be worrying about us,> Jordas sent. From this distance he couldn't

238

see her expression, but she was watching them intently and didn't see two Humanu from the rescue team come up behind her and lift her to her feet. They carried her, head turned towards the city as she protested, to the top of the slope and out into daylight.

"Soolkah!" But against the rushing of water and cries of other tribespeople Yado couldn't be heard.

"She will be fine," Jordas said. "They'll look after her. We can see her later." He hoped he was right.

"How should we leave here?" Aa'kam asked, pointing to the water rising against the chamber walls.

Jordas pointed to the slash in the rock. "Look! They come for us." Several rescuers were carrying inflatables downslope.

"What are they?" Hanook asked.

"*Mivattu*," Jordas said. *The word for boats from the time of Outside.* Like the words for stars and fish, they were so old they were only used in stories. The tribespeople watched open-mouthed as the inflatables headed for them.

"There's Gujas and her *amaaj*!" Yado had seen her amongst the Shiranu.

"Let's join them," Jordas said. He took Lorr's arm and walked towards the tribespeople gathered near the water's edge. Behind them, Yado led Jeene and Vru.

The first inflatable had arrived. Jordas watched as some of the tribespeople got in, steadied by the Humanu. They looked terrified. None refused assistance, despite the touch taboo.

The first boat left, powered by an almost-silent outboard motor. The next was filling up.

Jordas looked around. There were about twenty people left including themselves. He said to Lorr, "I'm sorry about your brother."

<They can't hear you,> Yado sent.

Jordas made a gesture, realised it was the one the tribespeople used for incomprehension, and shrugged instead.

They watched the tribespeople being ferried across the widening stretch of water. It had reached Jordas's thighs and the Naxadans' hips; the rock platform was half-submerged. Eventually, only a trio of Sargussi men waited with them.

"We can go this time," Jordas said. He helped Chixi's brothers board, then the rest of the tribesmen. Yado clambered in with some difficulty. Jordas followed him.

The inflatable swung about, caught in the battle between incoming currents and outflow from the city. As they set off, a dull growl belched from below and all around at once.

<Another quake!> Yado sent.

Jordas saw the fear on his face at the same instant as he felt it in his mind. *"Go!"*

In one corner, rocks tumbled. Water flowed in even faster. The helmsman touched the controls and the boat shot away from the crumbling city. Jordas turned for one last look.

Waters and tremor claimed Keramanthu equally. Buildings crumbled into a broth of rubble and filthy water as a tide slopped towards the cavern edges. Water swelled towards them, then overtook the inflatable. The next wave lapped higher than the last.

Peak followed trough followed peak, bouncing the boat on the waves. The level rose faster as stone displaced water. Jordas tasted Yado's fear, and felt him squeeze his eyelids together.

As the quake ceased grinding Jordas saw Yado open his eyes and stare towards the city. But it had sunk forever. Only a few shards of masonry pierced the waves.

*

Outside is cold. Hanook shivered in the wind funnelling between the mountains. The Humanu had given him a shining sleeping cloth to wrap around himself, but it only kept the chill off his skin where it touched.

He shielded his eyes with a hand and squinted around him. The light of glowcakes and ice caverns hadn't prepared him for this assault on his vision; his eyes filmed with moisture as his sight groped towards normality. *How did our ancestors live out here?*

A handtouch on his shoulder swung him round to face a Humanu. Hanook swallowed a furious order not to touch him as he squinted at him, saw his smile and the black thing in his hands which he laid across Hanook's eyes. The light was so much reduced that it was comfortable to look around now. Hanook nodded and adjusted the lightshield on his nose until it felt more familiar. The Humanu moved on to someone else. Hanook looked around. Now he could see how rocks sloped down the mountainside, meeting a torrent in the valley below.

As his sight returned it brought a surge of confidence. Hanook pulled the metallic sleeping-cloth more closely around him. It protected him against the wind, and warmed his skin.

Lorr passed him, eyes empty. Jordas held his wrist. Jeene and Vru followed Yado past Hanook along the ledge.

Hanook wondered where the rest of the tribespeople were. Although the ledge was crowded, there weren't enough people from either tribe there. He looked around in puzzlement, and found the Sargussi and the Humanu standing beside him. "Where is everyone?"

"They're in the silver beetles," Yado said, pointing into the air.

Hanook nodded, trying to seem as if he'd known all along. "My responsibilities weigh heavily on me at times." He tucked his legs under him and leaned back against the rockwall. "Sit with me, if you will."

Yado cast a glance at Jordas, then sank down beside him.

Jordas pushed Chixi's brothers gently to the ground, then followed his example.

*

Hands led Soolkah through the crowd, speaking words she didn't understand. No man or woman of her tribe would have touched her. *Humanu,* she thought. *Jordas's tribe.*

She'd seen Jordas and Yado beside Hanook. *They're safe, then.* She'd wanted to go to them, but couldn't pass through the crowd, jostled and swept away from the cavern exit. Currents of chill air buffeted her. She pulled her waterproof more closely about her as the fur rose on her legs. Her lightshield made the brightness more bearable, but she wasn't tall enough to see over the other tribespeople.

Above the ledge two great silver shapes hovered in the air, their heartblood throbbing in her ears. Reflections struck sparks into her eyes as she looked at them. They must be what Jordas had named *shuttles.*

The press of people on the ledge thinned as one shuttle scooped them into its belly. Soolkah looked around and saw the mountains for the first time. *So this is Outside. How big it is!*

A man at the head of the queue was counting people into its metal belly – half the size of a waystop cavern. A few at a time, the women and children were herded towards the basket which would take them away from their amaajnu and everything they'd ever known. Each time the basket returned empty, the man pushed the next few people towards it. Most of the tribespeople around Soolkah were weeping, fearful of permanent separation from their amaajnu.

The queue moved up as another surge of people came out onto the ledge. As Soolkah approached the head of the queue she saw the Humanu properly: he looked a lot like Jordas, but his head-fur was short, plastered against his skull by the drizzle; hairless face, skin speckled with golden-brown dots. He wore a silvery all-in-one suit, like the other Humanu.

"I'm Soolkah!" she cried, hoping they'd understand. "Let me find Yado

241

and Jordas! Don't make me leave my husbands behind!"

But the man just patted her on the shoulder as if to calm her, and ushered her towards the shuttle which crouched in the air like a squat silver umi-beetle. Soolkah sought Yado and Jordas, but the crowd obscured her view. *Surely I'll see them later*, she told herself, and turned her attention to the basket descending towards the ledge, swinging about in the wind which keened and blasted at her limbs.

The Sargussi woman nearest her was weeping, her children clustered around her, clinging to her legs and hands.

"Don't be afraid," Soolkah said. Her voice held a confidence she didn't feel. "They're here to help. It'll be all right."

There was a Humanu woman at the head of this queue, separating the crowd into small groups. Soolkah looked at her curiously, noting the single pair of breasts; like Jordas's chest. *Strange!*

Then she spotted Gujas holding her two youngest children against her for warmth, silver sleeping cloths wrapped about them. The boys, Juwan and Go'ti, were beside her.

She hurried over to Gujas's side. "I'm so glad to see you," she told Gujas. "Can I take Alsa?"

"Of course," Gujas croaked.

Soolkah scooped Alsa into her arms. She saw that the Humanu woman had noticed her changing groups; she caught her eye but didn't seem to be prepared to follow it up.

"Araz and Lagi and Ulon aren't allowed to come with us."

"Gujas, they'll come soon."

"I want them *now*!" Gujas's eyes were brimming over.

"I know," Soolkah said. "I want my husbands too."

More of the queue climbed into the basket and disappeared into the belly of the second shuttle: all women and children. The men queued up behind them on the ledge, but the Humanu stopped them from climbing. Every so often the basket would descend empty, or rise with a full load.

The group Soolkah was in dwindled rapidly until it was her turn to climb in. She clasped Alsa against her. Gujas clutched Teffen. Juwan and Go'ti followed them, clinging to their kilts.

Soolkah thought the wind would flay the skin from her as the basket was drawn up and into the flying beetle, but at last she stood inside it. There was metal all around her: walls, floor, and ceiling. The sights and noise were incomprehensible; but if Jordas understood and accepted these things, so must she. She was entering his world.

242

Another Humanu inside the shuttle led people to seats. Soolkah was strapped into one, then realised there were more people here than one harassed-looking Humanu could cope with. She waved to him to get his attention, then gestured at him – just as if he were one of the tribespeople – to show her how to strap people in so that she could help. After two or three goes the man caught her meaning and showed her.

Soolkah helped buckle in the next group to come aboard, then noticed Mnanga laid across three seats. Jordas's stained sleeping bag covered her; the sight of that brought a pang she couldn't ignore. Mnanga's face was whiter than usual with exhaustion and discomfort, but her eyes were open. She murmured occasionally to herself. The Humanu man spoke to her in a tone chosen to soothe, and Soolkah recognised the sounds of Jordas's language, although she couldn't understand him, and helped him buckle up straps to stop the Eldest woman from sliding about.

Aneera, Nazahl and Shan were strapped in nearby. Soolkah seated herself beside them, settling Alsa on her knees. "How is Mnanga?" she asked Aneera.

Aneera frowned. "She talks about the city," she said. "Something about the Prophecy."

"She said that earlier to me. Did she – say anything about me, or my husbands?"

Aneera shook her head and spread her hands palms down. "Are our husbands not coming with us?" she asked.

"I don't know. I'm worrying about that too."

The Humanu man passed nearby, checking everyone was strapped in.

Soolkah wanted to ask him what would happen to the tribesmen. *If only I could speak this tongue!* she thought.

The moment passed; the man took his own seat and belted himself in.

The shuttle lurched. Soolkah could see out through the spaces in the wall. She touched it and found a solid barrier. When she realised she could look out of the port without falling out she dared examine the scene below.

Her gaze explored steep valleys and upthrust peaks. The snow Jordas had told her about must have melted and flooded Kerui. There were no plants. No animals moved among the rocks. In the distance, lava spouted from a volcano like the one she and her family had farmed beneath, trusting heat not to engulf them. *Such a fragile alliance of heat, light from glowcakes, hard labour and plants was all that kept us alive for so long.*

A distant flame trail spliced the sky: terrifying, yet beautiful. For a moment she thought it was the other shuttle. But some fragments fell from it. She remembered Jordas's explanation to the tribespeople of what would

243

happen to their world, and understood fully. *We truly must leave. It's not safe to stay.*

And on the mountainside below stood the men of both tribes, most silver-wrapped, huddling together against the rain, the wind, the chill and fear. Momentarily the rocks twitched as the mountain shook again. Soolkah's stomach churned. She'd thought they'd all be safe once outside Kerui.

She easily picked out Yado and Jordas in their waterproofs. Then the shuttle moved, and Soolkah lost sight of them.

Will I ever see them again?

*

The sound of voices reached Jordas, along with the *smack* of bone on bone. He looked along the ledge. "Why are they –?"

"They're angry at being separated from their women," a man beside him answered. "I am, too. *Amaaju* should be together in a crisis."

"True," Jordas agreed. "My folk send women and children to safety first in danger, but it's not the way of the tribespeople." He stood up. "Let me through. I shall resolve this."

"I'll come with you," Hanook said. "Your tribe will understand you, but my tribe will listen to me."

Jordas stared at him for a moment, then nodded and shouldered his way through the throng, clinging to rocks for support where the ledge narrowed. Hanook followed. It took them several minutes to reach the fighting.

"Stop and listen!" Hanook's voice was quiet but held power.

His command stopped the fight mid-punch. The tribesmen fell back, shamefaced. Jordas saw a silver-suited man on the ground. Slowly he relaxed his arms which he'd raised to shield him.

"What's happening?" Hanook demanded.

"Our wives –"

"Our children –"

"QUIET! Fighting's too dangerous up here." Hanook turned to Jordas. "That's better. Tell them."

"They were sending your wives and children first for safety," Jordas said. "They don't understand about the *amaaju* – Humanu families have only one man."

Hanook turned to the nearest two men, pointing to the suited human. "Help him up and bring him to me."

"Are you okay?" Jordas asked the man.

"I think so." He wiped blood from a split on his lip. "Are you Jordas Krata? I'm Sam Mondel." He offered Jordas his hand.

"Do you need first aid?"

Sam shook his head. "Why did they attack me?"

Jordas explained the Naxadans' social set-up. "Even in emergencies they group according to families. Send the next shuttlefull with males as well as females and children and I'm sure you'll regain their goodwill. We'll help you re-organise them now."

*

Soolkah surveyed the shuttle, wondering if anyone else realised how final this leaving was. She'd known longer than any other Shiranu what would happen to Kerui. Because she'd spent more time with Jordas than the others she might find it easier to accept what was happening. *But it's still hard to bear*. Yado would probably adapt best of all; Jordas could help him.

A Sargussi tribeswoman strapped in nearby was sick. She wasn't the only one; and her three children were crying at the strangeness of it all, and calling for their fathers. The Humanu man unstrapped himself and walked over, clinging to hanging straps, a cloth in his hand. He wiped her kilt, then offered the cloth to the woman for her to clean herself higher up.

Soolkah wondered if Jordas's people also had taboos about touching each other. "I'll help you again," she told the man, gesturing to reinforce what she said. He seemed pleased and relieved as he passed a few damp cloths into her hands. They smelled of the stuff Jordas had sprayed into his wounds when she first met him, and dissolved the mess. She unfastened the webbing buckle, stood up and tottered to where he'd indicated, using the straps as she'd seen him do. Although the stench was ghastly in the confined space she knew she'd cope better with something to keep her busy.

She moved among her people, fighting for balance at times, sometimes feeling queasy herself. *But I'm strong,* she told herself. *I'll survive.* With an effort of will she rejected the weakness and nausea.

"It's hotter than a waterspring in here," one Sargussi woman complained to her.

"It is hot," she agreed. "Are you all right now?"

Without waiting for a reply, she removed the waterproof and tied the arms round her waist. When the Humanu turned, she thought his eyes registered shock. She remembered the Humanu woman on the mountainside. *And Jordas always keeps his chest covered,* memory told her. After that, she noticed he kept his eyes on her face whenever he passed her. *Did I do something wrong?* she wondered.

She turned back to check if Gujas was all right, and caught another glimpse of Outside. A fiery streak shot across the sky in the distance before a

245

ring of spray erupted from the water. Droplets spattered in all directions before the water extinguished the fire, and a wave swelled out from the impact. Soolkah watched, standing as if frozen to the spot.

The Humanu man had crossed to the port to look. She watched him. When he returned to his task, he couldn't quite erase the look of anxiety she'd seen often on Jordas's face. It was useless to talk to him – he wouldn't understand. But if *he* was worried, so was she.

When the man indicated she should return to her seat, Soolkah obeyed. She felt the shuttle turn in the air. That puzzled her. She was sure air had no substance for anything to turn against, but the sensation was unmistakeable. Nausea stirred again in the depths of her stomach. She felt the shuttle descend; perhaps they were approaching the shuzi, the collecting-place. As the shuttle settled onto a flat surface, Soolkah realised her guess had been right. She put the waterproof on again, longing for the protection of Kerui's caves.

Openings in the wall appeared. Mnanga was taken out first, carried by two Humanu. Then one by one the tribespeople stepped through the gap in the wall into the icy wind. Once more carrying Alsa, Soolkah looked up at the silver beetle they'd come from. *How can something so large and heavy hang in the air like that?* she wondered. *Perhaps that's why it makes that noise all the time.*

They splashed through knee-deep water towards a building. Despite its roof, it reminded her of Keramanthu's houses. Then the glare from above brightened again.

Soolkah held Alsa against her to hide her eyes, even protected as they were. Two or three globs of fire split the air and fell in the distance, but the Humanu faces wore expressions of worry as they hurried the tribespeople into the building.

Gujas made as if to catch at her arm as the Humanu men urged them inside. "Is it always like this Outside?" she demanded.

Soolkah hoisted Alsa more securely against her hip so that she could lay her arm above Gujas's shoulder. "I don't think so. Jordas's tribe seem afraid, and I don't think they'd stay here if they were always frightened."

"I want to go back to Kerui."

"You can't...Mother," Soolkah said. "Our place is gone." She watched the tears slide down Gujas's face, knowing there was nothing she could say to still her grief.

The door slid open. Soolkah followed her and the children inside. She sensed that the strangers wanted them to be safe. Behind her, she could hear the whine of the *shuttle* rising again as it prepared to leave. Perhaps it would return with Jordas and Yado.

Soolkah's tingling of anticipation dispersed with the hiss of another missile parting the air. It hit the water, but the percussion reminded her of a rockslide. At least in the *shuttle* they'd been spared the din of impact.

The door closed behind them. Inside, it was warm. More Humanu bustled up and led the tribespeople into a large room. Two men and a woman stood there holding boxes with glowing lights. To Soolkah's surprise, when the woman spoke into the box it reproduced her voice in Naxadan. The phrases didn't always sound natural, but Soolkah understood her.

"I wish you all a pleasant lighttime. My name is Wong Yuc Xiao. Please co-operate with what happens next. To provide you with suitable food, we must examine you. This won't hurt at all, or take long. Then we will bring you food, and treat your injuries." She paused. "Please sit down and make yourselves comfortable. We'll be as quick as we can." The woman and the two men passed among the tribespeople, pointing the boxes at them and speaking to each person in turn in calm and gentle tones.

Soolkah saw that the woman's skin was the colour of the digestive juices of a glowcake, her hair black as darktime. One of the men was as dark as Yado's complexion, and limped slightly. The second man was as pale-skinned as Jordas, with short yellowish head-fur. He smiled a lot; through the woman's speaking box he said he was a healer, and that his name was Tim.

"Will our husbands come here soon?" asked Soolkah. "We're all very worried about them. We can't understand why they didn't come with us."

"The shuttles aren't big enough to bring everyone together," Tim explained. "A couple more trips each and everyone should be here. Then we'll leave."

Soolkah could understand him easily enough, but something about his voice sounded different. After a while she identified that his accent wasn't like Jordas's. All these people spoke and looked different. "How unalike all the Humanu tribe are," she observed.

Tim laughed out loud at that, and everyone in the room turned to stare at him. "That's true," he said, still smiling. "We all are."

Soolkah looked at her origin-amaaj. Teffen and Alsa were crying, Juwan and Go'ti looked miserable, and tears streaked Gujas's face. Most of it was fear for the future, and for their fathers and husbands: fears she knew herself. The Humanu were afraid too, she remembered. But if Tim could laugh and smile, so could her people. She took Alsa back into her arms and said, "Shall we make up a story together?"

"Are we allowed?" asked Alsa. "All the stories we usually hear are true, and neither of us is the maaj'gar of the Eldest man."

247

"Today that doesn't matter – and anyway, Kayas isn't here yet. But don't make me give you kazmo'ra afterwards if I'm wrong!"

"What's the story about?" Alsa asked.

Soolkah wasn't sure until an image surfaced in her mind's eye. "Jordas told me about the place he comes from. This is a story about volcanoes."

"They have volcanoes there?"

"Yes, and he says people used to live in lava caves, just like us, if necessary."

With this evidence that the Humanu were so much more like them, Alsa lay back against her. Juwan and Go'ti looked interested and even Gujas was listening as she suckled Teffen. For a moment it felt as if they were back in their own sleeping-niche, and nothing had changed their way of life.

Soolkah drew a deep breath and began, "On Jordas's world, in a huge stretch of water the Humanu call *'the sea'*, is a land called *Iceland*. This is a story of the time before the winter ice departed those shores. The people that live there came from another land across the seas, and some were Jordas's ancestors."

Soolkah had a larger audience now than she'd intended. The Sargussi woman next to Gujas, and her four sons, were all listening. She smiled at her, acknowledging the right of all to share stories. "Iceland used to be much like here – snow and ice, volcanoes, and a place where the ground splits apart. Apparently the people were farmers like us, and also fisherfolk, but they sprang from sailors and warriors.

"On this particular day, the tribe's chief heard that another tribe was going to attack his people and take their animals and fish, and the news filled him with dread."

"What did he do?" Alsa's eyes were wide.

"He walked up to a huge waterfall to think how he could protect his people. But though he turned over one idea after another in his mind, just like the movement of the water as it poured down the valley, he couldn't think of a way to stop the raid.

"Then he walked across the land to a huge geyser which tossed water up in the air every few moments. But he found no inspiration in it. He trudged off in search of the place where, for generations, the Eldest of the people met to discuss things. But he still didn't know what to do. So he walked on, past the mouth of a lava tube.

"And as he came to the rift in the land, he had an idea as smoke and fire leaked out of the ground."

"What did he do?" Go'ti goggled at her.

"He saw the rift was wide, like a river. And he remembered the waterfall and the geyser, and the lava tube. And soon, he knew what he should do."

Now Soolkah had several family groups listening.

"He returned to his people and told the women and children to hide in the lava caves, and added that he had a plan to beat the raiders.

"Oh, tell us!" Go'ti was beside himself with curiosity. "What was the plan?"

"Who's telling this story?" Soolkah drew herself up and pasted a mock severe expression on her face. "Listen and you'll find out."

An indrawn breath from Juwan. "What happened?"

"The chief told the women and children to hide in the lava caves until the raid was over. Meanwhile he led the men, who were now more farmers than warriors, to the waterfall. They dug the rock away with farm tools and bare hands, and mounded the rock up above the rift. Some hid where the mountains met the sea at the shore, and the rest hid behind the dam.

"When the raiders arrived, they saw them drag their boats onshore. Some of those watching the shore ran down into the rift and along it. Others lit a fire they'd built.

"When the raiders saw the decoys enter the rift, they followed them, thinking they were few and would be easily beaten. The farmers in the rift ran far enough ahead that they could climb out and leave the raiders to their fate.

"When the farmers hiding behind the dam saw the fire they broke down the rock barrier. The water thundered down into the rift and boiled along it. It reached the places in the rift where flames came out of the ground and made eruptions of steam, and the raiders couldn't see.

"So they didn't see the water coming at them along the rift, or the fire that couldn't be extinguished – though they heard a noise like meltwater pouring into a cavern. They certainly didn't see the rocks that rained down on them and pinned them into the rift as the waters raged over them. Because the farmers had diverted the course of the river at the foot of the waterfall so that it would drown the raiders."

Gujas caught Soolkah's eye above Alsa's head. "How did you think of all that?"

"Jordas told me about the special places on Iceland, and I thought about how the tribes made the rock platform together, and I just made it up."

"Aren't you afraid, Soolkah?"

"Of course."

"You don't *seem* scared," Gujas said, smiling. "Soolkah, I never understood before! You weren't like other girls; you never did what I expected you to. I was ashamed when you did things I didn't understand or approve of. But today I am *so* proud of you."

"Proud of me?"

"Yes. Mnanga saw it, too. She's always been a strange one, as well."

"What is there to see?" Soolkah asked. "I can only be who I am."

"I know. *You* haven't changed; but *I* see you differently now. I worried when I heard you'd become amaajni with two foreigners. But now I think they'll suit you, even bring out the best in you. Mnanga realised that being different can be a strength, rather than a weakness."

CHAPTER 23

WHEN THE MOOD OF THE TRIBESMEN HAD CALMED, Jordas, Yado and Hanook returned to the back of the queue. The rain had stopped. Where before the press of people had deflected the cold, now there were more spaces for the wind to bite into. The tribespeople crouched or sat with hands clasped around knees or half-leaned against the rocks. Many shivered. Jordas and Yado were better protected from the cold, but periodically Jordas stood up and scrubbed at his arms through the waterproof.

"When will the shuttles return?" asked Hanook, wrapping his foil blanket more closely around him. "In two lighttimes, three?"

Jordas smiled. "It's not so far – and they travel fast!" He checked the time. "Each shall return before mid-lighttime, and again before darktime." He turned to Yado. "Would you go with this group or wait for the next one?"

"Although it's cold," Yado replied, "You would go in the last group, so I will stay too."

When Goram approached, Jordas took off his waterproof and offered it to him, then hauled the thermosuit out of his pack and struggled into it.

Goram stared, awed, until Yado pulled the waterproof over his head and rolled back the sleeves for him. "I'm honoured by this – gift?"

Jordas nodded. "Would you go with the next group?"

"My brothers and I will go when you do."

"And your wife, your children?"

Goram shook his head and leaned back against the rockwall. "Narunah and the children have already gone." He seated himself beside Yado and Hanook. "I'll tell my brothers."

"I shall be last aboard," Jordas said, "but we welcome your company."

"They say you and he are *maaj'garu*," Goram said. "How can this be? He's of a different tribe from you."

"From all of you," Jordas agreed. "I have no understanding of it either but it *is* true."

"I've an idea about that," Yado said. "Jordas is intuitive and sensitive, though his tribe rarely have telepathic ability –"

"A sort of free-range telepath, mayhap," Jordas murmured.

"When I lost my brother, if the connection stayed open instead of sealing off, that might account for him sharing with me."

Goram made no comment.

251

Jordas thought then what might have happened had he not been able to convince Marcus that he could communicate with Yado. *The sajamu are so powerful that I felt as if I was here before I set foot on-planet. Even if I hadn't come, I'd have felt it when he died. I'd feel the pain as the lava burnt me alive, or the last air was forced from my lungs as I drowned, and I don't know how I'd keep my sanity –*

He looked over at Jeene, Vru, and Lorr. *The* maaj'nag'ur *is how they cope,* he thought. *They shut everything out while they adjust to the loss. But being human, I may not have that option.* Then he wondered if Chixi's brothers would become telepathically linked to him as well.

<*They may have an open connection, but neither of us do now.*> Yado told him.

In the distance another light flare heralded a meteor screaming through the sky, followed by two more.

"Jordas," Goram began, "the fire in the sky –"

"I know, Goram," Jordas said. "Burning rocks. But they're small, and most fall into the water. We're safe enough unless one lands on us, and far enough inland to avoid any tsunamis they create."

Goram covered his face with his shrunken, crooked hand.

Jordas was surprised. "No need for fear! The Humanu Elders want to help your people survive, or I wouldn't be here now."

"I'm not just afraid," Goram said, voice cracking. "It hurts to leave everything I've ever known."

Jordas put his hand above Goram's shoulder as if to comfort him at the same time as he felt Yado's privacy shield close his mind against him. Yado squatted with his arms linked around his knees, face hidden against them.

Jordas hunkered down beside him. <Yado?>

Yado opened his mind to him suddenly. His grief was a wound that enclosed and suffocated him. <Outside weeps as we leave.> Rain pattered about them, mingling with the moisture on Yado's face, its rhythm broken only by the wind keening between the valley walls like a funeral dirge.

"It shall come right, in time," Jordas murmured.

*

Matt was in the main monitor room, checking seismographic readouts. There had been no quakes for some hours. The holotank was blank and dark. Although still tuned to the probe frequencies, they'd stopped transmitting some time before. *The floods must have destroyed them.*

With a sigh, Matt ejected the last holochip and dropped it into his pocket. *I'll pack that,* he thought. *There's bound to be a tank I can play it through on-*

board the ship. I should be able to get a look at the city.

He was about to switch off when John Wolfe hailed him. "Matt, the *Lady of the Lake* is calling –"

Matt linked the holotank to the ship's communications system. The captain stared into his face. From his expression this was no social call. "What's the problem?"

"The big fragments are still in formation, but Navigation reports increasing micrometeoritic showers crossing our orbit," Captain Thomas said.

"We saw that too," Matt said. "Can you adjust your orbit to compensate?"

"Implementing, but the shuttle will have to travel further to rendezvous."

"Can the shuttles divert to the ship without stopping here?"

Captain Thomas shook his head. "It takes as much fuel to leave the planet's gravity field as three runs between you and the rescue site. The *Guinevere* will have to refuel when it arrives. How many groups are left there?"

Matt sighed. "The last but one is eating hot food and resting now before embarkation. The last one's on its way back from the rescue site now."

"We'll get the *Guinevere* refuelled," Matt told Captain Thomas, "and send her up as soon as the previous group have embarked. But we need to keep the families together if possible."

"Fine," the captain answered. "I've told my crewmen there's no time to rest between trips." The tank darkened.

"Matt!" Abdel appeared at the door. "They're here."

Matt turned to him. "Tell the shuttle crew to refuel and be ready to take off again in half an hour." Abdel gave a thumbs-up and disappeared without wasting breath on a reply.

In the main hall, the refugees stepped through the door as if it would swallow them alive.

"Tim!" Matt called. "Have your patients left yet?"

The medic hurried over. "In the first group." He gestured towards the empty makeshift beds he'd set up. "These two groups need reorganising into families."

"I'll leave that to you, then." Matt turned to face the refugees. He soon spotted a human face in the crowd, stepped forwards and wrung Jordas's hand. "Good to see you again," he said.

"I'm *very* relieved to be here!" Jordas drew the tribesman forwards. "This is Yado, my...thought brother."

Matt extended his hand.

The tribesman looked at it before taking it. A look passed between him and Jordas. Then he squared his shoulders and copied the ritual handshake, a

253

smile softening his features at last.

Three Shiranu with blank eyes stood to one side. Matt shivered despite the warmth in the research station. Jordas didn't introduce them. Instead he indicated a small man with a withered arm and named him as Goram. He copied Yado's interpretation of the handshake using his left hand.

"Is he a thought brother too?" Matt asked.

"A friend."

Goram spoke, and Jordas replied.

Matt was surprised to hear the sounds coming from Jordas's lips. He hadn't realised how fluent he'd become in the tribal language.

"The family groups are worried about each other. Where are the rest of the tribespeople?"

"Resting in the staff quarters, though it's cramped. But we've sent most of the previous groups up to the ship now. Are you hungry?"

"Starving – and desperate for a fix of caffeine!"

"Then come this way for hot food and drinks, a shower and a change of clothes," Matt said.

"I could do with that – even a thermosuit doesn't work well over wet clothes!"

Having seen Jordas back to the room assigned to him, with Yado and Goram in tow, Matt returned to the foyer just in time for Abdel to report back.

"Refuelling's going well," he told Matt. "The *Guinevere* will be ready to embark shortly and the *Morgana*'s back. They said to get a group ready to leave for the ship."

"Right." Matt remembered Sam Mondel's call from the mountainside. *I don't need disorganisation at this stage, or any arguments.* "Go fetch Jordas from room twenty-three, will you, Abdel? He understands these people – he'll know what to do."

Soon Abdel returned with Jordas and the five Naxadans who apparently followed him everywhere. Jordas had removed his thermosuit, replaced his travel-stained clothing, and shaved and showered – though that hadn't removed the shadows from around his eyes or filled out the hollows under his cheekbones. But he looked less wild, more the civilised man Matt had greeted on arrival weeks before, though cuts marked his face.

"Can you organise them, like you did before? I don't want another *fracas* like Sam had out there. We don't want to antagonise these people."

Jordas nodded. To Goram and Yado he said, "Take a message to Hanook and Aa'kam to organise the tribes into family groups, ready to leave for the ship."

Matt watched them move through the crowd.

"They'll organise themselves now," Jordas said. He passed a hand across his face. "I need food and a rest, and time for myself," he added. "I've brought them this far." He sank into the nearest chair.

"I'll get you some food," Matt promised. "Stay there."

When he returned with a plate of steaming stew, Jordas was scanning the crowd as if seeking someone. "Who are you looking for?" he asked.

Jordas subsided back onto the chair and lowered his eyes to the food. "I just want to know Soolkah's safe and well."

Matt chuckled. "She's fine! She's helping dish food out. She wouldn't leave until you and Yado got here. Tim, Yue Xiao and Abdel recalibrated some food dispensers to suit Naxadan needs." He intercepted Jordas's look of inquiry with his own surprise. "She's got some of the other women helping, and a shuttle crewmen told me she helped on-board too," he said. "Would you like to speak to her when you've eaten?"

"Not if she's busy," Jordas mumbled, addressing himself to his food again. Matt had to strain to hear him above the hubbub in the room.

"I think she wants to talk to you," Matt said. "Your friend Yado's with her right now, but she keeps looking over here." *He seems to have become pretty close to some of these people,* he thought. *I wonder what really happened down there?*

*

Jordas looked around the almost-empty hall. <How many *amaaju* are left?> he asked Yado.

<Fifteen – about ninety people.>

Jordas yawned and stood up, stretching. He'd dozed after his meal but exhaustion still blanketed him; and now that he had returned to the surface and the society of his own people his emotions and position seemed uncertain. He felt as unequal to dealing with them as he had with the Naxadans, especially now Yado had helped him understand the tribes' customs. *I feel alienated from my own people's ways.* He groped towards a further truth. *No, it isn't even just that. It's how they'll deal with me as a human part of Naxadan society.* But he thought Matt would guess what his involvement had become, particularly within the confines of the starship.

"Shuttle's back!"

At the sound of Matt's voice, magnified by the station PA, Jordas looked up. The research team leader stood on a table to attract everyone's attention. The Naxadans jerked upright in shock at the volume as the universal translator echoed his words. "Please have your possessions ready for departure. We'll

255

leave when it's refuelled. Before that I want final reports from Frank O'Neill and John Wolfe."

Jordas could see Matt's astronomers approaching, and had no desire to hear their news. It wasn't going to be good. He reached under the chair to where his gear was stowed and hauled it out of his backpack.

Yado came and stood beside him.

Soolkah followed. Her smile for him was warm, if a little reproachful. "Where were you, Jordas?" she asked.

"Resting."

"I thought you might have spoken to me back there."

"I didn't want to distract you." He tried to concentrate on his surroundings. The scientists and technicians were going through a checklist of switches thrown and equipment deactivated. In a corner of the room, an argument had developed between the members of one *amaaj*.

Jordas closed his eyes, and saw himself bridging two societies: far enough removed from his own culture to be alienated from it, but not fully integrated into the Naxadan way of life either. He wasn't sure when he'd made the decision to leave Soolkah with Yado, but he thought it might be better for all of them if he didn't continue as Soolkah's *amaajne*, at least while on-board the *Lady of the Lake*. That might give him a breathing-space to decide what he wanted on a permanent basis...

And when we return to Goranon, what then? The question had been haunting him for some time.

He drew a deep breath, then told Yado his decision. <My tribe don't know about our – marriage.>

<Are you...ashamed?> Yado asked.

Jordas sensed his anger.

<I know marriage is different in your tribe, but I *am* proud to be Soolkah's husband. And I'm certain she's proud to be wife to us both.>

<I'm not ashamed,> Jordas protested, <but – I'm not sure how to explain to them. Or even if it's necessary right now.> That sounded defensive. Yado knew he'd deliberately kept away from Soolkah since arriving at the research station; and Jordas was sure he knew how much he wanted to spend time with her. The lack of privacy surrounding his feelings bothered him acutely at times.

And I still don't know whether my feelings for Soolkah are my own, or whether being Yado's maaj'gar *caused them...*

*

A percussion thundered overhead, penetrating Matt's thoughts. "What the hell was that?"

The station alarms shrieked.

Despite his exhaustion Matt grabbed his gear and shouted, "Jordas, we've been hit – get the Naxadans outside!" Above the hiss of pressurised foam he heard sizzling. He switched his thermosuit to cold. *But it's only a pebble, or we wouldn't be here!*

"The door's not opening!" Jordas yelled. "How do we get out?"

"Manual override – the box at the side."

Jordas yanked the cover off and jabbed at the controls. The door hissed open. He stepped through first, then stood counting as Yado helped the Naxadans outside.

At the back of the room, the ceiling peeled down in a layer of plasterboard. Fire licked the corner of the room. Matt felt heat on his face. Smoke billowed. Tears blinded him. He fought his way towards the brightness at the edge of his vision. Ahead, equipment spat sparks and crackles.

"Anyone hurt?" he demanded, gagging.

"A Naxadan man, over here." Yue Xiao. "Where's Tim?"

"Here." The medic touched his sleeve through the smoke. "Help me lift him, Matt. He's out cold."

He got one arm under the man's shoulders, feeling his head sagging against him as they edged through the smoke. A hand-held extinguisher hissed against the roar of flames.

"Where's Abdel?" he coughed.

"Smothering the equipment to protect us while we get out." He could just make out Tim's face.

"Leave it, Abdel," he choked. "Just get out now. Little Moon, where are you?"

"Here."

He felt her fingers touch his. "Let's go." He covered his mouth with his hand but his throat was already raw. They struggled through the smoke till the doorway loomed. They stepped through. Eager hands took the unconscious man from them. As Matt was helped through the doorway the irony came to him: *We're supposed to be helping* them –

His feet splashed into water. He felt its chill through the thermosuit and put up a hand to wipe his eyes. Jordas was speaking nearby to the Naxadans – probably sending them to the shuttle. People clambered through the doorway one by one without fuss. Most had little energy for upset at this latest catastrophe. The water level had risen centimetres since he'd last been outside. It was knee-high on the Naxadans, mid-calf level on the humans.

Matt blinked. His vision cleared. A crowd stood near the shuttle, waiting

257

to board.

"The fuel –" someone screamed. "Disconnect the lines *now*!" He saw John's shaggy form gesticulate.

"By Allah, yes, the fuel cache!" Abdel breathed behind him.

At that moment the main monitor room exploded. Jordas turned, ducking, hands raised as noviglass sprayed everywhere. Instinctively Matt shielded his own face with his hands. He turned. Jordas was bleeding from a gash on his cheek. Yado, Soolkah and the three Shiranu standing nearby seemed unhurt.

"There are still people inside!" Matt said.

Hands shoved at him. "Take these three to the shuttle – you'll need to lead them," Tim Perry said. "We'll get everyone out."

Matt saw he had a fire mask on, along with his thermosuit. "Make sure the shuttle's ready to take off."

Tim nodded and waded towards the shuttle, shepherding the three Shiranu.

*

Jordas glimpsed Yue Xiao assigning helpers to support yet another burn victim to the shuttle. The shuttle's engines whined above the roar of the fire. Almost everyone was outside. The drizzle couldn't dim the flares in the sky. Another bombardment breached the twilight. The Naxadans shivered, water up to their knees, hiding their faces with their hands, trying to purge their vision of afterburn images. Nearly all were huddled into foil blankets wrapped cloakwise around their shoulders. He sloshed over to Abdel's side.

"How many still in there?" he asked. "I make it we're missing six people."

"Me too."

Although he'd expected to hear that, Abdel's words hit him like a blow to the stomach. He didn't know what to say and tramped back to Yado and Soolkah. *At least the others got on-board ship safely – though I hope the ship's out of range of the showers.*

The shuttle had moved away from the flames marking the former fuel cache. The queue had followed it, with only a couple of *amaaju* still to board.

Overhead, light bloomed.

"Shit!" Jordas exclaimed.

Yado and Soolkah turned to stare at him.

<That's a heavy shower.> He pointed. <Depending where it falls we might need to navigate it.> Jordas knew Yado had picked up his alarm. He shut his eyes and breathed deeply. His heart thumped. He opened his eyes. The blaze of firestreaks in the sky looked nearer. *Or is it just my imagination?*

He caught Soolkah's hand and groped for Yado's mind at the same time.

<I've always been honest with you and your people, Yado. I wanted to treat you all as thinking adults in an adult world.>

<You have been honest with us,> Yado agreed, meeting his gaze with a sideways glance. <Same again?>

<Take Soolkah to the shuttle,> Jordas sent. <Look after Chixi's brothers. We'll finish up here.>

"Jordas, what will happen?" asked Soolkah. Her eyes were wide. "I'm scared."

"Me too," he said. "But you were safer away from the building." He paused, then added, "Go *on*." To Yado he added in the mindspeech, <If the shuttle gets damaged, we may be stuck here.> *It's as well they have the translators.* <Now go. Stay safe.> He watched them leave. He wanted to check where the shower was, but Tim Perry approached, half-carrying, half-dragging a Sargussi woman. Her children, a boy and a girl, followed her, crying.

"Is she alive?" he asked.

"Just. Here – take her."

Jordas lifted the woman out of his arms.

Tim looked round for Abdel. "Can you see the last three?"

"There can't be anyone else alive in there!"

"Just check, will you?"

Abdel pulled his mask down over his face and limped back towards the building, while Tim attached an oxygenator mask to the woman's face, hastily recalibrated for Naxadan physiology. "That should help," he muttered. Within moments her eyelids flickered open. She looked up at Jordas with an expression in her eyes that he recognised but couldn't identify.

"We're searching for your husbands," Jordas said.

The woman moved her head from side to side. "Save yourselves," she whispered. "I saw them burned alive." Her face was wet.

Jordas turned to Tim. "We should leave," he said. He beckoned Abdel.

Abdel tramped back, and Jordas explained.

"Let's go," Tim said. He scooped up one child under each arm. They struggled through the water to the queue for the shuttle. Only Matt and his colleagues remained to board. The hoist lowered again. Jordas felt ghost-fabric against his legs and a hand clasping his. Yado and Soolkah must already be aboard. The Sargussi woman slumped against him as she lost consciousness again, a dead weight in his arms.

They scrambled aboard the hoist. Matt pulled the gate fast behind him. The winch gear ground and squealed protest, but it clanked towards the underbelly of the shuttle. The waterlogged landing pad receded below them.

The cage clunked into place. Matt and his colleagues piled out. Someone lifted the woman from Jordas's arms.

"You deserve a rest now," a voice said.

They struggled up the companionway and into the belly of the craft. As they emerged from the central shaft, the human crew let out a cheer, then continued helping the Naxadans buckle up.

"Take-off in thirty seconds. Find a seat and strap yourself in," boomed the PA. The Naxadans cringed at the volume in the confined space. Jordas saw terror on every face. Children cried openly, clinging to their parents' hands. In one corner a woman brought her baby to the breast to comfort him.

Jordas spotted a seat on the far side of the cabin. He made for it, catching a hanging strap. But the shuttle lurched upwards; acceleration pressing down on him. He grabbed for the next strap and missed. His feet skidded on the floor. Free arm flailing, he dangled. The world shifted sideways.

Something clanged to aft. The shuttle bucked. The engines' scream faltered, then continued as if nothing had happened. Jordas heard shouts from the cockpit as the pilot and navigator fought to control the shuttle's seaward slide. His arm felt as if it would be torn off. *The pain's too much –*

Everything sounded far off. His vision whirled away to join the stars.

Abruptly the pressure released him. Hands hauled him to safety. His ears cleared slowly. When he could see again, he was buckled into a seat. Pain tore at his arm and shoulder.

"Jordas, what happened?"

"Couldn't get...to a seat in time," he mumbled. "What –?"

"Frank told the pilot you hadn't managed to get strapped in before lift-off and he was able to abort. But now there's another shower – we must wait for a launch window." Matt's eyes lingered on him. "How's the arm?"

"Awful. I hurt it when Yado nearly drowned, back in the caves."

Matt nodded. "We saw that."

Jordas gritted his teeth. Through the port opposite the sky was ablaze with a rain of flame. He felt movement again, though this time acceleration pressed him back into his seat.

"Hold now, I..." John's words were lost in the roar of take-off.

When the weight had lifted from his chest and he could think again, Jordas felt the craft turn as the pilot wove in and out of the meteor storm. One spin left Jordas gasping at the agony in his shoulder as his arm knocked the armrest, jarring the whole limb. His eyes sought Yado and Soolkah. Seated further along than he was, and only half-concealed by the armrest, Jordas felt Yado clasping Soolkah's hand. They looked terrified. They weren't the only ones to

260

break taboo.

The navigator appeared on the threshold of the cabin, eyes as wild as the course he'd plotted.

"Who's in charge here? We've just had a message from Captain Thomas."

Straining to hear brought Jordas's head up in a movement he instantly regretted.

"What message?" Matt demanded. "I'm the research team leader."

"The *Lady of the Lake*'s adopted a higher orbit to avoid the meteors." The navigator paused. "But the explosion forced us to disconnect early, so we don't have enough fuel to reach them."

CHAPTER 24

ANOTHER *CLUNK* AT THE REAR OF THE CRAFT. It jerked and slewed, then adjusted its course. Yado swayed in his seat. <What would that be, Jordas?>

<A fragment hit the shuttle's tailsection. They're trying to find a safe place to fly from to avoid the meteor storm. These are micrometeorites, but the fragments will become larger as the asteroid approaches.>

Yado saw Jordas's expression and felt his anxiety – along with his pain.

The shuttle shifted course again. Someone yelled from the control room. The Humanu lurched back inside it.

Yado's eyes watered from focusing on the silhouette against the lighted cockpit. He leaned forwards, ignoring the sajamu-ache in his shoulder. Through a port he glimpsed clusters of fireballs screaming groundwards. Their light pierced the darktime and scorched his retinas. The shuttle zigzagged through the air. Yado was flung against Soolkah, then Lorr, strapped in beside him. Lorr and his brothers rolled in their seats, oblivious. The other passengers clung to their armrests, toppling against each other like boulders in a rockslide. Without seat restraints they'd have been on the floor.

The shuttle steadied. Jordas was pale and sweaty. Yado was wrapped in sajamu he couldn't ignore. When Soolkah's hand crept into his beneath the armrest he returned to reality.

And now Jordas's injury was being dealt with. The Humanu healer Tim had got out of his seat and lurched towards Jordas, grabbing at hanging straps for support. He examined him, then pressed a tube against his neck. Soon the sajamu-ache faded from Yado's own arm and shoulder.

Tim moved among the injured, examining burns and scrapes, cleaning and dressing them. He even squirted a spray down Matt's throat before struggling back to his seat and fastening himself in. Then he leaned forwards to join the conversation between the Humanu with the face-fur and Matt. The other Humanu were all listening. The smile had left Tim's face for once.

Yado wondered what was happening.

<It's serious,> came Jordas's response. <Dodging meteors uses up fuel. We don't know if we can reach the rest of your people, now that the ship's moved further out.> He'd done his best to explain to Yado that they were going to a ship larger even than the caldera cavern of Keramanthu. "Yado!"

He saw that someone had wiped Jordas's face, and his eyes were focused on him.

"Remember giving me knowledge of your language? I'll sleep while they treat me for this injury, so I shall give you knowledge of *my* language."

"Good idea." Yado leaned forward, ready to concentrate.

The information flowed in, idea after idea, word after word, concept after concept. Sentences formed in his mind, ready to speak.

Thoughts were one thing, sounds a different matter. When he tried to speak aloud he found he knew how the words *should* sound, but they didn't come out as they should. The consonant blends were the hardest. The language of Kerui had few.

"Your language lies strangely on the tongue," he murmured.

"It shall feel comfortable soon enough."

Matt was saying something to Jordas. With a shock Yado realised that he understood. He nodded at Soolkah, dozing in the safety of the seat restraint. "She should l'arn too," he said, trying to copy Jordas's pronunciation. It sounded better; he felt encouraged by the small success.

<Pity we can't teach her that way,> Jordas agreed.

*

Soolkah's muscles had stiffened, and the air was stale. They'd drifted, out of the reach of the meteorites, for perhaps nearly a lighttime. Beside fuel, they'd also run out of pain relief. Almost half the tribespeople had some hurt, though their tough skins had prevented much harm.

Sweat sheened Jordas's skin as he lolled in his seat. Stubble had grown on his chin again; more than once Soolkah had seen Yado scratch at his own skin. The other Humanu had similar growths of face-fur. Every face was smudged with dirt and ash.

Yado stopped massaging his shoulder and rested his weight on the arm laid across his knees, cradling the other behind it. Jordas, Soolkah noticed, was doing the same.

A stir from the control room drew her attention. The pilot appeared at the threshold, clinging to the edge of the opening to stop herself from floating away. Since the shuttle had used up its fuel they'd drifted with nothing to hold them to the deck. Yado had explained to the tribespeople that for safety they should stay strapped in.

The pilot was speaking, addressing the Humanu. *Humans, they call themselves,* Soolkah reflected. *They call us Naxadans, but we can never return to Kerui...I mustn't think about that now.*

"What did she say, Yado?" she asked, proud that she could ask him to translate instead of Jordas.

"The ship comes for us!"

"Can you stand?" someone asked Jordas. "Can you walk?"

"Yes," he answered. Supported by a medic, he stumbled through the door. "Where are Yado and Soolkah?" He looked for them, but they were nowhere in sight.

"Keep still," the medic told him. "They're Naxadans? They'll be fine. You can see them later."

He either dozed or blacked out then; he came to when pain shot through his shoulder as someone moved his arm. He felt Yado's mindtouch and reflected pain.

He opened his eyes. Everything was blurred. He was lying encased in the medmachine. This must be the *Lady of the Lake*'s sick bay. A needle penetrated his forearm...

"Does anyone speak English?" one of the Humanu asked. "They're bringing a *universal translator*, but until then –"

Drawing a lungful of metallic-smelling air, Yado stepped forwards, rubbing his shoulder. "I do."

"Ask them to follow us."

Yado nodded and signed to the tribespeople. They'd clustered together, scared by the strangeness of their surroundings and the disappearance of familiar faces.

He was worried about Jordas. He'd tried the mindspeech but there was only blankness and a grinding in his shoulder as the dislocated joint was cranked back into place. The prickle of the drip in Jordas's forearm bothered him. As the Humanu made to move off he caught at his arm. He thought it would be acceptable; hadn't Jordas himself touched people before he'd known of the touch taboos of the tribespeople? "Wait! What about Jordas? Is he all right? When can we see him?"

"Is he the injured man? He'll be in sick bay. Food first, then medical checks. You can see him then. He'll be fine, don't worry!" the Humanu added, and moved off.

The tribespeople followed. Children cried at the strangeness of it all. The uniformed Humanu were people, yes, but with facefur, and clothes covering them from head to foot. Despite his mindlink with Jordas, Yado understood the tribespeople's uncertainty at the differences between them.

They entered a huge room full of seating-places and what Jordas had named *tables*. "Tell the others – we shall eat here," he told the tribesman nearest him.

The man nodded and with some satisfaction, Yado heard the information being passed on. The tribespeople murmured with excitement; after all, they hadn't eaten or drunk for more than a day.

The Humanu beside Yado checked with them that they'd correctly understood the nutritional differences between the tribes. Soon afterwards, food arrived.

Yado inspected the meat stew in his bowl. Soolkah's had vegetable stew. With the bowl came a metal object which he remembered the Humanu called a *spoon*. He began scooping the steaming food into his mouth, but screwed up his face as he tasted it.

"Ugh! Sweeter than Kerui meat," he told Soolkah. It was as much as he could do to swallow it, hungry though he was.

Soolkah said nothing.

He looked at her face. Although she was eating he saw no enjoyment, nor relief from hunger. Tears pooled in her eyes.

"Soolkah?"

"I've just realised," she said. "I'll never eat aldu bread or luthu again, or spicepods or chillcaps. It'll never be quite the same. However kind Jordas's people are, it'll never be like home."

Ghasru masaachifar, I am such a clumsy fool! Yado gripped her fingers under the table. "I know," he said.

They finished the food in silence.

*

Senator Gerrold Hartmann tossed the half-read progress report from Marcus Carlin on his desk and picked up his beaker of coffee. *Damn it! Every one of these reports has contained some complaint about the money not being there at the right time.*

He'd always taken care, both in government and at the Committee, to ensure security. No whisper of his activities had ever reached Asthorn or anyone else's ears. He hadn't been greedy. The money he used to fund his operations was returned to source as soon as he'd made his profit. *And up until now, it hasn't made any difference to the functioning of the projects concerned, because separately the sums involved aren't large enough to cause problems.* The litigation over the explosion of the Kiai ship had been covered, though he hadn't made his usual killing. And then World Senate business had demanded he visit that Godforsaken Mars colony, Apollinaris M, for negotiations lasting almost a week, and prevented him from starting his next couple of transactions sooner. *Had I been able to transfer funds in from another account, Carlin would have had nothing to bleat about. But I went straight on to the next visit,*

265

and didn't dare make calls from Mars – those damned robots run every security check known to man and some that aren't! Hartmann shuddered.

But the plan for this project was nearly completed. He sipped and pondered his next move. It was lunchtime, so he wouldn't be missed while he made two final calls. Then he'd be in the clear. He finished his coffee and breezed into his secretary's office. "Gianetta?" he said.

Gianetta was painting her lips with a scarlet lipspray. She had to stop to pout at him. One side of her mouth glittered.

"I'm going out for lunch," he said. "I'll be back at about half past two."

Gianetta put down the lipspray. "I can be ready in two minutes, Senator," she said.

"I have to meet someone," he said. "We'll do lunch tomorrow."

Gianetta pouted at him again, this time with disappointment. Ignoring it, he strode out of the door.

It was raining. Hartmann stood on the steps of the World Senate Building to open his umbrella. Raindrops fingered his collar. In a corner of the forecourt above the steps, at fountain level, a man stood studying a newsreader. His off-white rainjacket blended with the pale stone of the building.

Hartmann tripped down the first flight of steps. At street level he slowed his pace and soon integrated into the crowds on the sidewalk. This whole historic area had been designated as a technology-free precinct. Cars passed several times, but electronic pavements were not permitted here.

He crossed the street at the corner, heading for Kitchener's Restaurant, just outside the precinct, and strode towards a cluster of holobooths along the street. He entered one at random.

Hartmann withdrew from his pocket one of several pairs of spectacles and balanced them on his nose. The holotank flashed up a message: "PLEASE IDENTIFY YOURSELF". Although discretion required the silent facility to be available for financial transactions of all kinds, identification was always required. Hartmann spoke the name, then waited while the computer matched database details.

"Verify identification," was the next demand.

He leaned forward for scanning.

"Identification verified," the computer told him.

Works every time, he thought. *Well worth the initial investment.*

Once he'd accessed the bank account, he selected "transaction" from the options menu, entered the security code for the account destination and made the transfer. The account was now empty. *I'll close it from a public holobooth elsewhere in the city,* he decided, though he could have done so there and then.

He'd withdrawn cash to salt away as his profit the previous day.

He completed his call and left the booth after checking that none of his acquaintances were around and stowing the spectacles away. The only person he recognised was the man in the off-white rainjacket, slipping into the booth beside the one he'd used.

For a moment fear clutched at him. The Naxadan project had given problems all along. But the operating system had proved foolproof time and again. Hartmann mentally squashed down any possibility of problems and walked briskly back to Kitchener's.

*

After eating, the tribespeople were led along another metal corridor to what their Humanu escort told Yado was the *sick bay*.

Yado explained its purpose to Soolkah. Although she'd wiped her eyes, she was frowning. "Jordas is here."

Soolkah's face lightened. Yado was looking forwards to seeing Jordas again too; he was his lifeline in this unfamiliar place. He knew Soolkah felt the same; and surely the rest of the tribespeople did too?

But in the sick bay shock hit him. The patients weren't lying wrapped in sleeping bags like Jordas's, as he'd imagined, but were encased from the neck down in metal *boxes*. At first he thought they were all dead, but sajamu told him otherwise. The next blow was that although the first two *machines* were occupied by familiar faces, neither Jordas nor Mnanga were conscious.

"The pain would be too much for them," his Humanu guide told him, "so we keep them asleep until they're healed. Soon they'll be fine."

Yado remembered his awareness of the *machine*'s work on Jordas's shoulder, his half-healed cuts and bruises, and shivered. Granted, the drugs Jordas had been given dulled his perception of them; but he wondered again at the fragility of Humanu skin. Sleeping through illness and injury seemed a good idea, after all.

Aneera and the assistant healers of both tribes were there, perhaps helping with the healing in some way, though Yado wasn't sure how. *Will the Humanu know how to heal us?* Then he recognised the woman from the shuzi and the Humanu healer, Tim. Yue Xiao came forwards with the translation *box* he'd seen earlier. She, Tim, and the ship's healer examined each tribesperson, and asked about injuries, pain or other problems. They consulted often with Aneera and the apprentices. Cuts and bruises were sprayed against dirt and germs, then coated in the stuff Jordas had used to dress his ganzu puncture. It quickly hardened to form a layer which stood out as oddly against the pallor of short white Shiranu fur as it did against the darker, longer whorls of the Sargussi.

267

Yado wrinkled his nose in distaste at the smell.

When he asked after Mnanga, he was told her thigh was healing nicely. Tim complimented the tribal healers' skills. The Sargussi woman burned in the fire was in a *machine*, and would soon be fit. Her origin-amaaj were caring for her children. Even Matt was receiving treatment for breathing smoke, though he was seated, reading. A breathing *device* covered his lower face.

"What about these three?"

Yado realised the ship's healer was indicating Jeene, Vru and Lorr. "No," he said. "They aren't injured or ill, just grieving. They just need to be told what to do and they'll do it, until they come out of this state."

"We'll look after them, then," said Tim. "They can stay here, but we won't put them in *machines*."

Yado wasn't sure if that was acceptable until he caught Hanook's eye and saw his slight nod. "They're really my responsibility," he told Tim. "I'll come here every day to see how they are and spend time with them."

Azhee was being installed in a *medmachine*, amid protests from her husbands and wails from her children. She fought the Humanu healers, raising a red line with a talonslash on one of them.

"Help us!" Azhee's eldest husband appealed to Yado.

"How long must she be here?" he asked.

"One or two days," the ship's healer murmured. "Why is she so upset? Her injury will repair more quickly in the *machine*."

"Her husbands worry that she won't be able to feed the children," Yado explained.

The newborn howled as if in agreement.

There was a moment of silence. Then the ship's healer muttered, "We heard about the fight on the mountainside from Sam."

"You should understand that for Shiranu people, breast milk is the most important food for children up to five highwaters."

The healer's mouth opened and closed, then opened again. "That's not a problem. The drugs won't affect her milk. The family can stay here and we'll rouse her when it's time to feed the children. And we'll help watch them."

Yado explained to Azhee what the healer had suggested. "They would help us, not cause problems," he said. "It were better to sleep whilst your injury heals."

"All right," Azhee agreed. She lay back and allowed the *machine*'s upper layer to be fastened over her. "I don't like this – I can't move..."

"Relax," Yado said. "You needn't move, and you will feel better when you wake."

"Don't leave me," Azhee mumbled, but her eyes were closing.

Soolkah caught Yado's eye. "You're a good negotiator. Jordas would be proud of you."

"Speaking of Jordas," Yado murmured, "I understand now why he kept quiet about our relationship. The Humanu aren't used to women being married to several men. They surely won't understand one of them being part of an amaaj."

CHAPTER 25

THE JOURNEY TO GORANON took the usual five days. Jordas had spent two days sedated in the medmachine.

Tim helped him out of it.

Yado and Soolkah stood watching. He smiled, touched by their presence.

"We owe status-debt towards Chixi's brothers," Yado reminded him, pointing to them, seated nearby.

"Jordas should rest today. The drugs will still be in his bloodstream," Tim objected via the translator.

"I am tired. I must rest, but I haven't forgotten," Jordas said, yawning. "I shall help tomorrow."

"You don't have to, Jordas," Soolkah said. "I can help Yado."

"Tribal business, no Humanu allowed?" he asked, narrowing his eyes. "It was my *kazmo'ra* and Yado's – you weren't even there."

"I haven't forgotten, either," she said. "But Matt said you'd have other things to do when we asked him. I don't think he understands –"

"I suppose I'd better speak to him and Marcus before resting." Jordas got up, thanked Tim, and left the sick bay. He didn't look back.

Marcus requested a report, which Jordas sent from the Charidas Interchange. By the time the *Lady of the Lake* was in orbit around Goranon and the tribespeople had been transferred by shuttle to the spaceport at Rorvik, he'd had no reply and was beginning to worry.

But when he ushered the tribespeople towards the Arrivals desk, he realised his angst had been unnecessary. Marcus stood frowning beside a large marble desk constructed in one with the flooring. He peered around as if seeking someone among the throng in Arrivals. As he spotted Jordas approaching, his face creased into a relieved smile. He stepped forwards and wrung Jordas's hand. "I'm glad to see you're back in one piece."

Jordas shepherded Yado and Soolkah forwards.

"I think I recognise these faces!" Marcus smiled, extending a hand to Yado.

Jordas introduced them. <Shake hands!> he instructed Yado. Then he turned to Soolkah. With surprise he saw Marcus bowing over her hand, and caught the flash of jealousy in Yado's eyes, and its echo in his mind. *I should have warned Marcus not to do that.* Unaffected for once, he mindsent an explanation of Marcus's behaviour to Yado.

"We'll just get you processed," Marcus murmured. "Have the tribespeople all got identification documents?"

Jordas nodded. "Issued at Charidas." That had been exhausting for both himself and Yado, who'd fingered his ID as he puzzled over the marks on it in between acting as a translator. The tribespeople knew everyone else in their communities, but they were awed at the number of people. They'd begun to understand the need for retinal scans and handprints.

"Everything's arranged. There are stress counsellors waiting back at Axos to work with the Naxadans," Marcus said, finger-combing his beard.

Jordas realised he was anxious and wondered why, as the tribespeople filed past the officials. The worst was over; he'd brought them this far. Sargussi and Shiranu alike stared about them at buildings and scenery, and especially at the Humanu going about their business around them. The sight of Kiai or Vanjeynish drew much attention; and once, a Zarduthi in furs, leather and metal strode through the arrivals lounge, perhaps seeking some of his own people.

"So many different kinds of people. Perhaps there's a place for us here after all," Jordas heard someone say, and made a mental note to try to reassure the tribespeople.

"Look – the leaves are green and blue here!"

Jordas smiled to himself.

"There'll be a wait before the Naxadans can be resettled, I'm afraid," Marcus said as the immigration clerk began to process the Naxadans' documents. "Howerd has set things in motion, but he warned me that it could take some time to find a suitable resettlement planet."

"So – what will they do till then?" Jordas asked. "Yado and Soolkah could stay with me, but my house is small –" *And does anyone know the extent of my relationship with Yado and Soolkah? What would Marcus have to say about it?* he wondered. *And what will my community expect of me now that I'm back here?*

"I know they're special friends, Jordas, but I don't think the Committee will like it. Anyway, temporary arrangements are already in place."

"Oh?"

"Some prefabricated buildings at Axos have been set aside for them until resettlement – basic requirements but no unnecessary technology. The Naxadans will be confined to the area, with access to them restricted to counsellors and medical staff, our research team and Committee employees."

Anger and apprehension grew inside Jordas as he digested this. He thrust his hands into his trouser pockets, unwilling to let Marcus see it disturbed him.

"And how long will this state of affairs last?" His voice sounded subdued even to him, but he was turning angry words over and over in his mind, seeking the right ones. However comfortable their quarters, they didn't deserve virtual imprisonment, and wouldn't cope well with it.

"Perhaps a few months."

"Marcus, these people are nomads!" Jordas protested.

"There's nowhere for them to go here on Goranon. The terrain isn't suitable for that lifestyle," Marcus pointed out. "Every time *you* go climbing you first have to hack your way through the jungle to get to a cliff!" His voice softened as he added, "And we'll need access to them when Howerd gets here. Can you imagine trying to find them in that lot?" He waved a hand in the direction of the jungle. "The desert areas north and south of this belt won't support them. And food preparation's an issue. They'll be safe in the compound, though."

Jordas examined the ground, forced his mouth to relax, trying to swallow his anger so the tribespeople wouldn't see and become angry themselves.

"I passed your report on to the Committee," Marcus added. "They intend to hold an official inquiry to establish the cause and manner of that big Naxadan male's death."

Jordas stared at him. "Why?"

"Something to do with promoting good relations between the Naxadans and the Federal League. It was Senator Hartman's idea." Marcus sighed. "He's set it for next Tuesday and is coming here to chair it." He hesitated. "I've been told I must suspend you from work until after the inquiry. I'm sorry, Jordas. It wouldn't be *my* choice." For once, he couldn't meet his gaze.

Jordas's fists balled inside his pockets. Now he understood Marcus's anxiety. "I see," he said. "You know, Marcus, if trouble starts between the tribes again, it will be the Committee's fault for raising the matter."

"Why should trouble start between the tribes?"

"Because Yado is Sargussi and Chixi was Shiranu. We've already had some difficulties."

"You may have a point there, Jordas," Marcus said, "but it isn't entirely our problem. It's the Committee's, and I'm sure they'll handle it as best they can."

"With Hartmann chairing the inquiry?"

Marcus ignored the gibe, so all Jordas could do was to allow him to usher them towards the huge commercial flyer chartered to take them from Rorvik to Axos.

*

272

Yado rubbed the site of his anti-sunburn shot. "Shall we collect Chixi's brothers now?" He adjusted the fit of his *sunvisor*.

"They won't know the difference anyway," Soolkah answered. They stepped out of the *hut* together.

Jeene, Vru and Lorr shared the *hut* past Hanook's. As they passed, Yado saw the Shiranu Eldest man sitting on the steps of his *hut*, deep in conversation with Aa'kam and some of the tribesmen. Taloned fingers pointed at them as Soolkah and Yado walked past.

Yado did his best to keep his discomfort from showing. "I do wonder what your people think of you being amaajni with me."

"It doesn't matter what they think." A shadow passed across her face. "But I wish Jordas could be with us. It feels strange without him."

"He misses us too," Yado said.

They'd reached the *hut* where Chixi's brothers lived. The door was open, as usual. Inside, he could just make out Jeene, Vru and Lorr. He entered, his *sunvisor* adjusting to the gloom.

"Wake up," he called. "Jeene!"

"Will you bathe them?" Soolkah asked. "I'll prepare food."

Yado nodded. He helped Jeene rise and led him into the *shower room*. The Naxadans had all enjoyed this pleasant novelty. Water sluiced down onto Jeene's naked skin. *Even were it the custom,* Yado thought, *I wouldn't let Soolkah bathe* these *men!*

"Let's take them back to our *hut*," Soolkah suggested after they'd fed Vru, Jeene and Lorr.

They led the three brothers outside. A few paces away, two young Shiranu boys stood watching.

"Haven't you got anything better to do than watch us?" Soolkah inquired.

They shook their heads. One of them scratched at his side. "Where can we go?" he muttered. "The walls of this place keep us in."

"For our safety," Yado said. But there was no conviction in his voice.

"Safety, hah!" said the other boy. "What do you know about safety? You're the maaj'gar of the Humanu. You helped him kill Chixi."

"Who told you that?" Yado demanded.

"My fathers said Hanook told them the Humanu Jordas is believed by his people to have killed Chixi. That's why he hasn't come to see us."

"Hanook knows that's not true!"

"Then why are you caring for his brothers while they're in the maaj'nag'ur?"

Several Sargussi youths had come to stand nearby. Yado felt a frisson of fear, though not for himself. He looked at Soolkah, at Chixi's brothers, then at the growing group of Sargussi and Shiranu youths. His fear encompassed all of them.

"It's shame on our tribe that you owe kazmo'ra to a Shiranu," came the throatier voice of Imar's youngest brother. He'd had his coming-of-age just days before Yado, and was full of pride since becoming amaajne. "Just as it is to be wed to a Shiranu ganzu-bitch –"

"Stealing a woman," said the youngest of the Shiranu boys, "is *just* what a Sargussi would do!"

A shriek burst from his lips as fingers whirled out within the crowd and found their mark. Blood spurted from a talon-rake across his chest.

"I'll get you for that, Sargussi!" The youngest Shiranu's fist knuckled the Sargussi youth's eye.

The Sargussi took a pace back, hand over his eye, then tripped forwards and kicked, raising another bloody weal down the young Shiranu's flank.

His brother leapt forwards and grappled with the Sargussi. The impact of his body took them both onto the sealcrete compound floor. Neither noticed the impact. They rolled over and over, gouging for each other's throats. People joined the crowd all the time.

Yado's fists clenched. His talons pierced his own palms. He fought for control, knowing that if he allowed his own anger to spill over, he'd just make things worse. He wanted to touch Soolkah, tell her she'd be safe, but it wasn't necessarily true.

"I'll kill you, Shiranu!"

"You...kill me, and I'll...kill...you! Tribe of woman-stealers –"

"Enough!" Aa'kam's voice bit through the group to still Yado's anger. "Let me hear no more such speech!" His look was directed at Yado, but his words rang through the air. "Imar – pull your brother off him!"

"And Nulma – stop your son from fighting. Rokka's hurt." Hanook appeared, pointing, with Nulma at a run behind him. Nulma hauled his son away from the Sargussi. Heartbeats later, Hanook and Aa'kam spoke together. The tribespeople waited to see what they would do. The air was charged.

At last Hanook spoke. "I'm forced to impose kazmo'ra on you two," he said to Nulma's sons.

"To whom?" The boy's voice was soft with surprise.

"Gwa's amaaj."

"And you, Bessil, maaj'gar of Gwa, shall owe kazmo'ra to these two's amaaj," Aa'kam added, before either of the youths could comment, "to be carried out when we reach our new place. Go back to your amaaju, young ones.

Neither the Humanu Jordas *nor* Yado killed the Shiranu Chixi. It were best not to listen to such gossip."

Bessil allowed Gwa to lead him away, back to their *hut*. His eye was swollen and discoloured. As Nulma led his sons away Yado heard him say, "You've brought shame on our amaaj, my sons. Don't be so foolish again, or you'll owe *me* kazmo'ra as well!"

Yado stood beside Soolkah and Chixi's brothers. The sun beat at his skin in waves for many moments before he knew what must be said. "Jordas and I know we're innocent. But until the Humanu learn this truth, we may expect more trouble."

*

"Call for you, Marcus."

Marcus thanked Ray with a smile. "I'll take it on my monitor." He glanced around the monitor room. Ray was at his workstation, comparing seismic readings and spectrographic analyses, while John Wolfe, Frank O'Neill and Alleem Zheutal were using the large holotank to observe the impacts as the last larger asteroid fragments hit Naxada.

"Got it!" Hyperactive as ever, Ray seemed excited by the prospect of an eruption. "Magma on the move!"

"Where?" asked Alleem.

"Below Kerui. Take a few days, though."

"Before the final eruption?" asked John.

"We got the Naxadans out just in time, then," Frank commented.

Abdel, Matt and Yue Xiao were on leave in Rorvik. *Jordas should have been here too*, Marcus thought. He settled into his chair. Corah Whitley and Howerd Asthorn appeared in his projection tank. Corah beamed, though Howerd looked more serious.

They exchanged greetings, then Howerd asked, "How are the Naxadans?"

"They've mostly coped with being in the compound, but there have been a few scuffles between the tribes." Marcus frowned. "How can I help you?"

"We have some information for you."

"Oh?"

"I think you'll be *very* interested in it," Corah said, with a glance at Howerd. Her hair formed a mountain of curls today. It wobbled slightly as she perched on a seat. "When we looked at the other projects Hartmann has been involved in here, we found that Nevil Floyd's name cropped up in quite a few of them as Senior Administrator, and where it did, problems similar to those on your project also occurred."

"So why didn't anyone report them?" Marcus asked. "Surely someone

275

must have noticed?"

"Maybe not," Howerd said. "Each project had a different junior administrator, so nobody picked it up until now. And some projects are much larger than yours. It was only when 'Mr Floyd' got greedy and decided to divert funds away from smaller accounts as well that it became more noticeable."

Marcus fingered his beard. "So do you have any idea who would set up a series of accounts with a fictitious administrator yet?" he asked.

"Oh yes," answered Howerd. "Senator Hartmann divides his time between his work for the World Senate and the Committee. When he was in Washington recently I had our internal security department tail him as he's the central figure in all these projects. You should have had some more money enter the account in the last few days."

"Yes."

"Our security agents report that five days ago, Hartmann made two holophone calls from public facilities, both to a bank account opened in the name of Nevil Floyd. The first authorised money to be paid into the project account, to make it up to the correct balance. Unfortunately, of course, it was too late to make the difference to the project that it would have done earlier. The second, made just over an hour later, closed the Nevil Floyd account." He paused. "Three days ago he left Earth for Goranon to chair this inquiry."

"You mean – he's not in custody? Wouldn't it be cheaper and easier to arrest him on Earth?"

Howerd shrugged. "We're still investigating what he did with the money, and *how* he got his hands on it. He's instigated this Inquiry, which gives us a few extra days and hopefully will lull him into a false sense of security. By the time he's picked up, we should have all the evidence we need to deal with him."

"I see." Marcus leaned back in his chair. "I should say I'm not too happy about my assistant, Dr Krata, being suspended on Hartmann's instructions. Especially in the circumstances."

Howerd considered his words before replying. "I can understand that, but I think in view of the delicacy of this operation, that must stand."

"But Jordas hasn't done anything!"

"It's only a formality," Asthorn said. "But I don't want Hartmann's suspicions aroused in any way. I'm sorry." He paused again. "This would be normal procedure in any such inquiry under Committee regulations."

"Jordas is no murderer, whatever Hartmann may be trying to imply!" Marcus's vehemence surprised even himself. He looked around the room, but apparently none of his team had heard even that part of the conversation.

"I'm *sure* he's not," Howerd said. "In fact he's quite the hero for rescuing the Naxadans. But Hartmann has been working for the Committee for the last several years, and nobody suspected his involvement in this sort of...conduct. He doesn't realise we know what he's been up to, and I'd rather things stayed that way until our agents can pick him up."

"It seems unjust that an innocent man should be treated like a criminal while the real villain goes free! I don't like it, Howerd," Marcus said. "It's just not right. And what if Hartmann goes missing?"

"He's still being tailed. And it won't be for long. Senator Hartmann will arrive in four days' time. Your assistant probably needs some leave after what he's been through, anyway," Howerd said. "I...have read the reports," he added.

"I assumed you had."

"I'll call tomorrow. We should have what we need by then. In the meantime, don't mention this to anyone, not even your man Krata."

Marcus acknowledged his instructions with a curt nod, still feeling nettled on Jordas's behalf. "Goodbye." He fingered his beard again. *I still think Howerd's wrong about leaving Hartmann on the loose. If he can siphon money off like this, there's no telling what he'll do between Earth and here.*

*

Senator Gerrold Hartmann strolled along the plaza towards Lakshar's Bar. He was careful to look around him as if exploring the area, but in reality his stare assessed which, if any, of the space station's inhabitants might represent a threat to him. *I may not be an intuitive man, but I've been uneasy ever since closing the last account.* That was why he was here.

The bar was dead ahead. He took a timecheck from the old-fashioned brass clock mounted in the centre of the square. *A few minutes till the appointment.* Hartmann detoured to examine the clock. A fashion for nostalgia, even homesickness, had pervaded the architecture of certain human-established member-colonies of the Federal League, not least the Charidas Interchange. He walked all around it, watching the brass pendulum swing back and forth a few times. Then he meandered back towards the bar, and when the door slid open at his approach in an apparent gesture of welcome, he put his head inside and looked around as if he'd never been in it before.

It was almost empty. On the walls were a portrait of the revolutionary, Per Lakshar, and a painting of his organisation's symbol. In one corner a contingent of Zarduthi were drinking and negotiating in fierce gutturals with two Vanjeynish men. At another table a group of humans lounged, playing cards, drinking, or vying with each other for the attention and favours of the

277

bored-looking barmaid; Lakshar's eschewed the fashion for robot servitors. Two Kiai leaned against the bar, a pair of them –

That's Hlur. Hartmann sauntered towards them.

Hlur looked him up and down as he approached. His moustaches drooped well below his pointed chin, giving him a doleful air. His face had always reminded Hartmann of nothing so much as a bloodhound; but his ability to drive a hard bargain was legendary.

"Good trade to you," Hartmann said when he was near enough for his words to remain private. "Drink?"

"Indeed, kind sir." Hlur scanned the tariff, then pressed the touch-sensitive panel against one of the cocktails available. Hartmann selected a drink for himself and offered his credit chip to the barmaid, who had extricated herself from her admirers.

He turned back to Hlur.

The Kiai murmured, "And what might your urgent business be?"

*

Jordas wandered into the kitchen. It was lunchtime, but he had no appetite. He dialled a drink; he couldn't even face putting on the real coffee machine. Heat stung his fingers as he picked the beaker up.

<Yado? Are you there?>

<Where else were I?>

Yado's good humour was absent for once, and Jordas realised why at once. He'd been shocked to learn that the resurgence of conflict between Shiranu and Sargussi was being linked to their part in Chixi's death. And the tribespeople resented the loss of their way of life, though Yado had admitted they could see that Goranon's jungles were a major confining factor. Yado's anger was a threatening cloud in the background of his mind, and Jordas supposed that was probably how Yado perceived his own fury.

He wasn't just angry at his suspension, he was missing Yado and Soolkah's company. He'd felt hurt at their rejection of him on-board the *Lady of the Lake*, but remembered that he'd denied their relationship first. *I hurt them too,* he thought. *I wish I knew how to handle this. However I try to deal with it I make mistakes. And it's so important, on an inter-species level* and *on an interpersonal one.*

It felt strange to be alone. *At least Yado has Soolkah there with him,* he thought. *He can sleep with her, but I –* Misery and jealousy washed over him.

<Jordas, there is no need for these feelings,> Yado sent.

<I can't help it.> Shame followed the jealousy. <It's the way I am. It's not the Humanu way to share wives.>

278

<But we are *maaj'garu*, and fated to share. You saw the Prophecy.>

Jordas walked back into the lounge. <It's easy enough to say that, when you've spent your whole life knowing you'd share. I didn't. I never had anyone close when I was younger, except for my grandmother, and she died years ago.>

<Grandmother?>

<Mother's mother.> Jordas had forgotten how limited the bounds of acknowledged relationships were amongst the Naxadans. <When I came to Goranon I finally found someone to be close to, but she couldn't give me what I needed.> He sipped at the coffee, set it on a coaster on the half-moon table, and wandered over to the bookcase. He squatted in front of it and ran a forefinger over the spines of the books. <I'm in the same situation now.>

Yado didn't answer straight away. Then he sent, <I understand it's hard to adjust to this change in your life. We tribespeople are trying to adjust to changes in ours. But remember, however much it hurts you to share Soolkah with me because you want her to yourself, it hurts me just as much to know that.> Yado paused, then added, <But you *are* my *maaj'gar*, and we are joined until death. You need never feel alone again.> With that, he withdrew from Jordas's mind.

There was a sudden void inside Jordas as he thought about what Yado had told him. *He sees my jealousy as a flaw in my personality,* he realised. *Something that's not permitted amongst his people, and never happens anyway.* It felt like being judged and found wanting. *Perhaps a read will take my mind off all this for a while.* He was about to pull one of the volumes out when the phone bleeped.

"Jordas, it's Marcus."

A wave of relief at the familiarity of Marcus's voice brought moisture to his eyes. "I –good to talk to you, Marcus," he said, aware of the emotion in his voice.

"You sound...upset."

Jordas thought of what Yado had sent; his anger had jangled his nerves. "I am," he said, glad there was no visual contact. "You –" He stopped. "I want to come back to work."

"We could certainly do with you here. But I've just spoken with Howerd again. I told him that being suspended wasn't good for you, but he assured me it was necessary. I am *so* sorry – nothing I said could persuade him that you should come back yet. But he did say it was only a formality."

There was a pause, during which Jordas could think of nothing at all to say.

Marcus's voice filled the void. "I'm sorry, Jordas. It's not possible at present. Try to be patient." Jordas could almost hear the guilt in his voice. "I wanted to tell you that the Inquiry will be held tomorrow, at the Andromeda Hotel in Rorvik. We'll send a car to take you to the airport and meet you there for the charter flight."

*

"Where's Corah?" Marcus asked.

Howerd frowned. "Checking Hartmann out for possible anomalies in his government work. But we have enough evidence now for me to authorise Internal Security to pick him up." He paused. "Now, you haven't said anything to anyone about this operation?"

"Of course not!" There was more heat in his voice than Marcus had intended. "But the way Dr Krata has been treated is getting to him. He should have been told."

"Secrecy counts for a lot in an operation like this," Howerd murmured, then changed the subject. "Hartmann appears to have some odd connections for a politician – or perhaps not...Anyway, Corah found out what happened to the money he's been creaming off the project accounts, smart woman. She noticed there was an explosion on-board a Kiai ship carrying a valuable cargo of glassware shortly after the date when some money left the account, and suggested checking further."

"Oh?" Irritation pricked Marcus. "And what was the significance of all this?"

"Futures."

"Futures?"

"That's what Hartmann's been doing – raiding project bank accounts to buy futures in various goods, mostly staples. Shipments are often bought and sold several times before the ship carrying them docks – and if the trader's luck is in, the price keeps going up." Howerd inclined his head in a gesture Marcus interpreted as a request for patience. "Corah had a brainwave and found the various shipments he bought futures in by checking the ships' arrival dates relative to the dates when money re-entered the account. They checked with the companies involved and it all fitted a pattern. We're checking back into the Mourang debacle now."

"But you said the glassware was destroyed, so how could he make any money on it?"

"He couldn't, unless he claimed on the insurance, and that could take a long time. We assume he's still waiting, as Corah found his fake identity named as a claimant. So he had to make a profit elsewhere before he could pay back account funds. This wasn't the only physical shipment, but it was the only one he lost." Howerd smiled. "We reasoned that because of the amount of money going missing he couldn't have just bought one shipment at a time. It was the same story with *each* project account linked to him, and because all the transactions related to a particular project went through the same broker we were able to trace the movements of all the money involved."

"So Hartmann's been using the Nevil Floyd identity to speculate on the value of goods!" Marcus sat back and stroked his beard. "Hmm."

"And he's used a different identity again to set up transactions with his offworld broker," Howerd interrupted. "When our agents interviewed him, he hadn't connected Senator Gerrold Hartmann with the man he had periodic holophone contact with. He'd never even heard of Nevil Floyd. He never met Hartmann, though he knew who he was."

"So he used multiple identities?" Marcus mused. "But why not use several different fake names as Senior Administrators?"

"He needed someone with credibility within the Committee. The only way to get that would be by using the same person all the time. And if he'd used several aliases, eventually someone would have realised *he* was the linking factor in all the projects. As we did." Howerd smiled as he spread his hands in a throwaway gesture. "And of course, it would have been more expensive. He may even have been thinking to lay the blame on Nevil Floyd and somehow get off scot-free."

"Of course," Marcus echoed. "Does he always use the same bank?"

"Not at all – probably with good reason. None of the banks our inquiry agents have checked out so far have reported any irregularities in the way money was deposited or withdrawn. We're not yet sure how he fooled the identity scans, but when we do find out, it may have a bearing on your question."

"Hmm. Logical reasoning." Marcus shifted in his seat. "So where do we go from here?"

"Our agents will pick up Hartmann after the Inquiry. Just let everything run according to Hartmann's plans – we'll be able to set everything to rights afterwards."

That sounds very glib, Marcus thought. "And where's Hartmann now?"

"In the Andromeda Hotel in Rorvik. One of our security people put a tracer on him last time Hartmann was there." Howerd paused. "You haven't long to wait until he's out of your way."

CHAPTER 26

JORDAS LOOKED UP as Hartmann began to speak.

"Ladies and Gentlemen, we meet today to establish the truth about the death of the Shiranu, Mr Chixi. The only permitted translation of the Naxadan language will be that from my handheld translator. Dr Krata, please take the stand and tell us what happened at Keramanthu."

Jordas left his chair and climbed the steps into the witness box. Like the table they were seated around, it had been carved from a block of local hardwood; everything was in the grand style at the Andromeda.

He drew in a breath. Whatever he said would be recorded; it was the law. "Yado and I entered the city to holorecord the buildings – particularly the carved frieze – for later analysis, enhancement and reconstruction." He explained that this solution had been suggested when the funding for an archaeological expedition hadn't been available. No-one interrupted. Hartmann's translator kept up a stream of Naxadan in the background for the Elders, seated together opposite. Jordas noticed frequent spread-palms gestures pass between them as he spoke. Jordas described in detail Chixi's attack, how he and Yado had fought him off, and the subsequent accident.

Hartmann thanked him and turned towards Yado. "Take the stand, please, Mr Yado."

"One moment, Senator –"

Hartmann turned to face Tribune Milgar. His legal adviser wore a pin-striped collarless suit and bow-tie. A smudge of moustache adorned his upper lip. "Yes?"

"Senator, may I point out that Mr Yado is not subject to Federal League laws? As such, he cannot be compelled to give evidence in this Inquiry."

Hartmann narrowed his eyes at the lawyer. "Could you explain that statement further?"

"Indeed," said Milgar, gesturing at the Naxadans. "These people are not members of the Federal League as such yet, although under the protection of the Committee for Resettlement and Colonisation. Our laws do not, therefore, extend to them, although if they *wish* to testify, that is perfectly acceptable."

Hartmann nodded and turned back to Yado.

"Mr Yado, do you wish to testify on behalf of Dr Krata and yourself?"

"I do." Yado replaced Jordas in the witness box.

"Mr Yado, is my understanding that you were present during all of this correct?"

"Yes," Yado replied in English, "and I couldn't describe it better or more truthfully."

"Please try, in your own words and language."

Jordas caught Yado's irritation at being made to use Naxadan.

<He's compromised my status.>

<Just do as he says, if you want to improve things for us both.> Jordas picked up Yado's resentment; but then he bobbed his head in consent, and spoke. The translator followed him, as it had Jordas, with a smoothness which hadn't been there when Hartmann himself spoke.

When he'd finished, Hartmann said, "Mr Yado, we are here to decide what happened on that day. Your account has many points in common with Dr Krata's. You may recall that I did ask you to tell us what happened in your *own* words."

Jordas felt Yado's momentary loss of composure. Then Yado stood up and leaned forwards, hands on the desk, deliberately avoiding using English. "Senator," he said, "I *am* telling you in my own words, and it's the truth! What you must remember is that Jordas Krata and I are mindlinked. We share many things, among them each other's memories of that day."

"Anything else?" asked Hartmann.

"No."

"Then you may leave the stand."

Yado nodded, returned to his seat and subsided back onto it, watching the politician.

The backwash of his disquiet flowed into Jordas's mind.

<I see why you lacked confidence that this Council could go well for us,> Yado told Jordas. <Surely he shall believe us?>

<I don't know. We can only tell the truth.>

Hartmann stared at Jordas before his gaze flicked to Marcus. "Dr Carlin, can you confirm what happened from your hololink observations?"

"I'm afraid not. There was a lot of confusion during the evacuation. My colleague here might have something to add, but..."

"Dr Johnson?"

"Not really, I'm afraid," Matt replied. He shrugged, glancing at Jordas. "I spoke to Jor–Dr Krata by phone just before he and Yado went into the city. The tribespeople had built a rock platform below the escape opening. Our probes transmitted holovid recorded at the time, but Dr Krata and Yado are only shown leaving for the city."

"Show me. It may be relevant."

Matt inserted the holochip into the slot of the console. The projection tank was about a quarter of the size of the one in the monitor room at Axos. Despite the reduced scale, the clarity of the images was enhanced by the hotel's darkened windows.

Watching the tribespeople build the platform was strange. The Shiranu collected rocks; the Sargussi set them together without mortar. The holovid showed Jordas and Yado crossing the open area before the city as they made their way towards it. It finished among the tumbles of masonry inside the city.

"Is there more?" Hartmann asked.

"The rest is being processed for the Naxadans, though there are no further images of Dr Krata or Mr Yado on it," Matt answered, "or of Mr Chixi." He uncurled his hand; another chip lay on his palm. "But this is last chip recorded. I don't know what's on it, but it may shed light on events that morning."

Hartmann conferred with his legal representative for a moment. "Show it."

Matt replaced the chip.

Within moments the images filled the holotank: Chixi arguing with his brothers, the blow which had felled Lorr, Chixi stealing towards the city, then moving out of range.

"That's him – Chixi," Matt said, pointing.

"Now, I'm not disputing recorded events," said Hartmann, "but who, I wonder, followed whom?"

*

"Dr Krata, Mr Yado, do you have witnesses who can confirm these events?" asked the Humanu Elder, Hartmann.

His eyes held no expression. It made Hanook unwilling to trust him.

"There were no witnesses," Jordas replied, "though Eldest Hanook will confirm Chixi followed us. He dealt with the situation according to Naxadan customs."

Hartmann swung his gaze onto Hanook. "Mr Hanook, will you testify?"

Hanook thought of the fights between the younger tribesmen and nodded.

"Then please enter the *witness box.*"

Hanook hesitated, then walked over and climbed the steps. The *witness box* had been made for Humanu; he could only just see over the top of it.

"Explain those customs to the court, and how they pertain to this situation," Hartmann said.

Hanook looked around the room at everyone in turn. Everyone was waiting for him to speak. He was sure the Humanu Eldest, Hartmann, and his apprentice Milgar were the only strangers to tribal customs, but explained the system of kazmo'ra and the need for it.

284

"Dr Krata said you'd already dealt with the situation. How does the status-debt system affect Mr Yado and him?"

"Jordas and Yado are working off their kazmo'ra to Chixi's brothers." Hanook decided not to mention that most of the burden of the status-debt he'd imposed had fallen onto Yado, especially since Jordas's injuries and suspension.

"So even murder would be dealt with by the same system?"

Hanook nodded. "But why would Jordas or Yado risk the maaj'nag'ur by attacking –"

Jordas was on his feet, forehead as creased as a pricket nut shell. "Yado and I aren't murderers!"

Hartmann stared at him. "As I'm chairing this Inquiry, perhaps you'll let *me* be the judge of that."

Matt gasped.

Carlin stood up. His chair fell over with a clatter. "This is outrageous!" he said. "Under Federal League law –"

<Tell him Chixi's brothers know what happened,> Yado urged.

<But they can't speak now!> Jordas reminded him.

Hartmann glanced at Jordas. "Please sit down, Dr Krata."

"Jordas and Yado haven't done anything wrong," Matt said. "What about 'innocent until proven guilty'?"

Everyone in the room was speaking at once. The translation *box* struggled to keep up.

Crash!

The hubbub ceased. It was a moment before Hanook realised Hartmann had deliberately thumped his desk. Like him, Aa'kam, Aneera and Mnanga had their hands over their ears, their faces showing shock at the easy use of noise to restore order.

"Sit down, Dr Carlin! Let's deal with these matters in a civilised fashion." Hartmann waited.

Carlin righted his chair and sat down, arms folded across his chest. His eyes snapped hostility at the Senator.

Hartmann ignored this, turning back towards Hanook. "Who entered the city first?"

"The Humanu Jordas and the Sargussi Yado."

"Chixi followed them?"

Hanook nodded. "Chixi's youngest brother, Lorr, came to tell me this."

"Ah. And why is he not here today?"

"Chixi's brothers are all in the maaj'nag'ur. It wouldn't have helped to

285

bring them."

"Explain, please."

When Hanook had finished, Hartmann said with an edge to his voice, "All this maaj'nag'ur tells us is that Chixi is dead, not who attacked whom, since his brothers can't testify at present – even if this Inquiry could compel them to."

*

Senator Hartmann noted the consternation on Krata's face as he nodded to Milgar, who had risen.

"Do you wish to call further witnesses?" Milgar asked.

"I would like to question Dr Krata again."

Milgar nodded.

"Please take the stand, Dr Krata."

The scientist entered the witness box.

"Ladies and gentlemen," Senator Hartmann announced. He could hear the translator in the background; the Naxadans, he noted, were watching in awe. "We have established to date that Mr Chixi followed Dr Krata and Mr Yado." He swung round to face Krata. "Dr Krata, why would this man – Mr Chixi – attack the pair of you, as you claim?" asked Senator Hartmann.

Krata's silence stretched almost into oblivion. "Jealousy," he mumbled at last.

"Jealousy?"

Krata frowned at the wood of the witness stand, opened his mouth, then closed it again.

Why doesn't he speak? Hartmann thought. *Is there something here I can use for my benefit?* "I'm waiting for an answer. I should warn you that a silence will be interpreted as evidence of guilt in these circumstances."

Krata looked up, eyes luminous. "Senator Hartmann, the day you came to Axos research station, Soolkah ran away from her tribe." The scientist's hands were clenched on the witness stand.

"What's that got to do with Chixi's death?" Hartmann asked, remembering Travers' holovid.

"She was contracted to marry Chixi and his brothers. She ran away and met Yado instead and became his wife, and as you know, he later became telepathically linked to myself."

"But what's the connection between Chixi and *you*, Dr Krata?"

Krata was almost gasping for breath, and even the alien male Yado was perched on his chair, eyes fixed on Krata's face. *Are they sending telepathic messages?* Hartmann wondered. "Dr Krata!"

286

"You must understand the social set-up of these people, Senator. Any one of them, or Dr Carlin, or Dr Johnson, will confirm that there's a shortage of women amongst the tribes, which, along with the telepathic links between the brothers in each family group, has led both Sargussi and Shiranu Naxadans to practice polyandry."

Hartmann waited for him to continue, but he said nothing. "So how can that affect you, Dr Krata?"

Krata's head was bowed. He wouldn't look at anyone. After another pause, he said, "I'm telepathically linked to Yado, Senator. He's considered to be my maaj'gar – my...thought brother."

Hartmann regarded him for a moment, then glanced around the courtroom. The Naxadans sat, placid as babes sucking pacifiers; they probably didn't understand what was happening anyway. He turned back to the stand. "Dr Krata, am I to understand that the Naxadans consider Soolkah to be your wife as well as Mr Yado's? Is that what you're saying?"

He could barely hear Jordas Krata's answer.

"Yes."

"Does this mean that you have had sexual relations with this female?"

"Yes."

Carlin's face was blank as a mask, but his complexion was darkening by the second.

Johnson's gold-rimmed spectacles glinted with outrage.

Hartmann glanced at Carlin, then back at Krata. "But the Naxadans are an alien race, Dr Krata, moreover one under the protection of the Committee. They aren't full members of the League yet. It may be generations before they're ready. Their status is that of interstellar refugees. You were trusted with getting them out of danger. Surely having...sexual relations with one of them was not wise? Surely it betrayed their trust in you?"

"That's not how it was. They *expected* me to be Soolkah's *amaajne*. Especially Yado and Soolkah themselves."

Travers sniggered, the sound muffled at Carlin's frown.

Hartmann tried again. "But in view of the fact that they are – covered in fur, like animals –"

Jordas Krata lifted up his head to stare at Hartmann. "Senator, I'm telepathically linked to one of them!" He enunciated every syllable as if to emphasize his meaning. "There is *no* possibility that I could look on them as anything other than people – like you or I." He glared at the politician.

Hartmann looked away, aware of backing down. "Dr Krata, nobody is suggesting that these people are animals. But I find it...interesting...that you didn't see fit to mention your involvement in Naxadan customs in your reports, or to your colleagues." Hartmann saw that Carlin's face was purple now. He paused, then added, "Inter-species marriages aren't unknown, of course, but you do realise, don't you, that you've laid yourself open to allegations of a cover-up?"

After a silence Krata muttered, "I didn't think of it like that at the time."

"Dr Krata, please continue with your explanation as to why the Shiranu male Chixi should seek to kill you."

Krata lowered his eyes and stared at his hands on the wood of the stand. "Chixi regarded us as having stolen the woman he and his brothers intended to marry," he said. "He wanted her back, and would do anything to get her, including killing both of us."

Hartmann watched him, thinking. "Although we still haven't established the truth of what occurred on that morning," he said after some moments, "we do now have a motive for Mr Chixi's actions. However, the converse of that must also be true. If Mr Chixi would benefit by your deaths, so would you by his. You and Mr Yado would get to keep the female Soolkah, unless challenged again by Chixi's brothers."

"That's not possible," Krata said, "with the maaj'nag'ur."

"Exactly!" Hartmann stood, considering. *It doesn't look as if I can get away with pinning a murder charge on Krata and the troglodyte, but this might suit my own plans better. People prefer sleaze to murder.* He smiled. "Indeed." He glanced around the table. Travers' eyes were on Krata, his expression a mixture of disgust and fascination. Johnson's spectacles hid his emotions. Carlin's beard barely softened the disapproval that straightened his mouth and thinned his lips. The older Naxadans looked as if they wanted to speak but were bewildered, yet anger deepened the lines on their faces. The younger Naxadans looked mystified and anxious by turns. *It's obvious they don't understand all of this. Well, not my problem!*

Last of all he looked at Jordas Krata. The scientist was staring at the floor. *His humiliation will cover my escape,* he thought with some satisfaction.

"Ladies and gentlemen," he said. "We have not reached a firm conclusion about anything this morning. However, there seems to have been a cover-up. Dr Jordas Krata, I must recommend that you remain suspended from work until further notice, pending future investigation."

Hartmann checked the time. *Hlur will be waiting.* "In the meantime, this Inquiry is adjourned until Mr Chixi's brothers are able to testify – *if* they so wish." He surveyed the room once more. "Good day to you all." He bowed, turned on his heel and left the room.

288

Marcus got up. Tribune Milgar picked up his notebook and followed the politician. The silence thinned and parted.

"Why the hell didn't you say something?" Matt demanded. "The times are encoded on the holovid. There was no need for Hartmann's insinuations."

"Why didn't *Jordas* say something?" Ray snorted. "Should have told you what was going on."

"You can't just let him leave it like that!"

"What will happen to us, Marcus?" Yado's voice held an unfamiliar plaintive note.

Jordas stood, silent.

The tribespeople were speaking, but Hartmann had taken the translator and Marcus only understood Yado's question. And he was sure he wasn't just asking about the rest of his people

"I don't know," he said, shaking his head. "Matt, I wanted to say something, but – my hands were tied." *Still are. I hope they pick him up soon!*

"Well, mine weren't, and I damn well wish I'd said what I was thinking!" Matt's voice was choked with anger. "That 'Inquiry' was a farce, and you know it! Sir."

"I'll speak to Howerd as soon as we return to the monitor room." Marcus turned to Jordas. "You should go home till this mess is sorted out."

Dusk was settling around and infiltrating the house. At a word from Jordas a table lamp clicked on.

There was a tap at the door. He roused himself from his thoughts. *Who's come to see me at this time?* Hope leapt up in him that it would be Yado or Soolkah, or both of them. *Sajamu* and common sense told him that was impossible.

He went to the door, ordering the hall light on as he went. He blinked at its brightness as he opened the door.

Marcus stood before him. "Hello, Jordas," he said. "May I come in? I have news for you."

"Of course." Jordas cleared his throat and swallowed. "News?"

"Hartmann's disappeared." Marcus's gaze pierced Jordas.

"Disappeared?"

"Yes, on his way back to Earth after that load of baloney that passed for an Inquiry."

Jordas began to feel more charitable towards his superior. "Come in," he invited. "I have real coffee from Earth."

Marcus accepted and followed Jordas into the lounge. He looked around with interest before sitting on the couch, leaning back, fingers interlaced behind his head. "Nice place."

Jordas gave a non-committal grunt and went to make the coffee. "It'll be a minute or two," he said, as he came back into the room. He perched on the edge of his armchair. "Tell me about Hartmann."

Marcus was looking around the room. His eyes lit on the lamo-harp on the half-moon table. "You play that?"

"Yes. But what about Hartmann?"

"Of course." Marcus cradle his knee with both hands. "He should have arrived at the Charidas Interchange two days ago, but he hasn't been seen since the Inquiry. Committee Internal Security agents are searching for him – they tailed him, but a device placed on him has gone off-grid. They came to see me this afternoon before going after him. I spoke to Howerd again after they'd gone." He leaned forwards. "I couldn't say anything before, but we think Hartmann used the inquiry to draw the attention away from him –"

"You mean you knew all along? For Chrissakes, Marcus, I've been under extreme pressure! If I'd known what was going on I might have handled my situation better." Jordas heard the note of bitterness in his voice, and changed the subject. "The coffee's ready." He strode out into the kitchen, half-regretting the impulse which had made him offer Marcus hospitality.

He banged the fragile bone china cup down on the saucer and a chip ricocheted off the edge of the tray. *Shit!* His mouth tightened, and he breathed in, trying to calm himself. He was more careful with the second cup. The coffee machine had been his grandmother's; he kept it from sentiment. He set milk and sugar on the tray and carried it into the lounge.

"This smells good," Marcus said. "Incidentally, Alfred Grantham found that the Naxadans do have tougher skin than we do – enough to make their coming-of-age ceremonies very necessary and not just a matter of tradition. It's probably an adaptation which has arisen since they moved underground, to protect them from injury by the lava."

Jordas stared at him through narrowed eyes. *He's trying to set things to rights.* "You do believe me about Chixi's death, don't you?"

Marcus nodded. "I've never had reason to doubt your word before, Jordas." His pause gave Jordas a chance to study him; his beard hid no trace of subterfuge.

Marcus groped for the cup at his elbow, then changed his mind. "What *does* concern me is the situation between you and the female, Soolkah."

Jordas felt a twist of apprehension in his stomach. He folded his arms.

"It's not illegal."

"No, but Hartmann was right in a way. Your silence *could* be construed as a cover-up. Howerd's not too pleased about all of this, and it's rather left me with egg on my face. Why didn't you report it?"

"*Report* it?" Jordas echoed.

Marcus made a throwaway gesture. "Well, ask for advice –"

"It's a private matter, of concern to no-one but Soolkah, Yado and me."

"Seeing as I'm in charge of this project, any problems like this reflect on me, and you know how tongues wag in a backwater like Axos! If people get to hear of this –" Marcus broke off, watching Jordas's face. When he spoke again, his voice had softened. "What possessed you, man?"

Jordas turned away. It was moments before he could bring himself to answer. "You *know* how the *amaaju* work," he murmured. "A man without *maaj'garu* is simply not allowed to marry – he has no real status in the tribe. And to the Naxadans, status is wealth. A woman has no choice in the *amaaj* she is given to. Yet Soolkah ran away and became *amaajni* with Yado. In a way I suppose Yado wanted me to go with her as well to lend credence to his claim on her." He spread his hands. "I guess all three of us have gone against tradition."

Marcus watched him. After another silence, he said, "Break it off, Jordas! Can't you see –?"

"I have no choice." Jordas thrust his hands into his trouser pockets and turned away. He tried to blot out Marcus's presence by focusing on the square of darkness at the glass door to the garden; nightfall had cleared the noviglass to allow in starlight. "I tried to break it off when we reached the research station, but all that happened was that all of us were – are – hurt. I'm involved whether the Committee likes it or not," he said. "Yado is my *maaj'gar*...it means thought brother, but with the peculiar – talents – of Naxadans, there can be no separation of brotherhood from marriage for me. He's Soolkah's husband, so I am too...I have his sense impressions, his *sajamu*. Do you understand what that means? It means when he makes love with her, I feel it too!"

He paused to rest his elbows on his knees, eyes downcast as he raked his hands through his hair, pressing it smooth for a moment before it sprang back, unruly as ever. "I haven't slept with her since Keramanthu, but I know when Yado does. I feel it. I felt it last night, and I'll feel it each time, as long as we're both alive." He glanced up.

Marcus waited for him to continue.

But he wasn't sure what else he wanted to say. At last he added, "I didn't

291

understand any of this until I met up with them." He got up and paced the room until he faced the garden door. He stared through it for many heartbeats, not registering the sprinkling of stars above the plants. He remembered instead the night of his final joining to Yado, when he'd sat on the wall, plucking at the lamo-harp's strings, beaming melodies like messages into the darkness. *That was so long ago!*

"I see," Marcus said at last. He had moved to Jordas's side without him noticing. "I didn't understand either. I'm so sorry...you're in an impossible situation."

Jordas nodded. "It's torture at times." His voice was softer than a raindrop, and his eyes focused inwards rather than on the lush growth, or the dance of stars above. Beyond the glass door he sensed a greater harmony than he could understand, something he'd sometimes registered when he turned a telescope on the skies or watched new growth burst from soil.

And he wanted to be part of the harmony. But the notes eluded him.

CHAPTER 27

HANOOK SQUINTED through his *sunvisor*. He'd been waiting since lightbreak for the Humanu to arrive. "Aa'kam, we must impress on the Humanu that we need their help in *all* these matters."

Aa'kam nodded his agreement.

Hanook had found him a man of many silences, but much thought. "Fetch Mnanga and Aneera," he told Geem. "Tell them Marcus and Matt are here now." His son nodded and dashed off towards their *huts*.

The Humanu approached. Hanook was surprised to see a third figure with them, hand in Matt's. That shocked Hanook for a heart's beat, until he remembered that the Humanu didn't share their touch taboos. As they drew nearer he identified the shorter figure as the woman Yue Xiao. *Even better,* he thought. *There need be no further breaking of traditions.*

The Eldest women arrived almost at the same time as the Humanu did, Mnanga leaning on her new metal stick for support.

Marcus greeted Hanook with that strange Humanu custom, the handshake. The translator *box* he carried gave an approximation of his words. "Eldest Hanook," Marcus murmured. "It's a pleasure to see you. How are you?"

Hanook waited for the translation to finish, squirming with impatience. Then he said, "I am well, but my daughter Zuas is not. She's inside." He pointed to his *hut*. "We need your help once again, Humanu." His gaze included all of them.

"What's the problem?" Matt asked.

"It's the young girls. Perhaps..." Hanook hesitated. He'd noticed that Humanu women had equal status with men, with duties shared between the sexes. It would be improper for a Shiranu man to discuss women's problems when there were two tribeswomen and a Humanu woman who could do so. He indicated Yue Xiao and the two Eldest women and addressed Matt. "Perhaps Mnanga and Aneera can explain to your wife? Aa'kam and I must discuss other matters with you, and the women are better-suited to dealing with their own sex. They have the Words that a man doesn't."

Yue Xiao nodded. "Give me the other translator, Matt. I'll find out what's wrong." She followed Mnanga and Aneera into the room.

"What's troubling you so, Eldest Hanook?" Marcus asked.

Hanook bit his lip. "Much."

"Come!" Aa'kam said. "We shall go to my *hut*."

293

They set off towards the *hut* his amaaj shared. On the way they passed the one the other Humanu used. Alfred Grantham had seen many tribespeople over the past few days, including Hanook and Aa'kam themselves. Alfred waved as they passed, so Hanook waved back.

They reached Aa'kam's *hut* and entered. Inside it was cool, and dark enough, with *double-strength noviglass windows*, for Aa'kam and Hanook to remove their *sunvisors*. In one corner, Aa'kam's brothers Ghura and Jeeban flanked a Sargussi youth. In another a Shiranu boy crouched between Kayas and Brach. His cheek bore a bloody talonslash.

"This is the problem," Aa'kam said, indicating the youths. He seated himself cross-legged on the floor. Matt and Marcus lowered themselves down beside him.

Hanook realised from their fidgeting they weren't used to sitting on the floor. He walked over to the window and stared through it at his own *hut*. *Ghasru! Let the Humanu be able to help her,* he thought, pacing up and down. *If this daughter dies too my ignorance will be to blame yet again.*

"Well?" Marcus asked after a moment's silence.

"Marcus, there has been fighting between our tribes." Aa'kam indicated the two youths glaring at each other from opposite corners of the room. "These are the latest we caught, just today. Since Jordas doesn't come here, people think he and Yado must truly have killed Chixi. Old troubles have reopened between the tribes, just as we thought the past was behind us and a new start ahead. What can be done?"

"The tribespeople know what happened to Jordas?" Matt asked.

Hanook sighed. "That, also, was my fault. Some of them asked where he was after we came here, especially after the Humanu *Inquiry* – they knew we Elders went with you to it. I could not lie, so –" His voice shook. "I told them what happened. Aa'kam and I realised Chixi's death was an accident. He would have needed restraining in some way had he lived. But our peoples have lived apart for hundreds of highwaters, and before that, war separated the tribes. It's hard to overcome old ways of thinking."

"What did you do with the others you caught?" Marcus asked.

Hanook spread his palms. "All we *can* do is impose mutual status-debt, but it's no solution. It can't be carried out until we have a new home and can continue our usual way of life."

"Why not?" asked Marcus.

"Because I would impose work tasks on both young men, and we can't work here. We can't farm and the Sargussi can't hunt," Hanook pointed out. "Part of the trouble is, the tribespeople are idle. The result is, we have a backlog of kazmo'ra to carry out."

Marcus thought hard for a moment. "Deal with these young tribesmen in your usual fashion, so that I won't be seen to undermine your authority. Then we can discuss further strategy."

Aa'kam nodded. It made sense to Hanook too. The Eldest men spoke to the two youths together, explaining to them that their actions had brought a loss of status to each amaaj concerned.

"Go back to your maaj'garu," Hanook said. "Tell them neither Aa'kam nor I will tolerate further fighting. There are few enough of us as it is."

The Shiranu youth left, scowling. The Sargussi followed him moments later.

"How about patrolling the compound in pairs, and settling arguments before fights start?" Matt suggested.

"Indeed," Hanook told his brothers. "Walk among the *huts*. Don't allow fights to start. If you go in pairs, Sargussi with Shiranu, the people will see your friendship, and you can summon the others by mindspeech if trouble starts."

"That's a good idea," Kayas said. He and Jeeban replaced their *sunvisors* and left, followed by Brach and Ghura at a nod from Aa'kam.

"We knew adapting would be difficult, both here and in your new home. Perhaps a diversion is needed," suggested Matt. "Something to unite Shiranu and Sargussi."

Hanook nodded his agreement. "We know it too...But it's better to be alive here than dead in Kerui."

"I've something to show you," Matt said. He took something out of his pocket, pushed it into another Humanu box, pressed it, and sat back. "This is a *portable holotank* – like we used to watch you, when you were in the caves, and we were trying to work out how to rescue you. Look!"

The *tank* filled up with colour. Images flickered into life under the dim light from a pack-ice ceiling and ranks of dying glowcakes.

"*Keramanthu!*" exclaimed Aa'kam. "It's Keramanthu!"

The *holovid* played over tumbled walls whose incised images told the story as clearly as possible in the gloom. The Eldest men watched, enraptured, tears streaming down their faces.

"This is your city's – your people's – history. It won't be forgotten," Matt promised. "You'll all remember it, and so shall we. And a *hologram* has a big advantage over a model – it never needs dusting!"

"Call everyone together this darktime," Marcus said. "We'll bring a bigger *tank* to show everyone. Remind them that *both* tribes worked to build

295

the rock platform that allowed them to escape – it might unite the tribespeople long enough for the real problems to be dealt with."

Matt gazed at him. "You don't think this is a real problem?"

"Very much so, but until Jordas's name is cleared and he comes back to work, the trouble could continue."

"Marcus, I don't understand –"

Matt broke off as the Humanu woman appeared on the steps of the hut. Her face was creased with urgency and anxiety.

"Enter," Aa'kam invited.

Yue Xiao shook her head. "Marcus, Hanook's daughter needs immediate medical attention," she said. "Mnanga and Aneera have no more herbs to heal her, and are too embarrassed to ask Alfred Grantham for help because it's a women's problem."

"What's the matter?"

"I'll tell you outside, away from the translator."

Marcus followed her.

Hanook, Aa'kam and Matt watched them. Yue Xiao was waving her arms about and gabbling with urgency and some force. This reassured Hanook; he'd learnt that when Humanu made a lot of noise, it meant something would get done quickly.

When the two Humanu returned, Marcus said, "Hanook, you *must* agree to this, even though it breaks tradition. Zuas must have her coming-of-age ceremony now, or she risks severe illness and perhaps death. Tell Mnanga that it's all right to do that. Then we'll take her to our *medical centre* and make her well again."

"Take her away?" Hanook was confused. *Didn't the Humanu say we couldn't leave this place?*

"Just for a few days, until she's better. Like when Mnanga's leg mended quickly." Marcus paused. "When should she have had her coming-of-age?"

"That's part of the problem," Yue Xiao said. "Normally they would be able to reckon the time using the mother's menstrual cycle, but the tribeswomen have lost count since leaving Naxada, because the length of days is different."

"Zuas's mother died more than a highwater ago," Hanook added. "I have no way of knowing when she should have had her coming-of-age."

"Zuas is surely not the only one," Aa'kam said. "There are Sargussi girls, too."

"I understand," Marcus nodded, "but it isn't the big problem you think. I can check how the days match up here for you. Then we can work out their exact ages. In the meantime, can't you get all the young girls who need it together and let Mnanga and Aneera give them the coming-of-age all together, even if it's a little early, so the others don't become sick?"

Hanook locked gaze with Aa'kam. "Well?" he asked, wishing again that they shared the benefit of mindspeech together. "Strange times demand new answers. It seems sensible, if you agree."

"A joint ceremony would mayhap unite the tribes," Aa'kam murmured, "one for all the young women, and one for all the young men."

"Then there'll be marriages to arrange, though not yet for all of them," Hanook mused. "I'm not anxious to marry Zuas off – I want to keep her with me for now." He turned to Yue Xiao. "Ask Mnanga and Aneera to make arrangements with me."

"Can they deal with Zuas first?" asked Yue Xiao.

Hanook nodded.

"Yue Xiao will call for help when she's spoken to Mnanga," Marcus said. "I promise you'll have Zuas back safely soon, and I'll try to get Howerd to hurry things up."

"And the other problem?" Aa'kam asked. "I would prefer that no son of my tribe were blamed for a Shiranu's death."

"I understand that. May I speak with Yado?"

"He keeps to his *hut* to avoid trouble."

"So he's as isolated as Jordas, in a way," Marcus mused. "Well, can we go to him?"

"We shall come too," Aa'kam nodded.

At Yado's *hut*, they found him helping Soolkah to hand-feed Chixi's brothers. The Humanu men's expressions, when they saw the condition of the three brothers, perplexed Hanook. The tribes accepted that this happened and paid little attention.

Matt seemed particularly disturbed. "They can't do anything for themselves, Marcus," he muttered. The translator just caught it.

"I hope their maaj'nag'ur were almost over," Yado said. "If they could speak they would end this situation. I want to spend time with Maru and Jordas."

Soolkah put out a hand to Marcus, not quite touching him, treating him with the courtesy she would show another tribesperson. "You've helped us so much already, Marcus. But can't you help us a little more?"

"What do you need?"

"The tribespeople know the Humanu had an *Inquiry* –" Soolkah stumbled over the humanu word, and started again. "If Chixi's brothers could tell the

Humanu his death was an accident, the tribespeople would believe them and there'd be no excuse for fighting."

Marcus said, "The Inquiry was adjourned – I'll find out from Howerd when it will reopen. But remember, Chixi's brothers can't be forced to testify."

*

"How's Zuas?" Matt asked as Yue Xiao entered the monitor room. He tried the fine control again and swore under his breath.

"Be calm," Yue Xiao said, slipping off her linen coat and hanging it up. "I've just come from the medical centre. The problem was similar to toxic shock syndrome, but she'll be fine – they've got her fever down." She came over and kissed him before flopping into a chair. "But the infection caused some scarring, and she needs an operation. Good job Alfred was onsite and they asked him to call us."

"It was."

"Where's Marcus?"

"Gone to see his lawyer." Matt paused. "He seemed freaked by that frieze last night – with Jordas, Yado and Soolkah at the end." He thought for a moment, then added, "I was, too, eh?"

"How can someone dream something so far in the future?" asked Yue Xiao. "And it came true."

Ray breezed into the monitor room.

"I thought you went home," Matt said, frowning.

"Came back. Forgot my jacket – credit chip in it."

"Matt, what are you doing?" Yue Xiao got up and came to peer over his shoulder.

"Cleaning up the sound on this holovid to feed it through the translator." He sighed. "I'm not sure I approve of Jordas's involvement with Soolkah, and I think he should have at least told Marcus, but he's my friend and I intend to see him – and Yado – cleared of this murder charge."

"Mmm."

Ray shrugged himself into his jacket, then sauntered round to stand on Matt's other side. He picked up another holochip. "What are these here for?"

"I'm checking for any other evidence," Matt said. "Don't muddle up the piles, will you?"

"Tea, Matt?" Yue Xiao crossed to the drinks dispenser.

"Sure."

"Caffeine freeze," Ray said, eyes fixed on the tank.

"Help yourself – I haven't got three hands!" Yue Xiao held both beakers by the rims.

298

Ray shrugged and replaced her at the dispenser.

"Now what's this?" Matt picked up a chip. "There might be something useful on it." He inserted it. Seconds later, he saw an image he remembered turning off. Yado and Soolkah lay side by side, fur intermeshed. "Oh, that's the one with all the night-vid on. There won't be anything –"

The images had caught Ray's eye. "That's Jordas!" he exclaimed. He watched as Soolkah straddled Jordas, his hands touched her chest and her breasts began to swell.

"Shit!" Matt exclaimed. "You're not watching that!" He flicked the holotank off, ejected the chip, and tucked it into his pocket. "I should have left this behind on Naxada."

"One thing – proves Hartmann right about Chixi's motive for attacking Jordas and Yado –". Ray hadn't lost his chirpiness despite the rebuke.

Fury quickened Matt's speech. "Whose side are you on? Go home."

"But –"

"Your working day ended half an hour ago. I've chosen to stay here and work on this because I want to help Jordas. And the Naxadans. Giving free rein to your personal opinions helps no-one!"

"Pulling rank on me?" Ray sounded surprised.

"For once, yes."

Ray sniffed, swigged his caffeine freeze, then straightened his jacket and left the room, muttering.

"I didn't realise he was like that till we came here," Yue Xiao said. "But I've not had much to do with him."

Matt shrugged. "He's just envious because he doesn't have a girlfriend."

"Who'd choose such a sexist? Have you seen the way he treats Alleem?"

"I know. It's about time either she or Marcus cut him down to size." Matt slid his arm about her waist, sighing. "It was a shock to me as well, seeing Jordas and Soolkah together like that. I hadn't realised there'd be holovid –"

"It's not our business."

"Precisely – nor Ray's!" Matt snorted. "Did you see the look on his face?"

Yue Xiao sipped at her tea before answering, "I wonder how they cope with the differences between them?" She looked at him from under her lashes. "Oh, the physical differences obviously *don't* matter much. But the Naxadan culture's pretty low-tech and very different from ours."

"It's not physical *or* technological differences that bother *me*," Matt said. "It's the whole mindset." The morning's visit had been on his mind all day. "You know, Chixi's brothers – it freaked me out to see them like that. They're totally blank – they don't register anything! If you wave a hand in front of them it's like they're blind. I suppose that's what shocks me, Jordas getting drawn into that." He shivered and drew her closer. "With all our flaws, I'd rather be human than Naxadan."

"The Naxadans probably don't understand how we deal with things, either," Yue Xiao said between sips of tea.

*

"The Inquisitor is a Vanjeynish woman, Garat Frelox," Marcus whispered to Hanook, who was seated beside him, via the translator. "She's Howerd Asthorn's Vice-Chairwoman. He promised me she knows what she's doing."

"Some of you look very anxious, so let me explain first that the Committee is most concerned about the manner in which the original Inquiry was conducted, and why." The Inquisitor surveyed the room, as if weighing up the members by studying their faces. "A serious crime appeared to have been committed, and independent evidence was not available to refute that situation. The Inquiry was adjourned until it became available, so my remit is to investigate that evidence, and also affirm that as Mr Chixi died on Naxadan territory his death falls under Naxadan jurisdiction, whether or not Dr Krata was involved. I know it has already been dealt with as such, but also that this Inquiry's outcome will have an effect on the Naxadan social situation. Hence it has been reconvened as soon as possible." She glanced at the holocam recording proceedings for replay to the tribespeople. "My legal adviser also informs me that Dr Krata's suspension has been deemed unsafe, due to the circumstances of the previous Inquiry."

Marcus let his mind drift, remembering his calls to Asthorn on Thera 6. Across the room, Jordas sat, head in hands. *He's still worrying about his suspension. I must set that right.*

But Garat Frelox's voice recalled him. "Dr Johnson, please present your new evidence."

Matt stood up and entered the witness box. "Madam Chairwoman," he said, "I have been able to isolate relevant episodes from holovid recorded by our project. I have also clarified the soundtrack and will play it through the universal translator, so that all members of this Inquiry will understand the implications of this evidence." He paused and gestured to Ms. Frelox's assistant, standing beside the holotank.

The young man nodded and activated the console.

"The first clip, which concerns an argument between Mr Chixi and one of his brothers, Mr Lorr, who will be called as a witness later on, has been seen before, though perhaps not by yourself," Matt continued. "The argument was conducted in mindspeech, but you'll observe Mr Chixi throwing Mr Lorr off when he tried to prevent him from following Dr Krata and Mr Yado into the city."

Chixi's annoyance was plain.

When it had finished, Ms. Frelox spoke. "How does that assist your colleague's plea of innocence? I thought this was new evidence. I *have* viewed the holos from the previous inquiry."

"That piece isn't new," Matt agreed, "but it sets the next piece in context."

Ms. Frelox nodded. "Then proceed."

Matt nodded to her assistant again. The holovid played. "This shows Mr Lorr's conversation with Mr Hanook," Matt said.

"Eldest Hanook," Lorr's image said.

Marcus glanced across at him.

He was watching the projection, eyes like a child's at Christmas. "I'm sorry to bother you, but this is urgent. I'm very worried – Chixi has gone into the city."

"Where the Humanu and the Sargussi have gone?"

"Yes. He's following them. I tried to stop him, but he wouldn't listen. He hit me –" Lorr rubbed at his shoulder.

"This couldn't have happened at a worse time," Hanook muttered. "We need every fit adult to help with building the rock platform. Look how the water's rising! And everyone knows it's not safe to go into the city." He spread his hands. "But I can't ask people to leave off building the platform to search for your brother. I'm sorry, Lorr."

"I see," Lorr said. "Then my brothers and I must go after him ourselves. It *is* our rest-time."

"Only a madman would enter the city," Hanook replied. "I forbid it."

The holotank darkened.

"That's all?" asked Ms. Frelox.

Matt nodded. "It establishes beyond doubt that Chixi followed Dr Krata and Mr Yado into the city."

Beside Marcus, Hanook scowled. "I had a difficult decision to make there," he whispered. "I didn't want to split the tribe up again."

Marcus nodded. "I know," he said. "It was the right decision – in the circumstances."

The Inquisitor was watching them. When she'd got their attention again, she turned to look at Jordas. "Dr Krata, do you have anything to add at this point?"

Jordas looked up. "Actually, I do."

"Please take the stand."

Jordas did so. "My legal representative has advised me to point out that I had a gun in my backpack at the time of Chixi's attack, quite legally – I hold a licence for it, and know how to use it. I took it with me for my own protection, and could have used it on Chixi at any time, had I wanted to."

In the boardroom, no-one moved.

"I only used it once on Naxada, to scare off an animal which attacked me. To be honest, Chixi's attack was so sudden and vicious that it never occurred to me to use it."

"Can you prove this?"

"The gun has been examined by a ballistics expert," Jordas said. "My legal representative has a copy of the report."

"May I see it?"

Jordas's legal representative – Marcus's own lawyer, Milton Chalmers – stood up and passed the report across to her. She scanned it, then nodded. "This will need to be included in the body of evidence under Federal League law."

"Fine," Jordas said. "We expected that."

"Any more witnesses to be called?" Ms. Frelox asked.

"Yes," Chalmers said. "I call Mr Chixi's brothers into the witness stand."

"I was under the impression from the previous piece of evidence that they stayed outside the city."

"They did." Chalmers smiled. "But I rather think you'll want to hear their evidence, Madam Chairwoman."

*

"It's true," Lorr said. "Soolkah was contracted to marry all of us. It's..."

He was the last of the brothers to have been called to give evidence. The other two were back in their seats beside the Humanu stress counsellor who went everywhere with them. Ever since their awakening from the maaj'nag'ur only days ago he'd been there, helping them to come to terms with the strangeness of their new life.

He looked at each of the *Inquiry* members in turn. "It's our way, though we understand now that it's not yours." His eyes rested on Jordas Krata. He was slumped in his chair, looking at least as embarrassed as Lorr felt.

"These marriages are arranged?"

"They are."

"They cause problems for those concerned?"

"Sometimes, say if different members of the same amaaj have – inappropriate – feelings towards another member of the tribe." Lorr kept his eyes downcast.

"I see." Garat Frelox nodded.

Lorr thought it meant understanding rather than agreement. But it felt safer to look at her again than meet Soolkah's gaze.

"What happened on that morning, Mr Lorr?"

Lorr drew breath to speak. "Chixi hated the Sargussi and the Humanu. When he caught up with them he *told* them he was going to kill them."

"Did you agree with that, Mr Lorr?"

"Why do you think I was going to go after him? I didn't even stop to think of him perhaps being injured if he entered the city. I – I didn't want him to kill either of them. None of us did. But that was what Chixi intended, and he only needed to kill one of them." Lorr risked a sidewise glance at Soolkah.

She was watching him with such intensity that it almost felt like physical pressure.

"Why?"

"He knew if he killed one of them the other would be helpless in the maaj'nag'ur, since they were mindlinked. The floods would get the survivor, and he could claim Soolkah."

"Would that have been to your advantage?"

Lorr stared at the floor. "I suppose so, but I think we'd all have felt bad about claiming Soolkah under those conditions. Except Chixi."

"How did your brother die?"

"Th-the wall collapsed onto him when he fell against it. It...crushed him, and he drowned."

"And you're certain of this?"

"I remember how it felt. We all felt the pain, and then we couldn't breathe. But I can't remember anything after that."

"What do you think would have happened if the wall hadn't collapsed onto Mr Chixi?"

"He would have carried on fighting Yado and Jordas until he'd killed one of them. He was determined to marry Soolkah." Lorr's voice dropped to a whisper. "He didn't love her. He just wanted to own her. He'd have punished her for running away. He'd become obsessed with her."

At that Ms. Frelox thanked him and turned back to the other members of the inquiry. "Well, that confirms what Dr Krata and Mr Yado told us in the first place. Even Mr Chixi's brothers are sure his death was an accident. And we have confirmation that murder was Mr Chixi's intention. Does anyone else wish to add anything?"

Marcus Carlin stood up. "I do."

Ms. Frelox indicated for him to proceed.

"During the last inquiry, Dr Krata was accused of covering up the fact that he had become involved with Ms. Soolkah. I have known Dr Krata for four years and wish to refute that accusation. He is an extremely private person, and it simply wouldn't have occurred to him to cover up something he would regard as a private matter which didn't need reporting."

"Thank you. I've examined the minutes of the previous inquiry in some detail, and it's obvious that Senator Hartmann seized on this private detail and built it up into more than it actually was. Any other contributions?"

Lorr was surprised to see Hanook stand up. "I have one."

"Proceed."

"I have acted in the interest of the tribe's survival in this matter. The Eldest man serves the whole tribe." Hanook paused. "Therefore, at my request Jeene, Vru, and Lorr have told you what happened that day. In telling their story, they have sealed peace between the Shiranu and Sargussi, despite the fact that they now lose any claim they might have had on the woman Soolkah. They have served all our people, both Sargussi and Shiranu, with honour, and I wish this to be recorded as such in the Humanu way as well as in the tribes' way."

Garat Frelox smiled for the first time. "It will be so, Eldest Hanook." Then her features became solemn and business-like once more. "The *inquiry* into Mr Chixi's death is closed. *Verdict*: death by *misadventure*. If anything, Mr Chixi was the *architect* of his own destruction." She looked around the table at each person in turn. "I declare this *inquiry* closed. On behalf of the Committee I wish to thank everyone for giving up their time to attend it."

Lorr rose with everyone else, and followed Jeene and Vru, and Hanook. In the *foyer* Hanook turned to Marcus.

"I would like to invite all of you to a Naxadan wedding," he said. "We have negotiated for six new amaaju to be formed, to seal peace between our tribes with a celebration. Jeene, Vru and Lorr are to be wed at last."

Lorr felt dread shudder through him. *It's not that I mind Mzana, but I don't want to be married at all!* He stared at the floor while his brothers received the good wishes of Marcus and the others.

"And of course, now that the Humanu officially recognise his amaaj, Jordas should provide a home for Yado and Soolkah," Aa'kam said. "It's his responsibility as the Elder brother."

But that means I won't even see her any more! Lorr twisted his hands together. *Don't do this to me!*

Someone was standing beside him. Lorr blinked. It was Soolkah. Blood thundered in his ears, and he could barely hear her words.

"Thank you for helping to clear Yado and Jordas," she said. "It was a brave thing to do. You've earned much status today, all of you, but especially you, Lorr."

She looked after me all those lighttimes, and I didn't even know...

Lorr sucked his lower lip into his mouth so that it wouldn't tremble, and stared back at her. Soon he felt calmer. "I – we did it for the tribe," he said.

*

Jordas stared out of the taxi window, seeing nothing.

He'd had to try to explain what the various buildings were for Yado and Soolkah during the early part of the journey, but now they had stopped asking questions and were just gazing around in wonder. It gave him time to think about the implications of what he'd learned during the inquiry. Lorr's words kept coming back to him: that the arranged marriages caused problems for the members of an amaaj, "'…if different members of the same amaaj have – inappropriate – feelings towards another member of the tribe.'" *That means that their feelings can be different, too.*

For days before he'd met up with Yado and Soolkah he'd flayed himself for what he considered inappropriate feelings for another man's wife. He'd thought they'd been due to being mindlinked to Yado.

He rubbed his chin. The prickle of stubble helped his mind limp towards a truth: if Lorr could have different feelings from his brothers about Soolkah, as he'd seemed to imply, it could only mean one thing.

The feelings I have for Soolkah are my own, not because I'm telepathically linked to Yado. I really do love her. The realisation launched a tsunami of emotion which rioted through his mind and body.

The taxi stopped.

Jordas roused himself with an effort. The vehicle was outside his home. He breathed in deeply. "It's here." He indicated the house with a wave of his hand.

All three of them climbed out of the vehicle, the two Naxadans standing and looking on in bewilderment as Jordas handed the driver his credit chip. "Come with me!" Jordas swept on towards the door – the midday rains still draining from the ground – shepherding Yado and Soolkah before him. Behind their sunvisors their eyes were as wide as oceans. He caught a flash of Yado's emotions. After all that had happened to them, this was yet another new thing to take in. *It must seem stranger still to Soolkah.*

They stood to one side as Jordas laid his hand against the keyplate; the door whispered open.

"Come in." He ushered them through the door.

A command from Jordas activated the air conditioning. "Go in there." He waved at one of the doors. "Sit down. I'll ask Yue Xiao for the recalibration

305

details for the food dispenser." He waited long enough to see them enter the room before going to the phone.

When he re-entered the lounge a few minutes later, Soolkah was wandering round, not-quite-touching everything, wonder and curiosity mingled on her face.

"How could you leave all this? How could you live with us?" she asked.

"What?"

"We must – our lives must seem so – so wretched, compared to yours!"

"I didn't see it like that." He shrugged. "Your people needed rescuing and bringing to safety. There was no time to think how low-tech your ways were." He sighed. "But it feels good to come home now you're here too. This *will* be your home, too – were it your wish."

He glanced at Yado. He stood transfixed, mind closed. Jordas felt himself losing ground, and flung out a hand in appeal.

"Yado?"

"It's strange to me," Yado said, "though I see it through your eyes as well. But it can *never* be as Kerui was." He sighed. "We travelled all the while. I had no single place to call home, so this is just one more stopping-place on life's journey." Then his lips twitched. "But I admit, this part looks more comfortable than most!" He sank down onto the leather *couch* and leaned back experimentally, then relaxed.

Soolkah sniffed and laid fingers to the *couch*, then turned to face Jordas. "This is – the skin of an animal, isn't it, Jordas? I hope you don't expect me to sit on *that!*"

Jordas didn't know what to say. He'd hoped they'd both enjoy being in his house.

It occurred to him to offer them a drink.

This brought Soolkah back to herself; she followed him into the kitchen and watched him dial numbers on the food dispenser. "I should do that," she said. "It's *my* place to provide food and drink."

"How could you do that here?"

She looked so bewildered, so usurped, that he longed to put his arms around her.

"I will teach you how to use these things, if it makes you happier." He reached into a cupboard for a tray and put the drinks on it. "Take these in?" He saw her nod, the movement bouncing her hair in the way he loved.

She still looked disturbed.

Perhaps he'd been wrong to hope things would be easier with all of them living together here.

When he'd drunk his caffeine freeze, flavoured with rum, and Yado and Soolkah had drunk their zhahzhi, he showed them each of his treasures. He hadn't missed the curiosity on their faces, mingled with bewilderment as it was.

"People made these things?" Yado queried.

Jordas nodded.

Yado went to examine the crossed Zarduthi swords mounted on the wall nearby and lifted a thumb to the blade.

"Careful –"

Yado just smiled. "Where are these from?" he asked.

"The Zarduthi live in spaceships, travelling between the stars – they're nomads, like yourselves," he added. "Fierce warriors. You saw one at the spaceport. There are only a few thousand of them." He indicated the swords. "These are Zarduthi weapons."

"They're well-made, beautiful work indeed."

"And this is my father's gun." Jordas lifted the lid of the carved wooden box containing his revolver. The gun lay on its bed of worn velvet, its surface gleaming in the reduced light from the window. "You saw it back in Kerui."

Soolkah fingered the greenish-black glass of the Kiai pitcher which stood atop the bookcase.

"This is from Vanjeyno, where Garat Frelox is from." Jordas passed the brass dancing girl statuette to Soolkah. "It's a pleasure-planet. Many beautiful things are made there, including scent. Flowers grow everywhere there." He waved at the garden beyond the glass.

"Scents? People *make* scents?" Soolkah asked.

Another unfamiliar concept. He rubbed his hand across his forehead. "To make themselves smell nice..." He sighed. *This is much more difficult than I imagined.* "This is also from Vanjeyno. Listen." He mounted the lamo-harp on his knees and caressed a few strings. Notes floated out of its rounded wooden belly.

"What *is* it?" Soolkah whispered.

Yado smiled his half-knowledge. He'd discarded his visor and his eyes shone like citrines flecked with tiger's eye in the waning light from the window. "I've never heard such a thing before, either, though our amaamu had sound-makers before we lived in Kerui."

"It makes *music*." Jordas plucked the strings and the room resonated with another scatter of notes.

He thought he'd always remember the image of Yado's face, mouth agape at the sounds the instrument made; the wonder and awe on his face reminded him of his own pleasure in music as a teenager. Soolkah seemed as much affected as Yado.

He laid the instrument down. Then it occurred to him. *I shouldn't have shared my fascination at the beauty of music with them.*

CHAPTER 28

JORDAS PULLED THE DUVET to make a cocoon about Soolkah and himself. He stroked her hair. Its crimps felt as soft as he remembered. "It seems so long since Kerui. I hope I haven't forgotten how." His arms met around her.

Soolkah finger-stroked his face. "You can't forget something like that!" she smiled, imprinting kisses along his jawline. "Ooh, that makes my lips tingle! I'd forgotten your chin gets prickles," she said.

"Do you wish I were Shiranu or Sargussi?"

"I like you as you are," Soolkah said. Her fingertips explored his face. "Though I still don't understand lots of things about you."

"Such as?"

She hesitated. "I didn't understand why you wouldn't speak to me at the shuzi. I thought you'd changed your mind about being amaajne with me."

"I had no wish to hurt you, but on the surface again our time in Kerui seemed like a dream." He sighed. "And because I'm Humanu – not *just* from a different tribe – it's as hard for me to understand how a Shiranu or Sargussi woman feels about her amaajnu as it is for me to share you. It doesn't seem exactly...*wrong* to me, but even though he's my maaj'gar, I can't understand how Yado's happy to share you."

"Yado explained that perhaps your folk wouldn't understand about our marriage," Soolkah whispered. "I can see now how right he was. But *you* understand. You accept it –"

"That's different. I'm involved whether or not I want to be. But in my community women marry one man at a time." He shrugged. "That's why they don't understand Naxadan marriage customs." He stroked her hair, teasing the strands apart with his fingers. "When we met, I was unsure whether you really wanted to be my amaajni too."

Soolkah snuggled closer. "I admit," she said, "I was scared when Yado told me that I must be your amaajni too – a stranger, and a man from a different world. But now you don't scare me unless you're cold and distant."

"It were impossible to hold back for long when you do things like that!" His hand stroked her face and his mouth sought hers. Her lips parted and she kissed him back with an eagerness he'd never taught her.

Though Soolkah was as silent as ever while they made love, she clung to him. *She enjoyed it too,* he realised, with some satisfaction.

They lay side by side. Soolkah stroked his face.

"You do... seem glad...to be back with me," Jordas said between kisses.

"Of course. You're my amaajne," Soolkah said. "My Humanu husband." She stroked his face again.

I love the way she touches me – that purely Naxadan way of kissing me with her fingertips. I can't give her up now. She's in my blood. Jordas knew then – had been coming to the realisation for some time – that he would never be free of this passion for her, even if it weren't for the sajamu. He remembered the violence of that shock he'd felt – an earthquake throughout his body – when she'd unknowingly looked into his eyes through the holoprobe lens. That seemed like months ago now, though in reality it was just weeks since he'd become joined to Yado. *At last I know for sure. I can't doubt it after Lorr's evidence.*

"I love you, Soolkah," he said as his lips caressed hers again. "Whatever happens, remember that."

Soolkah laid two fingers along his mouth. "Hush, Jordas. Those are words from the time of Keramanthu and before. We don't use them now."

"Don't –?" Jordas found his fingers were trembling. "But how can your amaajne know you love him?"

Soolkah shook her head. "You can't know that, Jordas. I can't say it." She spread her hands. "A woman must treat each amaajne the same."

"Yado didn't – tell me that," he said.

"How would he know? He's a man. Only a woman knows these things, and only then because her mother tells her at the coming-of-age."

*

"In here," Jordas said, opening the door to the monitor room. "Come on." He slipped inside, Yado and Soolkah following.

It had been easy for him to agree when they'd asked that morning, but when Jordas saw Ray's stare as he closed the door behind them his confidence faltered. "Marcus, is it all right –?"

Marcus looked up, dismay veiling his face until he concealed it with a bright smile and a "Good morning," to Soolkah and Yado. "Come and sit here," he invited. His hand swept through the air to indicate the holotank. "This is where we first realised you existed. Alleem, pass me some of that holovid – in the tray tower."

She dropped a chip onto his palm.

He inserted it in the console. "Here." Images formed in the holotank.

"That's me! The day I ran away." Soolkah's eyes gleamed with wonder. "How could you see me?"

Her image gazed from the tank into Jordas's eyes, not begging him to intervene as he'd remembered her, but snapping defiance at her mother's news.

Jordas felt Yado's instant admiration for her spirit. <So you like that about her too?> He felt Yado's assent.

"Watch these while I bring Jordas up to date," Marcus suggested. He ushered Jordas outside. "I personally don't have a problem with this, although the Committee might. You know how keen they are to avoid cross-cultural contamination."

"Yes," Jordas admitted. "But it's not as if I'm bringing in Hanook or Mnanga! Yado already knows wherever I've been and whatever I've done, and could tell Soolkah about any of it at any time."

"True. But today's the worst possible day you could bring them in."

"Why?"

"What did we predict for Naxada after the impacts?"

"What's happened?" Jordas couldn't restrain himself. "Don't string me along, Marcus. Tell me!"

"The space telescope tracked the rest of the asteroid fragments as they fell. One of them struck the opposite side of the planet and triggered an eruption on Mount Kerui – and the magma chamber was already full."

Jordas felt as if he was choking. "Can I take them to another room to see the holovid?"

"Best idea, I think. We have a meeting later with the biology team. They probably won't find that too interesting, so –" He opened the door and beckoned.

Behind Marcus Alleem asked, "Ray, have you received the data from the telescope station yet?"

"It's still transmitting." Ray stared at his monitor again. "Uh – here it comes."

"What's the matter, Ray?" Jordas asked.

"Nothing...?"

"There must be *something* wrong. You never speak in proper sentences!"

"Jordas, we need the main holotank," Marcus interrupted. "Take Yado and Soolkah to room seventeen –"

"Incoming!" Ray muttered, ejecting the holochip and passing it to Jordas. Images boiled up in the tank: the shield of a volcano looming out of the glacier; a giant's bite into the volcano's flank; a huge steam explosion; lava pouring from the wound.

No-one moved.

"Caldera water level twenty-three metres and rising," Alleem reported. "That's three metres higher than this morning."

311

Ray breathed out hard. "Kerui blowing. Must have been unstable."

Oh, great! My first morning back to work and Kerui erupts under our noses. Jordas raked his hair with his hand.

Soolkah's eyes glittered like peridot and she was growing paler by the second. "Jordas, where is that?"

<Were that Kerui?>

Jordas couldn't deny it. He moved between Yado and Soolkah as if it would help him to protect them from the knowledge that their homeworld was changing irrevocably.

"Jordas! What does it mean?" Soolkah's tone made him swing his head round.

"As volcanoes erupt under glaciers they generate steam columns. It makes eruptions fiercer."

"Kerui – is erupting?"

Jordas nodded, trying to retreat from Yado. He needed time to think. He hadn't realised the catastrophe he'd feared all along would come so swiftly, but he'd always known they'd turn to him for support. *Can I give them that?* he wondered. *Am I strong enough?*

<Why shut me out just when I need you?>

With that demand and accusation Jordas came back to reality. <Sorry, Yado. I didn't realise –>

"Zoom fifty percent." Alleem's voice cut across their conversation.

The image swooped in to show crusts of lava piercing the edge of the glacier. From the jagged wound in the mountainside, a torrent of lava and debris raced downslope.

"Kerui!" Soolkah cried.

I was there. We all were. We only just got out in time. He felt as if he were trapped inside a bubble in time, unable to move.

"Jordas." Marcus came to him, trying to shepherd the three of them out of the room. "They'll be better off –"

"We're not children. You can't protect us now." Yado's eyes lingered on the holotank.

"He's right, though," Jordas said. "We should go."

"Take them to room seventeen and get them hot drinks. I'll call one of the stress counsellors over. When he gets here, come back for the meeting. Afterwards you should take them home."

Jordas dipped his head in assent. "Come."

*

"Ray, call Alfred and ask him to send one of the stress counsellors here urgently." Marcus checked the time. The meeting had been set for nine-thirty, and he'd wanted Jordas there to catch up on what he'd missed.

Pity Jordas hadn't asked whether he could bring Yado and Soolkah here today, he mused. *I could have put them off and they'd never have been any the wiser about Kerui.*

The monitor room had filled up for the meeting by the time Jordas slipped back in, face white as ice. *It's as if he's Naxadan, not human,* Marcus thought.

Jordas stared into the holotank. "They're okay about it. It's a good job we left when we did – the planet's virtually uninhabitable now." His voice sounded wobbly.

"Ah, good, we can get started." Though Marcus wondered if Jordas wouldn't be better off staying with Yado and Soolkah.

"Marcus, did you contact Howerd?" Jordas asked, over the whine of the drinks dispenser.

"He's away again. I had to leave a message with his secretary. He'll call me as soon as he comes back, but it seems they deal with these relocations in strict rotation." Marcus sighed. "It's a pity we got the rotten apple assigned to this project – someone with a bit of clout would have been very useful to get things moving. I don't mind admitting it, I'm worried."

"What about that Vanjeynish woman?" Alleem said. "From the second Inquiry."

"Garat Frelox, yes. Howerd's Vice-Chairperson." Marcus paused, sipping his drink. "She did seem sympathetic to the Naxadans' needs. I'll call her."

"I support what you're doing for the Naxadans." Alleem hesitated, then added, "My people haven't forgotten how the Committee helped us when it was first set up. We'll support any species in difficulties."

"Will you?" asked Marcus, surprised and pleased. "Is there anyone on Kiai you could contact to lend weight to our campaign?"

"There might be someone," Alleem said. "I could call my house-father, see if he could contact him."

"Support from Kiai might help swing things in the Naxadans' favour," Jordas mused. "I know other projects have prior claims on funding, but the tribespeople are so few, and if the Committee doesn't act soon they could be even fewer."

Marcus glanced at him. One arm was folded across his chest in a defensive position; his other hand held his caffeine freeze near his lips.

"It all hinges on whether a suitable uninhabited planet is available," Marcus pointed out. "If there isn't, they'll just have to wait. But Alleem – why don't you call your – house-father – from here, now?"

Alleem nodded. "I will," she said.

Ray slipped off his stool and strolled between the monitors. "One thing," he said as he reached the drinks dispenser. "Wouldn't make too much of Jordas being part of the campaign. Might not do much good after Inquiry."

There was a moment's silence in the monitor room.

"What d'you mean by that?" Jordas asked.

"*You* know – *ménage à trois* stuff. And *they* live with *you*. Others aren't allowed out of compound."

Marcus was on his feet, making eye contact and pointing to the door before he'd even finished. "Excuse us a moment," he said, and without waiting to see if Ray was following, strode through the door. He turned. "The project conference starts when we go back in. I don't need my time wasted like this." He closed the door.

"What's the problem?" Ray asked.

"You are. Or rather, your attitude is."

"Don't understand." Ray gestured, spilling his drink. "Damn! Said yourself you weren't happy about this Jordas-Naxadan thing."

"Ray, for an intelligent young man you can be extremely obtuse at times." Marcus sighed. "Jordas is an adult, and he's made his decision. It may not be what we'd choose, but it's not our business. Keep your opinions to yourself – and you'd better apologise to Jordas!"

Ray snorted. "But –"

"If you want to stay on the team, behave with more finesse in future," Marcus said. "Go back now. Remember what I've said." He thrust his hands into his pockets and watched Ray disappear into the room ahead of him. *That's the last thing I need.* He stood there for a moment, then followed Ray back into the monitor room.

*

This one, Jordas said. He'll be home soon. Soolkah jabbed at the panel on the food *dispenser*. She stepped back and stood watching it. The light came on inside to show that it was working, so she wandered over to the lounge door. Yado was seated cross-legged on the couch, examining another of Jordas's *books.*

"If only we could go back to the time when Jordas lived with *us,*" she sighed. "Everything was simpler then. I wish I had a stone to cook on. Jordas's house is beautiful, but strange. I don't understand a lot of the things here."

Jordas had spent several evenings coaching Soolkah in making food the Humanu way: how the food-maker worked, how to refill it every lighttime, how to change the settings for Naxadan and Humanu food. After the success

314

of yesterday evening's meal, she thought she'd grasped everything, but without knowing what the squiggles on the panel meant, she couldn't be sure if she'd worked it properly.

"Now, Jordas's *clothes*." She'd learned that this was the English word for everything that Jordas wore, as well as her cloth kilt and Yado's leather one.

"Are you talking to yourself, me, or the *machines*?" Yado inquired.

"I'm not sure." Soolkah spread her hands palms down and smiled ruefully. "I want to surprise Jordas by washing his things. I thought he'd be happier if I could do things like that for him –"

A muffled *thud* interrupted her. Yado dropped his book, crossed the lounge in two strides, and grabbed her. They clung to each other.

"What were that?"

"The food-maker!" Soolkah turned in his arms, expecting to see a lump of twisted metal, but the food-making machine looked normal. The light was still on. She released herself from Yado's hold and approached it. "It – doesn't make noises like that when Jordas uses it."

Yado had followed her. "Shall we stop it and see –"

"But how do we stop it? It usually cooks for a set time."

"I will ask."

"I wish we weren't dependent on Jordas here," Soolkah said. "In Kerui we were strong because we knew what to do. Here, I don't feel in control."

"He says press here," Yado said, pointing to one of the marked places on the food-maker. "He said don't touch anything else. He shall arrive soon."

Soolkah pressed the place Yado had shown her. The door swung open. Smoke poured into the kitchen. The food-container had exploded into several pieces, and blackened globs of meat-like stuff had stuck to the door, walls and roof.

"Your food!" Soolkah exclaimed. "I've burned it." She turned to look at him. "I'm sorry, Yado –"

"It matters not."

"But you said you were hungry!" Soolkah felt tears prickle her nose in frustration. "I want to be a good amaajni to you and Jordas..."

"You are –"

The door slammed, stopping Yado mid-sentence.

"What is it?" Jordas panted.

<I couldn't feel your thoughts as you approached,> Yado observed.

Jordas pushed between them in front of the food-maker, frown-marks etched between his brows. His skin was reddish and sheened with perspiration, and he hadn't got his breath back. There were damp patches on his *clothes*.

315

Soolkah could feel his body heat, and his scent was sharper than usual. "I'm sorry, Jordas," she said. "I wanted to surprise you –"

To her surprise, Jordas's features rearranged themselves. He laughed, yet moisture poured from his eyes. The sound filled the room. His body shook with guffaws which went on and on.

Humanu ways are strange. "What have I done that's so funny?"

"Jordas!" Yado exclaimed. "Calm down!" He seized Jordas by the wrists and shook him. "You're hysterical."

Jordas's laughter ceased. He made as if to pull Soolkah close, then stopped. He and Yado were mindspeaking again, from their expressions.

"Is the food-maker broken?" Soolkah asked.

"It's fine." Jordas's breathing and face were returning to normal. He turned back to the food-maker. "Who was this for?"

"Yado."

"Let's clean up." Jordas wiped his eyes, picked up a cloth and began to wipe the inside of the food-maker. "It was on a very high *setting*."

"Aren't you cross with me?" Soolkah asked.

"Why would I be cross with you? I can only blame myself for this."

"What do you mean?"

Jordas sighed. "Mayhap Ray were right. I shouldn't have brought you here."

"*Who* said this to you? I'm your amaajni, and Yado is your maaj'gar – you can't just put us aside! If we didn't live with you, what would we do?"

"You managed when I was *suspended*."

"Don't send us away from you – we're your amaaj. It didn't feel right at all when we couldn't live together."

"Nor to me. But I'm not sure what would." Jordas looked at Soolkah, and his face was sad and gentle. "You're unhappy here, and I don't know how to make things better. I wanted you both to enjoy living with me."

*

The night air cooled Lorr's skin, and for once a hubbub filled the atmosphere as each tribesman strove to make himself heard above his neighbour. With no further need for silence, both Sargussi and Shiranu tribespeople were learning to talk at greater volumes than in Kerui, and perhaps trying to outdo each other. Near Hanook and Aa'kam and their amaaju sat the Humanu: Marcus, Matt and Yue Xiao, Alfred Grantham and the younger Humanu, Ray. A tall, dark-skinned creature was with them, a woman of the Kiai tribe, according to Marcus. Mnanga sat on a pile of woven fabric on the other side of their group, next to Aneera and her husbands. Lorr let his eyes range across the amaaju-groups of the tribespeople. Soolkah was with her origin-amaaj for this occasion.

"Sargussi! Shiranu! Humanu and others!" As Aa'kam addressed the crowd the noise level fell. "I welcome Jordas Krata of the Humanu into the Sargussi tribe." He stood with Jordas and Yado on one side of him and Maru on the other, all grinning from ear to ear.

"Speech! Speech!"

Maru stepped forwards. "As the adopting father I am pleased to welcome Jordas into my amaaj, and to give my belated agreement to my bloodkin, Yado, and spirit-kin, Jordas, becoming amaajne with Soolkah of the Shiranu."

The Humanu began to smack their hands together, and, when they realised the gesture was an expression of pleasure, the tribespeople joined in. Lorr looked around at them. He knew he should, too, and felt distinctly unwilling.

To his shame, he was saved when Jordas stepped forwards, arms raised for attention. "Tribespeople, I'm very relieved that Alfred's confirmation that humanu skin is thinner means I've no need of circumcision!" Jordas waited for the laughter to subside. "Yado and I knew from the beginning that we were joined, but I'm delighted that this has been formally recognised at last."

Now Hanook stepped forwards. "On behalf of the Shiranu, I welcome both Jordas Krata and Yado into the Shiranu tribe as the amaajnu of Soolkah."

His words struck a chill into Lorr's heart. But the rest of the tribespeople clapped with the Humanu, this time without prompting.

"Have some dried fruit," Jeene said, passing a handful of what now passed for mathna globes to Lorr. He looked around. <And for the sake of the amaamu, stop staring at Soolkah! Try to look as if you're enjoying getting married. It's not very polite towards Mzana.> He knuckled him beneath his arm where no-one would see.

<I can't help it. I haven't seen her since she went to live with the Humanu.> Lorr sighed. <Anyway, I never wanted Mzana to be our amaajni.> He put one of the fruits in his mouth, frowning. He began to chew, then made a face. "Urgh! This may look like mathna, but it tastes like ganzu-shit!"

Jeene dug him in the ribs again. <Behave yourself! I know the Humanu can't quite get the taste of the food right, but it isn't *just* our wedding you'll spoil.>

Lorr nodded. How could he forget? He glanced around him. *Jeene's right,* he chided himself. *Five other new amaaju are being joined tonight. I shouldn't spoil their happiness with a sour face –*

Everyone was talking and eating, laughing, being happy.

Except me. Lorr felt his heart swell with sorrow until he thought it would choke him. He looked away.

A question from Jeene broke into his thoughts. "Why isn't Zuas being married as well? I'm sure there are plenty of Elder brothers who'd willingly have her."

"She's not well enough yet," Mzana volunteered.

Lorr had wondered earlier if she could talk at all, she'd been so silent all evening. *Perhaps the zhahzhi's loosened her tongue.*

"Don't forget she has the wheezing sickness as well," Mzana added. "She had an attack while I was with her last night, and had to lie down."

"Can't the Humanu do anything about that?" Mzana asked. "They have those healing *machines* –"

"Maybe they don't know." Jeene shifted position.

Lorr surprised himself by speaking. "I don't think it's just her health. I think it's because Hanook still blames himself for Nahru's death that he doesn't want to part with her."

Vru's glance penetrated him for a moment. Then his expression softened. "You're probably right," he said.

"The one I feel sorry for is the Sargussi woman," Mzana said. "How can the Elders do that to her? She must still be grieving."

"Is she the one whose husbands were killed in the fire at the Humanu Shuzi?" Lorr asked. "The Sargussi woman who's being joined to Temma's amaaj tonight?"

"Yes. Couldn't they give her more time?" Mzana shivered.

Jeene looked surprised. "Mzana, you know she must give more children to the tribe."

"Two of her husbands are younger than her. She must already be nearly thirty. She may only have a few more child-bearing years left," Vru pointed out.

"Well, I wouldn't want it so soon. And everyone must know it's political."

"Wouldn't you want Sargussi husbands, then?" Vru asked with a grin.

"I don't think so." Mzana turned to look at Soolkah. "At least *she* won't be the only woman with foreign husbands now. But I don't know how she can go with a Sargussi, let alone a Humanu!"

Lorr's teeth clenched on his lip.

"It'll be interesting to see if the Sargussi woman's son shares with any brothers she produces," Jeene said. "If a Humanu and a Sargussi can share, why not a Sargussi and a Shiranu?"

"That's the last thing I'd be bothered about," Mzana murmured. "I count myself lucky not to have been given to anyone I didn't like." Her eyes rested on Lorr.

He felt himself grow hot under her gaze.

Then she looked away and reached for another aggifruit. "Perhaps this would taste better if they didn't ready-cook it," she said. "Maybe we should get the food from the Humanu and cook it ourselves."

"It's an idea," Jeene said. "Why not suggest it to Mnanga when the lighttime comes, and see if she can arrange with the Humanu for us to try that?" He looked around. "I think everyone's leaving. Perhaps we should go, too." He rose.

Lorr saw the group of Humanu approaching them. *I'm not sure if I can stand more good wishes,* he thought. But he caught a warning fragment of mindspeech from Jeene, so he endured the *rice* scattered over him and the others, along with explanations that this was a Humanu custom for calling down good fortune on new marriages.

Vru picked a grain of *rice* from between the overlap of his kilt. "At least it's not meat," he said. "Come on." <My turn this darktime,> he reminded Jeene and Lorr. <Your turn tomorrow, Jeene, and Lorr's after that.>

Lorr didn't respond, but stared at Soolkah, now preparing to leave the compound with her foreign husbands. She had her back to him. He swallowed and tagged along after his brothers and amaajni as they threaded between the *huts*.

They stepped inside theirs. Someone, perhaps Mzana's mother, had lit the lamps. Mzana was trembling; for all her brave talk at the wedding, Lorr realised, she was as scared as any other new bride – or husband. *Perhaps the zhahzhi's wearing off now,* he thought. *And after all, she's only seen sixteen highwaters.*

Jeene walked over to her. "Don't be afraid," he said. "It'll be all right. We'll none of us hurt you."

Mzana tried to smile, looking around wildly – for the sleeping-cloths, Lorr guessed. He stood paralysed with fear that he would let his brothers down, while Vru guided her without touching her towards the pile of glittering sleeping-cloths the Humanu had given to each amaaj when they'd arrived at this place. She lifted them out one by one, and passed one to each of them. Lorr tucked his under his arm and backed away.

He heard a whisper: "More zhahzhi?" and remembered that it had been Jeene's idea rather than Vru's to offer for Mzana. He waited to see what the others would do, and when Jeene handed a bowl of the liquor to Mzana he lay down on his side and covered himself with the sleeping-cloth. He watched her sip from the bowl while the sleeping-cloth warmed him. But the heat of the zhahzhi he'd had earlier receded. He closed his eyes and felt Jeene lie down as well, then Vru with Mzana beside him. Vru blew the light out.

Lorr could feel Mzana's shivers as Vru held her against him, just as if she were in his own arms. He felt the softness of her short fur against his fingertips, as his brother's hands reached out to her.

Then the thing he'd dreaded for so many lighttimes began. While Vru groaned aloud as he entered Mzana, and Jeene used his own hands to coax out the stuff of life itself in rhythm with his Elder brother, Lorr fought the sajamu-sensations from them. Pleasure mounted between his two brothers, but Lorr lay silent, fists clenched and eyelids sealed against a stinging highwater of loss and regret. And as the liquid of life squirted out into the hot, wet muchuwa which wrapped Vru, so it pulsed under Jeene's hands.

But from Lorr's uchaan it spilled weakly, as if reluctant to be squeezed out. And from his eyes flowed tears which only spent their hot wetness on the floor.

CHAPTER 29

IF ONLY there was something to do on this crate! Gerrold Hartmann thought. *No women, no booze, nothing till we reach Galatea Station. Even the food's dreadful. And the crew jabber away in their own language.* Hartmann was glad he'd brought the universal translator and wireless earpiece so he could listen in on their conversations. *At least it won't be long now.*

Hlur had insisted he wasn't going straight to Earth no matter *who* Hartmann was. They'd been travelling far longer than he'd expected and his limited store of clean clothing and toiletries had diminished to the point of no return. He'd had steam showers, but Hlur had curtly informed him it wasn't possible to get his clothes washed, and Hartmann constantly registered the pungency of his own sweat.

He locked the cabin door and mooched along the companionway to the mess; at least he could get coffee there. The doorless area was deserted. He dialled himself a drink and carried it to a table near the viewport, secluded behind a support strut. He sipped, wondering if he'd ever felt so bored.

Along the corridor he heard voices, including Hlur's.

"Yes, that ship blew with a good bang!"

"Lit up the sky like a nova. Must've been all the glass on-board!" a second voice squeaked. Both Kiai laughed.

Hartmann remembered another space trip and a flashboard showing the latest news. It was just weeks ago, though it seemed months. He pushed the memory away and got up to go. But Hlur's next words made him sink back into his seat.

"It gives me such satisfaction to damage our so-civilised planet's trade. Almost worth losing the use of my testicles for that!"

"Makes no difference to me," the other Kiai squeaked. "I was castrated as a young boy, but then I wasn't a lord's son. But I just *love* blowing things up!"

Hartmann recognised him as Garrus. *So that's why Hlur needs him.* Hartmann had wondered whether smuggling was his only occupation when the Kiai captain had introduced Garrus as a weapons specialist.

"Yes, adult castration has a much more noticeable effect in some ways. You still look and sound like a man, but the equipment doesn't do the job any more. I savour my revenge."

"And you're getting it, aren't you? We've taken every glassware ship this quarter-year. They're afraid to send them out. We've blown their off-planet trade wide open." The drinks dispenser whirred. Hartmann heard the scrape of chairs as they sat down.

"Hmph! Funny smell in here. D'you notice it?"

"You know I have no sense of smell, Hlur."

"I forgot." Hlur's footsteps sounded as he prowled around the mess. He carried on talking anyway. "You know, I swear that smell's the vile brew that human drinks."

How am I going to leave without them seeing me? There was only the one entrance. *I'll just sit tight and ignore this.* He put his head on his forearms and pretended to be asleep in case they discovered him.

"He smells terrible anyway."

"He's paying you well enough," Garrus pointed out.

They *must have been responsible for destroying my investment.* Hartmann considered getting up and walking out, or confronting them. *Neither option's sensible. These are dangerous men with nothing to lose. And there's just me against two of them.* He stayed where he was, head on one forearm, eyes shut. He settled into the position, pushing his arms forward on the table.

As the beaker of hot coffee spilt on his forearm Hartmann leapt upright. "Fuck!"

The clatter of a toppling chair heralded Hlur and Garrus's arrival.

"Hartmann!" Hlur's eyes narrowed as he saw the earpiece. "Universal translator. How many of our conversations have you listened in on?"

Hartmann dabbed his sleeve with his silk handkerchief. "Damnation! My favourite suit!"

Hlur's moustache quivered with anger. "How long were you hiding here? How much did you hear?"

Garrus unholstered his disruptor.

He'd brazen it out. "I dozed off over my coffee."

Hlur shook his head. "No, human. I don't believe that." He turned to Garrus. "Tie him to the chair."

Garrus complied. His voice might squeak, but his strength made short work of Hartmann's struggles to evade the bonds.

When he was satisfied with Garrus's efforts, Hlur put his fists on his hips and stared at Hartmann. "Now, human. I warn you, Garrus is an expert interrogator. *What did you hear?*"

Hartmann stared back at him. "Enough."

"Enough? To do what?" Hlur's eyes bored into him. "Hit him, Garrus."

Garrus's fist came out of nowhere to land on Hartmann's nose. Hartmann felt it shatter, then felt the heat of his own blood. It dripped onto his chest.

"You realise I could hand you over to the authorities?"

"For what? I haven't done anything wrong."

"Again, Garrus."

This time the Kiai's fist met Hartmann's stomach.

"That's not what the newscasts are saying. They're after you, Hartmann – that's why we can't take you openly to Earth, or even Charidas – and, of course, it's precisely why you came to *me*."

Hartmann drew himself up as best he could. "I could do the same with you. The Committee promotes trade between planets, amongst other –"

Hlur nodded to Garrus. "Let him have it."

The blows rained down on Hartmann's head, neck, shoulders, chest and stomach. A few kicks found their targets on his legs, especially his knees. The pain mounted, to the point where he was barely conscious. His head sank onto his chest.

Hlur grabbed his head by the ears and forced him to meet his gaze. "You think they'll listen to *you* after you discredited them on Mourang – and that Naxadan business?" He laughed. "You think I didn't realise you were in trouble back there?"

"The reason for the 'Naxadan business', as you put it, was that you blew up a ship I had an interest in!"

"Oh, really?" Hlur smirked. "You collect glassware, do you?" He gestured to Garrus. "I'm tired of this. Deal with him."

Hartmann saw Garrus raise his bared arm. *This is it. Even if they drop me at Galatea Station, the antidote won't be available in time.* He made to swing his own arm up to ward off the blow from the extended poison spur at the elbow, and only realised he couldn't when his bonds cut into his wrists.

"Not that, you fool! Do you want them to tie this back to us when they find him?"

"Fine," Garrus muttered, and swung the butt of his disruptor instead.

The side of Hartmann's head imploded and he blacked out.

*

"Good morning!"

Ray looked up as Alleem breezed into the room. "Not morning yet," he mumbled, glancing at the window. "Still dark outside." He rubbed his eyes and leaned back in his chair, stretching to relieve the ache between his shoulder blades, then refocused his attention on the holotank, where a seismogram of quake swarms floated over the view of Naxada. Each swarm was of greater magnitude than the last. The eruption had rumbled on for days, but this episode was major.

"The ash deposits have completely covered the summit ice. Albedo reduced by thirty-five percent."

"How can you be so cheerful?" Jordas passed a hand over his forehead and raked his fingers through his hair, then yawned.

"Sleeping helps, though I had to break my usual activity pattern when I left Kiai." Alleem went to the drinks dispenser and selected a drink. "Where's Marcus?"

"Gone for a shower and change of clothes. Ray and I are off soon. Alleem, are you sure you don't mind holding the fort while we're at the conference?"

"Of course not."

Marcus had contacted Howerd Asthorn and explained why the Naxadans needed resettling as soon as possible. The Kiai government had lobbied on their behalf, and as two uninhabited planets had been found which might be suitable, Howerd had agreed to bring forward the resettlement conference. Ray checked the time. It was three hours away. Today, the location of the Naxadans' new home would be decided.

"What's that?" Jordas asked around another yawn as he joined Alleem at the drinks dispenser.

"*Grucht,*" Alleem said, holding the beaker towards him. "Kiai tea."

Jordas sniffed, then jerked back. "I'll play safe with a caffeine freeze."

"It is a bit of an acquired taste." Alleem reached her monitor.

"Gravity fluctuations increasing." Ray pointed to the space telescope monitor. "Spectrometers show massive amounts of gas emissions –"

In the holotank, the white-and-blue disk of Naxada had darkened to a dingy grey. The ice sheet melt was in full spate as the cinders on it absorbed sunlight instead of reflecting it. Gas and ash clouds, stabbed by lightning discharges, belched from the mountain.

"Zoom in."

At that moment, Mount Kerui exploded.

Ray waved towards the tank. "Look, Jordas!"

But Jordas stepped back as if reluctant to watch the destruction. The holo-image reflected the ash clouds off his features. His facial bones jutted like the skeleton of hopes lost. His eyes were full of shadows Ray hadn't noticed before, reflecting the cloven shield of the volcano as they fixed on the tank.

"It must be awesome, close up." Alleem sipped her drink.

"To watch a world die?" Jordas's face twisted. "We wanted to see what would happen, but it's a chain reaction and I didn't expect to feel so helpless. All we can do is watch as Naxada becomes uninhabitable. They couldn't go back now."

"What will Yado and Soolkah do when the others go?" Alleem asked, coming to stand between them.

"We talked about it last night. They're going with them." Jordas stood opposite Ray, mouth tight, hands thrust into his trouser pocket, face paler than ever. He stared at the tank, motionless as a boulder.

What Ray saw there chilled him. *Worked with him for four years. Changed on Naxada. Not himself any more.* With a throwaway gesture he said, "Best thing to let them go."

Jordas stared at him. "Best for whom?"

*

The door clicked to behind Jordas. *They're not up yet. I've got a few minutes.*

He'd left work earlier than agreed. "I've something to do," he'd told Ray and Alleem. They hadn't protested, but he was sure they felt his tension, and noticed the periodic tremor in his fingers.

The arrival of morning had shadowed the lounge purple and blue. He crossed it, eyes fixed on the carved box on the half-moon table. He lifted the lid, jerking upright as the hinges squeaked. He took the gun out, closed the box, and thrust a handful of ammunition into his pocket. Expecting to hear Yado's light tread at any moment, he thought he heard a sound behind him and froze.

The silence thickened. He turned, alarmed, almost guilty.

No-one there.

*

Yado opened his eyes. A few early-lighttime rays seeped through the *drapes* and chased purple shadows into the corners of the room. *What woke me?*

His arm pressed Soolkah back against him as he snuggled up behind her. She sighed in her sleep. Her body warmth reassured him against the cool of lightbreak and the strangeness of their surroundings. *There's much to learn about life beyond Kerui. Jordas can help me, but Soolkah is unhappy here.* He thought back over the argument the previous evening. They'd decided that when the tribespeople left for their new home, they'd go with them. *Jordas took it badly.*

Jordas was most likely still at work. He'd been asked to work the previous night, so Yado and Soolkah hadn't made love for fear of causing another embarrassing situation. He'd missed that.

He quested with his mind for Jordas, but found no parallel contact except sajamu. The blankness worried him. He didn't feel alone, though; sajamu ensured that never happened.

Yado let his thoughts drift until he dozed again. He dreamed that he was both Jordas and himself at once, looking down on the compound. Soolkah stood alone near the huts. The *fence* sprang up around it, dwarfing her, rising as she got smaller. He was flying above the compound. Emotion flooded and scorched in at once, a mingling of sorrow and passion – the greatest passion he'd felt in his life...

How can I leave her behind?

*

Jordas's nerves had lost their elasticity, stretched too far in recent days. *I must leave now.* For a moment his concentration slipped; his mindshield was fragile as a new scab.

Yado's dreaming. His dream resonated with such grief and yearning that Jordas almost laid the gun back in its case then; instead, he clamped his teeth in his lip and strode towards the front door.

He wouldn't say goodbye. He could only look ahead, lest he be turned from his purpose by everything he treasured. From the hall cupboard he collected his climbing gear and slung it over his shoulder.

Another step. *I'll never feel him touch my mind again.* He tamped the thought down, afraid Yado would pick it up. The fragments of the dream persisted, superimposed over the hallway like half-tangible sajamu-visions.

As Jordas reached the door he heard someone turn over in bed, felt Yado's hand touch Soolkah's breasts. *If they go away with the others I won't even be able to share her as I have up till now, but I'll know whenever he makes love with her. I have no other choice.* His foot crossed the threshold, and he cursed the expectations he'd nursed. Yado might survive in his world, but not Soolkah. *How could I have expected them to stay with me when the other tribespeople left?*

He stepped onto the paviors outside the house, struggling to move through a floodtide of emotion, drowning in a backswash which sucked him away from Yado and Soolkah. Tears washed away his vision. *I can't bear to lose either of them. There is nothing left but this.*

He wrapped the mindshield like a cloak about his consciousness and looked straight ahead.

*

Yado reached for Soolkah. Even asleep, her nipples hardened and her breasts swelled under his fingers.

A murmur told him Soolkah was waking. "Touch me, Yado!" She drew his hands downwards. "Touch me like you used to before Jordas came to be with us."

"D'you not like *kissing*?" he asked in some surprise.

"I do, but I like *your* way of making love as well. It's different from Jordas's. I like his way too, but I like it best from him." She paused. "Just touch me."

He obliged. "He's likely still at work," he reminded her, when she pressed closer.

"I know," she sighed.

Yado's mind returned to that blankness where the contact with Jordas should have been. It wasn't like the blackness of darkened noviglass which descended when Jordas slept, filled with dream-images. Though sajamu told him that Jordas was physically safe, its familiarity and strangeness worried him, like the contact between them had felt at first. It felt like something lost and only just found again. *Jordas has learned to raise his mental barriers.* It was inevitable, since all tribesmen had that skill. *But why did I not guess when he came home the other night? It feels so different that I didn't recognise it straight away.*

With the realisation that Jordas had learned another mindlink skill, he abandoned his worry. The privacy code prevented Yado from disturbing him.

*

A rap at the door returned Yado's thoughts to the present. "Hurry now! The *car* is here." Yado put on his *sunvisor*.

Soolkah scrambled upright; she wouldn't sit on the *couch*. She donned her own *visor* on the way to the open door.

A *vehicle* with darkened windows had stopped outside, but instead of Jordas, Ray Travers' straggle-furred figure climbed from behind the wheel.

They left the *house*. Yado sealed the door behind him with his handprint. The heat prickled his flesh and brought perspiration to his temples. Fragments of his dream returned; as he'd sat up it had slipped away, leaving only an impression of emotions lapping around him like water on a streamside – and an emptiness, as if he had no power to protect something he valued. He shook himself, and the sense of impending loss faded. "Where's Jordas?"

"Not with you?"

Yado shook his head, as sajamu gave him an impression of movement, bars of sunlight and shadow alternating on furless skin. "Oh, he's walking somewhere."

"Haven't seen him since this morning," Ray said. "Thought he was getting changed. Marcus sent me to pick all of you up. Should go now. Hop in!"

Yado swallowed his concern and they clambered into the *vehicle*. The *air conditioning* inside relaxed him. He looked sideways at Ray. His skin was

327

pinkish even in the grey light inside the *car*. Yado knew that in Humanu this indicated extreme emotion. "Are you *sure* you don't know where Jordas is?" he asked.

Ray coloured further. "Argument," he muttered, starting the *car*. "Left work when Mount Kerui blew again." He looked at Yado, his eyes wide. "Sure he's not in the house?"

"He hasn't been back."

"Kerui erupted this morning?" Soolkah reached for Yado's hand.

Concern at her stricken look quickly replaced pride in her growing knowledge of English. *Jordas warned us there'd likely be another eruption.* Ignoring Ray he squeezed Soolkah's hand.

Ray concentrated on the road. "Went up before dawn. Beaut, it was –"

"But what about Jordas?"

Ray shrugged. "Might meet us there." He swerved around a corner as they approached the fast route out of the residential area.

"Probably," Yado echoed, while his mind asked, *how?*

The *car* followed the contours of the road as it picked up speed. The colour had ebbed from Ray's face. Yado choked down his alarm and stared out through the windows. *I'd know if he weren't well.*

"Yado?"

He turned to look at Soolkah.

"If Kerui is gone, how will our people survive?"

Yado shook his head. "I don't know, but we agreed it were best to keep it to ourselves, remember?" The journey was completed in silence.

At the *conference venue*, a hotel in Axos, everyone looked as nervous as Yado felt as they filed into the room. Seats were laid out around an oval of wood. Ray read the names on the *cards* and pointed out their places.

Yado stared at the black marks on the *card*, then took his ID from his waist pouch and compared them. They were the same. Writing fascinated him. At the house he'd spent hours looking at the books, trying to puzzle the symbols out, but Jordas had insisted he'd be in trouble if he gave him the skill of understanding what they meant.

He surveyed the room. There were jugs filled with cool drinks at intervals along the table, and a beaker at each place. A large holotank occupied one wall.

The room filled up. Yado saw Ray had slipped into the seat on Soolkah's right, and a stab of jealousy made him resent the seating arrangements; then he remembered Ray was sitting in for Jordas. *Would I have such feelings were Jordas here? I don't think so!* He squashed the emotion down, then forgot it. Marcus and Alfred sat opposite, between the Shiranu and Sargussi Elders.

They were chatting to Hanook and Aa'kam using their translator. The rest of the Humanu milled about the room, chattering all at once so that Yado couldn't follow their conversations.

He was pleased when Matt smiled at him across the table, and raised his hand, nodded and smiled back, encouraged. He respected Matt for fighting to help the tribespeople.

"Where's Jordas?" he saw Matt mouth across the table to him.

Yado flipped his hands over in the "don't know" gesture of the Humanu and raised his shoulders.

At that moment, the buzz of speech quietened and people sought their seats as a man rose to his feet at the head of the table.

*

"Good morning, everyone. I am Howerd Asthorn, Chair of the Committee for Colonisation and Resettlement."

Matt Johnson exchanged a glance with Yue Xiao, seated beside him.

The universal translator kept up a stream of Naxadan. "I must start by explaining that as a matter of internal policy Senator Gerrold Hartmann has been replaced as Liaison Officer on this project." Howerd paused and smiled, his eyes meeting those of each person seated at the table, one by one. He introduced everyone seated at the table, including representatives of the various Federal League planets' governments. Then he added, with a glance in Marcus's direction, "I understand we have someone missing."

"Yes," Marcus said. "I've received apologies from Dr Krata, who regrets he is unable to attend the conference." He looked at Yado, and it seemed to Matt that a question hovered on his lips, but he didn't voice it.

Howerd continued. "The Committee's purpose is to supervise cases of necessary galactic migration and act as a clearing-house for all colonisation licenses within the Federal League. Another function is to find suitable worlds for settlement. We've helped in cases of overpopulation, disastrous wars, civilisations almost wiped out by famine, caused by crop disease or climate change. In the case of the Kiai, we supervised their repatriation and the rehabilitation of their homeworld. Now, I've met no case more desperate than that of the people of the planet we of the Federal League call Naxada, so named by its discoverers, the Zarduthi. We've never before had a situation where the planet has virtually torn itself apart through a combination of astronomical and geological circumstances. A successful rescue mission was mounted and the people living there brought to a place of safety." He indicated Marcus with a wave of his hand. "Dr Marcus Carlin will now deliver his mission report."

Marcus stood up and gave a summary of the background to the rescue

329

mission and problems the rescuers had faced. Then he addressed the Committee's resident experts. "And because of a history of mutual hostility between the Sargussi and Shiranu tribes, and the difficulty of avoiding cross-cultural contamination due to the delay in their resettlement, we requested that the Committee bring forward this conference. As leader of the Naxada research project, I wish to thank the Kiai government for supporting our campaign on the Naxadans' behalf." He sought the gaze of the Kiai representative and inclined his head.

The Kiai representative bowed back.

"Thank you, Dr Carlin."

Marcus bowed slightly to Howerd and reseated himself.

Howerd faced the Committee scientists seated at one end of the table. "These gentlemen have been gathering and analysing data and using it so as to decide which of the latest colony planets to be opened up should be set aside for the Naxadans."

Matt's eyes turned towards Yado. He was fidgeting in his seat. *He looks as if Jordas's absence is bothering him. I wonder why Jordas isn't here? Perhaps he couldn't bear to see the Naxadans choose their new home. I guess he'll be saying goodbye to them when they leave –*

Howerd interrupted his musings. "We haven't been able to find you a new planet just like Naxada, particularly in view of the urgency of resettlement."

The tribespeople looked at each other and whispered together for a few minutes, some signing across the table.

"They don't like that idea much," Yue Xiao remarked.

Matt caressed the back of her hand with his thumb in reply.

Yado voiced their worries. "We thought we would be going to a world like ours."

"I'm sorry. As far as we can determine, Naxada and its ecology are unique. There is no other habitable planet quite like it. Living underground sensitised the Naxadans' eyes to sunlight and they need certain dietary salts peculiar to their specialised environment." Asthorn's voice dropped to a whisper. "It was indeed a very special place. We can only offer you the nearest thing to it.

"But we've found two unpopulated possibilities. We are going to show you details of both planets now, in the holotank." He gestured towards it. "We'll ask you to choose for yourselves whichever seems most suitable. Our initial considerations were for a breathable atmosphere, adequate clean water for drinking, washing and irrigation, and a gravity comparable to the Naxadan norm – not too difficult. But daylight and temperature variation were prime considerations as well, along with both vegetarian and carnivorous food sources.

"We also wanted suitable resources for the Sargussi and the Shiranu to be able to practise and improve their particular skills, and isolation from other cultures so that the tribes could develop in their own way, without outside interference. That isolation will be strictly guarded and guaranteed as far as possible, as will support from us." He gave a voice command and the holotank displayed a 3-dimensional starmap. The graphic homed in on one star system, highlighting the planet.

"The first planet is called Rogata, fourth in the Ariadne system." As everyone watched, the view zoomed in and skimmed across a river valley whose marshes stared up at the smiling sky. Like Goranon, the light was tinged blue. In the background, forests lifted dense green-blue heads and waved to their unseen watchers.

"Rogata has few seismic disturbances and several large, mostly placid oceans. It is in a system with seven other planets, all uninhabitable. The two moons are close and large enough to affect tides on Rogata. The planet rotates slowly, so at twenty-seven hours and fifty minutes, a day lasts a similar length of time to a Naxadan day. A year lasts four hundred and forty days, so the timescales resemble those of Naxada." Howerd paused again to give them time to watch the graphic.

"How would we know when a year has passed?" Hanook asked.

"There are differences in tides and weather and changes in vegetation. Rogata's seasons are more defined than Naxada's. Now, as regards living underground: if you chose Rogata, there are caves in the mountains suitable to live in, but you'd need to farm on the surface."

There was silence when the universal translator had finished.

Then Yue Xiao pointed to the tank. Matt leaned forwards to see mountains sweep down beside a stretch of fenland. As the holocam angled in, he saw many cave mouths beckoning.

"You'll have a chance to see these views again," Howerd said, "so let's press on." A new graphic filled the tank. "Pramir circles the yellow star Cressida, with three other planets and several satellites. Its day lasts almost thirty Earth-standard hours, so a little longer than you've been accustomed to, but its year is similar to Rogata's at four hundred and forty-nine days." Howerd highlighted its position on the starmap.

Again the holocam swooped groundwards, this time to scrubland. Even the ground seemed drier, and as the holocam overflew them the bushes blended away into grasslands, then dune-populated deserts, and finally a beach beside an ocean. The light had a cleaner, sharper quality, and the view seemed lit as if from within.

"The two planets are similar, but Rogata has more forests and wetland areas and no deserts, while Pramir has several mountain ranges, with savannahs bordering some desert areas. Both have caves, though no ice-caves."

"What sort of things grow here, and is there game?" Mnanga asked. "We'll need both, since we must co-operate together for mutual benefit."

"We realise that," answered Howerd. "The soil is very fertile on both planets." He indicated one of the men seated opposite him, a human with darting black eyes and a moustache. "Professor Winsley is a horticultural science expert, and was part of the survey team."

The professor stood and greeted the tribespeople courteously. "We understand your concern at the lack of supplies of foods you're used to. A wide range of plants grows on both planets, including cereals and grasses, pulses, fruit, vegetables, and herbs. Various Terran and Vanjeynish crops will also grow quite happily on either planet, though different types suit differing regional soil types. Our research into edible and inedible native plants will of course be made available to you.

"At present we are conducting a feasibility study into whether and how to adjust for differences in your diet. For instance, apparently some people have an illness you call "the swelling sickness", and don't need the sulphur pills – their bodies don't produce the enzymes to incorporate and use that element, so it accumulates in fat and causes bodily swelling and other ill effects. So they need different treatment from the rest of you, and may recover without the constant input of sulphur.

"Amongst other things, we want to find out if we could use genetic manipulation techniques, to change plants and animals, or even you colonists. That would take time and your consent. In addition, you'll need to experiment with growing methods, so food will be provided as now for as long as necessary."

"You may have been wondering why these other people are here," Howerd said. "They are all experts in their own fields, and once I've introduced them to you, you can ask any questions you have to help you decide on your new home." He introduced several more scientists.

Matt and Yue Xiao watched and listened as questions were asked and answered. Finally, the Elders fell silent.

Howerd said, "Now, ladies and gentlemen, please consider what you've seen and heard while you take refreshments, so that you can come to a decision in comfortable surroundings. You can take as long as necessary, within reason..."

*

"I like the look and sound of Rogata," Hanook said. "I think I would choose that place." He looked at the other Elders re-playing the holovid over and over as they disputed amongst themselves.

"You couldn't use the wetlands for growing things," Mnanga objected.

"Nor could you farm in the deserts on Pramir," Aa'kam retorted.

"There are fewer game species on Rogata. I asked," Aneera said. She and Mnanga often sided together in debates since becoming friends.

"But more of each type," Aa'kam argued. "And larger animals feed more people with less hunting."

"Perhaps we should ask all our people what they think," Hanook suggested, "if we can't make a decision."

Yado smiled and looked across at Soolkah. "Which were your choice?"

She looked back at him, her expression serious. "I would choose Rogata. Which would you choose?"

"I –"

A flash of sajamu interrupted Yado: gloved hands clenched on rock outcrops, stone scraped his knees, muscles tightened as he reached for the next handhold. Once, the rock gave as Jordas pulled himself past a plant growing out of it. Stones showered around him, exposing roots. He never looked down, just ahead and upwards. He hauled himself over the lip of a ledge and lay gasping, sweating, staring at the trees which grew through gaps between boulders. Yado felt Jordas's muscles relax, the stones under his back. The sky was a dome of blue-tinged light. The rains had come and gone, and the ground steamed –

In an eyeblink the vision was gone. Yado was back in the *room*, though he could still feel the rock at his back and sunlight on his face.

*

Jordas realised his concentration had slipped for a moment. The mindshield was hard to maintain. *It doesn't matter. I've done my best for them, met their needs. Now I have to consider mine – even if it does seem like running away –*

He was wet through from sweat and rain and the wet rocks. He sat up, shrugged the rucksack off his back, reached inside it for his father's gift. He stared at it. The antique weapon had represented safety on Naxada; on Goranon it was an escape.

Jordas loaded the gun and checked the safety catch was off. *This is one of the last things I'll ever do.* A hollow sense of satisfaction settled around him.

They'll never find me here.

It occurred to him then that he could simply have let go when the rock shattered as he passed the brushplant, or at any time on the climb.

It had never crossed his mind.

*

The flash of vision came again. Jordas's presence felt peculiar for having been absent so long, and for a moment Yado's sense of self was dislocated. Then he became aware of someone speaking nearby, and fingers not-quite-touching his arm.

"Yado! What's happened?"

It was Soolkah, eyes misted with anxiety.

He smiled at her. "It's all right," he said.

*

Jordas gripped the gun more tightly. Sweat sluiced down his forehead and stung his eyes. It wasn't easy to stare down the barrel, he discovered.

His thumb trembled on the trigger.

*

Jordas has dropped his mindshield again. He can't hold it when he's concentrating on something else as well –

It wasn't all right. Yado felt the smile dissolve from his features. By reflex he shut his eyes against the sajamu-vision and flung up his hands.

"Jordas!" he exclaimed. "Jordas, *DON'T!*"

CHAPTER 30

YADO'S PRESENCE ERUPTED into Jordas's mind. Emotions pulsed into his heart, drumming in time with his blood. His mind named them for him without prompting. *Love. Passion. Jealousy.* He wanted to wall them away and couldn't. His hands trembled, then convulsed. <Leave me alone, Yado. You can't stop me. When I'm gone you'll have her all to yourself.>

<I shall not let you.> There was as much determination as desperation behind Yado's mindsending. <We were *made* to share.>

Jordas's mind named another emotion to him. *Fear.* Not just his own. He swallowed the lump in his throat and steeled his resolve. <This way's quicker and more certain than a drug. It won't hurt. I've no other choice now.>

<You're wrong. It shall hurt us both–>

The tremor shuddered into every part of Jordas, but still his thumb squeezed the trigger.

A sound like a thousand thunderclaps. Pain scored the side of his head. Gunpowder stung the backs of his hands. Darkness settled on him.

His legs buckled. He slumped on the ground.

*

Pain exploded against the side of Yado's head. He clapped his hands to his skull and keeled over. Blind. He hit the floor. Its chill penetrated his side, invaded his whole body. Pain scorched his brain, set his head on fire. His world became the fight for one gasp after another. The room was pitch black. Pain slammed down on him. Finally, heat ebbed from the sajamu-wound. He heard voices, far away, and a jumble of other sounds.

"Yado! Yado!"

Soolkah? She was a pale blur beside him. She spoke again, but he couldn't make sense of her words.

The door crashed open. Yado became aware of Marcus and Matt beside him. A foil blanket rustled around him.

Speech. Not his language. He understood anyway.

"He's not physically injured – it's just severe shock. I can't understand why, there are no apparent injuries –"

"Never mind that! Give him some pain relief or we'll lose them both." Marcus leaned over Yado. "Where is he?"

Shaking his head hurt too much. Yado abandoned the attempt. He hadn't the energy to flinch when someone pressed something cold against his skin, but if anything, it revived him. As the fire in his head cooled and the chill in his body warmed, so the sounds around him sharpened. The intensity of his internal sensations ebbed as senses balanced each other out. The mist cleared from his vision. The blur beside him resolved. Soolkah.

"Yado? Can you speak?" Her voice cracked. "Where is Jordas?"

Memory swirled back on a torrent of pain. "Jordas," he croaked. "Jordas..." He knew what his maaj'gar had attempted. It panicked him. *It's only sajamu!* he remembered. *This weren't real for me, but for Jordas it is. We must find him in time. I lost one maaj'gar. I shall NOT lose another –*

Resolve firmed his voice. "Could find him," he said. "Proximity sense –" Slumped against his *seat*, he felt for Jordas's presence. He fought the drug, opened his mind to the sajamu, though pain sluiced in. Rocks felt hard beneath him. Blood congealed at his temple. Against the tide of pain in his head, his hands smarted in time with his pulse. He couldn't move. Blackness swallowed sight and sound as death approached.

The only sense Jordas has is touch. Yado groped after one thought at a time when the torment in his head allowed him. He *must* tell them. If only he could mindsend it! It was so important. But his mouth disobeyed. Pain dazed him. His knuckles stung. Weakness invaded his whole body. He dared not accept too much of Jordas's pain, lest it destroy him, as Uvvuz' agony had for a time.

But it would at least draw him to Jordas. He concentrated. *I am the son of Maru the hunter.* In his mind he built images of his spear in his hand, his knife at his belt. But he sought not meat but his maaj'gar. He extended his proximity sense...He saw Jordas again, reaching out to him through the plangent notes that spilled from the instrument in his hands, walking towards Soolkah and him, coming nearer, ever nearer...

"Yado! You said you could find him." Marcus grasped Yado's wrist.

"He went climbing," he whispered. "He got onto a ledge, and then –" The blackness inside the gun's barrel disturbed him as much as a memory as it had as sajamu. "There are trees on the ledge," was all he could add.

"He's on a cliff in the jungle, then," he heard Marcus say. "But it's pretty dense. He can't have got far. Which direction?"

"Fly west." It was all he could do to mumble the words. Marcus released his wrist as he withdrew from his maaj'gar's mind and accepted the relief from pain the drug brought.

"Let's go!" Marcus repeated his instructions to the pilot, then turned to the medic. "We'll need you." He whirled on his heel, shouting for Ray.

Yado wasn't sure how they got him out of the building, because when he

336

next opened his eyes he was fastened into the safety web of the *flyer's seat*. Beside him Soolkah gripped his hand, her face in focus at last. Her talons dug into his burn-scarred palm, but the pain had eased. Relief brought mental clarity and definite knowledge. He felt hands on him, touching his face with love. *Only Soolkah would touch me so.* He hoped Jordas could feel her hands too. *It might just keep him alive until we reach him.*

The drone of the *flyer's jets* beat into obscurity as Yado dozed for a time. It faded back in around him as he roused.

"Yado! Are we close?"

Yado squinted at Marcus. "Yes." He had no energy to nod.

"I see him!" the pilot shouted. "Over there, on the ledge!"

Moments passed in a slew of half-heard sounds and barely-sensed movement as the flyer landed. Carlin and the medic jumped down.

"Go with them, Soolkah," Yado murmured. "Bring him back to us."

A chill against his side told him she'd gone. He drifted. There was little he could do now. *It's up to Soolkah.* As he tried to get more comfortable in the confines of the *seat*, he felt fingertips on his face, teasing the stubble studding his chin and wiping away the sweat and blood.

There was a clamour when they brought Jordas onboard. Yado opened his eyes and saw Soolkah swing into the seat beside him.

She held her hand out. "There was this," she said.

On the palm of her hand lay the gun.

"I didn't stop him once just to have him try again," Yado whispered. "Throw it over the ledge."

CHAPTER 31

THE EVENING COOLNESS WAS COMING. Ray Travers reached for the coffee beaker at his elbow. It was lukewarm. He pushed it across the workstation and leaned forward in his chair, cupping his forehead in his hands.

The door opened to admit Marcus. "Where's Alleem?"

"Gone home." Ray felt sweat gathering at his temples. He wiped a hand over his forehead and stared at the moisture on his fingers. "How is he?"

"Not good. He's still in surgery," Marcus said. "It'll be some time before he's fit enough to work. Pack his effects up for him, would you, Ray? I'll ask Alleem to stay on to complete the analysis work."

"Know why?"

"People don't always cope well with changes in their lives," Marcus answered after a moment's thought. "From what he's said, being telepathically linked to Yado has put him under immense pressure. I've been concerned about him for some time, actually."

Ray nodded. The scene in the monitor room that morning had imprinted itself on his memory: snapping at Jordas; Alleem's concern; his clumsy attempt to help. *Should have kept my mouth shut. Not my business.* His voice quivered as he mumbled, "Could have been my fault."

"Why?"

"Argument."

"When?"

"This morning. Just after Mount Kerui erupted. Think Alleem and I upset him." Ray put a finger to his mouth and chewed the hard skin beside the remains of his fingernail.

Marcus eyed him for what seemed like forever. "Jordas has had one thing after another to deal with. In that situation, the last straw that breaks the camel's back can be a very small one indeed. It could even have been the eruption that pushed him over the edge. After all, he was *there*, with them, for several weeks. For all we know, he may have begun to see himself as Naxadan, rather than human."

"Ought to apologise," Ray said. His voice was gruff. "Don't approve of them living with him – but no need for this!"

"He thought there was." Marcus sighed. "Why don't you approve?"

"Naxadans need to be all together." Ray kept the other reason to himself. The day's events had taught him the value of silence, especially in the workplace.

"True." Marcus nodded. "Your apology will just have to wait until he's fit. Where are the Naxadans going, by the way?"

"Rogata. Week's time." Ray stood up. "Better pack things up." He crossed to Jordas's workstation and put an electronic stylus and a book-cassette into a sample bag with a few other items.

Marcus took the bag and stowed it in his desk. "I'll take it with me when I go to see Jordas. Incidentally, Ray, do you know how a chip containing material supposedly deleted could have been found in Hartmann's possession?"

*

Yado looked across at the other *medmachine*. Today, apart, from the ache at his temple and the detached feeling the drugs gave him, he felt stronger. Even the sting of powder burns on Jordas's hands had eased.

The haze of nausea and pain he'd awakened to the previous day had overwhelmed him. They'd kept Jordas sedated all day, head concealed by the dome of the healing *machine*. When he'd asked about his maaj'gar's condition they hadn't been able to tell him much. The surgeon had looked away, a frown on his face as he'd explained that Jordas might be left with brain damage.

The door opened with a whisper of *hydraulics*. Soolkah walked in with Marcus. Yado sat up to greet them with an effort; the room whirled about him. Soolkah ran to him, touching his hands. He could see tearmarks on her face. He caught her against him. It didn't matter that Marcus was there; he wasn't one of their people. And Jordas slept on.

But Marcus was smiling when Yado pulled away; he even saw approval in the scientist's eye. *When I first met him, I thought Marcus was cold and unemotional. But mayhap it's just hard for him to express his feelings.*

"How is Jordas?" Marcus asked.

"They haven't told me much."

"That wasn't what I meant."

Understanding came to Yado. "I can't really tell what's happened to Jordas. All I know is, I feel his pain. But he's alive. If he were dead, I wouldn't be talking to you."

Soolkah had gone over to Jordas. Yado watched her caress Jordas's face with her fingertips. He knew she wouldn't put her mouth to his with an audience.

He *felt* Jordas's response: eyes opening to darkness which cleared slowly; terror at the possibility of blindness, agony throbbing at the side of his head, the struggle to remember...

Yado wrenched his consciousness from Jordas's with an effort. The sajamu receded. He remembered too late that Jordas was supposed to be sleeping. By penetrating his mind, he'd cut through the *machine's* protection. But he had to *know*.

"I shouldn't have done that," he said. "He's coming round. And he's scared. He can't see and he can't remember."

"Let's hope that's only short-term." Marcus crossed the room to the bedside. "Jordas, can you hear me?" he asked, bending over him.

The only reply was a blurred mumble.

He can't speak! Yado realised.

"What's he trying to say?" asked Marcus.

Jordas needs my support now. Though Yado feared the pain would crush him, he opened his mind again. <Jordas, I'm Yado. Your maaj'gar.>

"Who-oo?"

*

The medmachine was gone. Jordas lay back against his pillows, exhausted. Now that Yado and Soolkah had gone as well, it felt as if a lifeline had been cut, although he could hardly remember these alien people who cared so much about him. That made his sense of isolation worse.

At first he'd felt a strong sense of intrusion every time Yado had tried to mindspeak with him. But it had begun to come back: where he'd been; who Yado and Soolkah were; how he'd fought for their survival. The need to bring both tribes to safety, and the several true meanings of being a maaj'gar. He'd even learned to distinguish between the sensations of Yado's body and his own self-awareness again.

The anguish of not knowing whether his feelings for Soolkah were real.

Jealousy.

The confusion which had driven him to try to destroy himself.

And I failed, he thought. *I failed because of the very thing I could no longer bear. Where do I go from here?*

He dozed.

When he opened his eyes again, Marcus sat beside the bed. "Hello, Jordas," he said, his voice gentle and distant.

"Herro." The struggle to speak had almost defeated him; for several days he'd been unable to give voice to even one coherent sentence, though the thoughts whirled dizzily around in his head.

At least I can see again. Perhaps I'll be all right eventually.

"Yado said your memory's back," Marcus said. "He said he helped to restore it to you."

Jordas said "Mmm." It was easier than "yes".

"I have news for you," Marcus added. "Senator Hartmann's been stripped of his post and is under investigation at the World Senate."

"Wha...?"

"I thought you'd be surprised." Marcus permitted himself the faintest of smiles. "He was found by a robot cleaner, locked in a cupboard on Galatea Station. The robot entered the cupboard to refill its detergent cell and Hartmann was there, badly beaten up. He was critically ill at the same time as you were. He's just been released into custody for fraud and evading arrest."

When he spoke again, his voice was lower, almost conspiratorial. "It's caused a stink at Committee HQ – they're laying in security measures left, right and centre! Corah Whitley's being promoted to Senior Administrator, with extra responsibility for security, and Garat Frelox is permanently taking over the Naxadan resettlement project."

"She seem' fair," Jordas murmured. He allowed his eyes to close, still aware of Marcus seated beside his bed.

"There's something else. I've had to let Ray go."

"Why?"

"In Hartmann's effects, following his arrest, was a chip containing sensitive material that should have been deleted. It had Ray's handwriting on the label. Apparently he passed it to Hartmann on his visit. I've been unhappy about his behaviour for a while, but he knew very well that that was against the rules."

Jordas remembered Ray's critical attitude towards him. He shrugged, then said, "All of us...a bit wayward...sometimes."

"What will you do?" asked Marcus. "Alleem will stay on until you're fit, and of course, we'll keep your job open for you – if you want to carry on here. I estimate there are several years of data analysis still ahead, but if you want to finish and move on, I'll understand."

Jordas's heart wanted to cry out then, that it wasn't finished; it never would be. He'd always feel the pull of sajamu, even if he wasn't in direct telepathic contact with Yado; and to be apart from them would tear at him as much as being with them.

Nothing's changed, he thought, *except I'm hurting physically too now. I'm weak and ill, and I'm not sure what to do. I'm still alive, but I don't know how to cope with this, either. I can't even speak properly...* He opened his eyes and realised Marcus was waiting for an answer. It plunged him into panic. *At least with Yado, if I can't answer in words, I can use the mindspeech.*

"What other – choices?" he gritted out.

341

Marcus got up and paced to the window. He stood for what seemed an age, peering into the midday rains where mist veiled forests and cliffs. "I'm not sure there are any other choices."

"No? Father could trace back... to Vikings, but – married an English girl. Carrying...family fascination with foreigners to extremes." He sighed. "Been thinking...should go live with *them*."

Marcus swung away from the window and came back to his seat. "I'm not sure how the Committee would view that. They've recommended a period of immediate, discreet support once the Naxadans arrive on Rogata, followed by minimal contact. They know the Naxadans' society will inevitably change, and they want to limit that change so that it comes from within, when they're ready." Marcus shifted position in his chair. "*You* can't promise that. Look at it this way. The Naxadans have neither the wheel nor written script. You come from a society that has both, not to mention higher technology. If you lived with them, there'd always be the temptation to disrupt their development. The Committee could argue that even your presence would be a possible source of future cultural contamination."

"Some unavoidable, but I might...be able to prevent it – for all they know," Jordas argued. "Thing is, Marcus – can't cope, living apart from them. They weren't happy at my house. But I – miss them both. Need them. Thinking...my place is with them. Naxadan by marriage, according to their customs. Of the tribes now. And they *both* need me."

"Even though your confusion drove you to try to –"

"Yes!" Jordas didn't want to hear him say it. "*Was* confused," he added. The urgency of getting the Naxadans to safety had driven him on their planet. Now the rescue mission was over. "Had time to think – past few days. Perhaps what's important is – I *have* those feelings...joined to Yado and Soolkah forever. No matter they aren't human, they're my family – my amaaj." *It's a kind of acceptance, at least. Perhaps it will grow, in time, and I'll learn to control my jealousy.*

A thought occurred to him. "The gun, wha' happen' to the gun?"

"I believe Yado asked Soolkah to dispose of it."

The sense of intrusion was back for a moment, but when Jordas tried to picture the Colt in his mind's eye, he couldn't remember what it looked like. Yado and Soolkah's faces, however, he could see clearly.

This is change. I had to go through the suicide to learn this. The Naxadans have to adapt to their circumstances or die, but so do I. Yado wouldn't let me die, so I must adapt too.

It would take courage to leave behind everything he'd ever known:

language, customs, family, work patterns and colleagues. *The Naxadans have to do that now...But there is a precedent in my family.*

It was a long time since Jordas had thought about his father.

*

Lorr turned over and faced the wall, trying to ignore the sound of his brothers' breathing. *This place is strange.* The smoothness of the walls and floor bothered him.

Chixi should have been here. His brother's face gleamed off the polished wall at him in the darkness. *But Mzana wouldn't have married us if Chixi was still alive.* A twinge of guilt invaded his thoughts. He'd recognised some time ago that Soolkah's action in refusing to wed Chixi had probably given Mzana's parents the courage to refuse their offer for her while his Elder brother had lived. *And I'd still have been getting a beating every time things went wrong for him.*

He sucked air in and exhaled, trying to relax. His brothers were having no difficulty in sleeping whatsoever. *I wonder, is Mzana awake? It isn't that I have anything against her, but I still love Soolkah. And she's here on the ship with us.*

"Lorr?"

Lorr wasn't sure if he'd heard anything or not until the whisper came again.

"Lorr! Are you awake?"

"Mzana? What's the matter?"

"I can't sleep."

"Me neither."

"This place is too weird."

"I don't like it."

"It'll be better on Rogata," Lorr whispered. "Come over here, then you won't wake the others."

Mzana was invisible in the dense dark; yet Lorr felt her approach. Her hand brushed his shoulder as she reached the platform where he lay, wrapped in his foil sleeping cloth. He held it open.

"Don't be scared," he said. "It'll be all right. We'll soon be there."

"You don't remember your first time on a *spaceship*," Mzana said, snuggling against him.

"No." How strange to feel her lying beside him – as strange as being in the Humanu ship. *Nice, though,* he realised with surprise.

"You never take me when it's your turn," Mzana whispered, "but the others always leave me for you on those darktimes."

343

"I...wasn't ready."

"You still like Soolkah."

Lorr didn't respond, appalled that she knew.

"I told my mother I didn't want to be amaajni with a man who loved someone else," Mzana said. "But she said I'd be lucky to have two husbands who like me."

Lorr didn't know what to say. He couldn't be anything but honest with her. Although he'd never taken her, and had done his best to avoid being sucked into the loveplay between Mzana and his brothers each darktime, he knew she was a good wife to all of them: hardworking, never sharp-tongued, always willing to help however she could. She deserved his respect, even if his heart were given elsewhere.

He touched her cheek with his fingertips, shyness keeping his mouth closed, and felt a surge of anticipation course through his stomach when she explored his forehead and eyelids with gentle fingers.

"We're all lucky to be amaajne with you, Mzana," he murmured.

And then it didn't seem so hard to reconcile himself to her. He touched her face again and allowed the darkness to enfold them together at last.

CHAPTER 32

"PREPARE FOR SHIP-LEAVING! Prepare for ship-leaving!"

Hanook picked up the basket containing his possessions and opened the door of his amaaj's *cabin*. "Look sharp, Zuas! Boys!" he called to his amaaj. "Bring everything you need."

Zuas lifted her own basket onto her hip, her brothers Nadna and Geem did likewise, and they headed for the *door*. Hanook and his brothers followed them.

In the corridor Shiranu and Sargussi milled about, trying to stay in their amaaju. Everyone carried a basket or Humanu *holdall*, and there was little room in the *companionways*. But the only sound was of footfalls, the barefoot children's talons clicking against the metal floors, the adults' slippered feet softer. *The practice run yesterday was useful – everyone knows what to do and where to go.* Hanook spotted *stewards* knocking on each door, working their way along the corridor. Reassured that no-one would be left behind, he led his amaaj in the direction of the *shuttle bay*, where the tribespeople were to gather.

The *spaceship* had four massive *shuttles*, towards one or another of which each amaaju were directed. Although in their family groups, Sargussi rubbed shoulders with Shiranu. Hanook and his amaaj climbed aboard one *shuttle*, while Aa'kam, Mnanga and Aneera and their respective amaaju had each been assigned to one of the others.

When everyone was seated and strapped in, the Humanu *stewards* called everyone's names, to which the tribespeople replied. Then the *stewards* strapped themselves in and the *engines* thundered in the confined space of the *shuttle bay*.

Hanook's heart thudded. *We've waited so long for this – we're going to our new home at last!* He was as excited and apprehensive as the children.

The *doors* rolled open as soon as the precious air had been sucked out of the massive room, and the *shuttles* crept towards the star-studded frieze before them. Hanook was in the last *shuttle*; one by one the others leapt into the void ahead. Then it was their turn.

Hanook knew he'd never get another chance to see this, and gestured to the children to look all they could. His first glimpse of the world they had chosen in no way disappointed him: a ball of blue, brown and white which would be the stuff of future tribal stories.

All too soon the *shuttles* swooped down towards the land that would be theirs, levelled off their flight, and settled carefully on the soil of this foreign world.

Debarkation was the reverse of their entrance into the *shuttles*. Hanook was the first to step out onto the soil of their new home. He stood watching for the other Elders so as to call them together. "Do you remember the ceremony we agreed on?"

The others nodded their heads.

"We'll wait till everyone's off-board. Elders, return to direct operations."

When the tribespeople had gathered together, the Elders met again in the centre of the *landing area*. Hanook was amused to notice that the *shuttles* hadn't left and the Humanu *pilots* were watching to see what they would do. He stepped forwards and dug into the ground with his talons, then lifted a handful of soil to his forehead. "By the leadership of the Tribes invested in *me*, Hanook of the Shiranu, I bless the soil of this new world we shall call home!" The other Elders copied him in turn.

"Now," Hanook said, "we'll look for those caves." As he spoke, another *shuttle* was landing, as promised. The Humanu who debarked came straight over to the Elders.

Their leader walked smartly up to Hanook, saluted him, and shook hands in the Humanu manner. "Samuel Mondel reporting to aid in the *resettlement programme* for the Naxadans on Rogata," he said. Then he relaxed and smiled. "Good to see you again, Hanook."

*

I'm missing Jordas, Yado acknowledged. *At least he's alive, but he's still recovering. This is almost worse than losing Uvvuz! With him the pain of loss was sharp and sudden, but it was over quickly. This gnaws on me like a ganzu on its last meal. And I have real need of his support in welding together a group of people who don't always want to be united.*

He fought down the ache of physical separation and turned to Soolkah, crouched beside the cooking fire. She, at least, looked reasonably happy.

The tribespeople had been on Rogata for many lighttimes now. Down in the valley the Humanu were building a proper place for *shuttles* to land; here in the mountains the tribespeople were trying to rebuild their lives. The first "Rogatan" child had already been born, though conceived in Kerui.

Although the Humanu call this planet "Rogata", we have our own name for this lush new world...

"Yado!"

He turned. Mnanga stood at the entrance to their cave, leaning heavily on her stick. She'd aged sharply since their arrival; Yado suspected it was at least partly due to the shock of leaving Kerui.

"Hello, Mnanga. Shall you share food with us today?"

She accepted with a nod, but held up her hand in a warding gesture. "Only vegetables, though." Some tribespeople had changed their eating habits since arriving on Rogata, but most still clung to their ancestors' ways. Now, though, it hardly mattered. Each made their own choices since seeing that the Humanu ate what accorded with their views and values. There was plenty of game for meat-eaters, plus (admittedly strange) vegetables provided to tide them over until their first harvest. Nobody went hungry; and the Humanu shared food with the tribespeople when invited to eat with them.

Of course, the food tasted different from the meat or vegetables of Kerui. But the Humanu healers brought regular supplies of little yellow spheres with a strong flavour of home – they called them *pills* – and insisted the tribespeople would become ill if they didn't swallow one every day with their food.

Mnanga entered their small cave, squatting beside the fire and removing her *cloak* and *visor*. "It's chilly today," she remarked.

It's true, it is colder on Rogata than in Kerui, Yado thought, *but at least here we're alive and not living in dangerous conditions.* "The Humanu say it shall be warmer after the next highwater."

"How is Jordas?" Mnanga asked, as Soolkah put a wooden dish of food into her hands.

Yado sighed. "Improving. It's been many lighttimes since we mindspoke. It upsets us both to be apart. He has – his life to go back to – and mine is here now." His sight ballooned and blurred with sudden moisture.

Mnanga changed the subject. "The *house* of the Humanu is almost built. They have said that when they leave the *holo* of Keramanthu will remain there. We can go there any time then."

Yado accepted a bowl of food from Soolkah, using a small two-pronged *fork* to spear vegetables and a chunk of meat. "I know," he said, lifting the food to his mouth. "Yesterday someone told me a *shuttle* shall bring more Humanu today."

"Who else could come here?" Mnanga wondered aloud. "There are already many Humanu here."

"Have you not been in the *house*?" asked Yado. "It has many big *rooms*."

Soolkah seated herself on the floor of the cave, filled bowl in her hand. She began to eat, using the two-pronged eating-stick Yado had given her.

A roar overhead announced the expected arrival of the *shuttle*. Yado carried on eating, though his heart leapt with apprehension; the familiar warning of his proximity sense, combined with a thrill of intuition. *Why would*

347

a shuttle's arrival sensitise me so? He pushed the thought aside. "It seems strange to live in one place," he said, "though nice as well. And presently there's no need to move on."

"It feels strange not avoiding blow-outs," Soolkah said, "but at least we needn't carry everything all the time."

"Well, Yado, what do you think about the promises of the Humanu?" Mnanga asked, after a short silence. She dipped bread into the bowl, soaking up the thick liquid which remained.

"They haven't let us down thus far," Yado observed. "I don't know how long before they think we're ready to join the *Federal League*, mayhap generations, but were it of benefit to the tribes, I favour it –"

A silence had fallen between the women; their faces were turned towards the cave entrance. Suppressing that thrill of intuition again, shading his eyes with his fingers, he too turned to face the blaze of bluish sunset.

Silhouetted against it was a Humanu whose height made an instant impression. It was impossible to distinguish his features, even so close. But his black-purple outline held both familiarity and strangeness.

"Yado?" came a voice well-known, quiet and only half-certain of a welcome.

Yado put his bowl down and leapt to his feet in a fluid movement. Another brought him across the cave floor. How could he have failed to *know*? "Jordas!" he exclaimed. "I've thought about you so much –"

The light lay in blue creases on Jordas's clothes and face; but he was smiling, Yado realised.

"I learned to shield my thoughts from you a while back, but I had to relearn it after I came round. I thought I'd surprise you." Jordas paused, perhaps waiting to see Yado's reaction to this news.

It took a moment for him to realise Jordas had spoken in English.

Jordas's eyes strayed across the cave to Soolkah, then returned to Yado's face, an intensity in their blue depths. "I hope it's all right – I didn't want to leave this behind." He seemed anxious.

Yado looked down. In Jordas's hands lay the lamo-harp, its strings quivering slightly, sensitive to the air movements at the mouth of the cave, setting the atmosphere humming with faint but plaintive notes.

*

"Jordas, how did you –?"

Jordas turned to face Soolkah. Puzzlement mantled her features.

"Being mindlinked to Yado changed my life forever," he answered simply. "I realised I need to be here with you." He breathed in deeply before

348

adding, "If you want me, that is."

"Of course we want you," Soolkah smiled, "Humanu husband." She set her bowl down, rose, and crossed to the cave mouth. There, she gestured to him to turn and face her, so that the mid-lighttime sunlight fell full on his face. She raised her fingertips to not-quite touch his features one by one, examining him as if she'd never seen him before. Her eyes were sad and gentle as her talons traced the shape of the bluish furrow along the side of his temple in the air, millimetres from his skin. *It's the nearest she can get to kissing me in public, in the way of her people.* He felt fiercely glad he'd found the strength to come to them.

"So the Prophecy brought you back to us after all," Mnanga murmured. "The paths to the truth are many and strange, but the traveller always arrives in the end."

Jordas wasn't sure what to make of this, so he said, "Well met, Mnanga. Do you remember Dr Grantham?" he asked, looking from Soolkah to Yado to Mnanga.

Mnanga answered for all of them with her quick nod of agreement.

"He came with me," Jordas said. "He's with the other Humanu."

"It were good to see him again," Yado added. <But I welcome *you*, my maaj'gar.>

"Dr Grantham's working on the tribe's fertility problems and food," Jordas told them. "I'm here to work, too. I persuaded the Committee they needed an ambassador to the tribes, someone who knows the ways of the amaaju and can speak for them. That's what took so long." He smiled. "They even admitted there wasn't anyone else who could do the job better."

"Share food with us," Soolkah invited. "Sit here."

She patted a cloth-covered rock. Evidently she hadn't forgotten what his house on Goranon had looked like. Jordas hadn't regretted selling it, though. *This is my future.*

He drew nearer to the fire and seated himself. Soolkah put a bowl of food into his hands. It smelt strange but appetising. "This is good for Humanu to eat?" he asked.

"Would I give you something to eat that wasn't good for you?"

Jordas lifted his shoulders in a half-shrug. "You might be after my life assurance!"

"What is that?"

"Never mind – I'll explain later. I trust you, Soolkah!"

He met his maaj'gar's eyes again. They were smiling a warm welcome at him, and Yado hadn't missed the joke. *It'll be okay,* he told himself. *I needn't have worried. They do want me here.*

"I talked to many people to come here," he told them around a mouthful of food. "The Committee people thought I'd cause total culture shock in the tribes. But I told them that things will inevitably change for all of you – they already have – but we must make sure they're for better, not worse." He remembered that final, difficult interview with Howerd Asthorn, and grinned. "I said it was my destiny to stay with you, if only to stop the tribespeople from fighting each other! I think that was what persuaded them."

"Well, you did a good job on that before," Mnanga murmured.

When they'd finished eating, Mnanga stood up, thanked Soolkah for her meal, nodded to Jordas, and limped out of the cave.

"Jordas, you are going to live here with us – aren't you?" Soolkah faltered. "We thought that was what you intended."

Jordas's eyes followed Mnanga. "I am, though it'll be hard to get used to not living in a house." He got up. "Excuse me a moment, I want to ask Mnanga something."

"Sure."

Jordas hurried after Mnanga and caught up with her quickly.

"May – may I walk with you to your cave, Mnanga?" he asked. "I need to ask something."

"*You* need *my* help? After bringing us to safety and showing us new ways to live?"

Jordas nodded. "I need a new way to live now, Mnanga."

"Meaning?"

Jordas hesitated. "I must find a way to deal with my jealousy."

"Jordas, I know – I think – what you're asking me, but you'd best ask Yado."

Disappointment settled on him. "I think your answer means you *know* what I need to know. Why can't you tell me, Mnanga?"

"I may be old, but I'm still a woman, and the Eldest Woman at that. It's my place to keep the traditions alive. Ask Yado."

"But –"

"Go back now, Jordas. Rest assured I won't shame you by gossiping about our conversation. Sleep well, stranger-brother." Mnanga turned and hobbled up the hillside towards her cave.

Jordas stood looking for a moment, then turned back.

Back at the cave, he was surprised to see Soolkah and Yado moving about at its rear. <What are you doing?> he asked Yado. They'd piled sweet-smelling herbs on a layer of twigs and branches, softened with grasses. Soolkah covered it with woven cloth and Yado piled animal skins and more cloth on top.

<Did you think I were sleeping outside?>

<What do you mean?> Jordas could feel the panic rising in him. He hadn't thought of the consequences of his arrival; he'd just hoped that they'd accept him.

<It may be your turn tonight but I still need somewhere warm and sheltered to sleep. We liked your bed, so we made one here, and just now we thought we'd make a big one that we could all sleep in.>

<But – that means we'll all be in the same bed when we're –>

<Yes. And how is that different from sajamu?>

That brought him up short. <Not much, mayhap, but how will I feel when it's your turn?>

And how *do* you think you're going to feel then?>

<I...probably still a bit jealous.>

<I thought you might say that.>

<Yes, but –> Now that the opportunity had arrived it didn't seem so hard to ask. Jordas plunged ahead. <I thought about that story – about the first maaj'garu. I'm like them, but I must change to fit in here. I have to learn to see things in the Naxadan way, but it's difficult to learn something like that.>

Yado put his hand millimetres above Jordas's shoulder, smiling. <I think I can help.>

*

Jordas stroked the lamo-harp, and the strings sang.

"The whole tribe will know you're back," Soolkah smiled.

"Only one tribe?" Yado's head tilted to match his grin. He turned back to Jordas. "Play. We missed that."

So Jordas teased notes out of the instrument, and in the cave the music swelled and eased the fear of disgrace that still hovered in the shadows of his mind.

"That sounds lovely in here," Soolkah said. "It makes me feel sad and happy at the same time."

"I know just what you mean," Jordas said. "The echo suits the sound texture."

"Play more."

So he did. They listened in silence, but Jordas felt Yado's approval and could see Soolkah's. *That's good. They're pleased to see me.*

After that, they sat up late, talking, until the flames had burned low. Yado gestured towards the rear of the cave. "It's darktime." <Are you ready?>

The bed was more comfortable than Jordas had imagined, and smelled of sweet herbs. He pulled an animal skin over himself as Soolkah slipped in beside him. It seemed she wouldn't abandon the habits of a lifetime because her cover was of woven material, but Yado's was also furred.

Jordas lay there, feeling awkward. He wasn't sure who should make the first move. He felt Yado's amusement, but his maaj'gar said nothing until some minutes had passed.

"It *is* your turn, Jordas."

"I – I know, but I feel uncomfortable about you being here as well."

"Don't worry about that. Do what you feel."

"It's my *social conditioning*," Jordas said, and had to explain. "Your touch taboo is similar."

"I shouldn't perhaps tell you this because it's a piece of woman's knowledge," Soolkah said, "but in view of your problem, my mother once told me that when I became amaajni I shouldn't touch any of my husbands in sight of the others in case they got jealous."

Jordas thought hard about that for a moment, then said, "Something that's bothered me for a long time – and I understand better about it now – is that in my culture people who love each other tell each other. But I guess you can't tell either of us…"

Soolkah raised herself up on one elbow. Her eyes glistened, reflecting the emberglow. He was acutely aware of her gaze on him, so intense was her concentration. "Not *just* you, Jordas. But perhaps –" She paused and breathed in deeply. "I love you, Jordas and Yado." She lay back down between them and touched a hand to each man's heart. "Ooh! I've broken a tribal taboo, and it doesn't feel bad at all!"

"I – Oh, Soolkah, I love you so much," Jordas whispered. "It means a great deal to me to hear you say it."

"Me too, though I didn't realise it till now…" Yado admitted. <I thought she did love us both, but I hadn't realised how much it bothered you, and I'd never have thought of mentioning it.>

Jordas felt Yado's emotion brush the edge of his mental awareness. *Yado's as much affected as I am.* Inside him, he felt his heart expand with elation and confidence. He'd done the right thing, coming here, having the courage to discuss their differences in mindset and customs. *I can deal with those now, so this time our relationship has a real chance of succeeding.* Soolkah's expression of commitment had given him permission to enter into their customs more fully than before, because some of his own expectations had been met, if in an unusual way. "So – we get treated the same. And…in bed?" he asked.

"I shall participate too," Yado assured him. "Then you can when it's my turn with Soolkah."

"I feel embarrassed about that."

"No need – it's natural within an amaaj. We really can't help it!" Yado grinned in the fireglow. "I remember a similar conversation when we first became joined."

Jordas remembered it along with his embarrassment. He sighed. "Perhaps we've all got taboos to learn to break."

"All right," said Soolkah. "I'll go first. It's your turn, Jordas." She wriggled closer to him and laid an arm over his chest, then leaned up on her elbow and kissed him on the mouth.

And after all, who but us three will know what we do together? Jordas wondered, since his feelings were private to his amaaj. *And who would worry?*

Soolkah was stroking him all over now. "Come on, Jordas, this is as hard for me as it is for you!" she said.

He folded his arms around her. "I've missed you so much, Soolkah," he said. "You too, Yado, though we're never truly apart."

"We both missed you, Jordas," Soolkah said, and kissed him again.

They were both trying to make it easier for him. He pulled her closer and kissed her back, and as his hands moved against her flesh he felt the *sajamu-*touch of Yado's hands.

Afterwards he dozed off despite the strangeness of his surroundings, with the wind occasionally gusting into the cave and the movement of the twigs beneath him as he shifted position. A touch on his shoulder awoke him.

"My turn now," Yado whispered.

"Tomorrow night, I thought! Besides, Soolkah's asleep." With some surprise Jordas realised Yado was using the mindshield. *That means he doesn't want me to know what he's up to.*

"If we leave it till tomorrow night you shall become inhibited again." Ignoring Jordas's objections Yado reached over for Soolkah and stroked her face.

"Yado? What –"

"Come this side now." All he said to Jordas as she wriggled over was, "Participate."

Despite what had gone before, despite the darkness, and even the sajamu of rhythmic penetration, it was hard to make his hands touch himself. Part of it was fear, he realised, of losing self-control before either of them. *But I have to try or I'll never know if it works.*

Yado's mindshield was still up, and it occurred to Jordas that perhaps he was giving him a little privacy. His hands moved to his loins, and for moments he became an animal spirit, concentrating only on his and Yado's physical sensations. But as the pleasure grew more intense and Soolkah pressed herself closer to Yado and himself at once, he felt the mindshield slip away and Yado entered his mind fully as sensations rioted through his body. <Now tell me that doesn't feel good!>

It equalled, then surpassed, the most intense mutual orgasm he'd experienced. *Now I understand what Yado's been trying to tell me all along.*

And at last he could be glad of the sharing, instead of resentful.

*

White-blue sunlight filtered in through the cavemouth. Jordas felt Yado's intense gaze on him as he ate.

"It worked!" Yado said at last. "You're not jealous of me."

Jordas nodded. "I've finally learned to see things in the Naxadan way. I learned something new last night, and it changed my attitude and feelings. I have hope now, that if I can live at peace with myself and with you, the tribes can also learn to co-operate."

"I too have hope," Yado told him.

Jordas felt warm with more than just the heat from the fire and the steaming food in his bowl. *It's going to be all right,* he told himself again. He looked at Soolkah.

"Welcome to Kernami, Jordas," she smiled.

"That's –" Jordas began.

Soolkah nodded at him. "It means 'our new place'." She smiled again. "It's your new place too."

THE END

Floodtide is also available from Amazon as a Kindle e-book.

For further information about the universe of *Floodtide*, including starmaps, a timeline, and other forthcoming publications by this author, visit: **www.Zarduth.com**.

Look-out for Helen Claire Gould's next novel,
The Zarduth Imperative!

ABOUT THE AUTHOR

Helen Claire Gould has been writing since her teens, having read her first two Science Fiction novels at the age of nine. At the Peterborough SF Club, where she met her husband, she contributed to the club fanzine *A Change of Zinery*. After suffering some miscarriages in 1992 she began writing for therapeutic reasons, joining Orbiters (SF postal writing workshops) and setting up the Peterborough Science Fiction Writers' Group. She edited two small press collections of short fiction, *Shadows on a Broken Wall* and *Mother Milk, Father Flywheel*, organised a weekend workshop on writing for comics, and had book reviews published in the BSFA review magazine, *Vector*.

Returning to full-time education in 1995, Helen graduated in Geology and Planetary science in 2000, teaching Geology and Creative Writing evening classes, and editing further collections of short fiction by her Creative Writing students. In 2013 she organised and ran a series of writers' workshops for the Peterborough Arts Festival.

Floodtide is Helen's first published novel, but she has several more novels and short stories, most of which are set in her own fictional universe.